FOUR PISTOLS

THE PENSIONERS' ADVENTURES SERIES

Bruce W. Goodwin

We Authors llc
Troy, Ohio

We Authors llc
PMB #125 1841 W. Main. St.
Troy, Ohio 45373
www.weauthors.net

Publisher's Note: This is a work of fiction. Names, characters, places, corporations, institutions and incidents are the product of the author's imagination or, if real, have been used fictitiously without any intent to describe their actual conduct and are not to be construed as real. Although some names, characters, places and incidents are based on historical record, the work as a whole is a product of the author's imagination. Any resemblance to actual persons (living or dead), actual events, locales or organizations is purely coincidental.

Book Layout ©2013 BookDesignTemplates.com

Four Pistols / Bruce W. Goodwin. – Revised 1st Edition.
1st Edition, March 2015.
ISBN-13 978-0-9863497-4-4

10 9 8 7 6 5 4 3 2

*Many thanks to the current proprietors of
The Occidental Hotel in Buffalo, Wyoming, David and Jackie Stewart and
Dawn Wexo, for allowing me to use their fine establishment as a location
in this story; despite the fact that my characters ended up
leaving a few dead bodies in their basement.
Additional thanks to Dawn for allowing me to borrow her name for a
character. Please visit www.occidentalwyoming.com for
information on the actual history of The Occidental Hotel.*

In Memory

Dear Mike,

I thought that I would send you a quick note to wish you well in your new adventure and also to remind you of how important you were to the people who came to know and love you over the years. Do you remember how we came to meet in the first place? Well, I do. We met in Doc Hill's class at Defiance College standing out in the hallway talking about the old curmudgeon professor's class. We connected immediately. As the semester progressed, we found that we were in more than one class together and shared similar thoughts about those classes—not all flattering. We were almost polar opposites in that you were a bit older, a lot more worldly and unmarried, and most certainly less interested in impressing the professors than I was. But almost 45 years ago, the differences that we had somehow created a bond that forged a strong and unbreakable friendship. Then our friend Steve joined us shortly after we met and that was that. Three friends became brothers and even though we became separated by distance over the past several years, we were able to maintain that special connection that the three of us began so long ago. Once, a couple of years ago, when you found out I was having some health issues and called me, I said that you shouldn't worry about it and you responded, "Bruce, you are the closest thing to a brother that I have and we are family whether our blood is the same or not. So I will worry and I'll be praying my Catholic prayers to get you better." That was you being my brother.

I could probably remind you of the many interesting stories from our early years, but you already know them and hopefully they continue to put a smile on your face and warmth in your heart. I shared a few of them in my book, but whenever anyone asks me if they really happened, or if that "Mikey" really existed, I assure them that your character is just that, a character enhanced by literary license, because, after all, no one could really be that way or do those things--- right? Anyway, there was not a day that went by, or a time that Steve and I got together, that we didn't end up remembering and reminiscing about our brother. And we always will. Mike, you changed my life all those years ago and you will continue to be always with us until we meet again. God bless you and remembering back to that far away Shakespeare class where I met you, I borrow his words to say, "Goodnight sweet prince…May flights of angels sing thee to thy rest."

I will miss you terribly.

Bruce

*Horseshit! I'm gonna drink another tequila and beer
and go feed my chickens.*
—MIKEY

*Collateral damage was always acceptable to tie up loose ends
and to clean up details. Always...*
—BUD

CHAPTER 1

The gym was already incredibly hot as Bruce walked through the patchwork quilt of chairs and risers and music stands that had been put into place for yet another graduation ceremony. Actually, hot is not the right word to describe the heat—it was more than stifling!

How many of these have I done as a teacher, principal, and superintendent over a thirty-six year career? He thought to himself. *It seems like only yesterday that I was sitting out there myself listening to a supposedly motivational speaker that would send me on my way to the next step of my life—and then on to my future. How funny! I can't remember a word he said, and I can't for the life of me remember who he was.*

It had seemed at the time an exercise in futility to him because none of them, mostly the guys in the class, believed they would be doing anything but going to college, if they could afford it, or to the military—which certainly meant a direct ticket to Vietnam and a very real chance of not having a future at all. So nothing the speaker had to say really had any meaning for the class of '67, not the scholarship winners, not the athletes, and certainly not the average kids who were about to jump into the craziness that was the end of the sixties and the start of the seventies.

Bruce smiled at the memory and felt very much conflicted as he wiped the beaded sweat from his forehead and neck. He loosened his red-striped power tie and took off his navy blue suit coat that he believed made him look authoritarian—or at the very least like someone worth listening to. He felt conflicted because he knew that in a very short time, about three hours from now, it would be his turn to be the unknown speaker trying to spark some deep response and understanding from a group of graduating seniors who had a much different view of life than he had.

He thought to himself, *I was one of the lucky ones. I didn't go to Vietnam. I had a great family. And I was always able to provide comfortably for us. Plus, I truly loved how I have spent the last thirty-six years of my life in a comfortable routine of family and work.*

And that is what caused the conflict for Bruce as he perused his notes and tried to collect his thoughts. *How do you reach out and make a difference with kids that have a completely different future looking them squarely in the face? How do you get the kids to listen and take to heart the words from a person who is not a part of their generation and who really can't speak to what their future will be? This generation of kids very well may have fewer options that I did,* Bruce thought. *How can I get them to be able to move forward at this point, into hope and prosperity? I guess that's what these years have given me, though—a life view that I need to share with those I can get to listen and force feed to those that just want to get the hell out of Dodge!*

Finally feeling ready to go, Bruce grabbed his jacket and walked slowly off the podium, out of the stifling heat of the gymnasium and back to his air-conditioned office to await the crowds of enthusiastic and proud parents, friends, and family members that were about to converge on the sauna in the gym and wait impatiently for the ceremony to begin—but in reality for it to end!

So this is how it ends? Bruce mused as he walked back down the school hallway toward the packed standing-room-only gymnasium where he was about to give the final commencement address of a thirty-six year career that spanned four decades and thousands of students and parents. *Amazingly, this feels strangely like most of the other addresses I have given over the years—except for the fact that I know how this one ends.* He smiled. *And I am sooo ready for it to end. It's time for me to go a different direction and do for me and my family instead of giving all my energy to this place and these people.*

But it's funny how different things hit you. Instead of feeling the relief he so wanted, as soon as Bruce walked through the door and into the mass of sweaty family members, students, and staff members, a flash of thirty-six years' worth of sacrifice smacked him in the forehead, and he almost passed out.

Luckily, one of the teacher ushers caught his arm and guided him back into the hallway.

"You okay Mr. G? Do you need help? Let me get you some water. It's way too hot in there! You okay? Hey Jim! Get the EMTs to check out Mr. G."

"No, Chad, I'm good. Just haven't felt the greatest lately—probably a touch of the 'retirement' flu, if you get what I mean…" Both men chuckled, and Bruce gathered himself and once again headed for the podium.

It was the traditional setting for graduations at this high school—a portable podium set in the middle of the small 1957 gymnasium that was still referred to as the *new* gym even though that hadn't been the case for over forty years. Directly in front of the podium sat several rows of chairs reserved for family and friends of the graduates and which, by the way, had been filled up for at least two hours now. Just off to the right of the podium sat the old musical risers that would seat the ninety-plus graduates who just wanted to get this thing over with.

Bruce reflected, *At least that's how I felt way back when.*

And, of course, the high school band and choir were jammed into the space by sitting on the pullout bleachers that were also being used for spectators. It was a hot, uncomfortable place to be even with huge fans blowing from the hallways and across the main floor of the venue. But be that as it may, it was what it was, and the people of the community seemed to accept it as the way it's always been. "If it was good enough for us, it is good enough for the new generations of graduates."

So let's get to it, thought Bruce, and he stepped up to the podium to watch the graduates being shepherded into their seats by the student ushers from the junior class. *Wow,* he thought, *the more things change, the more they remain the same. My thirty-sixth class looks like a replay of my first class, and the thirty-fourth after that.* He smiled. *That is truly amazing.*

The ceremony proceeded at its normal pace, predictable in every way. Music, speeches from valedictorians, salutatorians, class officers, more music, and finally it was Bruce's turn.

But first, before he started his message, he turned to the graduates and out of nowhere, he screamed at the top of his lungs, "PAY ATTENTION!"

This shocked the graduates so much that a few who had fallen asleep in the heat and humidity of the day almost fell off their chairs.

"Oh my god, or OMG, as you say, what a great day for the school, the community, the state, and our great country—and what a great day for you!"

With perspiration soaking through his suit and with droplets of moisture dripping from his forehead and nose and falling onto his written speech, Bruce took off, diving into his speech, directing, sharing, cajoling, and using every method he could to maintain the attention of the ninety-plus students. As he wound his way masterfully through his message and drew close to his conclusion, he realized that the kids were actually still looking at him as if he were actually saying something that meant something to them.

So he stopped, in mid-thought and shouted, "Thank you! Thank you for listening in such a polite manner. And because of that, I am going to finish with two things I absolutely have to have you remember." And then Bruce asked loudly, "Will you please remember my name as your graduation speaker? Who am I?"

The class sat in questioning silence; then someone cautiously said, "Mr. G."

So Bruce asked again, "Who am I?"

And this time he was met with a full chorus of "Mr. G's!"

"Please remember that as you go through your lives into the future—after thirty-six years it would be a great legacy to me, to have you speaking about memories and saying, 'Do you remember what Mr. G had to say?' And finally, one last thought, and I want you to stand up for this. Come on and stand up please! Okay, so here it is—if you don't remember anything else but my name today, I truly want you to remember this—the most important thing you can carry from my message is: **You must be able to adapt to the changes and curveballs that this life will send your way. How you react to anything that happens from here on out is what will define your life and determine if you find success or not. Happiness and success are always determined by how you are able to handle the difficulties that you will encounter in this life. Because this life has no guarantees.** So what did I just say?" Bruce looked squarely into the eyes of the graduates. "Again, what did I just say? What's the key word? Say it together!"

The graduates yelled, "Adapt!"

"Do what?"

Again, they yelled, "ADAPT!"

"One more time."

"ADAPT!"

"Good luck and godspeed!"

The graduates and the crowd accepted his words with a tremendous outpouring of applause and appreciation. With that Bruce sat down and realized that this really was the last significant thing he would do as an educator. He wiped the emotion from his eyes, took a deep breath to pull himself together, and said to himself, "Now it's time to move on."

Hours after the ceremony was over, Bruce was still in his office boxing up the last remnants of his professional life into an assortment of containers. His shirt remained damp from the heat in the gymnasium, and he had lost the tie. The blue suit coat was hung neatly behind the office door, and the office felt like it was fast becoming an empty shell for the next visitor to occupy for however long that would be.

I've been here so long, he thought, *I was afraid it would be more difficult than it has been to pack up and leave this place, a place that I truly held dear to my heart. But it's funny; it really doesn't feel like I'm losing anything. I guess that just proves that it is finally time to go. The old guys who came before me were right when they said that I would know when it was time—how right they were. Now I'm one of the old guys, and it does feel right.*

"Hey, Brucie! Where the hell are you?" boomed a familiar voice that Bruce hadn't expected to hear at this place, right here and right now. "Hey, Brucie," came the call once again—louder and closer.

"I'm here, in my office," Bruce shouted back. "And who the fuck wants to know?"

Then he smiled because he had never used that word in his office before—always trying to maintain that professional image, that role model stereotype that seemed to come with his view of how his job should be handled. But Bruce knew that he was the only one left in the building, and he also knew who was yelling for him.

"Brucie, it's me, Mikey, and I got Stevie with me too!" returned the voice. "By the way, nice talk from an educator!" he chuckled. "See, Stevie," he heard the voice say, "some things never change."

Then Bruce heard Steve say, "Just depends on what hat he's wearing today, and obviously he is wearing the 'I'm retiring and don't give a fuck hat!'" Laughter came down the hallway as both voices got closer, and Bruce started to relax and sat back into his oversized administrator's chair and awaited the entrance of his two best friends into his office.

What a great surprise! he thought. *My buddies, here to see me walk out the door for the last time. I never expected this.* And it almost brought him to tears.

Trying to explain friendship is like the impossible task of all impossibilities. It's like trying to explain how love works—why this person loves that person, what makes them work, what magical power or connection brought them together.

It is impossible. But telling the story of a friendship is not, especially a forty-plus year friendship that began in college and has held firm since that time.

This unique triad began way back with Bruce and Mike in a Chaucer literature class that was essentially for English majors. Both guys were in the class but didn't make a connection until they sat fairly close to each other during one of the lectures and started a conversation that followed them out into the hallway during a break in the class. It was kind of an Odd Couple connection from the beginning.

Bruce was younger by several years, was slightly built with an athletic appearance, and wore his hair much like one of his favorite characters of the time—James Bond. In fact, one of his professors who fancied himself a James Bond scholar often referred to Bruce as a Mr. James Bond lookalike. Bruce always took the reference as a compliment because he did think Sean Connery was a good-looking man. But, he was also a serious student who was fueled by a desire to get on with his life and get a job that would finally relieve him of working the three jobs that it took to pay both the college bills and the family bills created by a decision to marry his high school sweetheart at age nineteen and soon thereafter to have his first child.

On the other side of this odd couple was Mike. He was shorter than Bruce by a few inches with a square, compact build that served him well as a high school wrestler and a club soccer player. However, just by the way he carried himself, you would not have picked him as an athlete of any consequence. But he did come across as the guy you would want to have on your side if you got into a tight situation. As it turned out, this was an accurate assessment. For over the years, Mike was never averse to being a part of a barroom brawl on occasion—oftentimes dragging his reluctant buddies into the fray and always fueling the fire by his propensity to drink those brain-killing boilermakers. Shots and beer—a nasty combination of "chaos and piss" as the song goes.

One day, out in the hallway after a Shakespearian class that Mike happened not to be taking, Bruce struck up a conversation with the eventual third member of the friendship trio—Steve. Steve came across as a happy-go-lucky, affable young man with a very quick wit. He was built like a comfortable down pillow and could have easily been described as fluffy. He was anything but athletic and walked heavily in large long strides as the two walked outside to go on break. He quickly lit a cigarette and took a long needy puff on the Pall Mall. As usual the conversation began with comments regarding the legendary professor of the class, Dr. Hill—a very difficult old curmudgeon who had long since passed his retirement age, yet kept coming to work each day. Either you loved him, hated him, or feared him. On most days it seemed that it was his singular responsibility to make his students as miserable as he could. And today was one of those days.

Dr. Hill had zeroed in on Steve and stayed on him for at least twenty minutes, questioning, ridiculing, and finally moving on to another target with, "You will kindly come more prepared for tomorrow's lecture—Mr. Sheeeeeeen—no more slothfulness!"

Steve wasn't used to this and was still smarting when they talked. Bruce was just glad that Mr. Hill hadn't pounced on him. So it was easy to commiserate about the old bastard's teaching methods. Steve and Bruce clicked immediately. And before long they were discussing themselves and learning more about each other. This became a pattern as the semester drew on, and Bruce found himself thinking that Mike was someone that Steve would probably feel very comfortable with. So Bruce proffered a meeting between the three at a local bar and, as they say, the rest is history. From that meeting over quarter drafts and 50-cent slabs of Swiss cheese a lifelong trio was born. And almost from the beginning, it became Mikey, Stevie, and Brucie.

It's funny how the brain works, thought Bruce. *Here I am, finishing up the last day of my professional life as an educator, and I'm flashing back to how my buddies came to be my buddies.*

Hearing their voices coming down the school hallway seemed to flip a switch and take Bruce back to those old days, and he instantly felt a calmness and security that he hadn't felt in some time. His impending retirement had been giving him the completely opposite feeling. He had been anxious and short-tempered with his wife of thirty-eight years whom he loved so dearly and with his staff that had provided him with so much support during his tenure. Switching gears was going to be challenging for him, and he knew it. Having his buddies close by to help him through it was the best medicine he could imagine. And the fact that they both were here to congratulate him on his last day made him very happy. Plus, when he last talked with Steve and Mike, they had mentioned that they had a plan in place to help him slide into retirement, yet continue to be productive. And to have fun—with them. He couldn't wait to hear what they had to say.

By the time his buddies had reached his office door, Bruce was bursting with anticipation. It had been a long time since he had seen Mike. Mike had retired a few years earlier and immediately packed all of his belongings and headed to Wyoming to live on a thirty-five acre tract of land just outside of Buffalo, Wyoming. Steve and Bruce were shocked by this sudden move, but that was Mike, impulsive to the max—always ready to jump and go a different direction on a moment's notice. Instead of waiting until he got his thirty years in at the local water plant, he suddenly decided enough was enough and took an early retirement at twenty-eight years, costing himself a boatload of retirement money. But to Mike, it was just business as usual. He had never worried about money, scraping by over the years, working and then not working. He could live a Spartan lifestyle and squirrel away money probably better than anybody Bruce had ever known. So it was going to be very interesting to see what Mike's plan of attack for the future would be.

Steve, on the other hand, was a different story. He had retired a couple of years earlier and seemed to love the life. Money was never an issue—his wife was still working a very good-paying job, and he spent his time golfing with the old guys, drinking fine whiskeys and wines, going to the casinos, and occasionally heading out on hunting excursions.

Plus, he and Bruce would find time to play their own version of golf together at least once a week in good weather and sometimes twice. And they always played for money. Bruce was a much better golfer, so Steve would dream up ways to even the playing field so that there was an equal distribution of the winnings each time they played. However, it always seemed that no matter how the game was rigged, Bruce still came out on top at the end of the playing season. Whether it was one dollar or a hundred dollars, it made no difference. Bruce would always come out ahead in the "screw Brucie" matches between the two friends. It was something both men looked forward to over the long Northwest Ohio winters. They only wished that Mike had not moved so far away so that he could have been a part of their lives on a more regular basis.

But you know, it's like they always say, "it's as if he never left," once us buddies get reconnected, Bruce thought. So it was time to reconnect.

Mike and Steve turned the corner and walked through Bruce's office door. Bruce bounded from around his desk and reached out his hand to Mike and shook and hugged in a quick man-embrace.

"Oh my god, Mikey! It is so good to see you."

Steve stood back, smiled, and said, "C'mon, Brucie. What? Don't I get a hug too?"

Bruce countered with, "Not likely! I see you way too much as it is...and I'm not about to start hugging you." Bruce took a step back and shot a quick up and down of his buddy Mike. "Wow, some things never change. It's been two years and you still look the same—well, maybe a little grayer. And even a little bit more like Wilford Brimley! But hey, what can you do, right? And by the way, thanks for not wearing your bib overalls to the ceremony—I didn't even know you still owned a tie. That's probably why I didn't know you were here. I haven't seen you out of those bibs for years!"

"Hmph! You are so funny, Brucie, that I forgot to laugh," Mike retorted.

"Well anyway, it is so good to have the three of us together again. Like a three-legged stool, Steve and I are never really balanced without you around to hassle."

The three old friends walked out of Bruce's office and down the hallway and into the next chapter of their lives—and what a chapter it was going to be for three small town guys from Northwest Ohio.

CHAPTER 2

The Dallas airport was nearly at a standstill—jam-packed as a result of no planes landing and none going out. The chatter of people in the terminal was growing louder by the minute, and the frustration level was growing too. Nothing would move at the airport until Air Force One and top government officials left to head back to Washington, D.C., with the body of the assassinated President Kennedy and the newly sworn-in President Lyndon Baines Johnson aboard. People were crying—people were swearing—and people were just generally in a state of shock. It was beyond belief that the President of the United States could be assassinated right here in Texas—Dallas, Texas. And by whom?

Already rumors were flying rampant while TV screens kept up a continual coverage of the crisis. To say that everyone was glued to the screens would be an understatement. The whole world was fixated on this crisis, and every time a newsman came up with more detailed accounts, it evoked a gasp from those watching for an answer. But there were no short answers—there seemed to be a suspect, or suspects, and there was a huge manhunt going on throughout Dallas. There were more reports of a police officer being killed. And then there was the discussion of presidential succession. All information that just fueled the anxious state of mind of those trapped on "hold" in the airport.

Far across the main runway, parked hidden from view from the terminal, a small Cessna was on hold just waiting for Air Force One to take off so those on board could fly out also. It was clear that all of the passengers were anxious and on edge. But they sat silently, just waiting for the go signal from the pilot. The passengers had all arrived in separate vehicles, all nondescript government-like cars that shouted "unmarked government vehicle" just by their plainness. Each car, a dark Ford sedan, had a driver wearing sunglasses and a cookie-cutter dark suit and skinny dark tie, and each driver pulled up to the private gate and dropped off one passenger wearing an equally unremarkable suit and carrying a small personal travel bag and a silver metallic-looking brief-case. The cars all arrived within a few minutes of each other. Each person who was dropped off followed the same procedure and walked the few steps to the gate, nodded at the three guards who were posted at the gate, showed them some sort of ID, and waited for guard approval, hurriedly walked to the plane, entered, and sat down in a pre-arranged seat. Once seated, each man pushed the carryon bag under the seat and held the silver briefcase on his lap. Then they sat in silence.

When the fourth man was dropped off, followed the same procedures as the first three, and took his seat, the three men at the gate closed it, locked it, and entered the plane—still in total silence. One man settled into the pilot's seat and started fiddling with the controls, while the second man headed for the back of the plane and sat in the last seat directly behind the four passengers with the silver briefcases. The last man to enter headed to the co-pilot's seat and before sitting, signaled to all on board with hand gestures that they should put on a large set of earphones that were located just above everyone's seats. The seated men scrambled quickly to comply, and when it was obvious all were ready, the man in the co-pilot's seat started to talk—very slowly—very quietly—but with an assurance that immediately made it clear that he was in charge.

He started, "Your country thanks you for your service today. I thank you, and the Director thanks you." He paused for a few seconds before continuing, "Our original plan of exit has changed somewhat. Instead of lifting off immediately behind the Presidential plane and following it back to D.C., we now have to wait several minutes and depart in a different direction. The secret service has established a no-fly safety zone around Air Force One, and no one can be within miles of the aircraft. So we are going to take a more northern approach and stay just outside of that no fly zone with the goal of rendezvousing with our contacts when we get to D.C. Our timing will be slightly altered, but we will still make it work. Your package will still be delivered to the same location and to the same recipient."

The man was finished talking, and he turned away from the other passengers, took off his headphones, and stared out the front window of the cockpit. Short, cryptic, and done. No questions, no nods of assent, just straight-ahead gazes by everyone in the plane. Then finally, after what seemed an interminable wait, Air Force One began to taxi down the main runway.

As soon as Air Force One retracted its wheels and slowly rose into the eastern sky, destined for Washington, D.C., the small plane that had been virtually hidden on a small back-alley runway entered the main runway and asked for, and received, approval to take off. There was obviously some juice behind this departure—because every other plane was still in ground mode. No one was coming or going. But it happened so fast that no one really paid attention or noticed. The control tower was taking orders from someone, but that someone would never be discovered—that is, if all went well.

On the plane, no one spoke, and no one looked anywhere but ahead as the plane corrected its course and headed due north. If Air Force One's course could be described as heading at three o'clock, then the small Cessna would be described as following a twelve o'clock course into the heartland of the country. The no-fly zone around Air Force One was being enforced by military jets, and even though it appeared as though the small plane was somehow a part of the political drama that was unfolding, the pilot steered a course that would keep it just outside that zone. He was intent on not being a part of the drama. As the flight continued north, the man-in-charge, still sitting in the co-pilot's seat, occasionally spoke into a hand-held radio that was distinctly separate from the headphone radio system that the pilot was using.

In a voice meant to keep the rest of the plane from hearing, the man-in-charge half whispered and half spoke, "We are progressing north and are still a little behind schedule. Please verify that all is in order."

A voice crackled back, "Continue the northerly direction."

The man-in-charge simply said, "Roger that." He stopped speaking into the radio and leaned into the pilot, "Follow the northern route as planned." The pilot didn't even acknowledge the order and changed nothing. The rest of the plane remained silent, and the men holding briefcases continued to hold them on their laps, exactly as when they entered the plane.

After about an hour in the air, the radio held by the man-in-charge crackled to life. "Things are getting a little dicey. Continue to fly north, but follow the Buffalo option."

Another "Roger that" from the man-in-charge. He leaned to the pilot and simply whispered "Buffalo." The pilot quickly changed course toward Buffalo, Wyoming, shook his head at his boss with a what-the-hell-is-happening look, and proceeded on. The man in the co-pilot's seat had no response.

CHAPTER 3

Mike led the way as the buddies entered the bar that they had spent so much time in over the years before Mike's move out West. "Oh my god! It hasn't changed a bit," he exclaimed. "We had some great times in this old place! Look at that—they still have all of the baseball scores posted from today's play and lots of postings from local high school sporting events. It's been five years since I've been in this place and probably ten years since the three of us drank some draft beer here together. And look who's still behind the bar—Hey, Shorty, how's it going?"

Shorty was the owner and bartender, and he came by his name honestly, by being the youngest and smallest member of the family that had owned the bar for three generations. He had been the only child interested in working in the family business and oftentimes confided to his regulars that he was beginning to tire of the long hours and the daily grind of dealing with drunks and unhappy people looking for someone to unload their problems on.

Shorty looked up from his task of making a hot beef sandwich with onions, something the bar was famous for, and did a double take. "Why, Mike, how the hell ya doin'? I thought you were long gone!"

"Me? Hell no, you can't get rid of me that easy! I thought you would be the guy who was gone," Mike shot back. "I'm surprised you're still working here—good to see you."

Shorty smiled, returned to his hot beef, and said, "Good to see you too, buddy. Be right with you troublemakers."

The guys sauntered to a table that was kind of tucked away in a corner of the bar where they could talk and not be overheard.

Bruce said, "I can almost guarantee that we sat at this same table almost forty years ago, watching Monday night football, drinking quarter drafts, and eating a slab of Swiss cheese and crackers."

"You could get a lot out of a buck back then," Steve added.

Mike snorted and chuckled at the same time as he said, "Sure as shit could, especially you, Brucie, since Stevie and I seemed to be the guys paying the bill."

"No question about it, boys," Bruce responded, "I was so broke; I would have never been able to go anywhere without you guys footin' the bill. My lovely wife reminded me all the time that she was stuck at home with the babies while I was out playing with my single buddies."

"Yep," Steve added, "Marlene was and is a saint to put up with you—just sayin'."

"Well, remember, many times it was the three of us and Marlene," Bruce said. "And then you guys had to pay double!" he laughed.

Steve quickly rejoined, "So what you're saying Brucie...is...that...You are buying! Glad we got that straightened out."

The three laughed as though they were never separated by time and distance. Bruce thought again how wonderful it was to be sharing such a great day, his retirement day, with his best friends. Shorty came over, took the orders from the guys, and made quick work of delivering it. So now it was time to get down to business. Or at least they were getting closer to business. Mike had to swallow a hot beef sandwich, a knocker sausage sandwich, and a couple of slabs of Swiss cheese and crackers first.

"So, boys, here's the deal." Mike spoke while he made loud smacking noises from the remnants of the food that he had just inhaled. He was never someone afraid to show his appreciation for eating—eating fast and furiously, that is. Steve and Bruce were just beginning to munch on their sandwiches, but Mike was already done and washing the food down with his second draft beer and his first shot of Jameson's.

Both guys gave each other that knowing look of "Oh no, we know how this night will end." They had seen many crazy nights start this way over the years, and both thought the same thing as Steve stated the obvious, "Brucie, buddy, isn't it crazy how the more things change, the more they stay the same?"

Bruce chuckled, nodded in agreement, and marveled at the fact that forty years ago felt like yesterday—the three friends wondering then what their future would be like as they sat in this very bar. And now here they were wondering what their next future would be like.

Mike continued on between swallows of food and drink and said, "Listen, we're all retired now, right? So we need to do something great together before we fade off into the sunset. I'm talking about an adventure for the three of us, with just the three of us. You two guys have enough tucked away to do whatever you want, and even though my circumstances are more limited, I can supply the sweat equity that is always necessary in any kind of venture."

Bruce and Steve looked at each other as if to say, *Where in the hell is he going with this?* Over the years, when the buddies got together, this was pretty much standard practice because you never could tell if it was the buddy or the booze talking. But they continued to listen.

Mike reloaded with another hunk of cheese and another shot and beer. And as he did, Steve looked at Bruce again and laughed out loud as both men caught the same image of the old days.

So Bruce yelled, "Wait, wait, wait, Stevie, you're thinking what I am—I know you are!" Bruce turned to Mike and yelled, "Hold that thought for a sec, Mikey."

"All right, goddam it!" Mike chortled. "Tell the story and get it over with."

And Bruce and Steve reminisced about the time in college when Mike had failed to appear for an exam in Victorian Literature because he made the trip down the hill from the college campus to a local bar that catered to mostly local regulars. He spent a couple of hours drinking boilermakers until he was so drunk that he could hardly navigate the hill back to campus and his exam. When he did arrive, Bruce and Steve were almost done with the bluebook exam. As he staggered into the exam room, he loudly proclaimed to the professor that he was sorry for being late, said "Hi, Stevie, Hi, Brucie," and then tried to take off his navy pea coat. When he did, an empty beer bottle flew out of his coat pocket and clattered across the room in front of a stunned group of exam takers. The professor never said a word and just continued to stroke his goatee as Mike loudly and profusely apologized and scurried to pick up his bottle and find his seat.

The three friends roared at the memory, and Mike, his chubby cheeks getting rosier by the second, said, "Steve, you need to write my memoirs for me some day!"

Bruce chimed in with agreement and said, "No question it would be a best seller. Sometimes when I'm in between things and think about Mikey being out in Wyoming, I think of all those crazy things that he put us through and I actually laugh out loud, as the kiddos say!"

"So anyway, now that we have that off the table," Steve said. "Go ahead, Mikey, if you haven't forgotten what you were going to say and tell us about this venture or adventure, whatever it is."

"Okay," Mike said as he feigned hurt feelings, "But only if you don't interrupt me again."

"Can't promise that, buddy," Bruce laughed. "Almost everything you say jogs some past memory that needs to be revisited. So go ahead, buddy, spit it out."

Mike let out a huge loud guffaw and, while still smacking his lips, he began, "Well, it's like this—we are all retired now. I live alone and have lots of time on my hands—you guys have enough time and money to do about whatever you want, so let's"—he paused and shot the shot of tequila that came with his mug of draft beer, "ahhhhhh."

Steve and Bruce shot quick glances at each other with silly-ass grins thinking *here we go again,* but didn't say anything and Mike continued. "So let's go on a gun hunt," he finally shouted with a little slur that was starting to control his speech.

Bruce said, "A what?" and Steve politely smiled.

"A gun hunt," Mike said again. Steve and Bruce looked at Mike with what-the-hell-are-you-talking-about expressions, and Mike continued. "Okay, it's like this. I've got an old gun buddy out in Wyoming who has a list of valuable old pistols that haven't been seen in years. There are collectors who are willing to pay big bucks to find the guns or to find the guys who own the guns so they can try to buy them." He paused for a breath and continued, "These collectors are looking for guys who are willing to do that. We'd be kinda like subcontractors who look for treasure!" He snorted.

"Oh my god," Bruce challenged, "a treasure hunter at my age? You have lost your freakin' mind—been living alone on the prairie too long."

But Steve jumped in and said, "Wait, wait, I know what he's talking about. I've read about these kinds of guys. And some of them are throwing big money around to find their special kind of guns."

Mike interjected, "That's what I'm talking about—just hear me out, and I think you'll get it, Brucie."

But Bruce wasn't convinced that it wasn't the shots and beer talking for Mike. His checkered history often took the three down roads that were colored by the tequila, or Jameson's, or the abundance of free-flowing beer. And in the morning, after the buzz was gone and the headache kicked in, the fantastical ideas soon faded into the everyday reality of trying to get by. Somehow, though, Mike seemed to be really focused on this idea, and Bruce sensed that Steve thought so too. In fact, Steve seemed to be getting very interested in this idea. He was the real gun nut in the group. He was a member of numerous gun clubs, subscribed to gun magazines, and had a wide-ranging knowledge of how the gun world works.

So if Stevie is interested, then maybe I should pay closer attention, thought Bruce. *And maybe Mike isn't just drunk-talking. After all, it would be great fun to get the three of us out on an adventure once again. It has been way too long since the three of us have been able to spend time together, except for the occasional short visits.* So Bruce said, "I'm interested, keep going. Just quit spitting on us as you're talking!" he laughed. It was one of those things that just happened—the drunker Mike got, the more you had to dodge the incoming spit talk.

"What are you talking about?" Mike said with an indignant laugh. "I'm not even close to being drunk yet."

But Steve and Bruce knew the telltale signs and knew that maybe the details of this adventure would have to wait until tomorrow, after Mike had time to regain his equilibrium. It was such a great moment, because forty years ago, none of the three would have imagined that they would all still be around and in good enough health to think about doing something as adventurous as this. In fact, Steve and Mike both took wagers that they wouldn't see sixty, let alone be ambulatory. So the mere fact that all three were here and somewhat healthy and in the same spot they shared so often forty years earlier was a minor miracle.

Steve stood up first and said, "I gotta get going…told the wife that I'd be home a half hour ago. Let's get together for lunch tomorrow and finish this conversation—if you are able to get around tomorrow, that is," he nodded to Mike as he spoke.

"I'll be fine," Mike spit-talked again. "Let'sss meet at Kissner's."

Bruce stood up too and said, "That works."

And Steve and Bruce walked out together, both thinking that it is so amazing how things change, yet stay the same. Neither could count the number of times they had to leave Mike when he got started like this. But both were also very intrigued by what he had to say and looked forward to tomorrow.

CHAPTER 4

The next day started hard for all three buddies. No one was used to drinking late into the night anymore, including Mike. So lunchtime at Kissner's came early. Bruce was the first to arrive at the bar-turned-restaurant. Forty years ago it was principally a bar, but as the generations of owners changed, it became a very good combination spot that served pretty good food throughout the day. Its décor hadn't changed over the years, with the exception of how much better it smelled. Bruce remembered having to leave his clothes in the garage when he got home from this place all those years ago—they had just reeked of smoke and fried food. But now it was so different—no smoking in the place and no rotten smell of rancid cooking grease.

Bruce took a seat at a corner table away from most of the busy lunch crowd so he and his buddies could talk without being listened to. Most of the other tables were on top of each other. As the lunch crowd grew, the noise level increased exponentially as people tried to talk over each other to be heard. He chose his seat carefully because it was common to run into people he knew and have them stop by to talk while he was eating. Today, he just wanted to be with his buddies and eat and talk in peace. As he waited he mulled over the idea that Mike had started to share with the guys last night and thought of the possibilities. Surprisingly, he kind of liked the concept. *It not only provided an outlet for keeping us busy in retirement, but also would reunite the "Three Amigos,"* he mused. *And if it made any money, or at least covered expenses, then it would be a great scenario for the three of us to have a final adventure in a pretty tame life up to this point.*

Bruce saw his two buddies come into the bar together. Steve looked great and well rested, but Mike had the familiar Oh-shit-I'm-too-old-for-this-and-I'm-paying-the-price-for-my-stupidity-last-night look. But true to form, after both settled in and were ready to order, Mike chose the hair-of-the-dog-that-bit-him approach and ordered a draft beer and tomato juice. Bruce and Steve had been there, done that, and decided that iced tea would be the more civil approach.

Bruce said, "Nice of you guys to finally join me. Any problems getting started this morning?"

"Not for me," Steve said. "But my compadre here seems to be struggling a bit."

"Horseshit," Mike snorted. "I'm fine. Just like in the old days you wusses had to run home to your wifies or get grounded." Then he shouted, "But I will admit, I ain't as young as I used to be. I think I might have stirred up the old liver a bit."

"And that beer will fix your liver?" Bruce asked with feigned incredulity.

"Nah—but it'll make me feel like it did—at least until later. Haw, haw, haw," Mike belly laughed. "Enough about that stuff, and let's get on with it."

"Yes," Steve chimed in. "Let's do it."

As Bruce and Steve listened intently to the winding tale that Mike was pitching to them, both men started to feel more positive about the potential for the "great adventure" as Mike called it. Mike not only had piqued their interest, but also had made them suddenly in a hurry to get started. And for Steve and Bruce, that was never the case with Mike's schemes. Generally, they were very wary. But there was something about this plan. It seemed to be calling the three buddies back together to work towards a common result and create some spice in their lives as they were doing it.

Steve spoke first. "So, Mikey, you are saying that your friend in Deadwood has a list of valuable guns that collectors are just chomping at the bit to get their hands on. And there is a bounty attached to each one. And all we have to do is bring the collector and the guns together to get paid this bounty. Right so far?"

"And there is already a set of clues that will guide us as we search?" Bruce added.

"Hell, yes!" Mike shouted over the din of the lunch crowd. This got many curious looks. But he kept on speaking loudly, as his ruddy cheeks turned even brighter red than usual. "It's about as goddam simple as it gets. We are the treasure hunters basically following a map and clues to the guns, and then we turn them in."

"So where's the map? And who pays us? And how do we get paid? And are any of the guns stolen? Or illegal?" The questions flowed from Bruce and Steve until they were about the only ones left in the restaurant.

Although Mike couldn't answer all of the questions, both men finally said, "Okay, what the hell, let's do it." And the adventure was set in motion.

CHAPTER 5

The airport in Buffalo, Wyoming, was a tiny local strip of blacktop that was only a couple of minutes from the immediate downtown of Buffalo. Actually, it was only seven minutes—at least that's how long it would take the two black nondescript vehicles that had been awaiting the arrival of the small plane to the Johnson County Airport. The airport was aptly named for the county that it was located in and was more recognizable by the Johnson County name—specifically because it happened to be the famed home of the Johnson County range wars of the late 1800s—where cattlemen fought sheep owners and other small farmers over the open range that had been in place for so long. The fighting had been so bad that the federal government had to get involved to stop the bloodshed by sending in troops to break up and arrest a group of hired killers that had been brought to Johnson County by the large land owners to terrorize the smaller landowners and sheep farmers. The town of Buffalo itself had quite a storied past as western celebrities, outlaws as well as famous lawmen, passed through the town on a regular basis. Most of these famous folks came to town to visit the historic Occidental Hotel on the main street of Buffalo to partake of its food and drink celebrated across the Old West.

But the history of Buffalo was certainly of no concern for the seven men approaching in the small Cessna about to land at the Johnson County Airport. Their concern was that the original plan had been changed to another option—an option that was really very far down the list of options that had been so meticulously worked and reworked over the days and weeks preceding today's history-changing event.

No one expressed this concern, though. Instead they continued to follow the commands of the man-in-charge as he matter-of-factly reminded them of what was coming next. "As soon as we land, you will take your carryon luggage and briefcase off the plane and immediately get into the two cars that are waiting for you. Two of you will get in the first car, and two will get in the second car. I will drive the first car, and my man, sitting behind you, will drive the second car. The pilot will wait at the airport for our return."

The pilot handled the landing in a skilled, but measured manner. Before starting the final descent, he circled the tiny airport with permission from the antiquated tower and took note of the two black vehicles parked near the end of the runway. Other than those cars, everything seemed to be in order, so the pilot banked and quickly went into landing mode and touched down in a textbook landing. As soon as the plane came to a stop, the man-in-charge had the door open and moved to his designated vehicle, and his man in the back did the same. The four men with briefcases and backpacks quickly followed suit and jumped into the vehicles with no comments.

Seven minutes later the cars stopped in front of an old western style building that appeared to be badly in need of a facelift. It was the old Occidental Hotel. Made famous over the years by outlaws and lawmen alike as they moved about Wyoming and South Dakota, it had become a neutral watering hole of sorts. And it was a great place to settle in for a break, a hot bath, and good food and drink. People like Buffalo Bill Cody, Teddy Roosevelt, Tom Horn, Calamity Jane, and Butch Cassidy and the Sundance Kid were very familiar with this place. But the hotel's best days were behind it, and there was growing evidence that the place was doomed and might be torn down in the near future—unless someone was willing to pour lots of money into refurbishing the old structure. On this night, though, none of the historical stuff mattered. It was all about accomplishing the mission.

As soon as the cars stopped, the man-in-charge said quietly, "Sit tight—I'll be right back."

He signaled for his colleague to follow, and they entered the building. Once inside, they walked up to the twenty-five-foot bar that had been put into place in the very early 1900s and said something to the bartender, who immediately went to the back of the building and retrieved another man, who acted like he was the owner and that he was expecting the two men.

He spoke softly, "How the hell did you end up here?"

The man-in-charge said, "Never mind—are you prepared?"

The owner grunted, "Yes, but I wasn't really expecting it to happen."

"Well, it did, and now we are here," answered the man-in-charge.

"Okay, bring the goods in, and I'll take care of it," the owner responded.

With that, the man's colleague went outside and immediately ushered in the four men in suits carrying their silver briefcases. Talk about being out of place! The six men were the only people in the place wearing suits and looked like they were searching for a church or an FBI meeting.

Nonetheless, the owner, shaking his head with every step, led the six men down the ancient staircase into the basement. Within literally seconds, all of the men re-emerged from the basement, quickly left the hotel, jumped into the two vehicles, and headed back to the airport. Fifteen minutes later, they were taking off and heading east towards Washington, D.C., still maintaining silence except for occasional comments from the man-in-charge.

The peculiar thing here is that each of the four men took a silver briefcase into the old hotel, and not one man had a briefcase with him when he exited the hotel, got into the car, and boarded the small plane.

Back at the hotel, the owner shook his head and wondered what he had gotten himself into and how he was going to survive this thing intact.

CHAPTER 6

"All right, Mikey," Bruce said as his buddy climbed into his already packed and loaded full-sized Chevy van. Mike had been using the fifteen-year-old van as his hotel room. He had thrown a mattress on the empty floor of the back of the van and then parked it in Bruce's drive for the few days that he was visiting. It was not what you would refer to as luxury sleeping arrangements, but that was Mike's style. Always had been and always would be. "As soon as you get back to Buffalo and meet with your mysterious fella, make sure you send Stevie and I a copy of the gun list and then we can get to work."

"All right, goddam it, I already said I would!" Mike growled. Then he lit a huge old stogie that he'd been carrying in his shirt pocket. "Haw, haw," he cackled. "This is a great cigar. Make sure you tell Stevie how much I appreciate the gift. Just me and a box full of ceeegars for the next three days on my way back home." Steve had supplied Mike with a full box of assorted cigars that he collected off the Internet—Maduros, 5 Vegas, Black Beauties, Obsidians, and more.

"It's too bad Stevie isn't here to enjoy one with us," Bruce said. "He just couldn't get out of his appointment."

"I know, but it's okay—haw, haw—more for me," Mike laughed. "Okay, pardner, time to hit the road." As he started to back out the drive, he blew a huge smoke ring out the rolled down window and yelled, "Can't wait to get this gig going and spend more time with you guys."

"Me too," Bruce yelled back. "Safe travels, buddy." And just that quickly, Mike was gone and heading home, leaving Bruce and Steve to contemplate what was next.

It would take Mike three days of driving to get back to Buffalo, so Bruce and Steve went about their lives as usual, knowing it would be at least four days before they heard from him. So they played golf three days in a row and worked around the house for the next day. Both were anxious to move to the next step.

When the phone rang, Bruce saw that it was Steve and said, "Sheen, What's up, buddy?"

"So the way I figure it," Steve said, "we won't hear from Mikey for at least another day. You know how slow he is."

Bruce answered quickly, "Could be a day, a week, or a month. It's Mikey—a leopard doesn't change its spots."

"But I do wish he'd move on this." Steve retorted. "It really sounds appealing to me."

"I agree," said Bruce. "I just want to get this thing going."

Steve responded, "Okay, I was hoping that you had heard something. Let me know as soon as you do, and I will do the same."

"Will do," agreed Bruce.

"Adios, count on it." Steve finished and clicked off the phone. Bruce went out to cut the grass, and Steve went back to shampooing his carpet. Later that night, as the sunlight was fading, the doorbell rang at both men's houses, almost simultaneously. Both men were relaxing and intermittently snoozing in their reclining chairs. Usually, they figured it was a package that their wives had ordered, and they didn't bother to climb out of the oversized loungers. But this time the doorbell rang again and again. So each man groggily and grumpily got up to answer the door and see what was up. It was the FedEx man just as they expected, but he was waiting with that magic electronic tablet for them to sign—and he carried an overnight envelope.

Oh my god, Bruce and Steve thought to themselves. *Is this the information that Mikey was supposed to send them?*

"Hey, buddy. How's it goin'?" Bruce responded to the request for his signature.

And back at his house Steve said, "Thank you. No problem."

The FedEx guys wanted to chat a bit, but both guys were in a hurry, grabbed the overnighted envelope, and headed back inside—saying "thanks" and "take it easy" to the delivery guys as they shut the front doors.

Okay, thought Bruce, *this is it.*

And Steve, *Finally, it's here.*

And both guys were right. Mike took it upon himself to send the same information to both of them. Incredible as it seems, they both scanned the information and grabbed for their phones almost exactly in unison. The timing was such that both guys were listening to the ring when their call waiting beeped alerting them that the other guy was calling.

So Steve pushed the button, and Bruce said, "Sheeeeeen."

Steve said, "It's here."

And Bruce said, "I got one too. FedEx?"

"Yep," Steve responded. "And it's quite a nice list."

"So what do you think?" Bruce asked. "Are these gonna be findable?"

"Well," Steve said. "It will all depend on the accuracy of the last known whereabouts of the guns that the guy provided." He continued, "And the great thing is that we will be hitting a lot of gun shows to get started, even some around our neck of the woods."

"Yes," Bruce said. "I noticed that."

"So now we need to go through the list," Steve said, "make a reasonable guess about which ones we should start with, including the cost efficiencies when we go on a hunt, talk to Mikey, and get started."

"Are you busy tomorrow?" Bruce asked. "I'm ready to go."

Steve answered, "No, I'm free. So let's get started. How about you bring the list and your laptop and come to my place about 11:00 tomorrow morning so we can drink some bourbon and go over the list. I'll work on a best guess find list, and we can draw up the plan—always subject to change though," he laughed.

"Sounds like a plan, buddy," Bruce said. "Let's do this thing."

Bruce arrived at Steve's place right on time, as usual, and hit the door chimes. He had the list and his laptop under his arm and a small bottle of Maker's Mark in the other hand. Steve answered quickly and said, "Well, it looks like you've got the right idea—I have several other choices for you to sample as well." He was referring to the Maker's Mark.

"Yep, I know, you are the king of booze connoisseurs—but I'll stick to the 'devil I know,'" Bruce stated as he entered the house. "So have you figured a method to this madness yet? The list looks pretty interesting, but I'm guessing the finder's fee on some of these guns will exceed the price that they will sell for."

"Wait," Steve said, "first things first." He pulled out a bottle of single malt scotch—Johnny Walker Red, poured it over a full glass of ice, took a sip, and said, "Now we can begin."

"I'll just stick with my Makers, thanks," Bruce responded as he opened the bottle and poured it into the ice-filled glass that Steve provided.

Steve returned to Bruce's comment about the gun list, "You are exactly right. Some of these guns may be hard to find, but not especially pricey. So it is obvious that the point here is this fellow has a list of guns that he wants to find before he dies and doesn't have the time or energy to get it done."

"But he does have the money to pay someone else to do it for him," Bruce added.

"You are correct," Steve continued. "My thoughts are that we get Mikey on a conference call and discuss the list and the process. What do you think?"

"Well, buddy, let's do it," Bruce said. "Give Mikey a call, and let's get rolling."

Steve pushed the speakerphone button, dialed Mike's number, and while waiting for him to answer, swallowed a couple long sips from the JW Red. "Oh man, this is good stuff," he smiled and said to Bruce, "You really need to try it."

Then Mike barked, "Hello."

"Mikey," Bruce shouted. And Steve, always more reserved, said, "Hey, Michael."

Mike responded, "Hey, boys, what's up? Did you get the list?"

Both Steve and Bruce answered back, "We got it."

"So now we have questions and need to talk about it," Steve said. "Do you have time now?"

"Hell yeah! Why do you guys think I sent it so quickly? It cost me a friggin' fortune to send it overnight."

"Okay then, buddy," Bruce said, "spend it if you got it," and laughed loudly.

"You are sure wound up, pardner," Mike said. "I'll bet you and Sheen are drinking something very good and expensive."

"Well," Steve said, "as a matter of fact, yes we are. But we are still sober enough to talk about our plans to get this thing going."

"Great," Mike said. "So what's on you guys' mind?"

"Okay, let's start with the list," Steve said. "It appears as though this guy could find most of these guns by himself, on the Internet, or at gun shows or gun auctions. There are only a few that stick out as very difficult or impossible. So I guess our question is, why does he need us?"

"Haw, haw," snorted Mike, "I knew you guys would see through that list. And yes, normally a collector does his own work—that's part of the fun. But this guy is pretty old now, and his health is not very good. I think this is his way of putting together a gun collector's bucket list of guns that he always wanted, but didn't have time to get. As you noticed," Mike continued, "some of the guns are really high dollar, but most are mid-range and affordable by average collectors. This guy can afford anything he wants, so money is no object. The problem is his health and age, and that's the reason he needs someone to complete his bucket list—someone he can trust to be confidential about his part or interest in a particular gun."

"Okay, we get that," Bruce said. "But tell us again how you got to meet this guy."

"Well, you guys know that since I've moved out to Buffalo, I've become real active in the Catholic Church," he explained. "And of course you also know that I have no money to give to the Church, so I have tried to make that up by using sweat equity. I run the fish fries, breakfasts, carnivals, and anything else I can do just to give back to the Church. I started seeing this old guy coming to some of these things and wondered who he was. I asked around, and nobody really seemed to know much about him, except that he may have worked for the government in some capacity and moved out here after he retired.

"Then one day I went to shoot out at the range at a time when I can usually be alone. As I was shooting, this old guy drove in, watched me for a while, got out of his black SUV, and walked over to me. I recognized him immediately and said, 'Hello, pardner.' He responded with a

"Hello, Mike," and said he recognized me from the church and noticed how active I always was in different capacities. He then apologized and said he was a people watcher who enjoyed trying to figure out who was really who he said he was. And he also said it probably stemmed from a long career in the people watching business. I asked him what he did, and he would only say that he was a public servant and worked for the government. Then he said that he was also a gun nut and a collector and wanted to see what I was shooting. But it was clear that he already knew from a distance what it was that I was shooting. The guy seemed to be testing me in some way."

"So what is his name?" Steve and Bruce asked simultaneously.

"I'm getting to that," Mike responded as he continued his story. Both men knew that you couldn't rush Mike on anything—especially a story that he was telling. So they settled back and let him continue—and swallowed another shot of scotch.

"We talked guns for a long time, and I told him that my two buddies were retired too, and both into guns," Mike continued. "He said we were all too young to be retired and that if we were looking for something to do, he had something. That's when the gun collecting list was brought up. And that's when I said I would talk to you guys about it.

"By the way, his name is Bud, or at least that's what he said to call him. I said to him after he brought up the gun thing, 'Hey, pardner, you have me at a disadvantage. You know my name, but I don't know yours.' The man said, 'My friends call me Bud.' And that was that.

"Then he gave me his cell number and said to call him after I talked to you. That's how I got the list. I called him and said you were interested, and he said he would send me a list of guns and information and see how we did. And here comes the best part—he wants to give us *thirty thousand bucks* as seed money to get started. Our expenses will come out of this and our pay—and remember all we have to do is to find the guns and let him know. He will do the negotiating and buying. Pretty sweet, right?"

"All righty then," Bruce laughed. "It sounds like you have the details all wrapped up in a little bow. I'm assuming we should meet him sometime, right?"

"Oh yeah, you're right," Mike said. "He wants you to come out to Deadwood, where he spends a fair amount of his time, and meet him. He'll give us the money, and we'll be good to go."

Steve chimed in, "Sounds like a road trip to me. I love Deadwood anyway, so we can combine our new business venture with a little fun."

CHAPTER 7

Bruce's cell phone started playing his ringtone from the Eagles' "Peaceful Easy Feeling." He checked the caller ID and saw that it was his buddy Steve calling.

"Sheeeeeeen, buddy!" he answered. "'What's up?"

"Why, Brucie, how are you on this fine day?" Steve responded.

"I'm good, Stevie," Bruce said, "just chomping at the bit to get started with this gun gig."

"Well, I know the feeling," Steve chuckled. "And that's precisely why I'm calling. I've been going over this gun list that Mikey sent us and think we should make an effort to find a couple of guns before we head out to Deadwood to meet with Mikey and Bud. What do you think?"

"I'm agreeing with you, buddy," Bruce said. "I think if we could find something from the list, it would make the old guy believe that we are serious about this thing."

"Absolutely! My thoughts exactly," Steve said with emphasis.

"So there is a gun show this weekend in Montpelier, and I know the people who run it," Bruce added. "I think that would be a good place to start. It's not a huge gun show, but there are a lot of old timers who frequent the place who have been collecting for years. If we take the list, pick the most likely for us to find easily, and make some contacts, you never know what may happen."

"Sounds perfect," Steve said. "Let's do it."

"Great," Bruce said. "I'll make a call to let them know we are coming."

When Saturday came, Bruce and Steve drove the twenty miles to the gun show in Montpelier, Ohio. It was located in a back building at the county fairgrounds and was easily located by the amazing number of pickups and cars that surrounded all sides of it. The gun show was the only thing going on at the fairgrounds that weekend.

"Wow," Steve said. "This is a lot of people for a country gun show in the middle of Bumfuck Egypt."

"Hey," Bruce responded. "These are my people. Show a little respect for rural America," he laughed.

Steve said, "Oh I respect 'em. They are probably all carrying a weapon of some sort."

"Count on it!" Bruce countered. "I'm just really glad there is a good crowd. We might have some good luck here."

After Steve parked his mini-van, both men picked up some home-made signs that they were going to carry around the gun show. The process was pretty simple—carry a sign that was easily readable that spelled out what you were looking to buy and start walking and talking. It was a universal method used at gun shows that buyers and sellers had been using since gun shows began.

"You know, I hope this works" said Bruce.

"Well," Steve said," it's a longshot that we will run into someone who has any of these guns, but the important thing is to get some leads. Most of these guys and ladies are pretty savvy about collectible handguns, and they all like to talk."

"That *is* the key," Bruce agreed. "Get 'em talking and hopefully someone will head us in the right direction. But first, before anything, we need to pay the five buck fee to get in."

The guys headed to the entrance to the old fair building and went inside. Before they took any steps, though, a voice called out, "Hey, there you are. Thought maybe you weren't going to make it." Bruce turned and saw a familiar face coming quickly to him. The young lady threw a bear hug on him and said, "Great to see ya."

Bruce responded to the bear hug politely and said, "It's good to see you too, Beth." Beth was a young lady in her early twenties, a brunette that Bruce had gotten to know through some political functions that he had gone to. She was built like her dad, square around her shoulders and cute in her face. Bruce had never seen her wear anything but jeans and long-sleeve shirts. She liked to work hard, doing anything physical that she could. And she wasn't afraid to tell you where she stood on anything. Beth was a gun-toting diehard conservative who helped run the gun show with her dad, Duane, a former county commissioner who always seemed to know everyone in every room or event that he attended. It was no different here. A steady stream of people came through the door, paid their five bucks, and talked briefly with Duane before proceeding out into the main hall. And they didn't miss Beth, either. She knew them all too. Bruce pulled out his five bucks and motioned for Steve to do the same and tried to hand it to Beth. But she leaned in close to Bruce and said, "You guys are my guests, put the money away."

"Are you sure?" Bruce asked.

"Put it away!" she commanded and added, "I'm happy you are here, and Dad says the same thing. I think it's neat what you two have going on, and if I can help, let me know. By the way," Beth said as she stuck out her hand to Steve. "I'm Beth—if you're friends with Bruce, you're a friend of mine." Steve stuck out his hand, and Beth gave him a powerful hand shake. "Thanks for coming over." Then she said, "I'll steer you to a couple of the boys who might have some suggestions for you, but I think you should start making your way around the aisles with your signs first. Let me see what you are looking for again. I'll talk to a few guys myself, too."

"Thanks Beth," Bruce and Steve both responded at the same time.

"We have ten guns that we eventually need to find, but we decided to start easy and go after the most common ones," Steve said. "So we are looking for a Smith & Wesson Chiefs Special model 36 and a .22 Colt Woodsman 4.5-inch barrel in particular today."

"Okay," Beth said. "And what else? Do you have a copy of that list so that I can check it from time to time?"

"Sure do," said Bruce, and he handed her the copy he was carrying.

Beth scanned through it quickly. "Oh yes," she said to herself quietly. "These are some nice guns to collect. And I bet some of my guys will have leads for you." She continued, "Although, this one set of guns doesn't seem to fit."

"What do you mean?" Bruce questioned.

Beth responded, "Well, this set of Uberti Cattlemans is a replica. And I've never seen any in this neck of the woods or heard of anyone even talk about them. So my guess is you'll have to go somewhere else for those. Actually, I'm not sure what makes them so collectible for this list. But gun collectors are hard to define by gun choice," she added.

Steve jumped in, "And that's exactly what I told Bruce already. So that's why we're trying to get these other two off the list now."

Bruce chimed in, "I agree, too, but it's the collector's list, not mine."

"Okay," Beth said. "I'll start to ask my guys about the Chiefs Special and the .22 Woodsman; you guys start down the aisles with your signs; and we will see what happens. You picked a great time to come here, because we are full up with dealers and buyers. This is one of the larger shows we've had in a while. I guess the Obama factor is still on these guys' minds," she said.

Bruce and Steve nodded a knowing shake of the head. Since the Democrat, Barack Obama, had become President, gun sales in the U.S. had skyrocketed, and ammunition prices had gone through the roof, with lots of guys stockpiling their particular kind of ammo for fear of new gun restrictions being implemented. Actually, Steve and Bruce often joked that the NRA and other gun lobbies should be donating campaign money to President Obama's campaign committee because of his tremendous positive impact on the gun economy. *And who knows, maybe they are,* Bruce always added to the thought.

Bruce and Steve picked up their homemade signs that said—**LOOKING FOR S & W CHIEFS SPECIAL MODEL 36** and **LOOKING FOR .22 COLT WOODSMAN** and started down the first aisle, while Beth headed out to talk to her guys. This gun show, like most of them, was jam-packed with individual booths for commercial and private sales. Counting the people working in the booths and the people milling about walking down the aisles, Bruce estimated over a thousand people wanting to buy, sell, or just handle some of the guns and knives on display. Plus, there were lots of people carrying signs, like Bruce and Steve, wanting to buy or sell.

"Wow," Steve said. "There are some rough-looking dudes in this place. Some of them look like they just crawled out of the woods."

"Yep," Bruce said. "But there are also a lot of guys who look just like us." Then Bruce smiled and added, "But I do believe camouflage is the color of the day, and long scraggly beards or weeklong stubble outnumber the clean-shaven guys by about three to one." Steve nodded.

Every booth that the guys stopped at generated questions about the guns that they were looking for. "Why do you want those guns? Has anybody made an offer yet? How much you willing to pay?" However, about halfway through the walk around, no one had any suggestions, and no one had either of the two guns that they needed.

"Well, so far, nothing good," said Bruce.

"But I've seen a lot of guns I'd like to have," said Steve. "I love these shows."

"Yeah, right," said Bruce. "I'll love 'em if we find the guns we are looking for. Let's get a hotdog and Coke."

"Absolutely, I'm starved," Steve said. "This work stuff is hard on an empty stomach," he laughed.

As the two buddies sat at a picnic table eating their hotdogs and drinking their soft drinks, Bruce spied Beth working her way through the crowd towards them. Bruce stood up and said, "Hey, kiddo, you got something for us?"

"What?" Beth shot back. "Are you kiddin' me? I always take care of my friends." She had on a big smile that clearly outlined a huge dimple on her left cheek, that wasn't noticeable unless she was truly happy about something.

"So what is it?" Bruce questioned.

"Well, see that old grizzly bear looking guy over there in the middle booth?" Beth asked. "He said he could help you with both of the guns."

"No kidding," Steve said. "Wow! That would be incredible."

"But," Beth continued. "He's suspicious of you two—says he never saw you around the gun show before. Thinks you could be ATF agents or something."

"Oh my god!" Bruce blurted.

"And then he probably thinks we work for Obama as spies." Steve said.

"Probably," Beth said. "But he says it like it is, and if he says he knows where you can get these guns, he definitely knows. So get over there and make friends. I already told him what you were up to and that you were okay. Just tell him your story again."

"Let's do it," Bruce said. "You do the talking, Stevie. You have a natural affinity with mountain men. I'll listen for the banjos," he laughed out loud.

"Oh, by the way, his nickname actually is Grizzly Bear, but he goes by Bear." Beth added. "He won't tell you his real name."

"Imagine that!" Steve hooted.

As the two guys moved down the crowded aisle towards Bear, they noticed that he had a whole array of guns for sale. He was obviously one of the licensed dealers who come to this gun show on a regular basis. He saw them coming and watched as they navigated through the crowd with him looking surlier with every step they took. When the guys got to his table, he looked them up and down before Steve said, "Hi, Bear. Beth said you might be able to help us. I'm Steve, and this is Bruce."

Bear responded with a half whisper, half growl. Coupled with his fully bearded face and three hundred-plus pounds packed onto a six-foot-three frame, it was easy to understand why he was called Bear. "Beth said you guys are okay, so that's good enough for me," he growled. "My growl is worse than my bite," he said and then let loose with a tremendously loud laugh that startled everyone within twenty feet of his table.

Neither man had heard anything quite like that before. Momentarily surprised, Bruce and Steve stepped back for a second. And then Steve joined in the laughter with a huge laugh of his own and before you knew it, the three men were talking like old friends, mostly about the guns on the table and the huge display of knives that Bear was showcasing.

Then abruptly Bear growled and whispered, "I can get you hooked up with both of the guns you are looking for. They won't be cheap, but I can get 'em."

"Really?" Steve questioned. "That's outstanding. And cheap is not a part of our vocabulary," he emphasized.

Again with the whispered growl, Bear said, "Okay, gimme a card so I can call ya when I got 'em."

"Perfect," said Steve, and Bruce nodded as he handed Bear the card. "How long do you think?"

"Soon," Bear growled. "No later than next week. I'll call you."

With that, the conversation had ended, and Bear went back to hawking his guns and knives. Bruce and Steve walked away feeling like they had accomplished something. When Beth saw the guys again and heard about their encounter with Bear, she said, "I *told* ya. It's a done deal, if he said that. Congratulations."

Bruce and Steve looked at each other and said "Yessssss!" but deep down, they both had a fear that Bear wouldn't come through.

Steve said as they exited the building and got into their vehicle, "You know that we shouldn't put these on the found list until it's actually done, don't you?"

"Absolutely!" Bruce agreed. "As Yogi said, 'It ain't over 'til it's over.' So we still keep working at it. But it's good to have such a strong lead on the guns."

CHAPTER 8

The Director had been monitoring the situation in Dallas all day and deep into the night. He had his most trusted lieutenants update him hourly in person and by phone. *No loose ends,* he thought to himself—*no loose ends.* That was his personal and professional mantra. *Tie it down; nail it down; details, details, details. Pay attention to details....* This ran through his mind over and over again as he contemplated the events of the day. And no one, absolutely no one, was better at details than the Director. By the time he had decided to sleep in his office, he had gone through three shirt changes, underwear changes, and suit changes. No wrinkles for anyone to see and no hint of perspiration, nervousness, or extreme concern. He kept telling himself that if you look like you are in control, then people will believe it. That's how he presented himself to his public throughout the day—always in control.

But there were a few items that were nagging at him a bit, not anything that couldn't be controlled, but just nagging thoughts of "What if" and "If this happens, then what?" He shrugged these thoughts off, at least momentarily. However, the Director knew that in the end, every single nagging thought had to be addressed and fixed. Take for example his call to the Attorney General to tell him of the catastrophic event in Dallas. *The little prick,* thought the Director. *Questioning why I was the one to have called him. Well, little Bobby Kennedy, it was because I decided to, and I had the power to do it,* he chuckled. *It had to hurt even worse than it might have because it came from me, a sworn enemy to the Kennedy clan.* He felt himself immediately start to heat up at the condescending attitude that he always received from the clan, as he referred to them. *Bastards,* he thought. *Nothing but a clan of bastards and little rich boys. So who's holding all the cards now?*

Then there was the worried communication with LBJ. *Who was the first person he communicated with after being sworn in as President? It was me! The by-god Director!* But the thought of that conversation tweaked him a bit. LBJ's veiled questions of "Are we sure everything is okay? Are you taking care of everything?" made him a little uneasy. He needed the President to be at the top of his game and let the Director handle everything else. *And I have!* he thought.

Then the phone rang—it was his beloved Clyde. "Clyde," he said warmly. "I've been waiting to hear from you. Do you have any good news?"

"Well, it's mixed, Mr. Director," Clyde said. "As you know, Lee Harvey Oswald has been jailed in Dallas for killing a Dallas police officer and for suspicion in the assassination. So that seems to have been handled, at least for now."

"That seems to be going in the right direction then, Clyde," the Director said with some relief. "But you know that I don't want that commie, Oswald, to get with the press at any time. And to have limited time with the Dallas police. For god's sake, Clyde, who knows what might come out of that guy's mouth if he's allowed to be questioned without us in the room. We need to take full control of this process and control the outcomes."

"Yes, Mr. Director, we are getting closer to that happening. I'm quite sure that we will be calling the shots, literally, in a short time," Clyde laughed.

"This is not the time for jokes, Clyde," the Director lectured.

"Yes, I know, sir, sorry. But it just fit so perfectly."

"Well, remember, it's always the details that get missed that make or break a case," the Director continued to lecture. "All right now, Clyde, what about our merchandise? Has that been handled adequately?"

"Actually, no, Mr. Director, it's not," Clyde stated matter-of-factly.

"Well, you need to get it taken care of then. What's the latest?"

"The merchandise had to be routed through one of the last available options because of the restricted air space surrounding Air Force One," explained Clyde. "But you know we have Bud running that operation, and I feel it's in good hands. There is no need to panic at this point."

The Director jumped on this comment, "There is never any need to panic, Clyde, just loose ends to fix. Loose ends need to be tied down, nailed down, and all details need to be taken care of. Now, Clyde, communicate with Bud and make the loose ends go away, do you understand?"

"Absolutely, Mr. Director, I will make it happen."

"Thank you, Clyde, you always do. You have my complete trust in this matter." The Director finished the call with, "I'm sleeping in my office tonight. Keep me informed. Goodnight, Clyde." And the Director hung up the phone and moved towards the couch that he often used when big things were happening in the country.

CHAPTER 9

When the small Cessna lifted off from the tiny Johnson County airport, the man-in-charge felt a tightening of his stomach. Not from the takeoff, for god knows he had been flying on these small planes for years, but from the mind-tugging thought that he didn't get the job done properly. Now there were loose ends, and he could hear the Director's voice, admonishing him about, "Nail it down, tie it down, and take care of all details—never a loose end." *But it is what it is,* he thought to himself. *Now it's my job to make sure it doesn't come back to bite us in the ass.*

He turned to look at the rest of his entourage and for a split second thought about lecturing them about how important it will be to follow his next directions to a T. Then he decided not to. These men were all handpicked for the mission—the best of the best. And he knew that they would follow through on the plan. So as they headed back to Washington, the man-in-charge ran through a variety of scenarios in his head to counter what just happened in Buffalo and to correct the loose ends. Just then the pilot turned to look at him and signaled for him to put on his headphones.

"Hey, we have another situation. I just received word from the guys in D.C., and we have to divert to Baltimore to land. I guess the secret service has the Washington airport on lockdown until Air Force One and Air Force Two plus the C-130 carrying the President's limo are all down and secure. Do we have contingencies for a landing in Baltimore?"

"We will have," the man-in-charge said. "How much longer do we have in the air?"

The pilot quickly replied, "About an hour and forty minutes."

"Okay, I'll be on the hand radio for a few." The radio crackled, and he spoke, "We will need transport for six from the Baltimore airport in approximately one and a half hours. I will confirm runway and pickup details about a half hour out."

The voice on the radio said, "Roger that. A team will be in place. Nothing will be different except the airport."

The man-in-charge smiled to himself and repeated quietly "details." Everyone on board heard the destination change from the conversation between the pilot and the man-in-charge. No questions were asked, and no explanation was given.

The pilot requested the obligatory landing instructions from the Baltimore airport. He thought that there would be some slight delays because of his late request for landing status. But, unbelievably, that didn't happen. Instead, about twenty minutes from Baltimore, he received permission and the information that he needed. He had requested one of the little-used runways that were clearly out of eyeshot from anyone who might have the slightest interest in paying attention to a small plane arriving from Buffalo, Wyoming. It couldn't have worked out any better. The runway was old, little used, and surprisingly close to an entry gate that was commonly used by delivery trucks and airport personnel. The pilot glanced quickly at his co-pilot and marveled to himself—*This guy has some juice.*

And the man-in-charge just smiled and thought, *Now the plan is back on track. Details, details, details.*

The pilot followed the usual protocol for landing, found his runway, landed the plane with no problems, and taxied towards a gate that had been swung wide open for several vehicles to enter. After shutting down the props and putting the stairs in place, the pilot said, "Now," and all of the passengers except the pilot grabbed their carry-ons, exited the plane, and hurriedly jumped into the two waiting station wagons. Both cars had heavily tinted windows, and it was impossible to see how many other people were in them. But two of the men got in the first, two in the second, and then a long black limo pulled up. That seemed to be the signal for the station wagons to exit the gate; and for the two remaining men, the man-in-charge and his colleague from the back of the plane, to enter the limo.

The pilot jumped back onto his plane, started the engines, and worked his way to one of the fuel stations where he immediately refueled. He then asked for permission for takeoff and summarily took off, leaving everyone else to take care of their business, while he headed for a destination that he had not been given yet. But he knew it would be coming soon. *Just another detail to be nailed down,* he thought to himself.

CHAPTER 10

Mike was just finishing breakfast with the last of the pancakes that he had prepared for the Sunday morning K of C breakfast at Buffalo's large Catholic Hall. Actually, he was swallowing breakfast, as was his nature. Everything slow and in moderation except when it came to eating and drinking. It was never safe to sit too close when Mike was in a serious eating or drinking mode. So as he was prone to do, he sat by himself, slurping the pancakes down with huge mouthfuls, and washing them down with full glasses of draft beer that had been left over from a wedding reception the night before. Mike was supposed to be watching his diet, and he was, except when he was eating or drinking.

As he was about to jam the last of the huge pile of pancakes into his mouth, he heard his name, "Mike?"

He turned to see Bud standing beside him. "Damn," he said. "You almost made me choke on my pancakes."

"Sorry, Mike," Bud apologized. "It's my nature to approach people quietly and quickly. My experience has been that I prefer to be in charge of all situations. Just an old habit from another life." He smiled.

Mike smiled back and said, "Hey, buddy, thanks for your help. It's hard to get new blood to get involved with these kinds of things. Everybody always has an excuse."

"No problem," Bud said. "I find that I learn a lot about people by watching them work and by watching them interact with other people.

Since we are kind of working together, I thought this was a good idea to get to know you a little better. So I am happy to be here."

"Well, hell yes," Mike snorted. "That makes sense to me," as he promptly swallowed the last of the pancakes and a whole draft beer at the same time. "Well, what did you learn?" he probed Bud. Then he promptly let go with a gargantuan belch, pointed at Bud as if to accuse him, and let loose with his signature laugh. "Haw, haw. Sorry, buddy boy," he apologized. "When nature calls, I answer."

Bud just smiled and thought, *If this guy just knew that he was part of a plan, a plan meant to collect loose ends and details from the past, I'm sure he wouldn't be calling me buddy boy.*

But for now, Mike was rather entertaining for Bud. He had never really been around someone like Mike. He thought to himself about how the guys in his past, always professional acquaintances, never friends, were always so serious about everything. Always. Plus, he really couldn't think of any friends, not that he really had any, who were like Mike either—they too seemed to always be "on" and conscious of every word and deed.

Always on, Bud thought. *I hated it, but at the same time, I miss that whole lifestyle. I really hope that these civilians aren't going to get hurt in this process. But it's time to finish what was started all those years ago. And there is almost always some collateral damage in a mission,* he thought somewhat wistfully.

"Hey, Bud, whatcha doin' this afternoon?" Mike asked. "I'm goin' out to the range and shoot a little. Want to meet me there?"

Bud hesitated, then said, "Sure, Mike, I can be there at three. Does that work?"

"Hell yes, buddy boy, I'll be there. What you going to shoot?" Mike asked.

"Well, as you probably surmised from that gun list I gave you, I'm a pistol guy, so I'll bring a couple of handguns to shoot," Bud responded.

"Great," Mike said. "See ya there." Then Mike turned to say something to one of his helpers, turned back to say something to Bud, but Bud was already gone. *Wow,* Mike thought. *This guy is wound pretty tight. It should be interesting to shoot with him, though.* Then he swallowed one last draft beer, wiped his mouth with his sleeve, hitched up his bib overalls, and headed home.

The drive home took Mike about fifteen minutes. He lived on thirty-five acres of land a few miles from Buffalo in a modular home that he had brought in when he made the move from Ohio to Wyoming. It was a modest home, but it met all of Mike's needs, and the thirty-five acres made him a gentleman rancher of sorts...kinda, sorta. At least that's how he viewed himself. He had built a couple of small outbuildings and fenced in a small area for chickens and goats. He had originally planned to raise donkeys on his small piece of ground, but found that getting started in this endeavor would cost way more money than he had to work with. So he became the chicken whisperer.

For a guy who was raised in the city and had never been around any animals except for a few horses that his dad owned, Mike had an amazing knack for working with chickens. He talked to them, and they followed him everywhere, just like small dogs. Rosie and Sally were his favorites, and when he would call them, they would come running, turn around, and back up close to him so that he could reach down and pet them on their backs, rubbing them until they almost fell asleep. It was an amazing sight to see how his chickens reacted when he was around. And that's why his buddies started calling him the chicken whisperer. Mike loved his laidback lifestyle. Nothing was worth rushing through life for. He had enough to get by and that was okay with him. The pittance of a pension that he earned from Ohio only went so far, though. So when the offer from Bud came for him to find some collectible guns, he looked at it as a nice little switch from the usual. Plus, he really could use the money that Bud seemed willing to spend on finding his guns.

Wow, Mike thought as he turned into his drive, *time is flying. I better get my ass in gear, or I'm going to miss Bud.* He hurriedly got his shooting stuff together: handguns—a Ruger 9 mm, a .38 S & W Special, and a new .45 caliber Colt with lots of ammo—hearing protection, and sighting scope. *This should be enough. It's been awhile since I've shot these guns. So it's time. They all need to be cleaned anyway.*

Mike picked up the gear, headed out the door, and was immediately surprised to see Bud standing outside of a large, shiny, black pickup truck parked in his driveway.

"Whoa, pardner!" he called to Bud. "What's up? I thought I was meeting you at the range."

"Hi, Mike," said Bud, as if talking to an old friend. "Yes, sorry, you are right. But I got around early and thought I'd come by to pick you up. I hope that's all right with you."

"Hell, yes!" Mike shot back. "It works for me."

"Great," Bud answered. "Get in, and we will go."

Mike stretched his short legs and stocky frame onto the truck's step and pulled himself into the passenger side, placing his bag with all the weapons and other gear at his feet.

"Hope this isn't inconvenient for you," said Bud.

"Hell, no!" Mike said quickly. "This is perfect. It saves me the gas to get there."

Bud just smiled. He'd never had to worry about saving gas or money for anything for that matter. "Well, good," Bud continued. "It also gives me a chance to get to know you a little more. Like where you live, for example. You have a nice location, Mike," Bud added.

"Thanks, pardner. But how'd you know where I lived?" Mike asked.

"Oh, I guess I just make it a point to know as much about my acquaintances as I can," Bud said, basically evading the question. "Especially guys who I'm going into business with," he chuckled.

Mike thought about that for a bit, and then said, "Well, I'm an open book, buddy boy. Nothing to hide here."

"Oh, I know that, Mike," continued Bud. "I'm just detail oriented—I guess as a result of my work in the past. But that's old news, Mike," Bud quickly added and then moved on to other chit chat about Mike's life on his mini-ranch.

But Mike felt the hair on the back of his neck stand up a bit. This was something Mike always said happened whenever something or someone didn't feel quite right. *And this Bud fella, even though he seems okay....Probably nothing,* Mike thought. *But I just have to pay close attention to this guy's words. It's almost like he says more in his comments than he is really saying.* Mike decided to probe a little bit more and brought the conversation back to Bud's comment about his past work. "So, pardner, what did you say you did for a living? Was it working for the government?"

Bud responded, "Well, Mike, you know, I really can't talk about it. But it was government related. You know the old saying, 'I'd have to kill you if I told you?' That's a joke, but in some areas of government business, it may be true. In fact, let's just say that I do know of situations that would require that. But again, I'm retired now, so I'd just as soon not go there. Capiche?" he asked with a wry smile and a slap on Mike's shoulder.

"Okay, pardner," Mike responded. "No problem. But it works both ways, so don't go asking me anymore about my story, either, because I may just have to shoot you—just for the hell of it though."

And Mike erupted into his deep full-throated bellow of a laugh, "Haw, haw, haw," until it caused him to cough so loud that Bud asked,

"You okay, Mike? Sounds like you almost lost a lung there." He patted Mike on the back.

"I'm good—too many goddam ceegars—if you get what I mean."

Bud nodded and smiled and just then they were at the range. Both men felt it was good timing, as they both had a sense of going where neither wanted to go at this time. Mike didn't want to piss Bud off and lose his money-making possibility, and Bud just didn't want to go any further down that road. Bud pulled his pickup into the drive of the range and went all the way back to the pistol shooting area.

"This is a great range, Mike," Bud said as he found a close parking spot. "Plenty of wide open spaces and protective bunkers to keep errant shots on the range and from traveling into unsafe areas."

"Yep," said Mike. "The members really stepped up when we needed them. When I got out here several years ago, it was a mess, and dangerous. I was able to get some good guys to be leaders, along with myself, and this is the result. It is completely revamped, and guys come from all over to shoot here now. And our membership is continuing to grow—we have leagues and kid's groups—you name the gun activity, and we've done it or are trying to figure out how to do it." Mike added, "I feel good about the work I've put in here. But that doesn't mean I can shoot any better," he added with a "Haw, haw."

"We'll see about that in a bit," Bud said as he unlocked the compartment in the bed of his massive pickup. He took out his gun gear first, hearing protection, shooting glasses, an eyepiece for checking accuracy, then a handful of targets that had shadow figures of a man as the focal point. He seemed to be waiting to bring out the handguns that he was going to fire, at least momentarily. Bud seemed to be more interested in what Mike was bringing to the party, so to speak. He spoke to Mike, "So what are you going to shoot, Mike?"

Mike was busy getting the targets set up and responded after a bit. "I have a .44 Magnum, the kind that made Dirty Harry famous; a .45 caliber Colt; and a Ruger .22 caliber plinking pistol. I can't afford to shoot the .44 and the .45 as much as I would like, so I bring the .22 so I can shoot longer. The .22 has a laser sight that works great too," he added. "And you, pardner, what did you bring?" he asked Bud.

Bud responded to the question by opening a silver gun case, which looked very much like a briefcase, and pulled out a Colt Single Action Army pistol, a gun favored in the old Wild West. And it was a very expensive original model.

"Oh my god!" Mike exclaimed. "That is an amazing gun. Where in the hell did you get that?"

Bud smiled and said, "This is my baby. I don't shoot it much. But I just felt the need to bring it today." He added, "It was a gift from a business acquaintance many years ago."

"That's a hell of a business acquaintance, pardner," Mike practically shouted. "Feel free to introduce him to me. I'm sure he'd like me enough to give me one too." He laughed and smacked Bud on the back.

Bud smiled and said, "I'm sure he would." As an afterthought he said, "But it would depend on how dirty your hands got." And then he thought again about how true the old adage about, "If I told you I'd have to kill you" was.

"Oh, pardner, my hands could get pretty dirty for a gun like that!" Mike shot back.

If this "civilian" only knew what kind of dirt I was talking about, Bud thought as Mike finished talking. Then Bud pushed a button on the briefcase and a false compartment opened from the top of the case and revealed the second gun he was going to shoot. It, too, was a Colt SAA Cattleman's 1873, but it had a 7.5-inch barrel. In fact, this gun was called a Peacemaker and was famous for its role in taming the Wild West. It was drop dead beautiful in any gun person's eyes.

"Wow, Bud," Mike exclaimed. "You're killing me. That is so amazing, so beautiful—I think I need to sit down."

Bud laughed out loud at Mike's response to the second gun. He pulled it out, grabbed a soft cloth to put on the shooting table, and placed both guns on the cloth. "These guns are both very important to me, and I would be happy to let you shoot each today."

Mike quickly and loudly said, "Hell yes, to that!" Mike started out to place the targets, but Bud quickly said, "I'd prefer if you used my targets—the ones with shadow figures on them. It makes it more real for me," he added.

Mike chuckled, came back, and grabbed a few of Bud's targets and took off again to place them—at ten yards and twenty-five yards. He thought it odd to be shooting at human figures. Almost universally at this range the shooters used circular targets. *But what the hell,* Mike thought. *I don't mind shooting at them either.*

When Mike got back, he and Bud loaded their weapons and took turns firing. Mike started with his .45, switched to the Magnum, and then when he was out of ammo, he went to load his .22. Bud just waited and watched as Mike was all over the place on the target, especially from twenty-five yards. Then Bud fired the Colt Army first at the ten yard target. Boom, Boom, Boom!

Mike yelled "Oh my god! Three in the middle of the forehead—Wow!"

Bud shot several more shots with the Army—and never missed the head—that is until he said, "Okay, one in the heart with the last shot."

And he did—straight through the heart. Mike watched in amazement. Bud then switched to the Peacemaker 7.5-inch barrel and shot again, this time at the twenty-five-yard target while calling each shot.

"Head," he called. (Boom!—dead center) "Heart," he called again. (Boom!—dead center) "Three to the throat," he called one last time. (Boom! Boom! Boom! —all dead center)

Mike exclaimed, "That's incredible!" and he started clapping.

Bud just smiled and started to put both guns away—then remembered and said, "Go ahead and shoot them, Mike."

It didn't take long for Mike to pick up the guns, load them, and empty the cylinders of both guns. He didn't come close to the silhouette on the target.

"Thanks, Bud," he said after handing the guns back. "Those are great guns. Obviously, they're too good for me."

Bud laughed, "It's just training and practice."

Mike thought to himself about those words, *I wonder what training and practice he is talking about.* But he decided to not push the point again. He was sure he would probably get the, "If I told you I would have to kill you" response again. Instead he said, "My buddies are really excited about this gun gig. They're already working on a couple of leads for two of the guns on the list."

"Great," said Bud. "It'll be good to meet them. We should probably start thinking of a time to get together. Deadwood is a great place for a meeting and some pleasure too."

Mike responded, "We are all just waiting for you to say the word, and we will be there."

"All right, then," Bud said. "I'll let you know soon. It will probably be next month. That will give you some time to do a little research. I'll get you details soon, and I'll get you some money to proceed."

"Works for us," Mike said.

"Well, let's get going, Mike," Bud said. "I have some things to get done." Both men carried their gear and guns back to the pickup, jumped in, and took off for Mike's place. "Thanks, Mike," Bud said as he dropped Mike off, "that was enjoyable."

"Take care, Bud," Mike shot back. "See ya soon." Mike went into his house and thought a couple of things, *How did Bud get to be such an amazing shot?* and *What the hell is this guy really up to?* Then he decided, *I guess we shall see how this plays out. Maybe I'm just being my old paranoid self. But something just doesn't feel right.*

Then he went out to feed his chickens.

CHAPTER 11

As the man-in-charge and his colleague from the back of the plane settled into the limo, he sensed they were not alone. The windows were tinted almost black, and the door light did not illuminate when the door was opened so it was impossible to see in the darkness. No light came in from the outside, and no light had been left on in the back portion of the cavernous limo. It immediately made him uneasy. He said nothing and waited.

"So Bud, how are you and how are things going?" came an unmistakable voice from the darkened back seat.

Oh my god! It's the Director himself, he thought. "Hello, Mr. Director. I'm fine and things are going well to this point." He forced himself to speak with the tone of authority and self-assuredness that he used with his men on assignment. "I'm surprised to see you here, sir," he continued. "Is there a problem?"

"Problem?" the Director repeated. "How can there be a problem if you have covered all the loose ends and carried out all the details, Bud? So I ask you now, do we have a problem?" But before Bud could speak, the Director turned to a darkened figure sitting next to him and spoke very quietly. That person then opened the limo door again and slid out quickly and quietly, like he had never been there. The Director repeated, "Bud, do we have a problem?"

Now Bud spoke as his colleague squirmed uncomfortably on his seat, "Sir, we had to use an alternate plan to leave Dallas and, as a result, we do have some unresolved details to handle. Those details will be handled soon though, Mr. Director."

"Handled, Bud?" the Director questioned with a tone of sarcasm in his voice. "Just what the hell does that mean?"

The tone in the Director's voice worried Bud. The thought crossed his mind, *Am I a loose end that needs to be fixed too?* He was always prepared for something like that. His was a dirty business, and he knew that the people controlling the dirty business were always on edge and wary. The easiest way to fix things was to eliminate the potential threat. *That could mean me,* he thought. He thought about the man who got out of the car. *Is he just waiting for an order?* It's crazy how a multitude of thoughts can race through your mind when the pressure is on. He got himself under control though and responded, "What it means, sir, is that you have one of your best men in charge of this thing, me, and I assure you I will fix it. I have never let you down before, and this will not be the first time."

The Director came close to a chuckle, but didn't, and said, "That's what my good friend Clyde said. And even though, I am apprehensive, I will follow Clyde's advice and leave it to you." Then he leaned forward, peered at Bud and his colleague out of the darkness, and ordered in a threatening tone, "You, my friend, will fix this goddam clusterfuck! And fix it immediately. That is why I am here with you now. I want you to have no misperception of what you are to do. And that is precisely **whatever... it... takes....**" He dragged out the last three words in emphasis and then said. "You can get out now. I have arranged for another car for you. Keep Clyde informed of every single move and every single detail. Goodbye, Bud. Goodbye, Howard." He acknowledged Bud's colleague for the first time.

"Yes, sir. Goodnight, sir," they both responded at the same time as they exited the car. As soon as the limo door shut, it was gone, and another took its place. Both men got in and gave a sigh of relief, feeling that they had been given a reprieve. Without speaking, they both knew that the reprieve could disappear at any moment, unless all of the details were dealt with and nailed down.

When the Director returned to his office, even though it was the middle of the night, his longtime assistant met him at the door and said he had an urgent phone call from the President.

What a woman! he thought to himself. "How did he reach you, Miss Gandy?" he asked as he walked into the office.

"I couldn't sleep," she replied. "With all of the events of the day, I knew you would be here all night, and I decided to come in to see if you needed me. Then I got his call," she continued, "but I couldn't find you or Clyde, so I waited."

"Next time, don't wait. Try harder to find me," he said curtly.

She responded to his rudeness with a simple, "Yes sir, I will, sir," and then, "Here is the number you can reach him at, sir." She knew he cared about her and respected her, but he just didn't know how to be that kind of person. Historically, the closer you were to him, the more he expected and the less he acknowledged your worth to him.

In his mind, though, he did. *Miss Gandy is indispensable. I shall take care of her some day for her loyalty,* he often thought. And he was thinking just that as he sat down to call the new President.

"Mr. President, this is the Director," he spoke benignly into the phone.

"What a goddam day!" the President said and repeated, "What a goddam day!"

"Yes, Mr. President, it has been that," the Director responded. "Remember, I am here to help you in any way."

"Thank you, Director. I appreciate that," the President went on. "The reason I called is to make sure we are all okay with this thing. Nothing coming to bite us in the ass, Director?"

"I believe we are good here, Mr. President," he said. "Clyde has been keeping me up to date around the clock, and I've met with our man on the ground in Dallas," the Director continued. "He flew back to D.C. behind Air Force One and Air Force Two and apprised me of his thoughts."

Acting like he hadn't heard a word that the Director said, the President continued, "Because you know that our asses will be hung out to dry if things don't look kosher, if you know what I mean."

The Director responded again, "Yes, Mr. President. You know I'll be paying attention to details."

This time speaking over the Director, the President continued, "You make sure your guys are setting the table and that this Oswald guy is locked in tighter than a drum. He's the key," the President continued. "Don't be letting the local guys close to the bastard and don't be letting the press create something that will get in the way of getting this done right."

The Director, now openly agitated with the attitude of the President, said again, "Yes, sir, I feel very strongly that we have it under control."

The President ignored the edge that was climbing into the Director's voice and instead continued, "And what about his brother? Can you keep him from smelling up the process? You know he'll be sticking his goddam nose in and stirring things up. I can hear him now, shaking that conspiracy stick to every reporter who will listen. You just need to control that, Director."

"I will do that, Mr. President," he reiterated. "You know I'll get things taken care of."

"All right then," the President said. "That's all I wanted to say." And he hung up while the Director was beginning to speak.

What a fucking prick! He thought. *He better realize who he's talking to. Next time, I will do the talking, and he will do the listening!* With his blood still boiling, he got on the phone to Clyde. He woke him up, recounted his conversation with the President, and immediately began to feel better.

Clyde reassured him, "You know he's just feeling the power now, sir. That will change as he realizes who is actually in charge of this thing. I guarantee his tone will change. We need to set a meeting with him tomorrow and make some things clear to him," Clyde continued. "He'll be up to his ass in everything else, but that's exactly why we need to make sure who is important to him."

"Clyde, thank you very much," said the Director. "You have given me a new perspective, and I appreciate that. I assume you will let me know when the meeting is set?" he questioned.

"Absolutely," Clyde responded.

"Good night, Clyde."

"Good night, sir.

CHAPTER 12

Steve and Bruce had been doing their due diligence in searching for the two guns that they had targeted from the list. After a number of phone calls back and forth to discuss progress and direction in their search, it was time to get together again. This time they decided to meet at a place in town called Jersey's. It was a quiet little restaurant that had been many different types of eateries over the years, including a popular dance club during the disco era. The three buddies would sometimes stop by during their younger years. As usual, Bruce was the first to arrive. The front receptionist asked about his seating preference.

Bruce said, "How about one of the tables in the back beside the bar? My buddy is coming, and we need to see the keno screen." Bruce really preferred a booth for comfort, but Steve couldn't easily fit his girth into a booth, so it was always a table when the two got together.

The receptionist smiled, "Right this way she said, and are you guys going to play keno today? I believe that this is your usual table, with the good view of the keno screen."

"Yes, perfect, thanks," Bruce answered back. He sat down just as he saw Steve entering the restaurant. He waved and Steve headed in his direction, with a knowing grin.

"Looks like you are in the mood to lose more money, buddy boy," he said to Bruce as he sat down.

"Nothing ventured, nothing gained," Bruce shot back.

"Well, it seems to be always venturing and no gaining." Steve laughed. "Just sayin'."

Bruce nodded in agreement and said, "You know, now that we retired guys are on a fixed income, maybe we shouldn't be doing this as often."

"Oh yeah, right!" Steve shot back with sarcasm. "Like you are gonna quit gambling."

"Nope," Bruce said. "I said maybe, and maybe does not work for me." Both guys then got up and went to the keno machine, put in their twenty bucks for their numbers, and settled in to lose again. But the losing wasn't the reason they came to Jerseys today. "All right," Bruce said. "What do you have? And then I'll go over my stuff."

"For starters," Steve began. "I have been all over the Internet gun sites and have found three potentials for the Smith & Wesson Chiefs Special model 36. I have discovered that they really are very hard to find. That is unless you want to settle for a gun that's shot out and marked up."

"Nope," Bruce said. "We need to get the best we can get if we want to make a statement to Mikey's buddy that we can do the job."

"Yep," Steve said. "I agree, and that's why only a couple of these are worth looking at. By the way, each of these three guns is going for about a thousand bucks, and that's a little high."

"But remember, we are supposed to be finding the guns, and Mikey's buddy will do the buying," Bruce interjected.

"Right, right," Steve said. "So I'll keep looking for the Chief and try to narrow it to the best choice possible. Now, as far as the .22 Woodsman goes, it appears to be an easier find on the Internet. There are lots more of these on the Internet sites. My best options are in very good condition, and all price out around twelve hundred bucks for the 4.5-

inch barrel. That will give us some potential with both guns, provided that our man, Bear, doesn't come through for us."

"I think you are right on, buddy," Bruce said to Steve. "I've been canvassing the gun shops all around the state, and I've found both guns at very near the same prices as you have. The kicker is I think our guy wants mint condition, and I couldn't find any like that. And it sounds like neither did you."

"Yep, you're right. Nothing in mint." Steve said. "But we do have some options to present."

"Yes, that's right, but I'd really like to impress the guy and find 'perfect pieces,' if you know what I mean. Let's give it a few more days of research, hope Bear calls us—the time should be about right—and then decide which ones to select."

"Sounds like a deal," they both agreed.

"Hey, look at that—I just got five out of ten numbers," Bruce shouted. "Winner, winner, chicken dinner!"

"Works for me," Steve said. "Remember, the keno winner buys lunch. I believe you just made me a winner too."

"Dammit, Sheen," Bruce said. "Every time I win, I lose around you. Okay, I'm buyin'—let's go. I'll call you tomorrow." Bruce collected his winnings and paid the bill while Steve gave him the victory sign as he went out the door.

Bruce was driving the few miles home from the restaurant when his cell phone rang.

"Hello," he said into the receiver.

A voice growled back, "Is this Goode?"

"Yes, it is," Bruce said, knowing instantly who was on the other end of the phone. That growl was unmistakable. "Bear, how are you?" he asked without hesitation.

The growl came back, "Not too fuckin' bad. I got your guns like I said I would," he continued to growl. "Three thousand bucks will get it done for you."

"Wow, that's great, but pretty high end," Bruce answered. "I need to check with my buddy to make sure he's on board."

The growl came back louder, "No need to check. You asked for 'em. I got 'em. Now you owe me three thousand bucks."

Bruce swallowed hard and thought, *This isn't the kind of guy to piss off.* Into the phone he said, "Okay, no problem Bear as long as they are the best out there."

"I'll say this once, cuz you don't know me too good," Bear responded. "If I say it, it's true. If I do it, it's done. And if you fuck with me, you're fucked. Got it?"

"Yes, Bear. I got it," Bruce replied.

"And, yes. They are the best," Bear continued to growl. "Brand new, in the box. That would be a hundred percent to you. Just what you wanted."

"Okay, buddy," Bruce said. "It's a deal then. When and where?"

"The next gun show starts on Saturday," Bear growled a little less menacingly. "I'll be there all day. Come with a cashier's check or cash. Make sure you bring your marshmallow buddy. I like him. He seems to know a little about guns."

"You got it, Bear," Bruce said. "We'll be there in...." And the phone went dead. Bear had obviously concluded the conversation. Bruce smiled and finished the thought in his head *...the morning.* Then he dialed his buddy, Steve.

"Hey, what's up?" Steve answered.

"Bear called, and he's got our guns."

"Really," Steve asked. "Did you tell him we were looking around?"

"I started to, but he wasn't taking that very well, and he said they were mint in the box." Bruce explained. "He basically said, or implied, that if we don't take them, we wouldn't get any more help from him. So for three thousand in the box, I think we should do it."

"That works for me," Steve said. "That's not too bad for being in the box and for building a good contact. Let's do it."

"Okay, good. Cause I already said yes." Bruce laughed. "His threats felt pretty real to me, and his voice scares the shit out of me."

Steve laughed out loud and said, "You are such a wuss!"

"We will go to the gun show on Saturday morning and get 'em," Bruce said as he ignored the comment.

"All right. I'll pick you up at nine," Steve said. "Let's go hear the Bear growl some more," he laughed again.

The guys pulled into the credit union to get the three thousand bucks for their purchase. Even though Bud had said he would do the purchasing himself, they thought that he would be more impressed if they gave him a done deal. So they were willing to upfront the cash to get it done.

"You know, buddy," Steve said. "We can't lose either way, if these guns are truly mint."

"Yep," Bruce responded. "If Bud doesn't like them, we will get our money back or even be happy to keep them as an investment."

"Absolutely," Steve said.

They threw their cash together in a small envelope and headed to the gun show. When they arrived, they parked in almost the same space as they had the last time and headed into the building. The first person they saw was Beth, who was busy checking in guns to make sure they were unloaded and taking the fees from a long line of folks eager to get into the show. She noticed them right away, left a line of guys standing, and came to give them both a hug.

"I see you've made it back," she said. "Did you find what you were looking for?"

Bruce responded, "We hope so. Bear said to bring money, so we brought money. By the way Beth," Bruce whispered quietly into her ear, "is he as badass as he appears?"

Beth never hesitated, "Hell to the 'H. E. double L' yes! You screw with him, and you might lose a body part, a sensitive body part," she laughed deeply.

"That's the sense I got," Bruce said.

"Well, good luck and let me see what you get. I gotta get back. The natives are getting restless. Bear is in aisle three."

"Thanks," Steve said as they moved towards the badass Bear.

When they spotted Bear, he had already locked in on them as they were walking down the aisle. He got up, waved for them to follow him, and went down the aisle and out the side door of the building. There were signs all over saying that you couldn't use the side door, but no one seemed to want to tell Bear that he couldn't. He was absolutely an imposing sight, standing around six foot three with huge broad shoulders, a long full black mountain man beard, and camouflage from head to toe. He weighed in easily at over three hundred pounds.

"There's our man," Steve said. "He is quite a sight. Don't piss him off, Brucie."

"I was just going to tell you the same thing," Bruce responded. "My god, he is a hell of a specimen, not someone you would ever want to run into by yourself, day or night, unless he counted you as a friend."

"Let's be his friend, then," Steve chuckled.

As they left the building, Bear signaled for them to come over to a huge camouflage-painted pickup that he was standing by.

The guys both said, "Hey, Bear, how ya doin'?"

Back came the familiar growl, "Pretty fuckin' good, if you got the money and we make a deal."

"We're ready," Steve said.

Bear reached into a lockbox on the bed of his pickup and pulled out two gun boxes that looked like new, set them carefully onto the tailgate, and growled, "Here they are. Open 'em up."

Steve hesitated a second, probably worried about getting too close to the half man, half bear, then stepped forward and opened the box for the Chief .38 special. "Wow," he exclaimed and let out a low whistle. "This is beautiful, and obviously in mint condition." Then he did the same for the .22 Colt Woodsman and let out another exclamation of "Wow."

Both guys looked at Bear, and Bruce said, "Here's the three grand. These are great."

Bear accepted the cash and uttered in a low growl, "It's what I said I would do. Don't ever doubt me." The growl continued, "Let me know if I can get you something else." He sounded threatening, yet willing to do more business at the same time.

The guys picked up the guns, and Bear turned and left to go back into the gun show. He growled something unintelligible as he left. Neither guy could make it out, but they were happy to have the guns. Both thought that Bear might come in very handy to them as they continued to search for more of the collectible guns on their list.

Even Beth was impressed with the quality of the guns when the guys showed her what Bear had found. "Niiiiice," she said. "I thought he might be able to help. But if you need him in the future, just be aware and be careful how you approach him. He didn't get his nickname Grizzly Bear because of his sunny disposition," she laughed. "But he does have contacts all over this country."

"Thanks again, Beth." Bruce said. "We better get out of here, before we get crazy and spend some more money on guns. We will be in touch." As they walked out of the building and jumped into the truck, both guys were very happy with the first fruits of their labor and were looking forward to setting that meeting with Bud.

"I think it's time to call Mikey again," Bruce said.

"Seems appropriate," Steve agreed.

CHAPTER 13

The Occidental Hotel in Buffalo had gotten its reputation as a meeting place for Old West outlaws and lawmen in search of those outlaws. Even though the saloon was a raucous and potentially dangerous place because of the copious amounts of alcohol consumed by its patrons, it was considered by almost everyone to be neutral turf. Oh, there were the occasional shootouts from frustrated and drunken gamblers, as evidenced by the numerous bullet holes in the walls and ceiling, but conflicts between good guys and bad guys just didn't happen. In fact, by November of 1963, the old hotel and saloon was well on its way to being a footnote of Wyoming history. The current owner was facing huge financial difficulties and could find no one to step up and float him a loan large enough to refurbish the building and save its colorful past. Famous people no longer stopped by, local folks had quit frequenting the place, and the owner was desperate.

Oh my god, the owner lamented to himself. *What have I gotten myself into?* The men dressed in suits and carrying the silver briefcases had just left, and now he had to wait patiently, but nervously, for the man-in-charge to pay him for his work. He thought back to how this all came about. *Work,* he thought. *This is really something else, not work.* He knew the feeling of breaking the law. He was no angel. So he felt it from the beginning when an old acquaintance from long ago called him and said that he needed help and that the owner would be rewarded quite generously for that help.

"How much?" the owner asked.

"How does ten thousand sound?"

"Are you shittin' me Bud?" he asked incredulously. "What do I have to do, kill someone?"

Bud responded coolly, "No, that's already been done." Then he laughed as if it were a huge joke. "But you do need to provide a safe place to store some merchandise for me for a while."

"What the hell is it?" the owner continued to question.

Bud responded with a cool directness that came from situations just like this, "I can't tell you, but you just need to keep the merchandise safe until I can get back here to retrieve it. It could be a day, a few days, or weeks. It just has to be safely stored and here, when I walk through your door. Got it?" Bud emphasized with a hint of threat in his voice.

The owner of the Occidental knew he had no choice. Without the money, he would have to close the old hotel's doors. With the money, he could hold off the seemingly inevitable for at least a while longer, until maybe he could access some other way to fund the redo.

"Okay, I'm in," he said. "What's next?"

Bud told him to sit tight and wait for his call. And the call came. And now he was in deep, with whatever it was that he had agreed to.

After he was sure that Bud and the other five guys were gone, the owner went back down the basement steps and into the corner room of the basement that was a monument to another time in history. The block walls were crumbling, and the wooden floors overhead were creaking with the stress of literally thousands of long-gone patrons from a bygone era. If you believed in ghosts, this basement would be the perfect habitation for the likes of Butch and Sundance, Tom Horn, Teddy Roosevelt, long-dead sheriffs from a wild Wild West, and too many outlaws to count. The owner switched on the switch in the room and looked at the merchandise that he had recently acquired. Four silver briefcases all locked with built-in combination locks, seemingly brand new and appearing to have never been unlocked. He hefted each to check the weight and noticed that they all carried a similar feel, that is, with one exception.

Maybe it's my imagination, he thought. *But this one has a different feel and weight to it. It's obviously carrying something, but the weight is just a little off from the other three cases. Hmmm, I just need to remember that it's none of my business to notice anything about these cases, except that they are stored away safely.*

Then he went to the far corner of that dilapidated basement room, grabbed a huge wooden dowel, and pulled on it. Incredibly, a false wall popped open to reveal a faux safe that had obviously been hidden away since the first reconstruction of the hotel. It was covered in spider webs and dust and had not been opened in years, probably decades, until the owner found it by accident many years ago. Inside, he had found a few pieces of early memorabilia from the Johnson County War and a couple of old pistols that had no markings to connect them to anyone from that era.

As far as hiding places go, he thought. *This was about as good as it could get. That is unless the whole place burned down or got knocked down by a demolition crew.* He smiled.

One by one, the owner picked up the briefcases and moved them into the safe, resisting the urge to shake each one. When he was done, he pushed the creaky door shut, pushed up the dowel to its lock placement, and sighed, *I guess I'm into it now. That son of a bitch Bud better be getting me some money real fast.* On his way up the basement stairs he wondered, *How did Bud pick this place and me to help him with whatever scheme this was?* "Oh god, I hope he isn't going to get me killed," he said out loud to no one as he reached the top of the stairs, turned off the lights, and stepped back into the nearly empty saloon.

Meanwhile, Bud was contemplating similar thoughts as his mind raced through the events of the day. *I hope like hell that I've made the right call on this move,* he thought. He felt like things were not as orderly and tied down as they should be. *My gut is telling me that I've missed a detail,* he worried. *But I can't for the life of me think what it might be.* The only prudent act was to get rid of the merchandise in an easily retrievable spot. *That's why I chose the Occidental,* he recapped in his mind. He smiled as he remembered how this place even became an option.

About five years ago, Bud was visiting an old buddy who had moved to Buffalo, Wyoming, from Seattle. The friend had been a long-time government employee, partnering with Bud on many occasions. The visit was supposed to be a friendly visit, but as usual, Bud never did anything without mixing in a lot of business with pleasure. He kept copious notes on everything in his life, including his supposed getaways. So it was quite natural for him to note all of the places and people that he met. Bud's friend happened to take him to the museum in Buffalo and to the Occidental Hotel. The museum was small and anything but boring to the inquisitive Bud. He loved conflict and the art of handling conflict. The museum was basically that—a time capsule of early American conflict on the plains of the Wild West.

As he walked through the small rooms filled with life objects from the early Wyoming settlers and peeked into the murderous lifestyles that brought death and tragedy to Johnson County residents during the Johnson County War, Bud said to his friend, "You know, I believe that I can learn a lot from the actions of these people—how they lived, how they died, and what motivated them to do what they did." He continued, "Not all that much has changed from then 'til now." *Disagreements over power, land, and love,* he thought. *These things got people killed in the 1800s and are still fueling the motives for almost every conflict up to the present.*

Bud looked at his friend, and his friend was shaking his head in agreement. Then he said, "Bud, why in the hell are you writing things down about Johnson County? It's all right here."

"Yes," Bud said. "It's all right here, but in my peculiar way of keeping track of things, I have to take notes, file them in my own notebooks, and check them from time to time—just in case I run across something that I can use when I need it. I know it looks crazy, but in my way of doing things there is a method to my madness," he laughed.

After the museum, the old friends went to get some lunch at the old Occidental Hotel and poke around a bit. They stopped on the sidewalk in front of the old façade of the hotel and marveled that it was still standing. Years of neglect and disrepair had taken a heavy toll on the building. But it was still easy to see the three sections that were an early part of the construction of the hotel. Standing on the street, looking from right to left, Bud's friend explained that the far right front of the building had been built in 1903, the middle in 1908, and the far left in 1910. He explained that the current owner was an old lady who had been running the place for years, since her husband and his father had won the business in a high stakes poker game. They asked the son's wife to run the place for a short time, maybe a month, until they could find someone or sell it. "That was back in 1918, and she's still running it," his friend laughed. "Her husband helps to run it on occasion, but she mostly doesn't want him around mucking things up and gettin' in the way."

Bud laughed as they entered the saloon portion of the hotel. *This is really a unique property,* he thought to himself. *It's the kind of place that might prove useful to me in the future,* as he continued to write notes to himself. His friend just watched and shook his head as he ushered Bud towards the truly eye-catching part of the building's interior. "Wow!" Bud exclaimed. "Look at that bar—it must be at least twenty-five feet long and made out of some sort of gleaming solid wood!" He rubbed his hand over the smooth wood bar and pulled himself onto an old high back bar stool.

"Back in the old days," his friend said, "most of the patrons would come in and lean against the bar. There were very few bar stools like you see here."

Bud added, "I'll bet there were a lot of conflicts started and maybe finished right here. Look at the bullet holes in the ceiling and the walls," Bud continued as he counted up to twenty-one."

"Yes," his friend said. "There were lots of legendary fights in this old saloon."

Just then an older fella came out from what appeared to be a kitchen area behind the bar. "Howdy, gents, what can I do for ya? Name's Smitty, and I run this place with my wife, who truth be told, is the real boss." He snorted out a laugh. "I hired her years ago, and I'm still payin' for that one. So what can I get ya?" he persisted.

Bud and his friend laughed with the old fella and ordered a buffalo burger and beer. Bud was finding himself more and more interested in this old place and started to talk with the old guy as he took notes and ate his buffalo.

"What the hell ya writin'?" Smitty asked and actually sounded a lot like his friend.

So Bud explained again like he did for his friend. But then Bud started to ask the Smitty questions, one after another: How old was the place? Who are the current owners? Where is your wife? Does she really call the shots? And finally, is the old hotel going to survive being torn down?

The old guy finally said, "Whoa, pardner, I can understand you're interested in the history of the place, but give me a chance to catch my breath. I'll be right back."

Bud finished a few notes and then got up and walked around the saloon and into the hotel portion of the building. "Wow," he said to his friend from across the room, "if anyone took a chance and put some money into this old dinosaur, I think this could be turned into an amazing place, much like it used to be all those years ago. I think the locals could support it, and the tourists would find it," he continued.

Bud's friend said to him, "What in the hell are you talking about? No one's got money around here to take that chance. And you certainly don't have time—you don't even take any time off without working on some project that you can tie into your work."

Bud responded, "That may be so, but I do have a feeling that this place has potential, as a business and for my job."

Smitty reentered the saloon from what appeared to be an old basement door behind the bar and said, "Sold—if you are interested and if you have any money. Just don't tell my wife I sold it until I have time to get outta town," he laughed.

Bud laughed back at Smitty and said, "Nope, can't buy it now. But let us know if you ever need some help to keep the old girl open." He nodded at his buddy and added, "My friend and I may be able to help." His friend shot him a what-the-hell-are-you-thinking look and shook his head "no way" at Bud. Then Bud asked, "Hey, Smitty, what's down those stairs?"

Smitty turned to the basement door, pulled it open, and held his hand out as if to usher Bud and his friend down the stairs.

"C'mon, follow me and I'll show you. Just watch your head on the low beams and cobwebs."

Bud was up and on his feet in an instant, hustling around the bar and following the old fella down the steps. His friend was trying to catch up to both of the guys. Bud noticed right away that it was quite a place—not nearly as dusty and dirty as he had imagined. "Smitty, this looks way better than I thought it might for a turn-of-the-century building."

"Well, it has been done and redone so many times that every once in a while all of this old junk gets moved around, and it gets cleaned up a little," Smitty explained. "For example, look over there." Smitty pointed across the basement to the far end. "Those walls have all been replaced, and all of that old stuff has been moved around. Sometimes my wife even brings some of that stuff up to the hotel and saloon to put on display. It may look like old junk, but it all has some historical ties to the early beginnings of this place."

Bud and his friend marveled at the huge quantities of old, old stuff that had, at some time or other in the history of the Occidental, been on display or had been acquired from some of the patrons to eventually be put on display. The expansive old basement could almost have been classified as a small museum of Johnson County and Buffalo folklore by itself. There were pictures and paintings of old lawmen and townsfolk. Old furniture and kerosene lamps lined the outer walls. Gun belts and holsters lay in a pile in one of the corners.

"We just collected those old things from drunken outlaws and lawmen alike," Smitty said. "If no one claimed them, we just threw them down here. Look at the rusty old weapons that we somehow ended up with too." He pointed at the wall where several old shotguns and rifles were leaning and then at a box that had a stack of handguns wrapped in oil cloths. "All of these guns were just left here after a night of drinking or after a fight in the saloon," Smitty continued. "I probably should have had them checked out long ago to see if they had any real value."

"It's not too late," Bud said. "If you can connect them to some of the Old West bad guys or good guys, you would definitely have some value there."

"Well, maybe I'll eventually get that done—or not," he chuckled. "But look here," Smitty said. "This is my favorite thing about this basement." He walked over to a wall and pulled on a long wooden dowel, and the wall opened up just like a door. Bud and his friend were immediately impressed.

"Wow, now that is pretty special," Bud exclaimed while writing quickly in his notebook.

"Yep," Smitty said. "This was put in sometime after the first renovation and was used as a secret safe for the owner. It actually had an old heavy metal safe sitting right there too," Smitty continued. "But I had it moved upstairs to make it more convenient to use."

Bud asked quickly, "Do you ever use this as a hiding place anymore?"

"Nope," Smitty responded. "Not since I moved the safe upstairs."

Bud wasn't through jotting notes and continued to write as Smitty finished the tour of the old basement. Bud's friend thanked Smitty as they came up out of the basement, and Bud said, "That was a very nice little tour." The two men shook hands with Smitty, and Bud gave him what looked like a business card. But in reality it was just Bud's first name and a phone number. "In case I can ever help you in some way," Bud said as he and his friend left the saloon.

Bud smiled at the recollection. *It's funny how often I actually find people who do need my help and who, coincidentally, can then help me.* But now it was back to business. He signaled to another car, and the car immediately turned to go back to the Occidental. When the car arrived, the driver, dressed like all of the other guys who just left, jumped out and entered the saloon quickly.

Smitty almost wet himself when he saw him enter, thinking for a brief moment that his prophecy about getting himself killed was about to come true. Instead, the man pulled out an envelope and said, "Bud said to give you this and to say that he will be back as soon as possible." Smitty's hands were shaking, but he took the envelope and watched the man leave as quickly as he came. *Now what?* he thought, as he took the envelope down to the faux safe, counted the money, and placed it with the four silver briefcases. Bud continued to the airport still worrying about loose ends.

CHAPTER 14

The pilot of the small Cessna was focused on the night horizon where some daylight still snuck through the western sky as he sped away from the Baltimore airport. He had started out heading due north, but soon started to angle toward the west.

Anytime, boys, he thought to himself, hoping for his destination orders, *I can only fly around for so long before I'll need a place to stop.*

Then the handheld radio crackled, and the familiar voice of his colleague, Bud, called out to him. "Turn the plane around and come back to Baltimore and pick us up. The Director wants us to finish our business now."

"Roger that," the pilot said into the radio. "I should be there in forty-five minutes. Can you get me something to eat and drink?" he asked. "It's been a long day and definitely will be getting longer."

"I will take care of it," Bud crackled back. "Just make it back here as soon as possible."

"Roger," the pilot responded and started his turn around. Then he thought, *I knew we weren't done yet. Things just felt too unfinished.* He went to full throttle immediately upon his change of direction.

Back in Baltimore, Bud quickly readied himself for the returning plane. He had Howard get some fast food and drinks while he took care of the details. He thought, *This should be quick and easy—nothing out of the ordinary.* He was thinking about how he was going to handle the situation. *That means I'll be using the best available tool to get it done. No guns—no noise—no suspicious activity.* He went to the back of the dark limo and opened the trunk. He always maintained standing orders for his subordinates that required any vehicles that he would be using to be fully stocked with weaponry of various types. Even though his plan was to not use guns, he loaded a duffel with an assortment of small weapons. *Always better to be safe than sorry,* he thought. Then he threw in a tightly wrapped body bag that essentially used up the remaining room in the duffel. *That should be enough to take care of the loose ends.* Then he lit a cigarette and waited for Howard to return with the food and the pilot to return with the plane.

As the pilot neared the Baltimore airport for his second landing of the night, he was thinking about the day's news. *Incredible,* he thought. *But mine is not to question, but to follow orders—blindly and without hesitation.* He had been with the special operations part of the Bureau for a few years now. Nothing could surprise him anymore. And if he just continued to do what he always did, he wouldn't find any surprises coming his way. He was a robot—much like a plane on autopilot. He got aimed in a direction, locked in, and told to go until he was told to stop. He never felt the need to question anything pertaining to his job, except this one time. Bud had always been square with him, but this mission seemed to be weighing on Bud more than he had ever seen before. *Maybe, just once, I could get away with a few questions of Bud,* he mused as he guided the plane through the last stages of his approach to Baltimore. Then a voice crackled through the hand-held radio again. It was Bud, asking for his time of arrival.

"What do you think?" Bud questioned. "We have a go directive and need to make it happen." His voice was more stressed than the pilot had ever heard it before.

"So much for questions," he chuckled under his breath, "not gonna even go there." He responded, "Touchdown in ten minutes, doors open; you getting on board and refueling another twenty. Wheels up in thirty total," he said in his most professional tone.

Bud said, "That's good. We are ready."

The pilot became a robot again—swooped in, landed, boarded his passengers, refueled, and lifted off in thirty minutes just as he had promised. When the pilot glanced at Bud, Bud just said, "Back to Buffalo, Wyoming," and looked straight ahead. "As fast as you can, get this tin can there," he added.

And that was the last word that was spoken until the pilot said, "Buffalo is just thirty minutes out."

During all that quiet time, though, the pilot had a lot of things on his mind. He worried that he had become involved in something that was so much larger than he was. The assassination of the President, the mysterious flight from Dallas with the obviously FBI guys with silver briefcases, the stopover in Buffalo, Wyoming, and the drop off of the four guys in Baltimore and subsequent return flight to Buffalo with Bud and Howard—all of this was off-the-charts strange, even for a highly trained pilot operative like himself.

I feel like I'm the driver of a getaway car who didn't know that his buddies just held up an armored car or something, he thought to himself during the silent flight. *My "Oh shit" beeper has been going off in my head since this thing began.* But he knew that he had no option but to keep silent. So he did—and he just flew the plane. When it came time to land the plane, the pilot tried to reach the control tower of the tiny Johnson County airport, but had no luck.

"They probably shut everything down, go home to sleep, and leave the lights on for late night landings," he said to Bud.

Bud responded, "Well, let's go in, park it in the dark, and wait for our ride." Then Bud got on the hand-held radio and said, "We are here and ready for pickup."

The Cessna landed smoothly, taxied to the dark part of the runway near an open gate, and shut down the engines. Almost immediately, an old pickup truck came towards them. Bud and Howard got out with the duffel, walked to the truck, and talked to the driver who quickly exited the running truck and walked out through the gate. Bud and Howard got in and headed into town. Ten minutes later they were parked in front of the Occidental Hotel. It was almost 4 a.m. Both men got out and went into the mostly darkened hotel lobby and awakened Smitty, who was sleeping soundly behind the check-in counter. The last time Smitty saw these guys, Bud had sent an assistant to pay him off, and Smitty almost wet himself from fear. This time when he awakened and saw who it was, the front of his trousers were instantly soaked.

"Oh my god," he exclaimed as Howard put his hand over his face and half carried and half walked him into the saloon, behind the bar, and down the basement steps. He tried to scream. "Please, what is going…," he started to say. But that was the last thing he would ever say as Howard snapped his neck and let him fall to the basement floor.

Bud quickly pulled the body bag out of his duffel and made quick work of stuffing Smitty into it. "Pull the wooden dowel on that wall, Howard," he directed. When the false door popped open, Bud and Howard looked inside for the silver briefcases. Instantly, they were in shock. Instead of finding the four silver briefcases, they found only three. They scoured the faux safe and the rest of the basement as best they could in the limited time they had. But found nothing. So Bud finally said, "Let's take what we have and get this over with." With that, both men dragged Smitty, tightly jammed into his body bag, into the false wall and squeezed him into a corner so that his body would stand up when the door was closed tightly against it. The special body bag and the already dank smell of the basement should help mask any smell from the body. "If Smitty was telling us the truth," Bud said to Howard, "and he was the only one who knew of this hiding place, then he should rest in peace for quite some time. We just need to make sure this place doesn't get torn down," he added.

The men grabbed the briefcases—Howard picked up two and Bud one and the duffel bag. Then they quickly but quietly climbed the stairs of the basement and walked out through the saloon. They climbed into the pickup and headed back to the airport where their ever-increasingly anxious pilot was waiting for them, engines running.

They ditched the pickup near the plane in the dark and swiftly boarded the plane, carrying the merchandise they had come to get. But even the pilot noticed that the merchandise was different—he counted three silver briefcases, not the four that the other guys delivered. *I hope that was meant to be that way,* he thought as he revved the engines for takeoff. However, when he looked at Bud and Howard, their faces seemed to tell another story. Normally unreadable and all business, the two assassins now looked flushed and flustered. *They certainly looked different getting off the plane than they do now,* the pilot judged. *No matter for me,* he continued his thoughts. *I ain't askin' nothing!* Then he charged down the runway and into the still very dark sky, and the Johnson County Airport became a tiny speck of light through his side window.

In the air and heading back to Baltimore, the pressure finally got to Bud, who let out a "goddammit" that was so loud that the pilot almost jumped out of his seat. Nobody else said a word. That's because neither of the other two men had ever seen Bud out of control, and both men feared what Bud was capable of. Luckily, though, Bud quickly regained his composure and continued to look straight ahead. He shut his eyes, but he wasn't sleeping. No, he was thinking of details and loose ends. *No need to go haywire yet,* he thought. *Not until I see exactly what I have here.* But he was unwilling to look into the briefcases yet. *That can wait until we get back to Baltimore, secure the merchandise, have time to put things into perspective, and see exactly what needs fixed.* He thought. *And, by god, I will fix it!*

The three men sat in silence for the duration of the long flight back to Baltimore. All three were spent with the tumultuous happenings of the day that didn't seem to want to end. But they were trained operatives and accepted extreme conditions easily. Even though they hadn't slept in what seemed like days, they were capable of continuing on until the mission was complete. Nothing seemed insurmountable, and every problem had a solution. That is until the hand-held radio crackled as they were entering Baltimore airspace. It was the sound that Bud and Howard had been dreading. It was the one thing they might not be able to fix. It was Clyde. He was calling for the Director, and he sounded agitated.

"Bud, are you there?"

Clyde was the next-to-last person that Bud wanted to speak to at this moment. He had been hoping to get on the ground, get to his safe house, see what he had, and then formulate a plan that he could relay to the Director. Talking to Clyde or the Director without a plan was not a good idea, and Bud knew it. So he decided to improvise a cover plan.

"Hello, Clyde," he said into the radio. "I'm surprised to hear from you."

"Hello, Bud and Howard. I'm just checking in for the Director. Didn't you say you would keep us apprised of what's happening?"

"Yes, I did," Bud shot back into the radio. "But now is not the time or place. Even though this radio frequency is supposed to be secure, there can always be other ears listening."

"I understand that, Bud, but the Director needs to hear something. And now!" Clyde said emphatically.

"Okay, okay, I get that," Bud said calmly. "So here is what you can say—Mission accomplished, details nailed down and no loose ends."

The pilot and Howard sat quietly staring at Bud as he flat-out lied to Clyde. Both understood that if the Director sensed that Bud wasn't being truthful, they would all be terminated—and that doesn't mean just being fired.

"You understand that if I tell the Director this, it had better be without question the fact of the matter?" Clyde probed. "Bud, I have gone out of my way to support you here because you have never let me or the Director down." Then silence. Then, "Okay, that's what I'll tell him. Let me know immediately when you are down, and I will set up a meeting to debrief."

All three men felt the relief flow through their bodies with that statement. "Roger that, Clyde," Bud said as he ended the conversation. But the men knew, even the pilot, that there was still a cocked and loaded gun pointed at their heads.

Bud looked at Howard and said, "We only get one chance here. If we can't fix it, history will not be our friend."

Howard shot back, "But we won't know it."

Everyone nodded in agreement.

CHAPTER 15

"MIKEY!" Bruce and Steve yelled into the phone together.

"Holy shit," came back the response. "I may be old but I ain't deaf! But I'll surely be impaired now."

Again both guys yelled into the phone together, "You have always been impaired you surly old fart." And then they laughed as they normally did when the three of them got together.

"Haw, haw, haw," Mike laughed with them.

"Hey, buddy," Bruce said. "We finally met someone as rough around the edges as you. He coulda been your brother. And his name was Grizzly Bear."

"Sounds like a wannabe to me," Mike shot back. "Many have tried to be like Mike, but very few have succeeded. So is this why you are bothering me on this fine Wyoming morning—to tell me that I have another fan?"

"Hell no," said Steve. "We have business to discuss. Remember, we are your business partners? This Bear guy was the guy we had to do business with to get moving on our gun collection."

"And even though he was scary as Hell," Bruce continued. "He took care of us."

"All right then," Mike said. "What did this Bear fella do for you?"

"He found us the Chief .38 Special and the .22 Colt Woodsman—in mint condition out of the box," Steve jumped in. "It cost us three grand, but they are beautiful."

"Wow," Mike responded. "That sounds great. A little pricey, but if the condition is that good, I'm sure Bud will be good with it."

"Well, if he isn't, we probably won't be able to please this Bud guy," Bruce said.

Steve nodded in agreement with Bruce and said, "I agree, Mikey."

"Speaking of Bud," Mike said. "I told him we were ready to get together soon, and he agreed. He wants to meet in Deadwood. I guess he hangs out there a lot now since he's retired. He said he will have some money for us and talk about the list he gave us."

"Perfect," Bruce said. "I've been poking around online to see about flights and found one to Denver that was pretty reasonable in two weeks."

"See if that works for him," Steve said. "I would rather drive, but it just takes too long to get out there."

"I hear ya," Mike said. "It's two nights on the road to get here. Let me connect with Bud," Mike continued. "And I'll get right back to you. By the way, I went shooting with Bud the other day. He makes the hair on the back of my neck stand up sometimes. If there wasn't pretty good money attached to this, I'm not sure I would want to be around him. He strikes me as a little eccentric and maybe even a crazy son of a bitch." The three guys laughed at that. For whatever reason, Mike had a history of drawing to himself what Bruce referred to as "strange rangers."

"So what?" Bruce questioned. "He's your kind of guy then. You can handle him, and we can make some cash."

"Oh, no question, I can handle him," Mike responded. "But I'm just saying we all have to have our 'bullshit' radar turned up to full go, by god!" He added, "Haw, haw, haw! I'm having so much fun already, and we haven't even really started yet."

"Hey, Mikey," Bruce said. "You wouldn't be drinking a beer would you? Cause I feel like there's a little spit-talkin' going on on your end."

Steve chuckled at that, but knew it was true too. That's how Mike rolled, always looking for a reason to catch a beer or two or ten.

"Well, hell yes! I certainly am. Just trying to relax a little from this taxing new job," and he "haw, haw, hawed" again.

"That's great, Mikey," Steve said. "Enjoy and check in with Bud and get back to us as soon as possible so we can make this trip happen. We gotta get going."

"Okay, boys," Mike said. "Thanks for the call, and I'll get with Bud right away. Take fuckin' care of yourselves." And Mike hung up while Steve and Bruce were still laughing about the next round of spit talk that was about to hit Mike's phone.

"Wow," Steve said. "His liver must be feeling a little better. He wasn't drinking for quite some time."

"Sounds like this job has him excited, and it's giving him a reason to celebrate a little," Bruce added. "Actually it sounded like a beer and tequila type of celebration."

"Yep," Steve said. "I'm sure it is."

"Let's hope that he doesn't go talk to Bud now," Bruce said. "We don't need Mikey trying to kick Bud's ass even before this little job gets started."

But it was already too late to worry about that. Mike was on the phone calling Bud, inviting him out to his place for a beer even as the guys were discussing his history of drinking and then wanting to kick someone's ass.

Bud answered his phone and Mike greeted him with a "Hey, Bud, this is Mike. I'm drinking a beer and thought you might drive out and drink one with me. Maybe even a tequila shot or two."

"Hello, Mike," Bud answered quietly. "Why yes, that sounds good. I was just leaving Buffalo and heading up to Deadwood. I'll swing by your house."

"Okay, see ya in a bit, pardner," Mike responded and hung up. Then he prepared for Bud's arrival by drinking another tequila shot. Bud, on the other hand, threw his luggage into the back of his pickup and headed out to Mike's wondering what this was all about.

You know, he thought. *Maybe Mike is beginning to trust me as a friend. If that's the case, this is working better than I had expected and faster.* In his old profession, duping people into relationships and then into actions was a daily occurrence. *Looks like I still have it,* he thought. *It's crazy, though, but it's certainly tougher to be completely detached personally than it used to be in the old days. Mike is an easy guy to like. I truly hope that I'll be able to get done what I need done without losing him to collateral damage.* That was a phrase he hadn't used for years, but in his prime, it was an everyday situation. *Collateral damage was always acceptable to tie up loose ends and to clean up details. Always....*

His mind jumped back to 1963 when he visited the Occidental to clean up a loose end. Unfortunately, it was a loose end that cost Bud some collateral damage in the form of the old fella running the place, Smitty. And then he had gotten hasty and failed to nail down the details before he acted. *I won't give up though, until it's fixed,* he thought, *and I won't be as impulsive as I was then. I just need to fix this before I leave this earth.*

Mike was waiting for Bud in front of his house when he pulled in the drive. "Hey, Bud, glad you could stop by."

"My pleasure," Bud responded. "It was very nice of you to invite me out."

Mike signaled for Bud to follow him around the house to a small deck attached to the back of his doublewide home. "Watch your step, pardner," Mike said. "How about that view?" He waved his hand as if he were a magician finishing his act.

"That certainly is impressive, Mike," Bud said. "The Big Horn Mountains just off your deck."

"Yep," Mike said. "I drink my coffee and have breakfast out here every morning when the weather is right. This is why I moved out here." Bud noticed that Mike had almost stumbled off the end of the deck. It was obvious that he had been drinking for some time before Bud arrived. "So Bud, bigtime government employee, how the hell did you end up here?" Mike questioned with the beginning of a slur.

Bud responded, "Well, Mike, I believe that I mentioned that I had some business out here in the past that never got finished and so I moved here to get that done. You know it's a thing of mine—to never leave unfinished business. But as luck would have it, I still haven't got that done. But I do truly love this area of the country. And who knows? Maybe someday I can finish what I came here to do."

"I hope me and my buddies can help you, Bud," he said with a spit slur that caught Bud a little too close.

Bud backed up a bit and answered, "Well, that would be wonderful, Mike. I hope you can too. We'll just see what happens."

"So, pardner, the reason I invited you out here, besides having a little drinkipoo," he laughed at his attempt at humor, "is to set a time for my buddies to meet you in Deadwood. They've been working on the list you gave them and have had some luck all ready."

"That sounds great, Mike," Bud responded. "I'm heading to Deadwood after I leave here and plan to stay there for two weeks. How about the Wednesday the last week of my stay in Deadwood? That will give you guys a chance to spend a couple of days with me there, and we can get all the business sorted out. I have access to a couple of rooms at the Silverado that I'll reserve for you, and we can spend some time talking about the list and also let you guys have a little fun. So what guns have they found so far?" Bud asked.

Mike stuck his thumb behind the strap of his bib overalls and continued to spit slur as he said, "Well, my good friend and pardner, they have already in their possession, the Chief .38 Special and the .22 Colt Woodsman. And," he added with tipsy emphasis, "the guns are in mint condition. How about that, buddy boy?" he asked as he moved closer to slap Bud on the arm. Bud had already started to move away, though, to avoid any further spray coming his way, and Mike missed with his friendly pat on the arm.

Still moving, Bud answered, "Well done. Especially if they are in that kind of condition."

"I told you my buddies would take care of you," Mike continued. "When the three of us get together and put our minds together, we always git 'er done."

Even Bud had to smile at Mike and his comical comments and actions. *He really is a likeable sort.* "That's great, Mike," Bud said as he swallowed his tequila shot that Mike had poured so generously for him. "I better get going. But I'll see you in a week and a half in Deadwood." Heading off the deck and walking briskly back to the front of the house, he turned and said to Mike, who was struggling to catch up, "I'm looking forward to meeting your friends. And having a few drinks together. Let me know when their travel plans are solid." Then he got in the pickup and headed out, waving at Mike as he turned onto the narrow access road to Mike's property.

When Mike staggered back around his house and found his chair on the deck, he immediately picked up his phone and dialed Bruce's cell. Bruce saw that it was Mike and answered immediately with "Mikeeeeeeey" like he always did.

"Hey, Brucie, just got through meeting with Bud, and he said go ahead and make your flight plans for Wednesday, the week after next."

"Oh my god, you talked to him while you are drunk as a skunk?" Bruce questioned.

"Hell yes, I talked to him," he shot back. "And I ain't drunk as a skunk. We had a few sociable drinks before he left for Deadwood."

Bruce laughed out loud and said, "Sociable my ass. You were already drunk before you met with him."

"Well, I might have taken a wee nip from my last bottle of tequila," Mike slurred back almost unintelligibly.

"And you didn't try to kick his ass?" Bruce questioned.

"Hell no," Mike said. "He and I got along quite nicely."

"Okay then, buddy, I hope so. So what's the plan?"

"You just get out here on that Wednesday, and we will work out the time and place for our meeting with Bud. By the way," he said, "well done for getting those two guns. He was quite happy with you."

"All right, buddy," Bruce responded. "I'll let Steve know and I'll get right on it. You, on the other hand, need to take a nap." Mike answered that comment with, "Horseshit! I'm gonna drink another tequila and beer and go feed my chickens."

"Okay, chicken whisperer, but check your liver first," he laughed. "It's probably swollen like a balloon."

"Haw...Haw...Hawww," Mike was even slurring his laugh now. "Over and out, pardner," and Mike ended the call and staggered out to feed his chickens.

Bruce was still smiling when he dialed Steve. When Steve answered he said, "Hey, Stevie, Mikey has it set up. All we need to do is to get out to Deadwood in a week and a half."

"Very nice. Did he like the fact we had the guns?"

"Absolutely," Bruce said. "So I'll get on the plane tickets, and you find out the best way to get these guns out to Deadwood."

"Sounds like a plan. I'll get right on it. Oh, and I just gotta know, was Mikey so far gone that he wanted to do his 'I'm gonna kick your ass routine' on Bud?"

Bruce laughed loudly and said, "That is so funny that you ask that. I asked him that too. But he assured me that he and Bud are great friends. Today that is."

"How nice for Mikey. Isn't it wonderful how tequila works? You can find friends and enemies, all in one small fifth of tequila. Okay, Brucie, I'll get working on the gun transport and you get the tickets. Adios."

CHAPTER 16

Bud's mind was swirling with a thousand thoughts as the little Cessna flew through the dark skies after his pointed conversation with Clyde. "Just think, Bud," he muttered to himself in a whisper, "walk through the possibilities." He couldn't help wondering about how stupid he had been to allow Howard to terminate Smitty so quickly without verifying the merchandise. *That's not how I operate,* he thought. *Maybe it was the fatigue from all that had gone down that day—and the second flight to Buffalo to fix things.* His mind was racing. *But that's not me. That's not how I operate. Okay, okay, get it under control,* he exhorted himself. *In a very short time, I will be sitting in front of Clyde and the Director again.*

He decided to speak with Howard, so he unbuckled and walked back to sit beside him. "Walk with me through this," he said to Howard. "We need to get a handle on the situation or at least be on the same page of a story that we can make work when we speak to our bosses."

"Okay, Bud," Howard said. "Let's do it."

"Number one," Bud said. "We had four guys drop off the four pieces of merchandise."

"Check," said Howard. "All were given to Smitty and accounted for when we left and when he was paid."

"Check," said Bud. "Except we didn't see Smitty put them in the faux safe."

"Big mistake," Howard added.

"But Smitty knew what could happen if the merchandise wasn't properly stowed away," Bud said emphatically.

"He did," Howard said pointedly. "So how did the merchandise get lost in the amount of time it took us to get to Baltimore and back here?"

"It doesn't make sense," Bud continued. "Smitty was scared shitless of what would happen if he screwed up."

"He absolutely was!" Howard said. "I believe it wasn't Smitty."

"I agree," Bud concurred. "So if that's the case, we have two other options to look at: The agent who was responsible for that case and Smitty's wife."

"I agree," said Howard.

"So, as soon as we land," Bud was thinking out loud now, "we need to get to the four agents, interview them as a debriefing, and then get back to Buffalo to check out Smitty's wife, who no doubt by this time has discovered that Smitty is missing."

"Okay," Howard said. "But what about Clyde and the Director?"

Bud answered, "We will explain that all of the loose ends are taken care of and that we left the most significant piece of merchandise in Buffalo, hidden away in a place so safe it will never be found by anyone other than me, you, Clyde, and the Director." Bud continued, "And the other three pieces will be put back where they came from."

"I think that will work," said Howard. "But you know that we will be grilled by the Director until he believes that we did it right."

At that precise time, the handheld radio crackled with the sound of Clyde's voice, "Bud, we need an estimated time of arrival in Baltimore." Bud looked at the pilot who indicated forty-five minutes.

"Hello, Clyde," Bud said. "It looks like forty-five minutes, and we will be on the ground."

"Good," responded Clyde.

Bud then responded to Howard's comment. "Oh yes, my good friend, I fully expect to be berated and mentally beaten down before this is over. And you better believe that he will be there waiting for us when we land." Bud continued, "He knows that the best time to get to us is when we are so tired that it is difficult to think straight."

Just then, the pilot announced that they were approaching the Baltimore airport. Bud returned to his co-pilot seat, settled in for the landing, and thought to himself, *It's not game over at this point, but game on.*

From his seat in the long black limousine, in the early morning light, the Director was watching the small Cessna come in for its third landing of a very long day that had bled into a second day. But the Director was as focused as he had ever been on any mission. Even though he had slept very little and fitfully at best, he felt sharp and ready to command. That's how he viewed it—he was a commander in charge of his troops. And he was always in command mode and eager to orchestrate the business of the day, especially when he had his trusted lieutenant by his side. He shot a glance at Clyde who was also focused on the impending landing and thought, *I am so lucky to have him, my friend, my confidant, my right hand. I'm not sure what I would do without him.*

When the plane landed, he signaled to Clyde to give the order to pull out of the shadows of the seldom-used runway and move towards the plane. As Bud and Howard looked out the window, they gave each other a knowing look and began to disembark. Bud picked up the duffel and the briefcase that he carried onto the plane, and Howard picked up the other two briefcases.

Before opening the door though, Bud said to the pilot, "Go park the plane and plan on staying local until further orders. Get some sleep."

The pilot nodded his head and said, "Good luck."

Just as the men stepped off the last step, the limo door popped open with an obvious invitation to enter. Bud and Howard didn't hesitate and climbed in, placing the merchandise on the floor in front of two men who were sitting quietly in the semi-darkness. Even in the darkness of the vehicle's interior, it was apparent that they were being greeted once again by the Director and his trusted sidekick, Clyde.

Clyde leaned forward and was about to speak, when the Director's right hand shot forward and grabbed his shoulder to nudge him back. Bud was somewhat startled by the suddenness of the move, but never showed it. Instead he waited for the Director's next move. The Director seemed to be searching for words—paying attention to details. He wanted to get it right. He wanted to make sure these men had done what they needed to do.

No loose ends, he kept thinking to himself. Finally, he spoke, "Gentlemen, it's been a hell of a day and night." He leaned forward so that Bud and Howard could see his eyes through the semi-darkness of the limo and said with an emphasis that carried a great deal of threat with it, "I assume you know why I am here personally at this airport, at this time of the morning, when I could have sent Clyde by himself."

"Yes, sir," responded Bud and Howard at the same time.

"Then excuse me for my profaneness, but you better goddam make me believe that you took care of business. All of our professional and personal lives depend on what you got done. So start at the beginning and tell me what you did and how you did it." He turned to look at Clyde and said, "Please feel free to jump in anytime, Clyde."

"Thank you, sir, I will," Clyde responded quickly yet forcefully.

Bud started to speak, and he spoke with an assuredness that came from countless operations over his tenure with the Bureau. He hoped beyond all hope that he was selling his confidence to the Director and his lieutenant. Occasionally, Howard would jump in with a detail, but it was up to Bud to outline the events of the day. He talked about being re-routed in midflight to the alternate location of Buffalo, Wyoming. He talked about the drop-off of the merchandise at the Occidental Hotel and the subsequent return to Buffalo after meeting with the Director the first time. He talked about Smitty and how he was a potential loose end that needed to be dealt with. And finally he pointed to the merchandise on the floor and said, "And this represents the sum total of details that needed to be accounted for."

Bud was watching the Director's face closely for his reaction to the story. It didn't take long. The Director's face took on an apoplectic red hue as he almost came out of his seat.

"Who the fuck do you think you're dealing with here?" the Director screamed at Bud. Clyde saw it coming and tried to restrain the Director, at least for a moment. "Do you think I am some naïve turnip farmer who just got off the boat?" he continued.

Bud and Howard were completely taken aback by this demonstrative reaction from the Director. Bud tried to interrupt the storm of words, "But, but, Mr. Director, what..."

The Director continued, "Even I can count to four, and I count only three goddam briefcases! So cut the bullshit and fill in the rest," he said in a voice that sounded every bit like he was suppressing another screaming outburst.

"Sorry, Mr. Director, but I wasn't quite finished. I was just about to tell you about the other briefcase."

Clyde placed his hand on the Director's shoulder, in a calming fashion, and it seemed to be working. In a much restrained voice that belied that there was ever a storm of words, he said, "Thank you, Clyde. You may continue, Bud."

With a sense of relief, but with also a sense of impending doom, Bud broached the loose end—the only loose end that he had to deal with—the missing briefcase.

The Director's eyes never blinked and never left the face of Bud as he spun a credible story of why the briefcase was not here. "Remember, sir," he said. "Only one briefcase held the weapon that was used to finish off the President. Rather than bring it back here where all sorts of negative things could happen, I felt it was more prudent to leave it far away from here and far away from the event. So I determined that we should lock it away in the Occidental with the collateral damage that we had to incur."

Clyde spoke up, "You mean you put it in the faux safe with the hotel manager?"

Without taking his eyes off the Director, Bud nodded his head and said, "Yes, sir. I believe that that is the safest place until everything calms down," Bud continued. "And we can get the other weapons back where we got them from at an appropriate time too."

Clyde looked at the Director and gave him a nod of approval. The Director hesitated, appearing to be in deep thought. Then he said, "Thank you, Bud. Thank you, Howard. I'll be in touch. You may go now." The two men bent to pick up the merchandise, but the Director said, "No, leave it. Clyde will take care of it." They stepped out of the limo and were left standing on the runway as the limo sped away into the new morning light.

Bud looked at Howard and said, "It appears that they bought it. But you know that we are now expendable. So watch your back." Howard shrugged and both men moved towards a parked car that was hidden away in the corner near the exit gate. *I know it was a good story, but the question is whether it was good enough to keep from becoming collateral damage, like our poor old friend Smitty,* Bud thought to himself. The men got into the car and drove out of the gate.

Meanwhile, the Director and Clyde were heading to the White House for a very important meeting with the new president. As they entered the D.C. area, it was apparent that security had been ramped up to an all-time high. D.C. police and men in dark suits with bulging suit coats hiding weapons were seemingly on every corner. Clyde and the Director took it all in as they finally approached the gate to the White House, but neither spoke. Only high-ranking government officials, or essential staff, were getting through and that was only after a thorough search of vehicles and their person. None of this intense security seemed to bother either man in the limo. In fact, when the limo approached the security gate, the Director quickly rolled the window down and without any questions was immediately allowed to pass through. The Director looked at Clyde and smiled at the irony. Here was a man who was up to his neck in the conspiracy to assassinate the President, and yet he was a large part of providing the security for that same office. "Power is an amazing drug," he whispered to Clyde. "It's also an amazing aphrodisiac," Clyde responded. Both men chuckled under their breath.

As soon as the two men exited the limo, they were greeted by an armed escort and led through the back halls of the White House to a seldom-used conference room just down from the Oval Office. *At least the newly sworn-in President is being very thoughtful of his surroundings,* mused the Director. *No telling who might be listening and taping conversations of the first day on the job.* He would have much preferred this meeting to take place in his office where he would be the one doing the taping. But he understood that on this day of all days, the President would not be leaving the White House for meetings. Clyde and the Director were seated in two overstuffed office chairs that seemed to swallow them whole.

Both men knew that this was purposeful on the President's part. The chair that he would eventually fall into was more regal and designed to give the person sitting in it a feeling of superiority that the people seated in the overstuffed chairs could sense.

"What a crock of shit," the Director said to Clyde. "I made this son of a bitch, and he's already playing power games.

Peering over the arm of the overstuffed chair, Clyde just nodded his head in agreement and said, "Yes, he is. But I assure you, Mr. Director, that it will be short lived. We will make our point—tell him his role and then let him get to it."

"There will be no negotiation here—just direction," added the Director.

The door opened as the Director finished speaking, and LBJ entered and fell into the chair provided for him. In this chair he towered over Clyde and the Director exactly as he wanted to do. Now that this thing was done and he was in charge, he wanted to make it very clear to them both. But this wasn't anything new for him. It's how he operated his whole political life. He was a big man, and he enjoyed looking down at people and commanding them with his presence. He was notorious for getting in their space and pushing until he got his way by intimidation or by just wearing them down. He was indefatigable as a person and a politician and seemed to have a sixth sense in determining what it would take to win someone over to his position. To deal with him, you had to have an edge, something to leverage him into agreement. Only then, when he realized that his opponent had the goods on him, could you make the deal turn in your favor. And that is exactly what the Director and Clyde were thinking.

"Good morning, Mr. President," the Director spoke first.

"Good morning, men," the President responded. "I'm sure you realize that I only have a few minutes before the shit storm starts all over again today. So tell me now what I have to worry about."

"We understand that, sir, and we will be brief," Clyde responded after looking at the Director. "Mr. President, we have contained the situation and have removed all potential threats to exposure."

The President was staring at the Director's face from his elevated perch and made no comment. His craggy face looked well rested given the circumstances of the last day and a half, with only his fire red, bloodshot eyes belying a fatigue that came with the kind of pressure that he was facing. Then, without taking his eyes off the Director's face, he spoke. "Now just what the fuck does that mean?" he drawled with his deepest Texas accent. The Director started to respond, but as was his manner, the President continued to talk over him. "That sounds like political bullshit speak. I said that I want to know the goddam down and dirty threats that I have to deal with—give me a straight answer."

The Director was boiling inside and stood up in front of the President to level the power position and said calmly, "Let me be very clear here, Mr. President. As long as I am Director of the agency, you will have nothing to worry about." He continued, now looking down at the seated LBJ, "But the minute that I feel threatened in my position or personal safety, all hell will break loose for you. That, Mr. President, is all that you have to deal with. Clyde and I will take care of all of the other details as we have up to this point. Do we have an understanding?" he asked as he locked eyes with the President.

LBJ never flinched, never lost his eye contact, and finally said, "That's all I needed to know. Keep me informed when appropriate, Mr. Director. You and I are locked into an agreement with the devil, and we will be eternally linked together in Hell and in our lives both personally and professionally." Then he stood up, looked at both men, slapped the Director on his arm with his huge hand like old friends, and left.

Clyde and the Director just looked at each other and smiled. Each man knew that they had made the point that they needed to make and were now in charge of their own destiny again. "Clyde, it's time to start cleaning up the loose ends," the Director said to his lieutenant as they started to exit the room. They were ushered to their waiting limousine, and when the two men were seated in the car, the Director said, "You need to start by putting the merchandise back into safekeeping and then follow up with Bud and Howard on their meeting with the four agents and then the old fella's wife in Buffalo. When we get those details tied down, we will be in complete control." Clyde nodded in assent, and the two men rode in total silence back to the Director's office, holding hands until they arrived.

CHAPTER 17

Smitty's wife awakened early the day after the assassination, readied herself, and drove to the Occidental to relieve Smitty of his task of running the front desk. She knew that he would be tired. He always was after an overnight stint managing guests and taking care of the mundane matters that cropped up in the old hotel. It seemed like there was always something to keep him from getting a full night's sleep on the cot behind the front desk or even sometimes in the old reclining chair that he had brought in from home. She worried about him being too old to do the job anymore. But they couldn't afford to hire a night man to take his place. So they took turns. Mostly it was Smitty, though, because he worried about her being there overnight by herself and only let her do it when he was too worn out. On her way in, she thought about the extra money that he had told her he was going to make from some kind of business arrangement that he had made with a stranger who was interested in historical buildings. *I really hope that comes about,* she thought. *Not only could we work on the building, but maybe we could also hire someone to handle the things that Smitty can't do anymore.*

When she arrived at the Occy, she parked out back in the usual space and entered through the back door. *This place really needs a facelift,* she thought as she passed by the worn, paint-chipped clapboard siding that hadn't seen a coat of paint in years. When she walked down the hallway with tattered, faded carpet, she started to call out for Smitty to let him know she was there to relieve him. "Smitty, dear, I'm here. Where are you?" She called again as she crossed into the hotel. "Smitty, are you still sleeping?" Still nothing. She walked into the empty saloon and called again. "Smitty! I'm here!" She was getting progressively louder, and a strange feeling of uneasiness and a sense of dread was starting to well up in her stomach. They had been together so long they could sense when something wasn't right with the other one. And this didn't feel right. Smitty wasn't a great worker, but he was timely. *This just feels wrong for Smitty to not be here,* she thought. Then she thought of the basement and quickly went behind the bar and yelled down the steps, "Smitty, are you down there?" She really expected him to say, "Hell, yes, watcha yellin' about?" But nothing came back to her, so Smitty's wife started down the creaky basement steps to take a look. *He is getting on in age,* she thought. *I hope to God that he didn't fall down the steps in the middle of the night.* When she got to the bottom of the stairs and started to survey the basement, it became apparent that there was no one there. *Where is he?* She was almost feeling desperate now. And she had a funny feeling like he was close by, but far away.

But Smitty was obviously not down in the basement. So after a few minutes of quickly looking around, his wife climbed back up the stairs and tried to think of anywhere he might have gone and why he would leave without letting her know. *I might as well get started with some things that I need to get done,* she thought. *He'll probably be back before long.* Before long never happened though, and Mrs. Smith found herself several hours later on the phone calling friends and family around Buffalo to see if anyone knew where he was. With no luck on the phone, Mrs. Smith got into her car and started driving to anywhere he could possibly be. Again she had no luck, and finally she called the city police and the county sheriff. No one had seen him.

"Wherever that old fart is and whatever he is doing seems to be a mystery to everyone who knew him in Buffalo," she told the police officer and the deputy sheriff who were dispatched to check into Mrs. Smith's concern. "I'm going to kill him when he does show up," she told the officers with a hint of tears in her eyes.

"Now Mrs. Smith, it's too early to get this fired up," they both said in unison. "We'll check around, and I'm sure he will show up as soon as he gets done with whatever he's doing," the deputy added.

"Stay by the phone in case he tries to call," the police officer said as they were leaving the hotel. "We'll be in touch soon."

But Mrs. Smith already knew in her heart that this just wasn't right and, as she went back to the front desk to get some work done, she said a quick prayer, "Dear Lord, if something has happened to Smitty, please keep him close to your heart, but if you can bring him back to me, I will be eternally grateful. Amen"

Everyone in town knew the Smiths, and once the word got out that Smitty was missing, they all pitched in to see if they could help. But as the hours turned into a day, and the day turned into the night, everyone started to believe the worst had happened.

Meanwhile, back in D.C., Bud finally got rested enough to start the process of tracking down the missing briefcase. He called Howard to set the plan in motion. "Hey, Howard, good morning. How are you doing?"

"Probably just like you," came the response. "Anxious to get this thing off our backs and take the bull's-eye off too. I've just been waiting to hear from you—well not really waiting," he corrected himself. "I've been waiting but also working. I have the agents who carried the briefcases on call and lined up to talk at your convenience."

"Well done," said Bud. "I particularly want to speak to the guy who carried the missing case. Call 'em in later today for a meeting in my office."

"Okay, Bud, consider it done," Howard responded. "What about the old lady in Buffalo?" he asked quickly.

Bud answered, "I imagine that she's pretty consumed by looking for Smitty at this point. So I think we should let that play out for a while, before strangers come back into town poking around and asking questions. I don't want the locals to start trying to connect any dots that have to do with us. I have a plan," Bud continued. "But it requires a little time for things to get right in Buffalo first."

"Okay. Gotcha," Howard said as he deferred to Bud's role as the man in charge.

"Let's just start with the agents and see where that leads," Bud said. "I'm heading into the office so get 'em in here."

"All right. I'll be on my way too," Howard said as he hung up the phone.

Bud's office was located in the FBI Building, but away from the normal workings of the FBI. It was hidden away in the bowels of the building next to other agents' offices who were considered special operations types. Most of the offices were empty most of the time because of the nature of the special ops that the agents had to perform. In fact, most of these agents considered their homes or cars their real offices. Bud only used his when he had to deal with official FBI business that required immediate contact with his superiors. Lately, that contact seemed to be only with the Assistant Director and the Director. So as he entered his office he fully expected a call or a visit from either one. Both had a system in place to let them know immediately which special ops agents were in the building. Instead, Howard turned the corner and entered his office.

"All of the briefcase agents are here, but in separate rooms," Howard said immediately. "None of them knows the other guys are here."

"Okay, let's get started," Bud said. "Let's deal with the three briefcases first and the one that's missing last."

As each of the three agents came and went, Bud was convinced that they knew nothing other than what their role was for the operation. Each agent was asked the same questions:

"Can you walk me through every detail from when you received the briefcase in Dallas through when you dropped it off in Buffalo?"

"Was the briefcase ever out of your hands or out of your sight until you dropped it off?"

"After you closed the briefcase in Dallas, did you ever open it again?"

"Did you then or do you now know which briefcase held the 'hot' merchandise?"

"Have you talked to any of the agents since you got back?"

"What did the old man do with your briefcase in the basement of the hotel?"

All three agents seemed to satisfy Bud and Howard with their answers. So now there was only one left. When the last agent entered the office, Bud immediately started with the same questions. However, he added a couple that seemed to pinpoint which briefcase was the one holding the 'hot' merchandise. Howard had not even been sure which one it was.

"When you put the 'hot' merchandise into the briefcase, did you put anything else in at the same time?"

"Yes, sir," the agent responded mechanically. "I put the bogus Dallas police officer's badge and the Dallas police's service revolver that you gave me in also."

"Did you notice the old man handle your briefcase any differently than the other ones?" Bud continued.

"Yes, sir," he answered. "He seemed to notice it was heavier than the others. He lifted it as if he was checking its weight. But he placed it on the floor with the other briefcases, and we left. You and Howard stayed a second more and followed us up the stairs and out into the car."

With that, Bud told the agent, "We're finished here. Keep yourself available, and we will be in touch. Thank you Gordon," he said as he used the agent's name for the first time. He never once used any of the other agent's names during their interrogation.

"So what do you think, Bud?" asked Howard when the last agent left.

Bud responded, "I think that these guys are all okay, and that the only thing that was different was Gordon's account of Smitty noticing the difference in weight. We were the last ones to see the briefcases, so we are responsible to fix it. The way I see it is that the Director will see these agents as loose ends that need to be fixed," he said. "These guys need to be protected in some way. So we need to convince the Director that they will be a necessary part of any future special ops regarding this endeavor. After all, these agents put themselves on the line for the Director. And guess who would be next if he gets caught up in the paranoia Howard?"

"You and me, brother," Howard said quietly.

"Exactly," Bud responded. "Plus, Smitty's wife will be expendable if he views her in that way too. And I would rather keep her around so that I can monitor things in Buffalo through her."

"I get that," Howard said. "I just believe..." Howard didn't get to finish his thought. The phone rang, and Bud knew immediately that it was the boss.

"Yes, Mr. Director," he said. "I will be right up." He looked at Howard and said, "You're not invited, but I'll let you know what happens as soon as I'm able."

"Okay, good luck," Howard said and walked out of the office as Bud headed up to see the Director.

"Good morning, Miss Gandy," Bud said as he entered the outer office of the Director. "Good morning, sir," she responded. "You may go in. He is expecting you." Bud opened the door, and the Director immediately signaled him to come in and at the same time yelled loudly to Miss Gandy, "No calls and no interruptions." Bud shut the door, and the Director, who was standing, motioned for him to sit. Bud thought to himself, *He's such a small man, probably five foot seven at the most, yet so powerful and so dangerous.* As the Director stood in front of Bud, looking down at him in the chair that he was occupying, Bud told himself, *Don't be intimidated. Keep control of yourself. But be careful.* It seemed like a very long time that the Director stood there. Bud had greeted him with a "Good morning, sir," but received no response in return.

Finally he spoke, "Bud, I have been waiting for you to call me. But I've heard nothing. Pardon my rudeness, but what the hell is going on? What's the real story with the fourth briefcase?" He continued to stand, peering down at Bud from his position of authority. "I need answers!" he almost growled as his eyes flashed with a smoldering anger.

"Yes, sir, I'm sorry, sir, but we just finished debriefing the agents, and Howard and I were putting together our report."

"You don't need to file a goddam report—you just need to tell me what's going on—right now!" The Director continued as he glared into Bud's eyes. Then he abruptly turned and walked behind his desk and sat down in his oversized chair. Even though he was no longer standing, he seemed to be looking down at Bud, always maintaining his position of power. He accomplished this by positioning himself behind a massive dark wooden desk and a huge overstuffed and oversized chair that almost appeared to be putting him on a pedestal. His black button-like eyes said it all for Bud. He was highly agitated, and Bud knew that he needed to calm the storm within the Director.

Bud began, "Sir, we have finished with the agents and feel that there are no issues with them to attend to. Their dedication to you came through loud and clear, and their recounting of the operation was spot on. They performed their duties flawlessly. The glitch comes into play with the old guy at the hotel. We trusted him to protect the merchandise, and he is the only one who could have moved the missing briefcase. I believe he separated the briefcase with the 'hot' merchandise from the others because he noticed a difference in weight and for whatever reason, decided to put it somewhere else. It is not clear where yet, sir," he concluded. The Director just stared down from his perch at Bud prompting him to continue, "My plan now, sir, is to let things calm down a bit in Buffalo and then reconnect with the old guy's wife. I plan to make sure that it's not unusual for me to be seen at the hotel, by becoming a benefactor interested in saving the historical value of the hotel. In that way, I can question, yet not seem intrusive. And I can make sure the building remains intact so that I can look around more thoroughly. At this time, Mr. Director, I do not feel that anything has been compromised. We will find that briefcase. If we don't, no one else will, and if by some slight chance it does reappear, there is no possible way to connect it to the Dallas operation." Not sure how his story was being received by the Director, he watched and waited.

Finally, after what seemed like an incredibly long silence, the Director threw up his arms over his head, interlocking his fingers, and leaned back in the huge chair. "Bud, this is still very worrisome to me," he said calmly. "Do you think that an unfortunate calamity, like a fire or some other form of destruction, would be helpful in Buffalo?"

Bud didn't hesitate, "No, sir, not at this time. I will let you know if that is necessary."

The Director added, "And concerning the agents, do you still feel a complete trust? Or do we have enough leverage with all of them to ensure the continued confidentiality of the operation?"

"Absolutely, sir," Bud responded quickly.

"Then, let's move forward. Thank you Bud," the Director concluded. "Miss Gandy, will you show Bud out?" He shouted through the closed door.

As Bud left, he noticed that the Director still had his hands above his head and was still leaning back in his chair. *He isn't happy with this yet,* Bud decided. *I'm sure that he and Clyde will be talking soon. I hope that Clyde can cool his jets and talk him into giving us time to get this tied up.*

CHAPTER 18

Bruce turned into Steve's drive at precisely 9 a.m. to pick him up for the trip to Deadwood. Steve and his wife, Becky, were obviously waiting for him to arrive and popped out of their house with a full set of luggage dragging behind them. Bruce's wife, Marlene, was also in the full-sized van and called out, "Good morning, you two" through her open window. The guys had decided to turn this trip into a mini-vacation because Bruce had found some pretty reasonable airfares from Dayton to Denver, and both of the women had been really looking forward to a vacation. Marlene and Becky had very stressful jobs and felt it was a great time to get away. Plus they enjoyed the laidback, easygoing atmosphere that was a part of the Deadwood experience. They were very familiar with Deadwood from several previous trips to see Mike and had always had a great time sightseeing and gambling at the local casinos in the old western town.

"Nice to see you're ready," Bruce said to Steve.

"I was born ready," Steve shot back. "But I do wish we were driving. It's never any fun for me to fly anymore—too cramped and uncomfortable."

"You'll be fine," Bruce said. "Just don't be offended though when you see people staring at you as you walk down the plane's aisle looking for your seat."

"What do you mean?" Steve asked.

"Well, buddy, I hate to say it, but you are *that* guy nobody wants to sit next to. You take up way too much space," he laughed.

Steve shot back a quick, "Bite me," and a middle finger that added more emphasis to the thought.

Everyone laughed and Marlene playfully chided Bruce, "You better behave. It's going to be a long trip if you are going to be a smart-aleck the whole way."

Steve laughed out loud and said, "You tell him, Marlene."

Bruce pulled out of the driveway and headed south to Dayton. It was a two hour drive and then an hour's wait at the airport before they took off. It was plenty of time to talk about their plans for when they got to Deadwood.

"Well," Steve began. "The guns are in the mail and should reach Mikey before we get there. I sent them FedEx. He will sign for them and bring them to Deadwood when he comes to meet us."

"Sounds great," Bruce said.

"Yep," Steve said. "It was less hassle than bringing them on the plane with us—too much paperwork and scrutiny. Believe me though, I'm all for the security measures."

"Whatever it takes to keep me safe on that plane," Becky chimed in. Marlene nodded her head in agreement.

"So Mikey will meet us in Deadwood tomorrow, with the guns and before we talk to Bud?" Bruce asked.

"Yes," Steve responded. "Mikey will drive up from Buffalo and meet us at noon at the Four Aces casino at the Hampton Inn where we are staying. We will then meet Bud and hopefully get our money and see if we are good to continue on this adventure, as I choose to call it."

"Sounds perfect," Bruce said. "And the ladies can just relax and have fun while we get done what we need to get done." Both Marlene and

Becky agreed to that with an adamant nod of their heads. It was going to be a nice break for them away from the daily stresses of work.

The rest of the trip to the airport was filled with mundane conversation about Mike, golf, and gambling, in that order. Everyone was anxious to see their old friend and hoped that this joint business venture among the three friends would bring Mike closer in some way again. Even though they talked frequently, they all felt that Mike's move out West had created a hole in that friendship. It was not easy to stay in touch like they used to or like they wanted to. Long distance friendships had to be worked at to be maintained. In fact, before this gun thing came about, it seemed like communication between the three friends was becoming more and more infrequent. They all, including the wives, hoped that would change.

The trip to the airport seemed quick. They arrived on time, checked in, and continued their conversation while they waited to board the plane. Steve and Bruce spent the time looking at the list of guns left to find and discussing the best way to proceed.

"I really think we need to present Bud with a plan of attack," Bruce said to Steve while the ladies chatted about their jobs. "He needs to see that we are serious and capable of getting this done quickly."

"Exactly," said Steve. "I think we need to split the remaining eight guns into groups of two like we did with these first two that we found."

"I agree," Bruce said. "And we need to focus on nearby gun shows and Internet listings first. But I do think," he continued, "that we will have our best results from our contacts at these gun shows, or our contacts on the computer. Some of these guys always seem to know someone else, who knows someone else, etc., and they can narrow it down for us rather quickly."

"That's what we need to get Bud to buy into," Steve said. "He needs to believe that we have all of these contacts all over the country who can and will help us in our search."

"Yep, that's the plan," Bruce agreed.

The call to board interrupted the guys' planning, and they all dug out their boarding passes and headed to the gate. Walking down the aisle to their seats, Bruce and Marlene were following Becky and Steve. Bruce leaned forward and whispered into Steve's ear, "Hey, buddy, don't take it personal, but I see lots of worried people looking at you with just their eyes, nervously praying—please Lord, not me, don't let that guy sit next to me."

Steve never looked back, but he stuck his middle finger up, pointed it at Bruce, and pretended to be scratching the back of his head. Bruce almost choked trying to hold back the laughter building up in his throat.

Marlene quickly reached out and poked him in the side. "What did I say?" she said with a mischievous smile.

The couple of hours flight to Denver was uneventful. Steve and Becky even lucked out and found themselves with an unoccupied seat next to them, which allowed them both to stretch out for the duration of the flight. No one really spoke of anything else either. The focus was on getting there, renting the minivan, and heading out for the five or six hours drive from Denver to Deadwood. The couples found that drive to be uneventful also and talked a lot about family and friends, and, of course in particular, Mike. He was always easy to talk about. Reminiscing about the good times they all had with him over the years made the miles fly by. His exploits were legendary to his friends, and they never tired of repeating old stories of Mike and the situations he usually got himself into with Bruce and Steve seemingly always by his side. It was the strength of that great and long-lasting friendship that brought them into this endeavor with Mike. Neither Bruce nor Steve thought that trying to find collectible guns with Mike would turn into anything big in the financial sense. But rather it was an opportunity to rekindle the relationship of all those years with Mikey, Stevie, and Brucie—three friends who had really grown into brothers over a forty year friendship. So it was not surprising that the stories carried the friends the six hours to Deadwood so quickly and painlessly.

"Wow," Bruce exclaimed. "I thought this would be a long drive, but that really went by fast."

"Yes, it did," they all agreed as they turned into the parking area reserved for hotel check-in at the Four Aces.

"Let's get checked in and settled and then meet for dinner in about an hour," Steve said.

"Sounds great," Bruce responded. "Let's do it. Oh, and Steve, bring the gun list so we can look at it a bit and draw up some ideas."

"You got it, buddy," Steve said. "See ya in an hour."

When they met for dinner, it was apparent that the only choice in the small hotel/casino was a "squat and gobble" buffet as Bruce liked to call them. Nothing special, just lots of food.

"I hate this type of buffet," said Bruce as they got comfortable. "Everything's very average and very filling. I always feel like a beached whale after I eat at one of these."

"Don't we all?" asked Marlene as Becky nodded her head in agreement.

"Yep," said Steve. "We'll have more time tomorrow to find a nice restaurant for dinner. So 'til then, I say dig in and enjoy." And with Steve leading the way, the friends worked their way around the buffet and more than satisfied their hunger.

When they were all finished, Bruce said, "Stevie and I are going to talk about our plans for tomorrow over in the bar. So you ladies are on your own. Have fun, sweetie," he said, and he gave Marlene, his longtime high school sweetheart, a quick hug and a kiss. "And be sure and make me a millionaire," he added with a wink. Then, the two guys headed to the bar and found a suitable table for talking and working, if you could call it that.

Steve pulled out his gun list, and Bruce produced his list to match. "I'll have your oldest malt liquor on the rocks," Steve said to the combination waitress/bartender.

"Hey, that sounds good, I'll have one too," Bruce chimed in. "And with that drink, our adventure in Deadwood officially starts."

"You are so right, my friend," Steve said. "Let's get down to business so we can get to some serious drinking."

"Well, maybe for you professionals, buddy," Bruce said. "But I'm going to hold off until Mikey gets here. I can guarantee that there will be more booze flowing then, and I have to last 'til then. So only one for me now." The guys laughed and started to talk business.

"Okay, let's recap," Steve started. "We have the Chief's Special and the .22 Colt Woodsman for Bud tomorrow—if Mikey got them on time from FedEx. We should get our three thousand bucks back plus the finder's fee, and then we should get the cost of our trip back at just over a thousand bucks apiece for flight, car, and rooms."

"Perfect," said Bruce. "So let's divide the other guns into groups of two to set up a search order and process for getting through the list."

"Right," Steve said. "Let's put the Browning Hi Power 9mm 80th anniversary with the Walther PPK."

"Then," Bruce said, "Let's do the Glock .22 9mm Model 19 and the Ruger Super Redhawk Alaskan .44 Magnum with the 2.5-inch barrel."

"That should work," added Steve. "So then let's do the Smith & Wesson .44 Magnum 6.5-inch barrel and my personal favorite, the Model 27 .357 Magnum with the 3.5-inch barrel."

"Right," Bruce responded. "And let's finish the list with the matching set of Uberti .45 Colt 1873 Cattleman Single Action Army revolvers. Those are great guns even though it's a replica set from Uberti."

"Oh my gosh, yes," Steve said. "And these early models have a very hefty price tag on them."

"So I wonder why a guy like Bud, who seems like he would be a purist, wouldn't just go spend the money on original Colt Peacemakers, rather than go for the replicas." Bruce questioned.

"Who knows?" the ever pragmatic Steve said. "Gun collectors are a breed to their own and have different reasons for liking different guns. It's not our job to suggest to him anything."

"He calls the shots, so to speak, and we try to do his bidding," Bruce added.

"Right you are, my friend, right you are," Steve chuckled.

"Well, buddy, I think we have an order and a process for Bud. Now we can make Mikey aware of our plans tomorrow, before we meet with Bud and get this party started," Bruce said, as he and Steve swallowed the rest of the seven-year-old malt scotch and headed out to find the ladies and check out the sights in Deadwood.

CHAPTER 19

Bruce was up at 7:30 a.m. the next morning, Deadwood time, and even though it had been a late night by his standards, he found himself surprisingly fresh and ready to go. The anticipation of seeing his old buddy and meeting Bud really had his blood flowing.

He whispered to Marlene, who was still sleeping, "I'm calling Stevie and hopefully he'll want to get some breakfast. Be back in a while—let me know when you're up." She stirred a little and responded with something that sounded like okay, so he gave her a quick kiss and went into the next room to make his call.

Steve answered with his typically Irish greeting and said, "Top of the morning, my son."

"Hey, buddy," responded Bruce, "get your lame, lost, and lazy ass up so we can get breakfast."

Steve laughed and said, "You know me so well. Okay, meet you downstairs in ten at the buffet." When they got there, it was crowded with senior citizens hovering with plates, diving into a fairly good-sized line to pull out bacon and eggs and biscuits and gravy.

"Shall we?" Steve asked. Then he grabbed a hot and still wet plate from the stack and proceeded to dive in also. Bruce followed suit and before long both guys had everything they wanted and more than they needed to eat.

"Oh my god," Bruce exclaimed. "We have to slow down. You know we will be eating with Mikey later."

"Agreed," Steve concurred. "That's enough for me. Let's head to the bar and relax."

At that precise time, Bruce's phone rang. "Guess who?" Bruce showed the phone to Steve. "Well, how nice," Steve said. "Who would have thought that Mikey would be on his way so early, or at least we hope on his way."

Bruce put the phone on speaker and answered, "MIKEY."

Mike countered in the same manner, "BRUCIE."

"Where ya at, buddy?" Bruce continued.

"Well, believe it or not..." Mike started but was quickly interrupted by Bruce yelling "Not!"

Mike continued, "Very funny. Ha Ha....Let me start again. Believe it or not, I'm going to be a couple hours late. I had to wait on the FedEx guy to bring the guns. I had to call 'em and give 'em some shit about getting that package out to me. But I finally got the guns, checked them out, and I'm on my way. By the way," Mike continued, "Bud can't meet us today. He's got something else going on, but he wants to meet tomorrow morning at Miss Kitty's casino. I'll give you details when I get there."

"Okay, Mikey," Bruce responded. "I'm losing you—see you when you get here," he said as the call got dropped.

"No surprises there," Steve said. "I'm just glad he stuck around to get the guns."

"Me too," Bruce agreed. "Hey, I want to take a break and head back to the room for a few since we have some time to kill. See what Marlene has planned for the day."

"Perfect," said Steve. "Let's get back together at one and see where Mikey is at that time."

At one o'clock, the guys met downstairs and walked out to sit on some wooden benches outside the casino. Actually, they had decided to sneak away and smoke one of Steve's magnificent stash of cigars that he had brought with him on the trip. Steve gave Bruce a Dark Shark, a fine long cigar with dark tobacco, and chose a 5 Vegas for himself. The smoke had just started to roll off the cigars when Mike called again.

"Hey, Mikey!" Bruce answered in his usual, somewhat annoying, manner.

"I'm here, Brucie. Where should I park?" Mike asked.

"Right in front of the hotel, across the street," Bruce said.

"Gotcha, be there in a minute," and he hung up.

"Where in the hell is he?" Steve asked.

"Said he was right here. But you know Mikey, so let's just sit tight and smoke these beauties."

Finally, after about twenty minutes, Bruce spied a single figure walking towards them from about three blocks away.

"There he is," he nudged Steve.

"Where in the hell is he coming from?"

"From the parking lot across from the hotel," Bruce laughed. "Oh my gosh, some things never change."

"Look at him—he's limping. What's up with that?" Steve asked.

"Don't know, but I think he finally sees us—he's waving," Bruce said. Both guys stood up and waved back, but Mike still had a block and a half to walk, or limp, anyway. After what seemed liked forever, Mike reached the guys.

"Haw, haw, haw," he laughed as he reached out to shake hands and give his buddies a man hug. "It's goddam good to see you two." Before Mike could say, "Did you bring a cigar for me?" Steve had one out and was handing it to him and lighting it. "Oh my god, that's good," Mike said as he took a long drag and blew it out.

Steve had saved a great cigar for Mike—an Estrella Cubana. The three buddies then sat down on the bench and, as always happened, it was as if they were never separated by the time and distance of their lives.

"Wow, it feels good to be here with my buds," Mike said.

"Yep, we agree, Mikey," Bruce said. "And by the way thanks for dressing up for us. Are those your dress bib overalls?"

"Why thanks for noticing," Mike shot back. "And yes they are. And I also got a brand new pair of sneakers on. Pretty snazzy, huh?" He lifted his feet up to display the shiny white, brand new sneakers. "Haw, haw, haw. Just for you, boys."

Steve admired the sneakers and the bibs and said with a chuckle, "Yes, you certainly are what could be considered 'Deadwood chic.'" The guys laughed the comfortable laugh of friendship and talked and relaxed and smoked their cigars for a long time.

"Well, boys, I think it's time to talk business," Bruce finally said. "What's the deal with Bud?"

"Oh yes," Mike said. "I guess we do have business to transact. We are supposed to meet Bud tomorrow at noon for lunch at a place called the Deadwood Social Club."

"Oh yeah," Bruce said. "Remember, Stevie, that's where we ate last time we came to visit."

"Yes, I do, "Steve said. "As I remember they had a nice selection of wines and some good steaks."

"Yep," Mike said. "That's the place. We are supposed to ask for Bud when we get there. He'll be waiting for us. And he wants us to bring the guns and our lists."

"Okay, sounds like a plan," said Bruce as Steve nodded in agreement.

"So, Mikey, have you gotten to know Bud better since we last talked?" Steve asked.

"Nope," Mike answered. "He's been traveling so he's not been in Buffalo for a while. But the last time I saw him, he seemed excited to be meeting you. Remember," Mike continued. "This guy is a little on the strange side and hard to get to know. He really keeps to himself unless he wants to get to know you. And he's just very secretive about his past life and about what's going on with him now. He sometimes makes the hair on the back of my neck stand up, if you get what I mean. I get these strange vibrations from him."

"Well, the good thing so far," Bruce said, "is that you haven't kicked his ass yet."

"Haw, haw," Mike laughed in the way only he could. "You are right, but our time together is still young. Haw, haw, haw."

"And he hasn't caught you on one of your tequila shots and beer nights yet," Steve added.

"Oh wait a minute, buddy," Mike shot back. "As near as I can remember he has, and I still didn't kick his ass."

"Well, then," Steve said. "He must be okay," and laughed.

"Okay, boys," Mike said. "Let's enjoy tonight, and we will work tomorrow. Somebody want to ride along with me while I go check into the campground?"

"I will," Steve said.

"Me too," Bruce jumped in. "Let's go and get the guns also."

The guys spent the rest of the afternoon helping Mike get situated at the campground. They set up his tent, gave him a lot of shit about how tight he was, and generally had a grand time at Mike's expense. Then they pulled out the guns. Mike had transported them in the case that Steve had shipped them in. It was briefcase-size and held the two guns perfectly.

"Wow," Bruce said. "These guns look as good as I remember them. Bud should be really happy with them."

"Oh yes," Mike said. "He will be."

"We will take the guns with us back to the hotel and put the gun case in the hotel safe." Bruce said. "The guns will be a tad more secure there," he laughed.

"Okay, boys," Mike responded. "That works for me."

"Just call us when you're ready to get something to eat and we'll come out to pick you up." Steve said.

Mike grunted okay to the guys and headed into his tent to take a nap as the guys left with the merchandise and headed back into downtown Deadwood. On the way in, both guys felt a strange tingle of excitement as they talked about the next steps on their adventure.

The next morning found Bruce and Steve a little bleary eyed and moving slow. It was a short night. Both couples and Mike had gone out to dinner and worked their way up and down the many small casinos that peppered the main drag of Deadwood. Each establishment presented another opportunity to indulge in the drink of the moment, and everyone participated freely, except Marlene, that is. She preferred to keep a clear head while throwing her cash at the slot machines that caught her attention. But even though she was sober, she had no better luck. From the Silverado on one side of town to Saloon #10 and on to Cadillac Jacks on the other, it became painfully obvious that Deadwood wasn't in the business of giving away their tourist dollars easily. No one had any luck. And unfortunately the next morning found those who hit the alcohol freely in even more pain from their losses. That is except for Mike. He stayed away from the slots and instead invested heavily in beer with tequila shots for chasers. But unlike everyone else, he was up and raring to go. When he got to the hotel for breakfast, he made sure his buddies came down to eat with him and never missed a beat as he heaped huge quantities of eggs, sausage, bacon, and biscuits and gravy onto his overmatched plate. Bruce and Steve savored their coffee as precious medicine and ate sparingly. They were suffering from the kind of night that no one in the group could remember for quite some time.

"Boys, boys, boys," Mike chortled. "Come on. You've got to perk up and get with it. You've turned into a couple of lightweights," he laughed.

"Oh my god, Mikey," Bruce groaned and whispered. "Turn the volume down just a tad, and I might survive."

Steve just nodded and said, "We'll be fine once the caffeine and sugar return to our bodies. And we'll be ready for our noon meeting," he added.

With that, Bruce and Steve got up to head back to their rooms to get ready for the meeting. "You know we only have two hours until our lunch meeting," Bruce said to Mike. "We'll meet you in the lobby in an hour. Don't go anywhere very far and please, no hair of the dog that bit you."

"Haw, haw, haw," he belly laughed and splattered eggs across the table. "You know me too well. I'll behave."

As was his custom, Bud was early to the meeting. In his other life as an agent, later was never an option, unless you wanted bad things to happen to you. He needed to survey his surroundings and the layout for the meeting even though he had no reason to believe that anything would or could go wrong. It was just ingrained in his nature.

After all, he thought, *I'm just dealing with a few country hicks who have no inclination to dig deeper into my motives. They just want to make a few bucks, and I'm throwing a long shot out there just in case they get lucky.*

Throwing out long shots "in case something sticks" was an old professional habit that he had developed long ago. In his past life, he had gotten lucky several times in situations in which traditional agency methods didn't work.

It's kinda like trolling for marlin, he thought. *It's a great big ocean, but sometimes you'll snag one.*

Bud checked his watch, the same engraved gold watch that he received as a retirement gift from the agency, "Thank you for your service—Bud," and noticed that he only had a few minutes left until the guys arrived at the Deadwood Social Club. He had chosen the place because he felt comfortable on the rooftop deck that was close to the martini bar. It afforded him a great view of the main drag of Deadwood in both directions.

First rule in any meeting, he thought, *always maintain a clear line of sight in all directions. And second rule, always have a safe way out.* The rooftop deck at the Deadwood Social Club fit that bill exactly. Plus, Bud loved to sit on the deck and watch the tiny microcosm of life bustle by. He spent many hours here sipping wine and people watching, trying to guess who was who, tourist or resident, and then sometimes if he found someone very interesting, he would venture down, pretend to run into them, and start a conversation. He loved to talk to people, and he loved to read into their lives. Bud liked to think this kept him sharp in case he was ever needed by the agency again. He truly believed he had a gift for telling who was a good person, a bad person, a trustworthy person, or a liar. He treated it like a game—and he always won.

From his seat on the deck, Bud could see the three friends heading towards the restaurant. He had told the wait staff to expect the guys, and he paid them to close the deck to other patrons. When the guys arrived at the restaurant, they opened the door to find a stairway that seemed to go almost straight up.

Mike let out, "Holy shit! Which one of you guys is going to carry me up these stairs?"

"Steve, you're up," Bruce said quickly.

"Right," Steve responded with a laugh. "You are on your own, big boy. But we will follow you up in case you fall backwards."

"Gimme some time. Don't rush me," Mike said and started to scale the flight of stairs one slow shuffling step at a time.

"Oh my god, Mikey," Bruce said. "I think you could crawl faster, you old fart."

"Hey, first of all, bite me, and second...kiss my hairy ass!" Mike barked back.

After what seemed like forever, the guys reached the top of the stairway and came to a landing where they were greeted by the waiter.

"Bud is waiting for you, please follow me," he said. The waiter led them past the martini bar and out onto the rooftop deck where Bud was standing to greet them.

He smiled and said, "Hello, gentlemen, so glad to see you've made it."

Mike responded with a loud belly laugh, "Haw, haw, haw. Pardner, you damn near killed us with those steps."

Bud smiled, ignoring Mike's loudness, and said, "You must be Steve and Bruce."

Bruce nodded and pointed, "Steve, and I'm Bruce."

"Nice to finally meet you," Bud said calmly. "I hope your trip went well. Please, have a seat, and let's order some drinks to start with."

"Sounds good to me, pardner," Mike jumped in.

Bruce and Steve instantly looked at each other thinking about last night's drink-a-thon. But Mike went right for the "hair of the dog" and ordered a beer and tequila chaser. Bruce and Steve shook their heads in amazement, even after all these years, and settled for moderation with a quiet glass of Riesling.

Bud started the conversation, "Thank you for agreeing to do this for me. As you can see, I'm getting on in years, and I find it hard to go full speed ahead with my gun collecting as I did in the past. I used to enjoy the hunt for the guns as much or more than finally owning them. But now my interest is in building my collection. And that's where you fellas come in. I'll create the lists, and hopefully you can find them for me. Normally I would negotiate for the guns myself after you find them, but I'm open to your doing as much of that as you want. Probably, I'll get involved as the price goes up."

"That's great," Bruce said, "because we took it upon ourselves to negotiate and obtain the first two guns on our list."

Bud smiled and nodded, "Let's see what you got."

Mike flopped the gun case onto the table, spilling a little tequila, "Whoa, sorry about that, boys," he chuckled.

"I know," Steve said. "You hate to waste the good stuff."

Mike ignored the comment and said, "Take a look, pardner—what we have here is the Chief's Special and the .22 Colt Woodsman. Check out that condition, brother," Mike continued as he pushed the gun case holding the two guns towards Bud. Bud slid the case towards himself and popped the closers on the case to reveal the guns. He picked each up, turned them all around, studying seemingly every facet of the guns.

When he was through, and after he placed them back into the case, he said, "Those are very nice pistols. You men have done a very good job, and I am pleased. Mike had already told me that you have three thousand in them, and that's quite acceptable to me." Then Bud reached into his pocket and pulled out a wad of one hundred dollar bills and began to count and place them in three separate stacks. Mike's hand flew to his heart when he saw the stacks of hundreds growing.

"Oh my god, pardner!" he exclaimed with his predictable belly laugh. "Haw, haw, haw. That's more freakin' hundreds than I've ever seen in one spot before!"

"That totals ten thousand dollars apiece," Bud said with a smile. "Make sure you keep track of your expenses from this point on and use this money for that. I'll pay for the other guns myself, after you locate them and negotiate a deal. But if you need cash quickly to finalize a deal, use this money, and I'll reimburse you quick as I can. Nice job, fellas. After we eat, we can talk about your strategies for the rest of the guns on that first list."

"Sounds great," Bruce and Steve said at the same time. Mike had just ordered his third drink and held up his glass in a toast to the new venture.

The lunch was wonderful. Bud was picking up the tab, so everything on the menu was in play with his full approval. That meant Steve got the roasted pheasant, Bruce the salmon plate, and Mike the rib eye steak. Bud ate a vegetarian style entrée of stuffed portabella mushrooms and salad.

"Wow, that is so good" became the phrase of the day. Everyone relished the food, the conversation, and the drink. As the guys enjoyed the open air dining on the rooftop deck, it was easy to keep an eye on the main drag down below.

"What a great place to watch the comings and goings of the locals and the tourists," Bruce said as he leaned back in his chair.

Bud responded, "Yes, it is. That's why I choose to eat here when I'm in town."

"Speaking of which," Steve began. "How did you find yourself settling in this neck of the woods?"

Bud too began to lean back into his chair, but he could still see all directions from where he sat. "Well," he said. "Back in my professional life, I had some dealings out this way that I never really was able to complete, so I've made this town and Buffalo my home bases when I'm tired of the rat race in D.C."

"You still working on something from the FBI?" blurted Mike. Bud looked at his new friend and patiently said, "Now Mike, I told you I'd have to kill you if I let you in on that little secret."

The table became silent and uncomfortable for a moment. There was a sincerity and resolve in Bud's voice that made them all feel a chill for a second.

That is until Mike jumped in and said, "Bud, I love ya, but you are almost as full of shit as my buddies here are." Then, came the laugh, "Haw, haw, haw," and the uncomfortable moment passed as Bud reached out and slapped Mike on the shoulder and gave him a calming smile.

He thought in that moment that it was a shame to be bringing these clean, law-abiding citizens into a mess that he was so heavily involved in so long ago. *But business is business,* he sighed, *and more than likely they will do their little gun collecting thing without the success I need, and they will all move on to the next part of their lives.* He continued to think as he looked out over the railing to the street and sidewalks below, *unlike me, who desperately needs to tie up that loose end.*

"All right gentlemen," Bud said suddenly. "Let's talk about your plans for the rest of the collection."

"Perfect," Steve responded as he pulled out the list that Bud had sent them. "We decided that you would be better served if we broke the list into small goals, like concentrating on two guns at a time."

Bruce jumped in, "And by doing it that way, as we go to gun shows and surf the Internet, we should be able to move quicker and more efficiently. It's certainly easier to ask guys about two guns at a time instead of all eight. Plus as our network of collectors grows, we will also become more proficient in reaching our goals."

"That sounds like a good plan," Bud said. "Tell me, how do you keep Mike involved from such a long distance?"

Steve responded, "Wyoming is such a tremendous gun state that we believe he can develop leads here while we develop leads near our neck of the woods."

"And we will be staying in touch weekly through Skype," Bruce added. "Then when we are successful, we'll let Mikey know, and he will consult with you in person, if you are close by."

"If you are out and about, pardner," Mike jumped in, "we will use your contact numbers to track you down."

Bud nodded in approval at the planning the guys had put into this venture. *Who knows? Maybe I've been selling these fellas short,* he mused. "Sounds like you have a plan, gentlemen," he said. "And believe me, it's all about the plan in life." He smiled when he added, "Just pay attention to the details."

"Oh yes," Steve and Bruce answered in unison. "We are detail people."

"Okay," Bud said. "Just one more thing before we adjourn here. Do you mind if I ask you to move the Colt .45 Uberti's to the top of the list? They have been of particular interest to me for many years now. And please note that I need them to be the exact serial numbers that you see on the list."

"Well, sure, Bud," Steve said. "No problem. We'll go after them first."

"Perfect, gentlemen," Bud continued. "Now I'm afraid that I need to rest for a while. Unfortunately, I seem to tire easily nowadays."

"No problem, pardner," Mike slurred to Bud. "We are all getting a little long in tooth. Haw, haw, haw," he laughed. "I used to be able to drink more than I can now."

Bud smiled as he got up from the table, "I noticed you were only able to drink six beers and six tequila chasers. It's tough to get old," he laughed as he shook hands with the guys and wished them a fun time in Deadwood with their wives. Then he slipped out a back door on the rooftop deck that no one had noticed before. *Now we will just wait and see what happens next,* he thought as he disappeared from view.

The three buddies were excited with how the meeting went.

"Great meeting," Bruce said.

"Absolutely," Steve added.

"Right on, brothers," Mike agreed as he threw back his last tequila of the lunch.

"Oh no," Bruce added with feigned chagrin.

"What?" Mike asked aggressively. "What?"

"Oh nothing really," he said. "I just forgot to wear my wetsuit to protect me from the spit talk."

"I got your spit talk, right here," Mike shot back as he pointed at his zipper.

They laughed as Steve yelled, "Incoming!" And then they headed back to the Four Aces to relax and throw some more money into the slots. It had been a good meeting for the guys.

CHAPTER 20

Clyde and the Director met almost immediately after Bud had briefed the Director on the four agents and Smitty's wife, and now widow. The discussion was intense and sometimes bordered on the absurd as the Director leaned heavily on his faithful lieutenant for his input. As he looked into Clyde's eyes, he found a comfort that he desperately needed at this point in the operation. He was so afraid that the unfixed details and the missing merchandise were going to send everything spiraling out of control. He had seen it happen so many times over his professional life. The smallest detail, mistakenly overlooked, had brought down many criminal enterprises and many high-ranking politicians during his tenure at the Bureau.

"But, Mr. Director," Clyde said with patience and calm, "Bud has everything under control. I don't believe that it is time to raise any eyebrows by more collateral damage. The agents are suitably leveraged and completely loyal to you. And the widow is being scrutinized by Bud and Howard and will soon move on as she finds nothing to help her answer her questions about her husband. I have the merchandise and will be returning them as soon as I feel confident that there will be no questions involved and no reason to wonder why we have them. So, Mr. Director, I think we sit tight and let Bud and Howard do their work," he concluded. Clyde looked directly into the Director's eyes as he finished and sensed that his friend and mentor was still not satisfied. His dark beady eyes seemed to be focused elsewhere. When he finally spoke, it was with some deference to Clyde and his friendship, but it was clear that he wasn't buying totally into Clyde's confidence in how the operation would play out.

He said dramatically, "I understand what you are saying, Clyde. But, by god, I will not sit by and allow some tiny piece-of-shit detail bring us down! I have too much experience in these things to know that it can happen, and it often does. I will give Bud and Howard some time, but one day I will wake up and finish this myself if I still feel this way. Eventually, and very soon, I need to feel safe in our undertaking and know that we can move forward."

Clyde shook his head in assent, "Yes, sir. I know, sir. Whatever you need to do, sir."

The two men shook hands, embraced quickly, and Clyde opened the door and left the Director standing in deep thought, absolutely aware of the impending eruption that was boiling inside him.

On his way out, Clyde stopped by Miss Gandy's desk and inquired quietly, "Is the merchandise I gave you stored safely? And readily accessible?"

Miss Gandy answered quickly without even looking up, "Why yes it is. I can get it for you on a moment's notice."

"Thank you, Miss Gandy," Clyde said as he exited the outer office, "that's all for now."

As soon as Clyde got back to his office, he was dialing Bud's private number. Bud knew that he should answer, and he was right.

"Hello, sir," Bud answered quietly. He knew that it had to be either Clyde or the Director. No one else had this number.

"Bud," Clyde said quickly. "Get your ass out to Buffalo now and assess the situation!" he said with authority. "I don't want the Director to go deeper into this yet, and I have a sense that he will very soon, unless you can convince him otherwise after talking with the widow. Do it now!"

Bud responded, "Yes, sir," to an already dead line.

Clyde hung up immediately. He didn't want to discuss anything at this point. He just wanted it done. Bud felt that it was too soon, but didn't hesitate and immediately called his pilot friend.

"We are heading back to Buffalo. How soon can you be ready for takeoff?"

The pilot said, "Give me three hours and meet me on the back runway at Baltimore."

"I'll be there," Bud responded and hung up. He called Howard and said, "Back to Buffalo. Pick you up in an hour."

Howard grunted an, "Okay, I'll be ready," and hung up. The average person couldn't possibly have made that deadline. But these guys were always ready to go at a moment's notice. Bags with essentials were always packed and ready to be grabbed to head out the door.

Shit, Bud thought. *This is way too soon, but it's obvious the director still has a bug up his ass, and no one or nothing is safe until he feels better about this.* He said the same thing to Howard when he picked him up.

Howard responded, "I know the feeling. I'm starting to feel the same way. Maybe it's time to torch everyone and everything that may lead to trouble for us."

Bud shook his head knowingly, because he knew that it wouldn't be long before everyone involved with the operation would be fair game. There would be plenty of targets for the guys at the top, and whether Howard thought so or not, he and Bud would be a part of that list.

At the airport, Bud and Howard jumped from the black sedan, grabbed their bags, and headed for the parked plane.

The pilot said, "Long time no see," and laughed out loud.

Bud responded seriously, "Back to Buffalo." Then he said, "Sounds like a song. A sad song." Nobody laughed or even smiled as the pilot taxied for takeoff. This was going to be serious business.

The flight back to Buffalo was uneventful, yet stressful all the same. Very few words were spoken, and even the pilot, who had so many questions to ask, was all business. He just wondered to himself, *How many more freakin' flights are we gonna have to make to get this right?*

Bud received no radio calls and assumed it would be up to him to get back to Clyde as soon as his business had been taken care of. *I hope to God that Clyde can keep the Director calm and rationale,* he thought. *The easiest thing in the world for the Director to do would be to slash and burn everyone even remotely close to this operation. Dead men tell no tales,* he thought. *I can do that,* Bud's mind continued to wander. *But guess who would be included in that line of action—me and Howard—after we took care of the rest. I need to fix this or control this to the Director's satisfaction. Or Howard, the pilot, and I are all dead men,* he continued to think as the plane landed again at the Johnson County Airport. As the plane came to a stop, everything seemed all too familiar to the three men on board.

Howard said, "Yogi would be saying, 'It's déjà vu all over again,' wouldn't he Bud?"

The pilot laughed, but Bud just grunted as he clambered out of the plane, looking for their car.

"Who the hell is Yogi?" he muttered as he saw the waiting car. "Let's go Howard," he yelled as both men jumped into the car. "Back to the Occidental," he told the driver, and they were off again to fix what needed fixing.

When they got to the Occy ten minutes later, the driver parked in a spot immediately in front of the hotel. It had recently been vacated by one of the local police vehicles, but Bud noticed that there were still a couple of local law enforcement cars parked in spaces nearby.

"This is just what I was afraid of," he told Howard. "Let's not raise any red flags. I'll do the talking and you will be my friend," he continued.

"Let's do it," Howard agreed as they entered the lobby of the saloon. Both men noticed quickly that there were at least five men in uniform from the local police and sheriff's office. They were talking quietly to an elderly lady that Bud recognized immediately as Smitty's wife. When they saw Bud and Howard, that conversation stopped abruptly and they moved swiftly to intercept the two guys as they walked deeper into the saloon.

One of the uniformed guys with the biggest belly spoke in Bud's direction, "Gentlemen, can we help you?"

As agreed, Bud spoke and said, "Why yes, fellas. What's up? We're in town on business and wanted to stop in to see our friend Smitty. Hope everything is okay here."

"Well, actually," the big-bellied officer with a badge that identified him as the chief said, "we do have a bit of a situation. You say you are here to see Smitty?"

"Yes, sir," Bud responded with feigned respect. "Whenever we get to town, we love to stop here, grab lunch or dinner, and see what Smitty's up to. I certainly hope he is all right?" Bud questioned.

"When was the last time you saw Smitty?" the big-bellied officer continued as he avoided Bud's question.

Bud thought to himself, *See, this is what I was trying to avoid. Waiting for this to die down would have kept us off this radar.* He answered the officer with, "It's been a few days, I guess. We had a great visit with him at this saloon, and he even showed us his old basement with all the old stuff he has saved down there."

Old Big Belly kept at it for a while, asking lots of questions while his buddies took notes. Bud was so used to interrogations that he knew the answers to the next questions before they were even asked.

What a local yokel! he thought. *He's about done with the questions for now,* he thought to himself knowingly.

On cue, Officer Big Belly said, "I think that about does it for now, fellas. Hope you don't mind giving your contact information to my guys," he continued.

"No problem, sir," Bud answered quickly as the officer moved away toward the bar where Smitty's wife was still standing. Bud and Howard watched as he talked quietly to Mrs. Smith, who then looked up and motioned for the two guys to come over to see her. When both guys got close, Bud held out his hand and introduced himself and said, "Is something wrong with Smitty?"

Mrs. Smith responded, "I hope not—but he seems to be missing. It is very unlike Smitty to do something without telling me. So I'm very worried. That's why the police and sheriff's guys are here helping me sort this out," she continued.

"I see," Bud said as Howard nodded sympathetically. "We would be glad to help in any way," Bud continued. "Did Smitty tell you about our interest in your hotel as a part of history?"

"No, unless you guys have something to do with his scheme to get the old place up and running again," she spoke softly with a lost look in her eyes. "He was always trying to come up with some way to get us back on track. But nothing seemed to work. It always came down to too much to do and too little money to do it with."

"Well," Bud said, "maybe we are a part of that scheme. We talked to him about wanting to help financially through some sources that I have who are interested in preserving the historic buildings and local sites that are a part of the Western folklore from the region. He said he was interested, so we got the ball rolling and found a ten thousand dollar grant for him. We gave it to him a few nights ago. Did he tell you this?"

"You gave Smitty ten thousand dollars?" Mrs. Smith practically whisper screamed. "Oh my god," she continued. "Did anyone see you give this to him? That's a lot of money for these parts." Mrs.

Smith's agitated response to this revelation was catching the eyes of the local cops again. They started to move closer to the conversation, but she waved them off. Bud hesitated to answer her until the cops were once again out of range.

Then he said, "No one saw me give him the money. Besides it was in an envelope, because it was given to me in cash to be given to Smitty. He took it down into the basement, and I never saw it or Smitty again. That's why we stopped back today—to make sure he was using the money like he said he would. He never told you about it?" Bud pressed again.

"No," she said. "If he would've I would have put that money in the bank as quick as I could."

"Okay, then," Bud continued. "Do you have a place in the basement where Smitty could hide the money safely?"

Mrs. Smith replied, "We used to have a safe, but he moved it up behind the bar because he was getting tired of going down the steps to lock things up. So there is nothing that I know of," she continued. "Just a lot of old stuff from years and years ago."

"Can we go down and look?" Bud asked.

"Yes," she said. "But let's wait 'til the officers leave. They still think Smitty ran away, and if they hear about the money, they will quit looking for him."

"Okay," Bud agreed. "Sounds like a good time to get something to eat."

"Please do," Mrs. Smith said. "I'll get my girl to take your order at the bar. Have a seat."

As she walked away, Bud looked at Howard and whispered, "Poor old lady has no clue what happened. Remember, when we get her down to the basement, she is not a target. We are just looking around, with her help."

"Got it," Howard whispered back.

"I'm betting that the money and the briefcase are in the same hiding spot," Bud continued. "If we find nothing, I will make her an offer that I know she won't refuse. And if she agrees, I'm recommending a watch and wait approach to Clyde and the Director."

Howard added, "The best case scenario is to find the briefcase and let her have the cash."

It didn't take long for the local cops to move on. Bud was sure, though, that they were trying to check out who Bud and Howard were at this very moment. But both men had fictitious names from any number of special operations with the Bureau and so were very confident that the locals would find nothing suspicious about them. As they sat at the bar, finishing lunch, Bud couldn't help but think back to the first time he came to the Occidental and sat in this very spot talking to old Smitty.

I really hate that the old fella got caught in the middle, he thought. *And I'm still pissed off that Howard acted so rashly without knowing if all of the T's were crossed. If Howard had waited until we had the briefcases in, hand, we wouldn't be here now. Smitty would have told us in a heartbeat why the one case was missing. Now we have this bullshit to deal with,* he sighed as he finished his thought.

Mrs. Smith reentered the saloon and walked up to the guys. "I think it's safe to take a look now," she said as she waved them around the bar to the basement doorway.

As Bud and Howard walked around the bar, Howard whispered to Bud, "Feels pretty familiar, doesn't it?"

Bud nodded and didn't respond. It did feel familiar, but it wasn't a good familiar. He would have been quite happy never seeing this bar or stairway, or basement, ever again in his lifetime.

Unfortunately, he thought. *This may become a permanent part of my life, unless we can secure the merchandise. I just hope that this isn't what shortens my life.* At that moment, the basement smell that he remembered hit him square in the nose—musty and dusty. That was okay though because he was fearful that it would be another smell that he hoped to God had been dealt with by the bag and secret closet. *So far so good,* he thought.

Mrs. Smith, though, did smell something. "Smells like we have a dead rat down here," she said. "It happens on occasion because I put out poison to keep them under control."

Perfect, thought Bud and Howard after an initial start.

"Sorry," Bud said to Mrs. Smith. "My nose isn't very good, so I don't smell anything."

Howard grunted in agreement.

"No matter," she said. "It always goes away after a few days." Bud and Howard just smiled.

With all of the lights turned on and with the flashlight that Mrs. Smith was carrying, the basement was pretty well lighted. It was really a huge space that followed the contours of the saloon and hotel. There were separate rooms with tall ceilings and short ceilings. The rooms with short ceilings generally led to what could best be described as crawl spaces. Plus, there was a very large open room expanse at the very center of the basement.

"Mind if we just wander around and look under some of the old stuff?" Bud asked Mrs. Smith.

"No, go ahead," she said. "I apologize for the terrible condition of the basement. It was always on Smitty's to-do list to get down here and clean up the place. He was convinced that there were valuable antiques to be found amongst all of the junk. Oh my god, listen to me," she suddenly exclaimed. "I'm talking of him as if he was gone for good." Then she said, "I need to go back upstairs in case the police come by again."

"Okay," said Bud. "We'll poke around a bit and let you know if we find anything." When she was gone, Bud looked at Howard and said, "Look at this damn place. I would bet a thousand dollars that there are more false walls that Smitty found down here that he could have used as another hiding place."

"Hell yes," Howard said. "No question that that is probably what he did. He separated the heavy briefcase and put the money with it."

"Let's get busy," Bud said and started to pull and push on every piece of wood that they saw. They rapped on walls, looked under piles of old stuff, and scoured every inch of the place...but to no good use. They found nothing. "You know what we have to do next, right?" Bud asked Howard.

"Yep, let's do it." Howard said and walked over to the room holding the false closet that held Smitty's remains. He pulled on the large wooden dowel and stepped back as the door creaked open.

Bud fully expected to be hit by an overwhelming smell of death, and he feared that it would be noticeable to anyone coming down the stairs into the basement. But amazingly, it seemed as though the body bag was working the way it was supposed to. *No smell!* he thought. *Outstanding! Mrs. Smith was probably right when she said there was a dead rat smell.* As hardened as he was to being sensitive to things that normal people would find emotional, he still felt a twinge of remorse or guilt for what they had done to a perfectly nice old fella who just got caught up in something that was bigger than he could fathom. He almost felt like a grave robber for disturbing Smitty's remains. But he had to. He had to look again at the closet to be sure there were no more secrets being hidden in there.

"You watch the stairs to make sure we don't get walked in on," he said to Howard. Then he squeezed into the small narrow space and surveyed every inch, up and down. "Nothing!" he sighed. "Okay Smitty, your turn," he said as he grabbed the body bag. It felt like a balloon because of the gas being created by the beginning of the decomposition process. But it was very heavy too. And it also felt slippery inside. "Oh shit," he said. "I'll be done in a second Smitty old boy." He looked under the bag and deep into the corner that the bag was blocking. "Nothing again!" he said.

"You about done?" Howard yelled. "I hear voices at the top of the stairs."

"Yep," Bud said as he struggled with the body bag and squeezed Smitty back into the corner of the closet. "Rest easy old fella," he said and slammed shut the door to the false closet. "It looks like we move to plan B," he said to Howard as they turned off the lights in the basement and headed for the basement stairs.

As the two guys reached the top of the stairs, they ran into Mrs. Smith and Officer Big Belly. When Big Belly saw Bud and Howard coming up the stairs, he gave Mrs. Smith a look like, "What's up with that?" Mrs. Smith caught the look and quickly responded. "I asked these gentlemen to take a quick look around the basement to see if there is anything of value to sell or preserve down there. Remember, they are interested in historical preservation?" she asked Big Belly.

The officer responded, "Yes, I do. You know, fellas, I tried to check you out, but couldn't find anything about you anywhere."

"Isn't that good Officer?" Bud asked.

"I suppose it is, but given the timing of your showing up here, well, it just makes a guy curious. You know what I mean?" Officer Big Belly said with a smile.

"Of course, sir," Bud responded. "As I told Mrs. Smith, we are happy to help in any way." Bud was thinking, "I could have done this so much more discreetly and quietly if the Director had just been a little patient and allowed me to wait a while before I came back here." Then Bud asked, "Is there anything specifically we can do for you, sir?"

"Nope, not just now," the officer said as he followed his stomach out the door of the saloon.

As soon as he was gone, Mrs. Smith asked Bud, "Well, did you find anything?"

"No, sorry, ma'am," Bud responded. "But there is so much stuff and so many places to hide things that I'm sure we could have missed something. Do you mind sitting down to talk for a moment?" Bud asked her kindly.

"Okay, sure," she said and led them to a square table in the corner of the bar.

"So here's what I can do for you, Mrs. Smith," Bud began. "The people that I work for have deep pockets and are seriously interested in helping historical sites like the Occidental remain a viable part of the Western culture for generations to come. The ten thousand dollars that we gave Smitty was a first installment to get the Occy back on its feet. Now we can't replace that, but we can offer you a grant or stipend of several thousand dollars every year to make sure that you can keep the place up and running. Our only stipulation is that there will be no physical changes to the building without our approval—no exterior changes, no interior changes, and no basement changes unless we give you specific approval to do so—in writing."

"Just what does several thousand dollars mean?" Mrs. Smith asked. "How much money will that be?"

Bud answered quickly, "I am authorized to send you two thousand dollars every month."

"Oh my heavens," Mrs. Smith said with tears in her eyes. "I could keep the doors open and get by with that amount of money."

"Yes, you could," added Bud. "The only other stipulation is that if you would decide to sell, we would need to approve the purchaser because the grant is for the operations of the building and would go to the new owners if they agreed to our terms."

Mrs. Smith sat for a moment in deep thought. She knew Smitty would jump on this offer and actually already did. When he comes back, if he comes back, he will agree. *I know he will,* she thought. She said, "Okay, I agree." Bud and Howard smiled. "When do I sign the agreement?" she asked.

Bud shook his head from side to side and said, "No signatures, no written agreement. If you don't follow the agreement, the money will just stop coming in. I will be your sole contact and will make sure you get the money every month," he added.

Mrs. Smith was smiling and crying at the same time. "Thank you so much. Now I can concentrate on finding Smitty since I know that the Occy will be taken care of."

"Good luck with that," Howard said with a smile as he shook her hand.

Howard really is a son of a bitch, thought Bud. But he too shook her hand as they headed out the door. *And I guess so am I.*

CHAPTER 21

ack in Washington, the Director was in his office watching his array of black and white TV's and listening to the latest news chatter of the assassination. It was still wall-to-wall coverage days after the incident that rocked the world. Oswald was dead, Jack Ruby was in jail, and the dead President had already been buried with royal fanfare. And the FBI, under direct orders from the Director, was wrapping up the investigation.

There will be no conspiracy concerns, the Director thought to himself. *The sooner we get this thing closed, the fewer questions there will be. LBJ should be quite satisfied with our progress so far, and when he supports our findings, it will be virtually over.* The Director leaned back in his overstuffed chair and had just a hint of a smile on his face. *I will make quite sure that our investigation is the only one of value and the only one that has the President's support. Details, details, details,* he smiled. *Nobody takes care of details like me.* Then he thought of the lost merchandise out in Wyoming, and he called Clyde.

"Hello, Mr. Director," Clyde said answering the phone.

"Clyde, I need to know what's happening in Wyoming," the Director said sharply.

"Well, sir," Clyde continued, "I haven't had a chance to fully debrief Bud and Howard yet, but in a quick conversation by phone, Bud indicated that he felt the situation was under control."

"I need to know what 'under control' means, and quickly, Clyde," the Director exclaimed.

"Yes, sir. I know, sir," Clyde answered. "As soon as Bud and Howard touch down in Baltimore, they are coming straight to my office."

"That's what I want to hear," the Director said quickly to his old friend. "I know you will keep me apprised. I need to call the President soon, and I want to know that every single detail has been taken care of. The President and I both want this investigation done and over with as soon as possible."

"I will let you know the moment that I do," Clyde said in a calming tone.

"Oh and, Clyde?" the Director continued. "I am going to have Miss Gandy take care of returning the merchandise. I think that will look more like business as usual to the folks who look over this stuff."

"I agree, Mr. Director," Clyde said quickly.

"Goodbye, Clyde," the Director said.

"Goodbye, sir," responded Clyde.

As soon as he hung up, the Director yelled "Miss Gandy, come in for a moment." As was her custom, Miss Gandy responded quickly to the Director's directive.

"Yes, sir," she said upon entering the office. "What can I do for you?"

The Director was staring off into space as he continued to listen to the latest news broadcast that was hypothesizing all kinds of future action by the FBI, the Secret Service, and the ATF. When the news reporter started to use the word conspiracy, it was all the Director could do to not pick up the small TV and throw it into the wall. But he maintained a semblance of control as he said to Miss Gandy, "That is precisely why we have to finish this investigation!"

"Yes, sir," she said calmly but with deference. He turned to her and said, "I need you to return the merchandise that we borrowed from my personal gift collection, Miss Gandy. The three briefcases need to be returned today." He emphasized.

Again Miss Gandy said, "Yes, sir."

The Director continued, "If any of those simpleton bureaucrats question where the fourth briefcase is, tell them that I have decided to keep that particular gun as a display gun and have taken it home to put with my collection. Is that clear, Miss Gandy?"

Again came the reply, "Yes, sir," as he dismissed her with a wave of his left hand and went back to watching the broadcast. He knew she would get it done and done right. Over the course of his long tenure, the Director had come to rely on Miss Gandy's professionalism and loyalty for virtually everything big or small that came out of his office. She never questioned; she just got it done. So it came as no surprise when she immediately gathered up the briefcases that she had strategically hidden around the office and headed to the storage area that was created for gifts to the Director specifically or to the FBI in general. Actually, it was a common view that any gift to the Bureau was a gift to the Director, at least for anything of value. Located in the Department of Justice building since 1935, the FBI had become pinched for space, and the Director had been lobbying heavily for a new building that would only house the FBI, and it appeared he was going to get that done. Until then, though, the Bureau was making do with what was available, and that was pretty limited.

Storage of gifts was not a major priority for the Director. It was pretty easy for him to say that since there was such limited storage available that, "I'll just take that home with me for safe-keeping," and he did. His home was a virtual museum of valuable gifts sent from all over the world. Plus, he had a penchant for having his anniversaries recognized by his people, as he called employees at all levels of the FBI—the higher the rank, the more expensive the gift that he expected. Because of that, Miss Gandy felt very comfortable taking the briefcases down to the basement storage area, signing them in with the bureaucrat assigned to keep track of the gifts, and suggesting that the Director decided to keep one of the cases for display in his home.

"The Director decided that he wanted to keep one of the guns for a while," she said to the man keeping track of the gift log.

"No problem," he said back to her. "Please sign the log and note what he is keeping."

"That's fine," she responded. "He may want the other briefcases in the future so please store them in an accessible spot. He truly has a strong love for early weapons that represent our Western heritage," she continued. Miss Gandy perused the log for the date that the guns were signed out. When she finally found it, she noticed that it was September 8, 1962, and also noted that Clyde was the borrower at that time. He had signed the guns out and noted that they were two matching sets of replica Colt .45's donated to the Director by Uberti Manufacturing with serial numbers R80001, L80001 and R80002, L80002. Then she signed the log and wrote, "Returned 3 silver briefcases with matching replica Colt .45 revolvers in each—donated to the Director by Uberti manufacturing. The Director kept one for personal display with serial number R80001." Miss Gandy then handed the briefcases over to the agent keeping the log. He quickly looked into each case and placed them into the room.

"I'll find a good spot for them, Miss Gandy."

"Thank you," Miss Gandy said as she headed out of the room and down the corridor to the stairs.

As soon as she stepped into her office, she heard the familiar, "Miss Gandy, come into my office."

"Yes, sir?" she said in her usual totally professional way.

"Miss Gandy, is the merchandise back in place?" the Director questioned.

"It is, sir," she replied. "I signed it in and noted that you will be keeping one of the guns for display for a while."

"Very good, Miss Gandy," he said. "Please create a file noting the borrowing and the return of the gifts."

"I will do that immediately Mr. Director," she responded.

"That will be all," he said as he turned in his chair to continue to follow the assassination coverage. "Oh, one more thing, Miss Gandy," he yelled out through his open office door. "Call Clyde and see if he has connected with Bud and Howard yet. This is taking way too long."

"Yes, sir," she said and dialed the number.

"Hello, Miss Gandy," Clyde answered. "Is the boss getting antsy?" he laughed.

"Yes, sir, he is," she answered without a hint of humor.

"You can tell him Bud and Howard will be there in thirty minutes," Clyde responded. "They just got here."

"Thank you, sir," she responded and then relayed the information to the Director. He grunted with no other response.

When Clyde ushered Bud and Howard into the Director's office and shut the door, it had been almost forty-five minutes since Miss Gandy had spoken with him.

"Sorry we took so long, Mr. Director," Clyde said apologetically. He knew that the Director was adamant about being on time. However, the Director's mood seemed to be unaffected by the men's tardiness. He was still very much impatient, but he was civil to the men as they recited their stories about their trip to Wyoming. In fact, as Bud spoke, he sensed that the Director was actually pleased with the results and the solution that Bud and Howard had put into play.

"So, gentlemen, you are telling me that you feel very secure that the loose ends have been taken care of and that all we need to do is continually monitor the situation with an occasional infusion of cash?" he restated for the men.

"Yes, Mr. Director," Bud responded and Howard nodded.

The Director looked at Clyde, "All right then," he said to Bud and Howard. "Good work and thank you for your efforts. You are excused. Clyde, please remain for a moment."

"Yes, sir," Clyde said as he got up and closed the door after Bud and Howard left. Clyde looked at the Director and tried to read his face. "You look satisfied, Mr. Director. Are you?"

"Well, Clyde, I think I am," he responded. "I plan to call the President very soon and tell him I'm quite confident that this thing is contained and that it should be business as usual in short order."

"He should be very happy, sir," Clyde said. "Do you need me to sit in on the conversation?"

"No, I'm quite confident, Clyde," the Director added. "He and I will come to a complete understanding. Thank you. You can go."

With that, Clyde left the office, and the Director was immediately dialing the President. When the President came on the line, the Director said, "Hello, Mr. President, this will only take a minute."

"Hello, Mr. Director, I've been waiting for your call."

The Director responded, "I told you that I would let you know as soon as I felt everything was in order and that all variables had been contained. Mr. President, I feel that is the case."

The Director could almost feel the hint of a smile in the President's voice as he acknowledged the comment. "That is very good news. Now I'd like to speak to you as brothers and ask for your insights as to when the FBI's investigation will be completed. That is, as you know, one of the most important priorities for me, and I need you to get that done."

"Well, thank you, Mr. President, I am quite happy to be speaking to you as brothers," the Director responded. "Because I believe that our mutual interests have been served well by our relationship in this operation, as I like to call it. And yes, sir, I am very close to finalizing the official report. However," the Director continued, "as you know, I am very much interested in continuing to serve our great country as your Director as I have for the last few decades. So I need to have your assurance that I will continue to be your brother-in-arms and in service for you during your tenure in office."

The President knew exactly what the Director was asking and immediately responded, "Absolutely, my good friend. I will be needing you to continue to serve with me throughout the coming years. No ifs, ands, or buts, you will be my Director of the FBI, and I will issue a statement of complete support immediately."

Feeling in complete control now of the situation that had been so recently created, the Director said, "Thank you Mr. President for your confidence in me. And yes, sir, my report, the official FBI report, will be released soon and, in my opinion, will completely defuse and debunk all those conspiracy theories that are running rampant out there."

"Now that eases my mind, Mr. Director," the President said. "Thank you for your service and your continued service. We will talk soon."

"Goodbye, Mr. President," the Director said with a celebratory smile on his face. He leaned back in his chair and looked at the TV's and the reporters as they continued to talk conspiracy and thought to himself, *Screw you and your conspiracy theories! I'm still in charge.*

CHAPTER 22

After the meeting with Bud, the three friends enjoyed more of the Old West flavor that Deadwood provided for the tourist crowd. They ate well, gambled a lot, and went on some sight-seeing trips. Mike, unfortunately, missed out on much of the festivities because of his frequent rendezvous with his old friend, "Jose Cuervo." Bruce and Steve couldn't count the number of times over the years that Jose had ended an evening out for Mike prematurely. But Mike kept going back to his buddy. He used the old lip-sip-suck method for drinking his tequila. When the two buddies saw Mike licking his hand below his index finger, pouring salt on it, chugging the shot of tequila, then sucking on the lime, it was always clear to them that it was going to be a short night, or a long one depending on how you looked at it. So whenever they couldn't find Mike in Deadwood, they assumed that he had run into Jose. Nevertheless, "a good time was had by all," as Steve said when the three guys got together for the last time before Bruce and Steve headed back to Ohio.

"Hell yes, boys!" Mike concurred. "This has to rank with one of the best times ever with my two buddies. Haw, haw, haw. And I even got some money in my pocket. So tell me," Mike continued, "shouldn't we be planning the next step in our search?"

"That's why we are here, Mikey," Steve said. "We thought we should break down each of our next steps and get moving on Bud's request to move the Uberti's up on the list."

"Well, pardners, you just tell me what to do and I'll get 'er done," Mike said. "You can see that Bud likes me, and I think he likes you two miscreants too."

"Whoa there, mighty big word you're using," Bruce laughed. "Yep, we think so too."

"You know," Steve began. "I find it odd that he moved the toughest to find guns up on the list. You'd think he'd let us get down the list the best we could before focusing on those guns."

"Yep, I agree," Bruce said. "These two guns are the only guns to have serial numbers on them, which will make it incredibly more difficult to find them. All the other guns can be generic as long as they are in good shape."

"But you know what?" Mike asked not expecting an answer. "Bud is the boss, and as long as he's sticking cash in my pocket, I'm for doing whatever he wants and not worrying about the reason why. When I get back to Buffalo, I'll get Bud out on the shooting range again when he's back in town and try to get inside his reasoning if I can."

"That's great," Steve said. "Just don't piss him off by asking too many questions. I sensed that he doesn't want to get into too much about why he wants the guns."

"Haw, haw," Mike laughed. "When have I ever pissed anybody off?"

Bruce and Steve just looked at each other and shook their heads.

"Oh my god," Bruce said. "Okay, buddy, do what you think is all right."

"So back to business," Steve said. "Mikey, we want you to start talking to your gun buddies at your shooting club about any of the guns on your list. And start getting out to gun shows in your neck of the woods. Brucie and I will get with our connections in Ohio, try to communicate with Uberti Manufacturing, and get on the Internet with the Uberti serial numbers too."

"So even though the Uberti replicas are our first priority, if we run across any of the other guns, that would be great too," Bruce said. "Is everybody onboard with that?"

"Great," Steve said. "So now before the wives get down here and we head out, let's light up one more stogie together."

"Hell yes," Mike exclaimed as Steve passed out three huge cigars. "I'll take that Estrella Cubano," Mike said with a very bad Spanish accent.

Bruce opted for the Maduro, and Steve said, "I'll suck on this Cinco Vegas."

"I love it when you talk that way," Bruce chuckled.

Then Steve said, "Mikey, thanks for setting this whole thing up. It's been great fun so far. So here's a full box of assorted cigars, from us."

"Enjoy," Bruce said.

"Oh my god," Mike said. "Thank you, thank you!"

The boys sat back and enjoyed the rest of their cigars in silence, relishing the precious bond of friendship that they all shared. When the cigars were smoked, and handshakes and hugs were exchanged, Marlene and Becky appeared, and Bruce and Steve loaded up the minivan for the drive back to the Denver Airport. They left Mike standing on the sidewalk, waving goodbye to them in bib overalls, white tennis shoes, and the remnants of a most satisfying cigar.

What a great few days, Mike thought. What no one knew, though, was that Bud had been watching them all from the parking lot across the street from the Four Aces and listening to their every word from a device he had planted on the bench that the guys were seated on.

Nothing left to chance, he smiled as he watched the minivan drive away.

The ride back to the airport was uneventful and seemed to take less time than it did to get to Deadwood. Most of the conversation was a rehashing of everything that the couples did while in Deadwood. But

Bruce and Steve would sometimes fall back to the gun list and Bud. Both men would comment occasionally on the gun list, discuss where they were going to go first and how they expected the search to go. Eventually the ladies would get tired of that conversation and steer the guys toward something else.

"Can't we take a break from the gun talk?" Becky asked. "You guys are BOOORING!"

Marlene laughed and agreed, "You two will have a lot of time to talk when you get home."

"Sorry," Steve said. "But you two do know that we wouldn't be on this trip if we weren't using it as a business trip to try to make some extra cash."

"That's good, Stevie," Bruce whispered. "Throw those dollar signs at them."

"We heard that," both ladies said at the same time and laughed.

"Okay, okay," Bruce said. "We'll be good boys and change the subject. No more gun talk until we get home."

"Perfect," responded the ladies, again in unison.

"But we would like to know more about this Bud character," Becky said.

"Yes," Marlene agreed. "You've hardly mentioned him. So what's his story?"

Bruce looked at Steve and both men shrugged. "You know, we really don't know much about him," Bruce said. "He's kind of mysterious and eccentric at the same time. Mikey said that when he presses him to find out more about him, he basically clams up and jokes that he'd have to kill Mikey if he told him."

"Oh that's great," Becky chimed in.

Steve said, "He's really old, I'd guess in his eighties, but very articulate and low key. But you get the sense that he had a lot of power at one time in his life, as an agent of some sort. Mikey said that he's always talking about details and crossing your T's and dotting your I's."

"I hope he's safe to be around," Marlene said.

"We hope so too," Bruce shot back. "But one thing we do know is that he was true to his word about paying us for our work. Until he gave us those stacks of hundreds, we were just hopeful. By the way, it was so funny when Mikey saw that wad of money. His eyes bugged out, his mouth opened up, and he says he damn near had a heart attack."

"It was hilarious," Steve said. "Wish you could have seen him."

"Mikey is one of a kind," Bruce continued. "But you know, even with all the silly, crazy things that Mikey said to Bud, Bud would just smile and watch."

"It will truly be interesting to see how long this lasts and where it will go," Steve said. "Especially since Mikey will be our live connection to Bud as we move forward."

"Well, it has been fun so far," the ladies agreed.

"But you two boys need to be careful," Marlene said.

"Oh, we will," Bruce said as the friends pulled into the rental return area at the Denver Airport and prepared for the flight home.

CHAPTER 23

Back home in Ohio, Bruce and Steve took a couple of days off from the gun hunt to recuperate from the Deadwood trip. They did chores around the house, played golf, and generally lived the life of retirees with fixed incomes. After a week of this, both guys were getting antsy and decided to get going again on the search.

"Hey, Stevie," Bruce said into his cell phone. "Are you ready yet? Let's get busy."

Steve answered, "Hell yes, I was born ready," and laughed. "I've already started looking on the Internet," he continued.

"Great," said Bruce. "Then I'll get busy and start calling our gun show people."

"Okay, buddy," Steve said. "Let's meet in a couple of days to discuss what we turn up."

"Perfect," Bruce said. "I'll be in touch," and hung up. He immediately dialed his friend Beth to see what was up with her gun show. "Hello, Beth?" he said as she answered her cell.

"Hey, stranger," she quickly responded. "How's the gun hunt going?"

"Good, good," he answered. "And that's precisely why I called you. You must be clairvoyant," he laughed.

"I am, if that word means smart and wonderful," she laughed back at him. "So what's up Bruce?"

"I just wanted to pick your brain a bit about a couple of the guns we are looking for and when your gun show cranks up again," he answered.

"Sounds good," she said. "So whatcha lookin' for now?"

"Well, I showed you the list, but you probably don't remember exactly what was on it," Bruce said.

"You're right," she said with a laugh. "I can't remember my own birthday on most days."

"I hear that," Bruce said and continued, "The list had a couple of replica guns of the Colt Peacemaker. They had a serial number attached, so my guy wants these specific guns. They were made by Uberti."

"Okay, now I remember, because I thought it was strange for a collector who didn't care about cost to want a replica," Beth said.

"Yep, it seems like he has a personal attachment to these pieces. So do you ever see anything like this come through your show or any other shows?" Bruce asked.

"Sorry, but I've never had any come through our show," Beth responded. "But guess who is an expert on Colt models and who travels all over the country to buy and sell them?"

"Not my new friend Bear?" Bruce questioned.

"Yeppir," she responded quickly. "Your good buddy Grizzly Bear."

"Actually, that's great because I think we treated him right on our purchase of his two guns earlier," Bruce said. "And he seemed to like us."

"Well, I'm not sure he liked you," Beth laughed. "He doesn't like anyone. But I think he would put up with you again, if it could make him some more money."

"You're probably right," Bruce said. "Okay, when is your next show that he will be at?"

"Actually, it starts next week," she responded.

"Perfect," he said. "I have his number, but I'd rather talk to him in person. So we'll plan on getting over to the show and seeing Mr. Bear."

"Great. See ya then," she said as she hung up.

That's really not bad to get someone who travels the country interested in helping us find these guns, Bruce thought. *Especially someone who has already proven to us that he knows what he's doing.* With that thought, he got out his other gun contacts and started spreading the word about his interest in the Uberti's.

Steve, on the other hand, was hunkered down in front of his computer screen, scrolling through pages of gun websites trying to focus in on the specific Uberti's that they needed. It wasn't easy, and it was very time consuming. There were any number of Uberti replica Colt .45's out there, but trying to track down the serial numbers was a dead end so far.

I wish I would get a response from the manufacturer, he thought with frustration. *It should be easy to track down the serial numbers to these specific guns, but not getting a response from the company is just pissing me off,* he thought. *So I guess my only shot is to keep running through websites and listings until I hear from them. Wonder what Brucie is finding?* Steve tried to call Bruce, but got no answer. So he decided to call Mike and see what was happening out in Buffalo?

"Hey, pardner," Mike said when he answered the phone.

"Duuuude," Steve intoned slowly into the phone.

"What's happening?" Mike asked.

"Well, that's exactly my question to you. I'm kind of stuck here for the moment. Can't seem to get through to the Uberti manufacturing company to check serial numbers. So I thought I'd see what you are up to."

"Pardner, I'm up for anything you need me to do," Mike said. "You know I'm all about sweat equity, haw, haw, haw. Never had a nickel to invest, so this is normal for me."

Steve continued, "Since I can't seem to find anything yet, I think it would be a good idea if you would kind of run into Bud and try to dig deeper into his interest and find out why he has to have these specific

Colt .45 replicas. More information might help lead us in a better direction. What do you think?"

"Why hell yes, I can do that, buddy," Mike answered. "I'll see where the old fart is and maybe see if I can get him to come out to the shooting range again. That's where this whole thing got started anyway."

"That would be great," Steve said. "Any tidbits of info would really help."

"Yep," Mike said. "I'll git 'er done, pardner. The old fart loves me. I'll give him a call and after we meet, I'll let you guys know. What's Brucie doing so I can update Bud on what you guys are doing when I talk to him."

Steve responded, "He's working through his gun show contacts and looking for guys who may be collectors of these replica kind of guns. Believe it or not, there is a whole world of replica collectors out there. Mainly because they are so much cheaper and in better condition than the real thing."

"Oh that I know, pardner." Mike said. "Okay, sounds like you boys are doing what you can. I'll get to it and give you a call," he repeated.

"Talk to you later," Steve said as he hung up.

Mike didn't waste any time in trying to connect with Bud and dialed his number. He got no answer, but left a message.

"Hey, pardner, this is Mike. Give me a call when you can. I'd like to get together and maybe go out to the range again." He decided to jump in his pickup and head up to Buffalo to see if Bud was hanging out at the Knights of Columbus hall, catching some breakfast. When Mike pulled into the parking lot, he noticed Bud's vehicle right away.

"Hah," he yelled out loud to himself. "The old fart's here." Mike hustled in to the hall and along the way was harassed by his old buddies from the K of C because he took the week off from cooking breakfast with them. Hustling meant limping and creeping along at a little faster limp than usual. And that caught the eyes of his buddies too.

"Hey, Mike, slow down, you're gonna pop an artery," one of his buddies yelled.

Mike just smiled and yelled back, "Don't you worry about my arteries, pardner. I could still beat you in a race."

The guy yelled back, "Yeah, sure, only if it was a wheelchair race."

"Haw, haw, haw," Mike laughed. "Don't you guys have work to do? And by the way, bite me!" he shouted to all of the guys on his way to Bud's table.

Bud had seen Mike enter the building and watched the comedic exchange between Mike and his fellow workers. He noted that Mike had a special way of getting people to like him, and Bud was fascinated by that capability.

In my line of work, there was never any of that camaraderie thing happening, he thought. *It was all serious, all of the time.* Getting to know Mike and his buddies was really a refreshing interlude for Bud in a life full of failed relationships, serious business day after day, and generally bittersweet outcomes. *I really hope this fellow doesn't get hurt in this operation,* he thought as Mike got closer.

"Hey, pardner," Mike shouted at Bud as he got close to his table. "Didn't you get my message?"

"Well, Mike, how are you doing?" Bud replied. "Yes, I did, but I didn't have time to answer you yet."

"Right," Mike shot back at him chuckling. "Eating breakfast at the Knights of Columbus just ate up your time."

Bud smiled, "Yes and no. I do enjoy doing it as often as I can, but I was also trying to make a spot on my schedule to go shooting with you. It seems that even though I'm officially retired, my old bosses have an occasional need for my services."

"I figured that was the case," Mike said, then guffawed. "Haw, haw, haw. None of my old bosses ever wanted to see me back again after I left. I don't understand why."

Bud gave a rare laugh out loud and said, "Well, Mike, I can't imagine why either."

"Okay, Bud, enough of the bullshit chit chat," Mike responded. "Are we going to shoot or not?"

"As a matter of fact, I can make it happen tomorrow morning," Bud said. "Say ten o'clock?"

"Pardner, you read my mind," Mike shot back. He shook Bud's hand firmly with his huge meat hook palms as he turned to leave and said, "I'll just meet you there. Bring those old Colts again."

Bud nodded and said, "I believe I will. See you then," and watched his new friend in the bib overalls limp-saunter away.

The next morning Mike was the first to arrive at the shooting range. He busied himself preparing his guns and setting up targets. When Bud pulled up in his shiny black pickup, Mike had everything ready.

"Hey, pardner, good to see ya," he shouted as Bud climbed out of the truck and grabbed his gun cases and ammunition.

Bud responded, "You too, Mike. It's a lovely morning." They spent the next couple of hours firing their revolvers and rifles. Bud never missed, and Mike hardly ever hit the target.

"By god, how do you do that, Bud?" Mike finally asked in exasperation.

"Lots of training and practice on the range, Mike," Bud responded.

"Well, pardner," Mike said. "I'm tired of missing so I brought this just so I could hit something." He unzipped his gun case and pulled out his twelve gauge shotgun. "I brought some of my double aught shells, and by god, I intend to hit that freakin' target!" he exclaimed.

"Well, I'm sure you will," Bud said. "We called that load the man killer load when I was working. Fire away!" he said.

Mike picked up the shotgun, aimed, and fired. The sound was thunderous, but Mike fired twice more, completely destroying the head and torso of the target silhouette and said, "That's what I'm talkin' about!"

"I believe that you can say confidently that you hit that target," Bud said. "Now picture what a man would look like after being shot with that load."

"Hell yes, pizza face and chest!" Mike shouted.

Bud quickly flashed back to one of his early operations where he had to use that weapon. *That's one I'll never forget,* he thought as the grisly result of his weapon jumped into his mind. "It would not be a pretty sight," he said matter-of-factly to Mike. Mike didn't hear him though. He forgot to put on his hearing protection, and his ears were ringing like church bells on Sunday morning.

"Goddam it," Mike yelled. "Next time remind me, please. I'm gonna pay for that. Let's take a break."

"Okay on both counts," Bud responded and put his weapons away. When Mike had done the same, the two men walked over to a bench and sat down. It was a cool Wyoming morning, and Mike had put on a camouflage wind jacket under his bib overalls. Bud noticed and couldn't resist a jab at Mike's fashion sense. It was in stark contrast to the expensive shooting jacket and khakis that gave Bud a snappy buttoned up look. "Mike, I just have to say that I have never seen a shooting outfit quite like that," Bud said with a smile. "People from my neck of the woods would call that unique."

Mike took the comment well. He was used to people talking about his choice of clothing. "Well, Bud, since you are a friend of mine, I won't say 'fuck you and the horse you rode in on.' But I will say, 'Fuck you very much!' and I am very much unafuckted by what you think of my choice of shooting clothes. Haw, haw, haw. You know, Bud, for a stuffed shirt, I kinda like you."

Bud laughed out loud at the rudeness of Mike's comments. It was obvious that he liked Mike too. "You are definitely one of a kind Mike," Bud continued to laugh. "I have never really gotten to know many folks as friends. Lots of acquaintances, few friends. I'm sure my line of work had lots to do with that. But that's ancient history now," he mused and changed the subject. "So what's up with the gun list?" he asked Mike quickly.

Mike jumped at the question like it was a bluegill nibbling on his fishing line. "Hey, glad you asked. I didn't really want to talk business while we were shooting, but since you asked and we are done, I guess it's okay."

Bud interjected with a laugh, "And since I'm paying the bills."

"Haw, haw, haw, hell yes, that too. Wait a sec though," Mike said and jumped up and limped to his truck to get a couple of cups and a thermos of Jose Cuervo. "A quick hook of this will keep us warm while we talk," he chuckled.

"It's a little early for me, but go ahead and pour me a shot anyway," Bud said.

Mike responded with his "it's five o'clock somewhere" comment and both men laughed as they swallowed their shots. Then Mike asked, "Well, my buddies and I have been working on the Uberti Colt replicas and are finding that the guns with the specific serial numbers are very difficult to find."

"Mike, if it were easy, I would do it myself," Bud smiled.

"Yeah, yeah, I know, but what is it about the specific serial numbers you are wanting? We can get you any number of other Uberti Colt .45's in perfect condition, but are having a hell of a time with these particular numbers."

Bud replied, "I knew it would be difficult. The reason I want these specific guns..." he hesitated for a moment. "The reason I want these specific guns is because they were a part of a top secret operation back in the day that was completed but could potentially cause me problems if they got into the wrong person's hands." He leaned back on the bench, thinking to himself, *I must be getting really old or demented. I just said more than I have ever said to anyone about the guns.* He sighed inaudibly, *This puts my relationship with Mike on a whole different level. And not necessarily a positive level for Mike.* "Mike, you can share that with your friends, but you must make sure that they repeat that statement to no one as they search. No one!" he emphasized again and looked squarely into Mike's eyes.

"Holy shit, Bud!" Mike exclaimed. "I need to know more."

Bud responded quickly, "Sorry, Mike, I've already shared more with you than I have ever shared before with anyone. Frankly, my good friend, it would probably be better for you guys not to find the guns," Bud said with a muffled laugh.

Mike just stared at Bud for what seemed like minutes. Then he asked, "Pardner, do we have to be worried about our safety in this little scavenger hunt?"

Bud shook his head no, but thought to himself, *if you only knew how dangerous this was...* "I'll protect you guys, Mike," he said. "No worries as long as you guys can keep this under the radar. Besides, you have all the protection you need in that big ass double aught twelve gauge shotgun—the man killer!" He laughed out loud hoping to make Mike feel more at ease, but he was pissed at himself for talking too much. That was not how he did business.

Mike said, "Yep, I'm always locked and loaded."

Bud couldn't resist lightening the moment and said laughingly, "Loaded maybe."

"Haw, haw, haw, good one, pardner," he guffawed. "Yep, me and my friend Jose."

Bud then stood up and said, "Well, my friend, this has been pleasurable as usual. Thank you for inviting me," as he shook Mike's hand. "Time to get some retirement work done up in Deadwood," Bud yelled back at Mike as he walked to his pickup, climbed in, and drove away.

Mike yelled back, "Take care of yourself!" and then added under his breath, "and me." He couldn't wait to let the boys know what he had found out.

CHAPTER 24

The more the Director watched the national news networks, the more convinced he became that he had to get a report out as soon as possible. Conspiracy theories were growing by leaps and bounds. In his mind, he was confident that the FBI report would put an end to all of that nonsense.

My integrity and the integrity of my FBI are unquestionable by the American people, he thought to himself. *If I say there was no conspiracy, it will put an end to it all.*

He picked up his phone and dialed Clyde. "Clyde, we need to get that report out. Where is it, and when will be done?"

Clyde responded as he always did, with a "Hello, Mr. Director," said with the intent of calming and slowing him down a bit. "I have men wrapping up the details as we speak. But it will still not be possible to release it before early December."

The Director jumped on that and said adamantly, "Clyde, you need to direct the investigators and shortcut the process. As you know, the President is also commissioning a select committee to investigate."

"Yes, sir, I know, sir," Clyde replied calmly. "But I also know that many of the members of the commission are reluctant to serve on it, and Chief Justice Warren will be very methodical in how he approaches the commission's investigation. It will not be done before ours, sir."

"I know, I know," the Director replied. "But if we are first and loudest in our investigative results, then I believe the public will back our report. If we set the tone, the other investigations will follow our lead, because of the fear of going up against us. Don't you see that?"

Clyde answered quickly, "Yes, sir, Mr. Director, I do see that. I will make it happen," he added.

"Thank you, Clyde, I can always count on you," the Director responded. "Now, what do you think about our situation with Bud and Howard?"

"Mr. Director, I think we should discuss that in your office," Clyde said solemnly. He knew where this was heading, but didn't want to go there—yet.

"Please come over immediately, Clyde," the Director said and hung up the phone.

When Clyde arrived, Miss Gandy nodded and said, "He's waiting for you."

Clyde walked through the doorway, greeted the Director, and shut the door. "Mr. Director, it appears that you have some continuing concerns about the loose ends that Bud and Howard were working on," he said matter-of-factly.

The Director responded, "Clyde, you know me so well."

"Yes, sir, I do," Clyde said. "And that means I know that you are not yet satisfied that all of the details have been adequately addressed."

"You are absolutely right," the Director agreed. "I believe that we need to eliminate more of our threat liability. The way I see it is that we have nine loose ends."

Clyde had a puzzled look on his face and asked, "Nine, sir?"

"Yes, Clyde," the Director said quietly. "Follow me on this. There is the missing gun, the old lady in Buffalo, and seven of our operatives."

"Seven, sir?" Clyde asked again.

"Yes, Clyde. We need to include Bud, Howard, the four agents, and the pilot."

"Okay, sir. Yes, that makes nine, sir," Clyde said.

The Director continued, "I probably should include the President, but he is just as culpable as we are, so I feel he is not going to be a problem."

"All right, sir," Clyde said worrying about what was going to come out of the Director's mouth next.

"It's a very simple equation, Clyde," the Director looked him squarely in the eyes and leaned forward on his desk. "Eliminate all nine loose ends, and we have zero threat from within. Or eliminate the highest risks among the nine and hope for the best." The Director leaned back into the overstuffed chair and put his arms up in the air with his hands cupped behind his head. "Well, Clyde, which is it?"

Clyde knew his boss and friend intimately. And he knew that he had been thinking about this since the beginning, even before the complication with the gun. However, he had hoped that the meeting with Bud and Howard had alleviated his concerns. *Obviously that is not the case,* he thought.

"Mr. Director, I can see that you are committed to this clean-up," Clyde began. "But I believe that the more limited action would be the prudent and cleanest way to go. I believe we need to use Bud and Howard as our scrubbers and then keep them close to us to continue to watch our backs. I believe that they are indispensable to us and the agency."

"On the other hand," he continued, "the four young agents are the most expendable and potentially our biggest risk when investigative agencies start to poke around. The pilot should be included with these agents. But, sir, I have to tell you, I would be perfectly happy to continue to monitor these young men and only move forward with the plan if there is the slightest hint of compromising the operation."

The Director turned away from Clyde, staring at his black and white TV, for what seemed like an eternity for Clyde. "What about the old lady and the missing gun in Buffalo?" he asked Clyde without turning to look at him. "I have a strong sense that we should burn the hotel down with the old lady in it and comb through the debris under the guise of some sort of investigation." The Director turned back to Clyde and looked at him sternly through his beady dark eyes that even Clyde saw as evil at this moment.

Clyde stared back and answered, "Sorry, Mr. Director, but I feel that we should let that sleeping dog lie. I'm afraid it will draw unwanted scrutiny if we show up there again. Bud and Howard have a good plan, and I think that's what we need to do at this point." Clyde could sense the Director's mind was swirling over the possibilities. They both sat in silence for a few minutes.

Finally, the Director spoke, "Okay, Clyde, as always I trust your judgment, and I feel comfortable with the partial fix. Have Bud and Howard eliminate the risk from the agents and the pilot. Then make it very clear to both that the situation in Wyoming has to be controlled, or we all fall into the abyss together."

Clyde nodded his head, reached out to shake the Director's hand, but instead pulled him close and gave him a strong hug. He whispered in the Director's ear, "I'll protect you at all costs. Never doubt that."

The Director smiled and said, "Thank you, Clyde, I know."

Turning to walk out the door, Clyde reflected over what he had to set in motion. He would have done whatever the Director wanted, but he had gotten a compromise and that made it not quite so bad. *It is what it is,* he thought as he headed towards his office.

When Clyde got to his office, he reflected on the two directives that he had been given to complete—get the official FBI report on the assassination out ASAP and terminate the potential threat from within. The report posed the most difficult of the two assignments because he had to first get the copy from his investigators, then rework it to meet the Director's needs, have him approve it, and then get it released for all the world to see. It was a time-consuming process under any circumstances, but making sure the report would do and say what the Director and President needed it to say made it that much more laborious. As for the internal threat, that was easy. All it took to set it in motion was a call to one of his black ops subcontractors.

When he dialed the number, all he said was, "This is number two. I am sending you information on a cleanup that needs to be done immediately, but quietly. You will receive the pertinent information later today at the usual Post Office box. Only respond if you see too much risk to get it done in a timely manner. Otherwise, I will assume it will be done. Payment will appear at the usual time and place, upon verification of completion."

Then he hung up and thought, *It's as simple as that. Now for Bud and Howard,* and he dialed Bud's number. "Come to my office immediately," he said matter-of-factly into the phone. The curt directive from Clyde caught Bud a little off guard.

What's up now? he thought. *Normally Clyde is very professional and undemanding on the phone. He always prefers to do business face to face...* but the tone of his voice led Bud to think of all sorts of scenarios as he hurriedly left his own office and headed towards Clyde's office. *I'll bet the cleanup is about to begin. Or maybe Howard and I have become targets of the paranoid Director, and Clyde is just giving me the heads up. Or maybe I'm the target along with everyone else involved in the operation.*

Bud's mind was still racing with possibilities when he approached Clyde's door. Clyde was standing in front of his desk near a round office table that Bud had sat around many times hashing out plans for past operations. When Clyde saw Bud approaching, he motioned for Bud to take a seat at that table and closed the door. He started talking immediately, dispensing with the formalities of welcome. It was time to get down to the business at hand.

"Bud, I just met with the Director, and he is still hung up on the loose ends of our operation. I have been ordered to fix them." Bud started to speak, but Clyde talked over him. "This is what is happening now. The four agents will be neutralized by an outside subcontractor, and so will the pilot. You and Howard will monitor the Wyoming situation and keep us informed of everything that happens there. And I mean everything," he emphasized as he looked Bud squarely in the eyes. "Bud, you and Howard are still in the Director's line of sight. Your future at the agency—your future in general, depends completely on how well you contain this situation."

Bud took advantage of Clyde's pause and asked, "Are Howard and I in jeopardy here, Clyde?"

"Make no mistake, Bud," he answered. "We are all in jeopardy if we don't do this right. I am sorry for sacrificing our young agents in this situation, but it is the only sure way to know that they are contained."

Bud wanted to stand up and scream, "What the hell are you murderous bastards thinking?" But he maintained his cool and only responded with, "I understand, sir."

"By the way," Clyde continued. "The Director wanted you and Howard to handle the agents and the pilot. But I felt an outside intervention was more suitable for our needs."

"Thank you, sir," Bud said. "I agree."

"Are there any questions, Bud?" Clyde asked.

"No, sir. I will get with Howard and draw up a more specific plan for Wyoming and get it to you soon," Bud responded.

Clyde nodded, and Bud got up from the conference table and walked out of the office thinking the whole time, "Did I just dodge a bullet or did I just delay it?"

Clyde, on the other hand, got right to work on the other directive. *Gotta get that report done!* he thought as he dialed the number of his chief investigator on the assassination report.

"Hello, Bill? This is Clyde. I'm coming down to talk," he said and hung up the phone. When he got to Bill's office he stomped in like a man on a mission. He wanted to look serious, and he was.

"Mr. Deputy Director, is there a problem?" Bill asked.

"Not yet, Bill, but there will be if I don't get that goddam report, like yesterday!" Clyde responded with urgency in his voice.

"It's coming together, sir," Bill said. "But it is very basic at this time. There are a lot of angles that need to be looked at yet, and that's going to take time, sir."

Clyde stared at him from his standing position, looking straight down on Bill who was almost cowering behind his desk. "Goddam it, Bill, I don't give a rat's ass about other angles! What I want is a clean report that says there are no stinking conspiracies and that Oswald is the guy who did it—no ifs, ands, or buts! We need to have this report out first," he said emphatically as he slapped his hand on Bill's desk. "Now when do I get the first draft?" Clyde continued.

"Sir, I can have a first draft to you by the end of the week," Bill said. "That's the best I can do, and it will be very basic, sir."

Clyde responded, "Get it to me by Friday, and make sure it's very close to being the final version." And then he stomped out, leaving Bill, an accomplished investigator with years of experience wondering, *What the hell just happened?* He had never seen Clyde be that agitated.

CHAPTER 25

Mike waited until he got home to make the call to Steve and Bruce. He was still fired up from the conversation with Bud, though.

Wow, he thought. *Not only are we three old retired guys having a little fun, but we may also be three old retired guys involved in a top secret government operation."* Unbelievable," he whispered to himself. Mike couldn't reach either of his buddies, so he left a message for them to get together so they could conference call.

When Bruce listened to his message, he immediately called Steve. "Stevie?" he said as Steve answered the phone.

"Dude," Steve responded in a long drawn out hello.

"Mikey has a scoop for us, so can you get over here and set up a conference call for us?" Bruce asked.

"I'll be there in fifteen minutes," Steve replied and hung up.

When he got to Bruce's house, he quickly readied the phones for the conference call and told Bruce, "I got a call from Mikey too. He sounded all excited about what he found out."

Bruce added, "I hope he got some info that will help us find these guns."

"We shall see momentarily," Steve said as he dialed Mike's number.

Mike answered right away. The phone didn't even appear to ring. "Hey, boys," he said. "That didn't take long to get back to me. You musta been napping," he laughed.

Bruce answered, "Nope, not yet, but soon. That's what we retirees do," he chuckled. "So what's the big news flash?"

Mike quickly responded, "Oh my god, listen to this. Bud said that the Uberti's were used in a top secret operation years ago for the agency, and if the wrong person got hold of them, he would be in deep shit."

"Really?" Steve said. "What about us if we find them?"

"Bud said we would be fine," Mike said. "And I even got the feeling that he really doesn't expect us to find them. He's been looking for a long time."

"Wow," Bruce exclaimed. "That explains why he wants precise serial numbers and specific guns. And it does sound kind of impossible. If this professional can't find them, who are we to get it done?"

Steve jumped in, "Well, I think we should keep trying. We don't really have anything to lose here. Bud's the guy with the baggage that could get him in trouble. Not us. If we find them, we get them to him immediately, and we're out of it."

Bruce hesitated then said, "I agree. Let's do our thing and if lightning strikes and we find them, it's Bud's deal, not ours."

"Do we all agree to keep looking, then?" Steve said.

"Pardners, you know I'm in." Mike said. "This is the most fun I've had in years."

"Me too," said Bruce. "Let's do it."

"Okay then, Mikey," Steve said. "We will continue doing what we've been doing."

"Thanks, Mikey, keep us informed, and we will let you know our progress."

Mike responded with, "Adios, pardners. I'm out of cigars. Just sayin'." and hung up.

Bruce and Steve laughed out loud and Steve said, "I'll get some cigars to the boy as soon as I can. I just ordered a bunch of dark Maduros, and they should be here anytime."

Bruce nodded his head in agreement and said, "Don't forget about me," and walked with Steve out the door. He leaned into Steve's car window and asked, "Are you ready to hit that gun show again so we can catch up with our friend Bear?" Bruce asked.

"My guess is that he is a great place to get restarted in this hunt," Steve said. "Just let me know when," he continued as he started to back out of the driveway.

"You got it," Bruce said and went back into the house to check the dates of the upcoming gun shows and, in particular, the gun shows where they might find their new buddy Grizzly Bear.

When Steve got home, he immediately went to his computer and checked again to see if he had received any response from Uberti Firearms regarding the Colt .45's.

"Dammit," he said under his breath when he found none. "Okay, guys, I'll just send another request," he murmured. "And then I'm gonna start calling you until you respond."

With that, he hit the send button and picked up his phone to dial the only number he could find for Uberti. At that moment his computer chirped to show a response from his request so he hung up the phone and checked it out. It was an acknowledgement of his request, "Thank you for your interest in Uberti Firearms. We will process your request as soon as possible. Please be advised that it may take several days to complete the request. Have a nice day."

Well, crap, Steve thought. *I thought I might get a real person. But at least this is some progress.* He then picked up the phone to dial the contact number. *No sense waiting for a response if I can get it done in person,* he thought as he dialed.

The phone rang several times and then a voice answered, "Benelli USA and Stoeger Industries." And followed that up with a bunch of phone options from purchasing to warranty contacts. *This is exactly why I would rather deal with companies through the computer,* he thought. Steve stayed on the line hoping to speak to a real person, but after several minutes decided to try later. It was obvious to Steve, though, that Uberti did business in the United States through the companies that were listed on the phone greeting. *Let's hope I get somebody who knows something about the history in this country.* On an impulse, he dialed the number again and, amazingly, *Oh my god, a person!*

"How can I help you?" the voice asked. Steve explained what he was looking for, but didn't get the answer he was looking for.

"Sorry, buddy," the voice said. "We only started importing for Uberti in the early 2000s. And I have no idea who imported for them before we got involved. I think you got to talk to the company in Italy to get what you are looking for. Gotta go, nice talking to you man," the voice said and hung up.

Steve still held the phone in his hand and said, "Well, shit, shit, shit. Okay then, I guess that's where I go."

Bruce wasn't having much more luck with his gun show contacts from around the state.

Everybody seemed to have the same opinion, "Don't know, buddy, you need to talk to the manufacturer. We don't pay attention to specific serial numbers. Email the company in Italy. Why do you need specific serial numbers? Did somebody steal them? Were they used in a crime?" But so far nobody was able to give Bruce a lead he could use. Plus, they all wanted the collector's name, probably to cut Bruce out if they found something. One thing he did find out is that the gun collecting/finding business could be very cutthroat. Because everyone in the business was so knowledgeable about price, the only real money that could be made was in finding a specialty collector like Bud, who was willing to finance the search. After almost depleting his call list, he was getting close to calling it quits for a while and waiting.

I think I need to talk to the Bear and get him involved. My wheels are just spinning here. He made one more call and that was to Steve.

"Dude," Steve said in the familiar monotone greeting that he always used for Bruce.

"Hey, buddy, you doing any good?" Bruce asked.

"Hell no," Steve responded quickly.

"Well, I'm putting it on hold for a while, until we can meet with Bear at the gun show this weekend. Does that sound okay to you," he asked.

Steve jumped at the break he was being offered and said, "Yep, let's go play golf. Pick you up in an hour?"

"Perfect," Bruce shot back. "We need to work at our other jobs for a while—retirement that is."

Steve laughed and said, "Let's do it. I'm afraid our retirement skills are eroding—you know, use it or lose it."

"That comment fits many of our skills," Bruce chuckled back at Steve. "See ya soon."

Actually, playing golf was a very good thing to do at this point. It gave the guys a chance to unwind and compare notes and discuss their next steps in their endeavor. It also gave them a chance to reminisce about their Wyoming buddy's success as a golfer, or lack of success. "Mikey was probably the worst golfer I've ever played with," Bruce said. "And yet, I always had a great time with him."

"Me too," Steve said after he missed a two-foot putt.

"Nice putt, by the way," Bruce jabbed at him.

"Bite me, Bonzo!" Steve rejoined. "Remember that time you and Mikey were playing at St. Mike's and the swarm of wood bees attacked you?"

"Oh my god! Yes, that was terrible," Bruce remembered.

"Mikey went into that wooded ditch bank to look for his ball, and the next thing I knew, he came running out with a swarm of bees flying around his head and stinging the shit out of him." Bruce laughed out loud at the memory. "And then I dropped my club and went running to help, and they started to attack me. It was absolutely terrible and scary. I was swatting them on Mikey, and he was swatting them on me. It was crazy, but we finally got away from them and had stings all over our faces and arms. It looked like we had been beaten up, but we finished the round. And the best part was when we got back in the clubhouse looking like that, one. One of the guys came over and said, "I thought you two were friends. What the hell were you beating each other up for?"

"Yep," Steve said. "That was hilarious and probably one of the many reasons Mikey gave up the sport."

"Oh yes, and the other reasons were all about being no damn good at it with no chance to ever get better."

"He wasn't built for it."

They both laughed and continued to reminisce about all of the adventures the three buddies had before Mike left them for Wyoming. The two buddies finished the round without another word about the guns, but with an agreement to make the gun show with Bear a priority.

CHAPTER 26

The response to Clyde's communication with the agency's black ops subcontractor was swift and decisive—and merciless. None of the agents knew what hit them. At least that was the indication from the report of the terminations that Clyde received on his desk through a special courier. It was marked with a top secret stamp that also read "For the Assistant Director's eyes only." When Clyde started to read through the report, he was taken by the cold, impersonal description of how three of the agents lost their lives. It appeared that all of the young men were involved in deadly accidents that were unavoidable and certainly unquestionable to any coroner's report. Even though the report didn't give all of the particulars of each event, Clyde found himself reliving the so-called accident for each of the agents.

Agent number one was the first to go. He had been staying in a so-called FBI safe house that was designed to protect agents from harm while on special, black ops assignments. He never ventured out without taking all of the usual precautions of masking his true identity. Even people he knew wouldn't have recognized him when he did the ordinary kind of things that the civilian population did routinely. But he did all of these things on foot or on his bicycle. When he went to the grocery store, all he carried on his person was his FBI badge and wallet. Nothing outwardly connected him to the Bureau in the least. When he worked out with long power walks or long bicycle rides, he was always just an anonymous person, nondescript and unnoticeable.

Clyde thought, *The only way anyone could have found this young man was through the Bureau. He had learned his craft well and was on his way to being a great agent for us. What a stupid way to do business. Take our best and brightest, train them to accept whatever the Bureau throws at them under the guise of patriotism, and then throw them to the wolves.*

"And I am one of the wolves," he muttered under his breath. "What a waste!"

He continued to read about the accident, "The agent was riding his bicycle on a quiet suburban side street when a large truck of some sort, with huge mirrors on its sides, came driving by at a high rate of speed. The agent was riding his bicycle in the driving lane going with the flow of traffic, but oblivious to the large truck when it suddenly veered to the right," *And with almost the same precision that a surgeon might use in an operating room,* Clyde added in his mind. "The mirror struck the agent from the rear with such force as to decapitate him instantly."

Oh my god! Clyde thought, and he had to fight back a wave a nausea that had come over him with the picture of the "accident" that appeared in his mind. Clyde knew that even though he hadn't witnessed the termination himself, the picture of the agent's severed head and headless body wrapped around the bicycle would haunt him forever. The report of the first agent's demise continued tersely with, "The accident is still under investigation by the Bureau."

Clyde was unnerved by the first part of the report and the viciousness of the termination. He didn't want to look further into the report, but felt compelled. After all, he had been the guy who had set this special operation into motion. So he willed himself into a modicum of composure and read on.

The report continued, "Agent number two had sequestered himself in a safe house located in a dicey part of D.C. He went out every day to exercise and stop by a local coffee shop. He was unrecognizable to the population of mostly middle European immigrants. However, during one of his many trips outside the confines of the safe house, technicians came to the house to make sure the gas furnace and other gas appliances were working properly. They left him a note explaining why they were there and asked him to restart the furnace when he got back. The agent did as instructed. Unfortunately, the technicians had accidentally left a gas valve partially open, and when the agent pushed the igniter, the gas combusted and the agent and his safe house were completely obliterated, leaving behind nothing but a charred body and a pile of clapboard sticks of wood and shingles. The FBI is continuing to investigate this terrible accident."

Unbelievable, thought Clyde, *but so efficient and so thorough.* It actually made Clyde wince a bit at his own mortality. *My god, they made this happen so easily,* he thought. *Who's to say that someday my name might appear on a list like this? I guess it's better to be the decider of these actions than the receiver,* he sighed to himself.

But the more he read, the more he felt like a man who had given up his humanity for a life of self-serving convenience—and for selfish love. Clyde was clearly flushed with guilt for what he had set in motion. But he needed to continue reading to see it through.

The report continued with a description of the third agent's demise. It read, "Agent number three was placed in a safe house in a very wealthy part of the D.C. metro area. Of all of the four agents, this man followed the rules scrupulously. He went out very sparingly and only when necessary. He wore different clothing and always sported some sort of hat to make it less easy to identify him. He always ate in, only going to nearby grocery stores, and then, only in and out. He followed different schedules, never doing anything or going anywhere in the same way or at the same time. This agent was a skilled operative in every sense of the word. However, he made one mistake in the early morning hours of his last day on earth. The agent decided to leave before dawn to walk to a different coffee shop further away from his safe house. Believing that he was living in one of the safest parts of the city gave him a false sense of security. On his way, walking through the darkened city streets and sidewalks, he was accosted by a gang of hoodlums who took his money, and when he tried to resist with his weapon, they shot him dead on the sidewalk. He had no chance. The perpetrators have not been found, and the FBI continues to investigate the untimely death of one of their agents."

Clyde mumbled incoherently to himself and then said, "Three down and two to go." When he turned the page, he was surprised to see that the report was incomplete. "Now what?" he muttered to himself. "Just what the hell does this mean?"

He read the final words of the report that said, "This is a preliminary report, not the final version. The final two phases of the operation are still in progress and will be a part of the next and final report. Every effort will be made to conclude everything in the next couple of days."

"Shit, Shit, Shit," Clyde exclaimed under his breath. *As horrific as this report is, I needed to see it completed—and now! The Director will not like having this operation open and only partially completed. It's just another damn loose end that will bite us if we don't get it done soon. I can hear him screaming at me now!* Clyde thought. *Well, it's the best we can do at this point. But I gotta let him know,* and he headed out of his office towards the Director's office with the report in his hand.

Gordon was the last agent standing in a surreal situation that most people would have never seen coming—and even his highly trained agent friends missed it. *That's why they are probably dead and I'm still alive,* he thought. He was still alive because he was even more ruthless and merciless than the subcontractors sent to make sure that he was no longer a loose end. His longtime buddy, Howard, had warned him coming into this operation that he could possibly become expendable.

"No problem, Howard," he said at the time. "I know how to take care of myself."

And take care of himself he did. Bud and Howard had given the agents an emergency communication code so that they could contact each other in case something went sideways while they were stored away. That was the first thing that Gordon did after he was assigned a safe house like the other three agents. He set up a regular check in time with the other guys and while they pooh poohed the need, he made it very clear that it had to be done. Then he used the safe house as a shield for himself. He never set foot in the place except to see if anyone was checking on him. After checking into the safe house so everyone could see that he was there, he quickly left and found himself a hotel room in close proximity to the safe house. From there, he conducted regular reconnaissance forays past the safe house. So instead of being the prey, he became the predator. *And I'm damn good at being a predator,* he thought to himself as he made notes about the goings on around his safe house. So when Gordon couldn't contact the other agents as called for in their emergency plan, he knew that the shit was about to hit the fan. And he was ready.

On the same day that he couldn't contact any of the other three agents, he saw three men dressed in black and carrying pistols covertly enter the safe house under cover of darkness. "Well, shit, it looks like I'm missing the party," he muttered under his breath. "Time for me to make an entrance."

He was well armed with knives and pistols with silencers and slowly worked his way to the open back door that the three operatives had used to enter the safe house. Upon entering, he noticed that all three were just coming out of the bedroom and were splitting up to comb the rest of the house. *Perfect,* he thought. *Now I gotcha, one on one.* He stepped forward as one of the men walked past and strategically placed the blade of his huge Bowie knife into the guy's back above the kidney. "Shhhh," he whispered into the guys ear and slit his throat. *One down, two to go,* he thought. When one of the other guys came to check on his buddy, Gordon stepped forward and put a silenced 9 mm into his temple, caught him, and lowered him to the ground, and then gave the last man a forehead shot when he came to check on the noise. "Wannabe's," he spoke out loud. "You shouldn't have come out to play with the big boys." Gordon didn't bother to clean up the mess he made. He was quite sure that a cleanup had already been planned. But it was his cleanup they were expecting, not the three intruders.

On his way out of the house, Gordon had already decided to follow through with the rest of his plan. When Howard informed him of the potential for a full-scale cleanup after the original operation, Gordon prepared himself for the inevitable. He knew he had to disappear and devised a foolproof plan for his protection. He headed immediately to the hotel where he had been staying and rapped a coded knock on the door.

When the door opened, a man greeted Gordon with, "What's up man? It's really early."

When Gordon entered the room, he just looked at the man and said, "Okay, it's show time. Time to make those big bucks I've been promising you. Get ready now. We only have a few minutes." Gordon watched him as the man quickly threw on the pre-arranged outfit and thought, *Perfect! He could be my twin—same height, build, and facial structure.* He grabbed the guy's arm and said, "Come on, we gotta go."

The man grunted, "Let's do it," and walked out with Gordon.

Gordon led the man quickly back to the safe house, made sure it was still secure, and quickly ushered the man in the house through the darkness. When the man saw the bodies strewn about the house, he turned to Gordon and began to say, "What the hell....?" But that was the last phrase he would ever say as Gordon used one of the silenced guns from the intruders to neatly put a hole in the side of his head.

"Sorry, buddy, no big bucks here."

When Gordon had heard about the potential for his termination, he scouted the homeless population until he found the right fit, promised a big payday, and gave him food and shelter. If he needed to use the guy, so be it. If he didn't, he would cut him loose. Unfortunately for the man, he needed to use him. So in death, the man would assume Gordon's identity, and Gordon would disappear.

"Thanks for your help, buddy," he said as he maneuvered the bodies into the right positions and placed the weapons where they would be expected to be found. Then he emptied the can of accelerant he had already placed in the house, threw down the match, and walked quickly to the street. It was an inferno almost immediately, and he was quite certain that he would be proclaimed dead after any sort of investigation. As he walked quickly away from the flames and heard the sirens coming closer, he allowed himself to feel a little smugness and satisfaction at his handiwork. Even though his life had just changed forever, he was alive.

It always comes down to paying attention to details, he thought. *Never send boys to do a man's job. Thank you, Howard,* he continued to think. *I will be calling you very soon. Don't want you to be too weepy eyed at my funeral,* he laughed out loud as he disappeared into the darkness.

After the unexpected extra cleanup at the safe house and the confirmation of a charred corpse matching Gordon's description, the subcontractors felt secure enough to proceed with the final phase of the operation. So a plan was put into play to terminate the pilot. However, much like Howard felt the need to help Gordon, Bud just couldn't get the young pilot out of his mind.

I can't let that happen, he groused to himself over and over again. *He was like the driver of a getaway car. He knew something was up, but he knew none of the details. I just can't see how his elimination is good for any of us.*

He brought his concerns to Howard over a discreet coffee in the middle of the morning. He breathed an inward sigh of relief when he raised his concerns and saw and heard that Howard shared the same concerns. "Howard, will you help me save this kid?" he asked.

"Yes, I will, but you have to know that any sign that we didn't fully support the Director in this operation will bring it all down on us. We are walking a very fine line as it is," he emphasized. "But you know what, I say fuck 'em! Let's save the kid." He took a long drag on his Pall Mall, blew it out slowly, and dropped his own bomb. "I helped save Gordon," he said matter-of-factly with a wry smile.

Bud was swallowing some coffee and nearly choked and spit at the same time. "Say that again," he whispered, as if suddenly all eyes and ears in the place were on the two guys.

Howard obliged, "I helped save Gordon. I warned him of the termination order and wished him luck. He did the rest. He is a goddam good young agent! And I couldn't see him sacrificed."

Bud didn't know quite how to respond to this revelation. But as usual he gathered himself inwardly and whispered again, "So Gordon is alive?"

"As of last night," Howard responded. "But he'll never be Gordon again and that pisses me off."

"Wow, wow, wow," Bud muttered to himself. Rarely at a loss for words he fumbled around for a bit before he spoke again. "Okay then, if you are with me on this pilot thing, I'm quite sure that we can protect each other's asses. But we have to move quickly."

Howard agreed, "Okay, let's move on it then. Here's my take on this. If I'm doing the termination and don't want any questions, and my target is a pilot, I can tell you that there will be a plane crash soon. No muss, no fuss, difficult to identify a body. Are you with me here?" Howard continued.

"Yes," Bud said. "So we'll need a body double, right?"

"Correct," Howard said. "We just have to be prepared to make a switch with someone who is expendable. And I think I got that covered too. I have a slime ball pilot who has been ferrying drugs for some mafia boys. We'll keep our guy's plane under surveillance and keep him hidden away. That way, the subcontractors will only have one option to get our pilot, and that is when he's flying. We'll make the switch before takeoff; the mafia pilot will be none the wiser. We'll give him his destination, and he will think he's doing what he usually does. And then we'll see what happens. Most likely they will tamper with his instruments and have the engine fail in some way. They might use a bomb, but that would draw too much attention."

Bud agreed with the plan and said, "Perfect, let's get the surveillance going. I'll talk to our pilot, and you get the dead guy walking," he chuckled. Then he thought, *It's pretty rude to see humor in someone's death. But it will be humorous to know that we got one over on the thugs who are in charge of this operation...again!* he thought as the men exited the coffee shop.

Both men went about their assignments like the professionals they were. Bud met with the pilot, who was completely caught off guard by what Bud had to say. And yet he was very willing to go along with the plan, especially after Bud said, "You have no other options; we are trying to save your life. It's a simple equation. Your knowledge of the events of that fateful day equals the need for your complete silence. That can only be achieved through your death."

Finally grasping that he had to go along with the plan or die, the pilot said, "Thank you," and moved his mind past the why to the how.

Bud didn't give him all the details, but he did say, "We have it all covered. Just be ready and follow our directions explicitly."

Things happened very quickly after the conversation with the pilot. Howard had already contacted the rogue pilot, had him convinced that it was a drug run for the mafia, and had him stashed at the Baltimore airport in the hanger closest to where the FBI pilot generally flew. Bud had the FBI pilot prepped and ready. Now it came down to a waiting and watching game. The plane that the FBI pilot was assigned to was sitting on standby outside the hanger on a secluded parking pad. This created the perfect visual for Bud and Howard. Each had his pilot tucked away awaiting a go order, and each expected things to happen fast. To make sure that the subcontractors came after the pilot now, Bud had his pilot file a bogus flight plan with the FBI and with the airport. *That's what I would do,* Bud thought. *I'd get the target as quickly as possible and with as little potential for discovery.* Then Bud contacted Howard over the hand-held radio to double-check their communication, and almost immediately after everyone was in place, a group of men drove up to the unattended plane and proceeded to enter the cockpit with a full set of tools. They were dressed in airport mechanics coveralls and appeared to be quite proficient at what they were doing. From a distance, it didn't appear that they were connecting a bomb.

Bud spoke quietly into the radio to Howard, "Looks like it's going to be some sort of failure in the cockpit, like fuel or altitude control, or whatever else might cause the plane to crash en route to its destination."

"I agree," replied Howard. "Let's bring out the real pilot so they can see him, and he can make some small talk about the flight."

"Roger that," Bud said and went back to his pilot and said, "Showtime. Go over to the plane and when they leave, taxi it to the front of this hanger, keeping the pilot side towards the hanger door. As soon as you stop, jump out, and the other guy will jump in and go. You okay with everything?"

"I'm okay with getting to live," the pilot muttered as he left the hangar and went to the plane.

Meanwhile, Howard had the rogue pilot move to the end of the hangar where the plane would stop. *This guy thinks it's business as usual,* Howard thought. *He's used to doing clandestine things to move the mafia drugs. He has no idea what's going to happen this time though,* Howard smiled. *Pretty good trade—slime ball for FBI pilot.*

As the FBI pilot worked his magic with his would-be assassins, Bud and Howard were on pins and needles. "Oh my god, the only thing that can go wrong now is if they somehow put a bomb on the plane and it never gets off the ground," Bud whispered to Howard.

"Yep, all we can do now is let it play out," he responded.

And that's exactly what Bud and Howard saw. The situation played out—the right way. The guys in the mechanic uniforms left the plane, got in their truck, and pulled away. The pilot taxied to the hangar, blocked the view of anybody watching, and jumped out.

Howard yelled at the slime ball, "Now, get in that plane, get clearance, and get the hell out of here!"

The switch was made, the plane took off, and Bud and Howard breathed a sigh of relief. The truck full of mechanics had stopped further up the runway to watch, probably congratulating themselves on a great job. Bud and Howard shared a moment of laughter and triumph as they steered the seemingly safe pilot through the back of the hanger and into a waiting vehicle.

Bud spoke first and said, "Congratulations on your new life," and handed him a briefcase with his new identity and a plane ticket to Denver, Colorado. "Other instructions are included," he continued. "We'll be in touch as soon as we get word about an FBI plane crashing somewhere over a large expanse of forest somewhere in the Northeast," he said with a large seldom used smile. They dropped him at the terminal and it was over.

CHAPTER 27

When Steve picked up Bruce to head to the gun show, he brought along a specially wrapped box and sat it prominently on the console between the seats. Bruce noticed it immediately and took the bait. He had to ask Steve what was in the box.

Steve just smiled and said, "Just got my new order of Maduros in and I'm sending a bunch to Mikey."

"Wait, buddy," he whined. "You aren't sending him all of them, are you?"

"Ha," Steve snorted. "I just had to hear you beg. Don't worry, my good friend," he continued with his big Irish grin. "Look on the back seat."

Bruce swiveled around and just exclaimed, "Oh man, you are such a good guy! No matter what everyone else says." On the back seat was a box filled with dark Maduro cigars. "I can't wait to suck on one of those."

Steve cracked up laughing and said, "I love it when you talk that way."

Bruce picked up the box and said, "Thank you, buddy. You know what else?" he asked. "I think we need to start our dealings with Bear by offering him one of these."

Steve said, "Perfect, I'm sure he is an aficionado. Guns and cigars go well together."

"Okay then," Bruce said, turning the conversation back to the gun show. "Where are we so far on the Uberti?"

Steve answered, "I don't know about you, but I'm pretty much still at square one."

Bruce nodded his head to imply that was exactly where he was. "Everybody wants to know why we are looking for specific serial numbers and who we are looking for," he said.

"Don't tell 'em," Steve said. "They'll just try to steal our client."

"No way, Jose," Bruce laughed. "As soon as they start fishing, I move on. I'm really counting on Bear to show us a path here."

Steve said, "Well, he did a great job with the other guns. I say it's worth a try. My Uberti folks are not getting back to me. It would be so much easier if they could give me a quick point of sale reference, or shipping order, or just anything with a matching serial number."

"Well, Steve," Bruce interjected. "I believe that if it were easy, Bud would have already found the guns years ago, and he wouldn't have needed us."

"Yep, you are so right," Steve agreed.

"So let's shake the Grizzly Bear bush for a while," Bruce said as the two guys pulled into the familiar gun show in Williams County.

The parking lot was just starting to fill with the members of the gun lobby, as liberal talk shows and news reporters seemed to always describe anyone attending events like this. There were lots of familiar faces from the last time that Steve and Bruce made the trip to talk to Beth and eventually to their main contact, Bear. However, they couldn't find Beth.

Her dad noticed the guys coming in and said, "Oh, she's around here somewhere. Probably making a deal on some ammunition. Man that stuff is hard to get now—and expensive. When she comes back, I'll let her know you are here."

"Thanks, buddy," Bruce said and then asked, "Is Bear here yet?"

Beth's dad responded, "Yep, always one of the first. He's in his regular spot on the floor. Keep walking that way and you'll see him."

The two guys nodded and made their way through the aisles to where they remembered Bear had set up his table of guns and ammo. "There he is," Steve said first as both men spotted him together.

When they got to the table, Bear grunted at their greeting of "Hey, Bear, how ya doin'?" Bear just stared at them and then he growled, "Are you here to make another deal?"

The guys looked at each other and then at Bear. They were a little taken aback by the unfriendly greeting from Bear. They knew though that this was just who he was, a grouchy old son of a bitch with no people skills.

So Bruce responded, "Why yes, Bear, we are. Do you have a sec to talk?"

Bear nodded and growled back, "I always have time to talk if you have the money to make a deal. Whatcha lookin' for now?"

Steve responded, "Well, our collector liked those last guns you found for us so well, we decided to see if you can find us another set that he has been looking for for years."

Bear just stared at Steve and then at Bruce and then growled in his meanest tone, "Just give me the collector's fuckin' name, and I'll get it done for him. I don't need you two pussies slowing the process down."

The guys were again taken aback and didn't know how to respond. So they just stood for a minute looking at Bear as Bear stared intently at the two of them.

Suddenly, Bear let loose with his signature guttural laugh that seemed to disturb everyone in the building for a second and made Steve and Bruce jump, "Haaaaaaaaa. Haaaaaaaaa. Haaaaaaaaaa. Don't mind me. I'm just fuckin' with ya. Tell me what you need," he growled as he was still chuckling over his little joke.

Steve and Bruce felt somewhat relieved, and Steve said, "On that list we gave you, was a Uberti-made set of Colt .45 replicas."

Bear bent down under his table and retrieved a small cash box, opened it, and pulled out the folded list that the guys had given him earlier. "I keep this as a reference in case I run into one of these guns in my dealings. You guys pay pretty good," he said with a hint of a smile. "But to tell you the truth, I never thought you'd be really looking for the replicas."

"Our collector moved them to the top of the list, so that's why we're here," Bruce said. "What do you think?"

Bear gave him a quizzical look and answered, "What do I think? Well, I think I'll find the goddam guns for you. I got the serial numbers right here," he pointed at the list. "And I have your phone number. I'll get started," and then he sat back down and started to negotiate with a guy wanting to buy one of his shotguns.

"I guess we're done here," Steve said and shrugged.

"Me too," Bruce said. "Let's go."

On their way out, they still couldn't find Beth, so Bruce told her dad, "Tell her we stopped by and I'll give her a call....Oh shit!" Bruce exclaimed.

Beth's dad said, "What?"

"Oh, I just had something for Bear and forgot to give it to him," Bruce said. He motioned for Steve to give him the cigar they had brought to give to Bear.

"Glad you remembered," Steve said as he handed the cigar to Bruce.

"Me too," Bruce responded. "I'll be right back." When he got to Bear, he saw that he was done with the guy negotiating on the shotgun and said, "Hey, Bear, we forgot to give you something for your help."

Bear looked up, saw the cigar that Bruce was holding out to him and for a quick second a genuine smile crossed his face. "Well, by god, that's mighty nice of you," he said with a kinder and gentler growl. "I'll be smoking this as soon as I get outside. These pricks and the government pricks who made the law won't let me smoke in here. It's goddam unconstitutional and un-American." Then he let loose with that laugh again, drawing attention from the whole building. "Haaaaaaaaa. Haaaaaaaa. Haaaaaaaaa."

Bruce just smiled and said, "Enjoy, buddy," and started to walk away.

Bear yelled after him, "Hey, thanks," as he took the cigar out of the wrapper, smelled it, and stuck it in his mouth to savor the tobacco taste.

When Bruce got back to Steve, Steve asked, "Well, did he like it?"

"Absolutely," Bruce responded. "He even smiled."

"Good deal," Steve said as they left the gun show and jumped in the truck. "It never hurts to grease the wheels a bit."

"Yep, I've got a good feeling about Bear," Bruce said. "He could very well have contacts that will get him those serial numbers."

"Time will tell," said Steve.

"When we get back home, let's give Mikey a call and see what's up out there."

"Sounds good to me," agreed Steve.

Meanwhile, Bear was leaning back in his chair at the gun show, chomping at the bit to get outside and light the cigar. His mind was running at a hundred miles an hour thinking about the contacts that he could reach out to in order to find these serial numbers.

The only way I know to find those serial numbers, he thought, *is to start with the original point of sale through Uberti and find which importers handled the deal. I've got to start with some of my buddies in the import end first,* he mused as he continued to mouth the Maduro. He bent over, pulled out an old satchel from under his table, and grabbed an old manila file folder. He quickly eyed a list of contacts and phone numbers, but made no move to call anyone. *I just have to smoke this goddam cigar first,* he thought as he walked towards the exit of the gun show. *Then I'll get busy.*

Outside, Bear lit the dark Maduro cigar, inhaled deeply, blew out the smoke so that it wrapped around his face and head like a shroud, breathed deeply again to suck all of the smoke back into lungs, and growled to himself, *Mmmmm, mmmmm, mmmmm. Those pussies and I might be able to work together for a long time, if they keep me in cigars like this.* Then he pulled out his cell phone, looked at his contact sheet, and dialed an old contact from Cimarron, a recognized importer of Uberti guns.

A man answered immediately, and Bear growled into the phone, "Hey Jim, this is Bear out in Ohio."

"How they hangin' brother?" Jim laughed and responded, "I'd recognize that Grizzly Bear voice anywhere. What's up, buddy? Watcha lookin for?"

Bear growled back into the phone, "I need some help tracking down a couple of specific Uberti pistols. I got a collector who's attached to the serial numbers and wants just those guns."

Jim asked, "Did you try dealing with Uberti yet?"

"Hell no," Bear growled louder into the phone. "I never get anywhere trying to deal with those crazy bastard Italians."

"Okay, gotcha," Jim said. "Give me the serial numbers, and I'll give it a shot. But if they are pre-1980, we probably don't have records for them, and I'm sure we didn't import them."

"Tell me something I don't know," Bear shot back. "I'm calling you to help get to whoever imported them. I'll have a nice finder's fee for you if you come through for me."

"Okay, I can look into it and get back to you," Jim said.

Bear added one more growl, "Do it fast, and I'll make it worth your while. If you don't, I'll find you and cut your nuts off."

Jim was quiet on the other end.

Then Bear growl-laughed, "Haaaaaaaaaa, Haaaaaaaaa, Haaaaaaaaa. Just jokin' Jim. Let me know ASAP. See ya." And he hung up.

Bear continued this same line of communication with buddies at Stoeger and Benelli, also common importers of Uberti. Finally, satisfied that he had a good beginning in the search, he took one long last drag on the Maduro, stubbed it out, put it in his pocket for later, and went back into the gun show.

As soon as Bruce and Steve got home, they placed a conference call to Mike. When Mike responded to the call, both guys yelled, "Hey Chicken Man."

Mike laughed and said, "Thank you very much. I take that as a compliment."

"You should," Bruce said. "It's not everyone who can speak chicken," he laughed.

"Well, I've got your cocka doodle doo for you!" Mike retorted with a laugh. "What do you two Neanderthals want? Did you find the guns?"

Steve said, "No, not yet, but we have Bear on the hunt for us, and he seems to have a lot of contacts. What about you? Anything new out there with Bud?"

Mike answered, "Not really. I check in with him from time to time, but I get the feeling that he always knows where I am and what I'm doing. He just sorta shows up when I'm out and about. It gives me a strange feeling."

"Maybe he's got you under surveillance," Bruce said. "It would be second nature for an old spook to keep tabs on the people he's working with."

"Well, if he's got me bugged, all he's hearing are chickens and farts after I've been drinkin'," Mike laughed out loud.

"You're right," Steve said. "But it probably beats watching TV for him."

"So when you run into him, what does he say?" Bruce asked.

"Mostly just small talk, but he always asks about the Uberti's and how you guys are doing," Mike said. "And he hasn't given me any more details about the guns, except that once he said that he believed that they would turn up in Wyoming or South Dakota for some reason. I asked him why he felt that, and he said, 'It's just a gut feeling I have.' He is a strange duck. But I get the feeling that he knows more than he's telling us. It's almost like he's throwing out morsels of truth for us and then standing back watching where it takes us."

"Well, that's fine with me," Steve said. "As long as he keeps the money flowing."

"Yep, me too," Mike said. "But I do think we should keep looking for the other guns on the list too, while we are tracking down the Uberti's."

"All right," Bruce said. "Let's keep the Uberti's first, but still look for the other guns. You go over the list with Bud again, see if he will prioritize beyond the Uberti's, and stay in touch with any new developments."

"Okay," Mike said. "Talk to you later."

"See ya, Chicken Man," the guys responded and hung up.

Steve got up to head home and said, "Hopefully, I've got a response from Uberti when I get home and check my email. Uberti is really where it's all going to begin for us in this hunt."

"Yep," Bruce said. "They have to have something that says when these guns were made, which importers handled them, and maybe even who first purchased them."

Steve said, "Sure. In a perfect world of perfect recordkeeping. But obviously, in my opinion that's why Bud hired us. I bet he already tried Uberti and struck out."

"We shall see," Bruce responded. "And soon I hope. Good luck, Stevie."

CHAPTER 28

Clyde entered his office and saw the folder immediately. It was stamped for his eyes only. Taking a deep breath, he walked around his desk, fell into his chair, and reluctantly flipped open the file folder.

"Sure enough," he sighed. "It appears to be done."

Clyde read the report that was now marked as "Final." In it he saw the words that he knew would be there. "Target terminated." He saw those words twice and much more when he read the preliminary report. It was all he could do to keep from heaving all over his desk and the report.

Oh my god! he thought. *Two more dead agents that I am completely responsible for!*

Pulling himself together, he read the report's details so that he could respond to any questions from the Director. In the description of Gordon's death, he noticed the extensive damage to the subcontractor's men involved in the termination. And he wondered under his breath, *Who were these guys? Did they have families? Were they patriots? Or were they simply sociopathic assassins who had no regard for the lives they were taking?* Then he thought about the fire that pretty well eliminated any chance of identifying Gordon's body.

That worries me a bit, he thought. *But if the subcontractors are satisfied they got their man, then I guess I have to be also.*

Continuing on, Clyde read through the report of the FBI pilot who had a tragic accident flying over the thick forests of Vermont. The ensuing investigation by the FBI found a body matching that of the targeted pilot, but it too was impossible to fully identify because of the horrific nature of the crash. The report documented engine failure as the preliminary cause of the crash and the final lines of the report read, "Both operations were successful in terminating the targets. There will be ongoing investigations by the FBI, but the matter should be viewed as a success and subsequently closed." With those words, Clyde slammed the file closed, picked it up, took a deep breath, and headed out of his office to brief the Director.

Miss Gandy was working at her desk when Clyde approached.

She quickly greeted him, "Hello, Mr. Assistant Director, the Director has been expecting you for some time now."

"I'm sure he has," Clyde responded.

"You may go in," she continued as she rose from her desk to chauffeur him towards the Director's office. "Mr. Director, the Assistant is here to see you," she said leaning into the office.

The Director had been reading through the latest newspaper reports, trying to ascertain if the conspiracy thing had started to die down.

He quickly pushed them aside, leaned back, and said, "Hello, Clyde, I've been anxiously awaiting your report on our loose ends and how that is going."

Clyde responded, "That is precisely why I'm here, Mr. Director. May I close the door?"

"Certainly," the Director said. "Then let's get to it. You know how waiting like this disturbs me."

"I do, sir, and I think you will be feeling less disturbed with the results that I am bringing to you." Clyde handed the folder over the desk to the sitting director and waited while he quickly perused the contents.

When he was finished, the Director looked up with a smile and said, "Well done, Clyde. I know how much this operation troubled you, but your loyal service and successful implementation please me very much. I am concerned about fully identifying the bodies, but the nature of their demise will probably limit that. All in all, I am feeling much better about the details....and the loose ends. Now I will call the President and inform him of our progress. Going into this operation, we had seven potential problems—now we have two. But Bud and Howard have too much skin under their fingernails to go rogue on us. So I feel good about that too. However, I do want to meet with them, in your presence, to look them in the eyes. Can you set that up for me, Clyde?"

"Absolutely, sir, consider it done," Clyde responded.

With that, the Director dismissed Clyde, called for Miss Gandy, and said, "Please file this report accordingly in my personal file, Miss Gandy. Make sure it's protected for my eyes only. Thank you."

"Yes, sir, immediately," she responded as she grabbed the file, coded it, walked it to the Director's personal files, and placed it with the special personal files of the Director.

Meanwhile, the Director had already dialed the President's personal line.

"Mr. President?" he asked when the familiar Texas drawl responded to his call.

"Well, hello, Mr. Director. I assume you are calling about our last conversation."

"Why, yes, sir, I am," the Director responded. "I have just been updated about our concerns and wanted to brief you as soon as possible."

"Thank you. As you know, I have been waiting, and rather impatiently, I might add, for your call," LBJ slowly drawled into the phone.

"I have been pushing things on our end and want you to know that I believe we have completely taken care of what I considered to be loose ends," the Director said. "And you will be pleased to hear that we are going to issue our report this week. Clyde and I will be signing off on it within the next day. I am sure it will meet with your approval."

"Well, that is good news, Director," the President continued to drawl. "Will there be a moment for you to brief me in person regarding the substance of this report?"

The Director responded quickly with, "Absolutely, sir, I will bring it to you personally prior to its release. Again, sir, I am fully confident you will approve."

"Thank you, Director," the President said, then added, "I am counting on you to get this horseshit conspiracy talk stopped—and the sooner the better."

"Believe me, sir, I understand completely," the Director countered.

LBJ grunted and hung up.

The Director felt that the conversation went as well as could be expected. But it always pissed him off when he wasn't the one hanging up first. LBJ used it as a display of power and made it his little goal to always hang up on the Director first. *After all, the Director was still only a bureaucrat serving at his pleasure—so why not make a statement when he could?* he thought.

As soon as he got off the phone, the Director had Miss Gandy contact Clyde again. Intuitively knowing why the Director was reaching out to him so quickly, Clyde gave her an appointed time to meet with Bud and Howard and a tentative time for them to sign off on the report.

"Hello, Miss Gandy, please schedule Bud and Howard to meet with the Director at 0800 tomorrow, and please follow that up with a meeting to sign off on the report." Then he added, "Can the Director hold a press conference tomorrow at 1400 to release the report?"

Miss Gandy responded, "Yes, sir, he can."

"Okay, then, please schedule that and then please schedule the Director to meet with the President prior to the news conference," Clyde continued.

"Yes, sir," Miss Gandy responded. "If he has further issues, I will be back in touch immediately."

"Thank you, Miss Gandy," he said as he hung up. When Miss Gandy informed the Director, he smiled and thought to himself, *Things are coming along quite nicely. Tomorrow will be a big day in terms of moving forward.*

When Bud got his call from Miss Gandy, he promptly answered, "Yes, Miss Gandy, I will be there. Are you planning to have anyone else there too?" he questioned.

Miss Gandy deferred the answer, not knowing what the Director was planning, by saying, "At this point, I cannot confirm or deny that question."

Knowing that it served no purpose to push Miss Gandy, Bud just said "Okay, thank you," and hung up. He immediately dialed Howard, though, fully expecting a busy signal.

Instead, Howard answered with, "Hello, Bud. I am to attend a meeting with the Director tomorrow at 0800. I assume you are too, and that's why you are calling?"

"Exactly," Bud said. "So we should meet prior to the meeting—breakfast at 0700 at the Diner?"

"See you there," Howard said and hung up.

Both men had a sense of dread, thinking about the meeting. *Howard and I need to be absolutely, perfectly on the same page,* he thought. *This may be our last chance to prove our value to the Director as assets and not liabilities.*

Arriving at the diner at precisely 0700, Bud saw that Howard had already been seated and was sipping on an oversize cup of black coffee. He looked calm and completely in control.

Bud thought *I hope I look as cool and calm as he does.*

"So, good morning, Howard," he said while taking his seat in the oversized booth, as far away from the busy breakfast crowd as possible. Both men chose this particular booth so that they had a good view of the interior of the diner as well as the entrance and exits. They were always the consummate professionals when it came to their craft. Speaking low and slow, Bud said, "Let's go over our stories first. I'm sure the number one question will have to do with our feelings about the agents and their termination."

"Yes, and that's an easy one," Howard said. "They needed to go for the greater good—good patriots who died heroes for their country in unfortunate accidents."

Bud continued to press, "And no specific mention of Gordon or the pilot, right?"

"Hell, no," Howard said. "We know nothing, only that it was handled."

Bud pressed further, "And our plans for the missing merchandise? And the old lady?"

"Same as before," Howard calmly stated as if this were no big deal.

"What was the same as before?" Bud continued.

"We will support the old lady with a monthly stipend that will appear as though it is historical in nature, keep an eye on the old hotel and the lady, and stop by periodically to snoop around. If the old lady does know where the merchandise ended up, our surveillance will let her lead us to it. Otherwise, it is probably lost, and even if it is found, it will have no relevance or connection to its use."

With that, Bud nodded his head, satisfied they were ready to meet with the Director. Two more cups of coffee and the usual scrambled eggs and bacon brought the meeting to a close. Bud left first and headed to the Director's office. Howard lingered awhile, so that they would not come in together. They wanted to avoid any appearance that they had conspired with their stories.

Clyde was already in the Director's office behind the closed door when Bud arrived. Miss Gandy acknowledged his entrance and quickly dialed the Director who responded with, "Wait 'til Howard gets here too. Then send them in."

"Yes, sir," Miss Gandy said. "It'll be a minute," she said to Bud. But almost immediately, Howard entered too. Miss Gandy knocked on the door, and the Director yelled from his overstuffed office chair.

"Come in, Bud and Howard." Upon their entry, Clyde stood and moved to a side office chair, where he could see both the Director and the men.

He said, "Good morning, men. Thanks for coming so promptly."

The Director leaned back, put his hands over his head, and clasped them as he stared at each man before speaking. "You know why you are here, I presume." Both Bud and Howard nodded while the Director continued. "At this point, you two are the only people privy to the facts of our operation besides me, Clyde, and the President. Unfortunately, the other agents involved have met with some untimely tragedies—in other words, the four agents on the operation and the pilot of the operation are gone. This was not a part of the original plan, but sometimes fortune smiles on good deeds, and that's how I prefer to look at their demise. All five were patriots, all five were heroes, and all five will never get their deserved recognition for their work in this endeavor. For us, their deaths, although cruel in every sense of the word, will help us tie up all of our loose ends and serve to protect all of us that I previously mentioned." He continued, "So now it is up to you, Bud and Howard and Clyde, to preserve what the President and I began."

All three men responded, "Absolutely, sir."

From now on, you two will keep Clyde abreast of any changes in the lost merchandise. As long as it is missing, that will be your highest priority, above all else, for as long as it takes. Do I make myself clear?"

"Yes, sir," they both responded.

"That will be all," the Director said and signaled for Clyde to open the door and excuse the men. "Clyde, please stay a bit longer."

As Bud and Howard walked out of the office and down the hallway, neither spoke, but each was thinking the same thing. *Did we just escape a date with the guillotine, and are we truly safe to go about business as usual?*

On the street, Bud spoke first, and said, "That was not how we drew it up. That man is off the charts impossible to read."

Howard agreed and said, "Yes, but I'm feeling like we have gotten a pardon here, and we should both plan to make the most of it. We just have to make damn sure the two guys we rescued never, ever, surface while any of the key players he listed are still alive."

"Agreed!" Bud said emphatically. "We need to have a meeting with each to underscore that very fact."

"The sooner the better," Howard retorted.

When the door to the Director's office closed again for Clyde and the Director, the Director immediately threw open an extensive document that Clyde had handed him, that was labeled "The FBI Investigation of the Assassination of President John F. Kennedy."

"Well, Clyde, here it is," the Director said with a nod to the document. It was a four-hundred page, five-volume work that had been fast-tracked to get ahead of the conspiracy theories that were steadily gaining ground. "Thank you for pushing it through for me," he continued. "What do you think of it?"

Clyde sat down, leaned back, and said, "As reports go, it is a very lame piece of work. It's loaded with evidence that places Oswald as the lone conspirator. It covers his history, his connections with the communists, and his penchant for guns. But it is weak in every other sense of the word. Sketchy factual evidence on the actual shooting. Very little actual investigation of the different threads of the assassination itself. And basically it is just a statement from us, the FBI, that we are totally committed to the fact that Oswald is the guy who did it and he is the only guy involved."

By now, the Director was seated behind his mammoth desk, thumbing through the pages without comment. When he finally spoke, he said with some agitation, "Well, goddam it, Clyde, that is exactly what the President and I want. I want people to read this and say, 'well if the Director of the FBI and the President support this report, then we do too.' It's what we need at this time," he said while slapping the softbound volumes in front of him. "Did you sense any problems from the investigative people involved, Clyde?"

"Not a lot, sir," he responded. "As always, they wanted to do the best job they could for you, but I explained that we needed this to be done and released, like yesterday. Oh there might have been some negative comments after I left, but that's how it always is. And they did exactly as I asked them to do—for you."

"Thank you, Clyde. I can always count on you. Now I need you to do something else for me," the Director continued. "I need you to leak the guts of this report to the press so they can start supporting this document in print. You know how it goes, make the son of a bitch that you leak it too feel special so he will jump on and support it even prior to its release."

Clyde responded with a nod and said, "Yes, sir, I will immediately, sir. When do you plan to release it to the world, sir?" The Director leaned back, put his clasped hands over his head, thought for a moment, then said, "I'm going to memo the President that it is completed, summarize it for him, and get it out on December 9. And that, Clyde, should put an end to the conspiracy theories so that we can move on and get back to governing this great nation."

"Sounds perfect," Clyde said as he stood up to open the door. "It's a major step forward, and although it's not a loose end that can hurt us, it is a positive thing for us to get this done."

"Absolutely, thank you, Clyde. Please send Miss Gandy in." When she entered, the Director said very simply, "Please memo the President and say both that the FBI report is complete and that I plan to release it to everyone on December 9. Its major focus is on the assassin, Lee Harvey Oswald, and there is no indication of any further conspiracy. I will be calling the President soon, after he has had a chance to review the document."

Miss Gandy took the information as she always did, efficiently and professionally, and promptly put the memo into play.

After LBJ read the memo and quickly read through the highlights of the report, he didn't wait for the Director to call him. "Mr. Director?" he drawled into the phone.

"Yes, Mr. President," came the response.

"I've read through the report and want to thank you for getting it out so quickly." As the Director started to reply, the President talked right over him and said, "But in my opinion, this report just won't cut it." Almost sputtering now as he tried to get in a word to respond to the President, the Director finally gave up and just listened. LBJ continued, "It does a good job of incriminating Oswald, but it's short on evidence. So I'm going to follow through with that commission that I talked about and put some good people I can trust on it and that will just add to this report's credibility."

"But Mr. President," the Director finally spluttered over the President's words. "I don't think that's a good thing to do yet, until the dust settles from this report. You'll just get more people cranked up to look further into this. I believe my report will stop that. People trust the FBI and me, and with your support for my report, I believe all of the conspiracy crap will go away."

Not even acknowledging the Director's comments, LBJ continued talking over the Director and said, "The commission will supplement your report and validate it. Two reports saying the same thing will be just what the public needs. When I finalize the members, I'll let you know. And, Mr. Director, I am in agreement with your release of the FBI report on December 9. Thank you," and then he hung up again on the Director, whose face was now the color of a fine red wine.

"Miss Gandy," he shouted out into her office. "Make sure that the President doesn't get through to me, until I say so, and do not give him anything he requests until I approve it. That Texas hillbilly needs to learn his place!" he shouted. "Please bring me his file."

CHAPTER 29

After leaving the Director's office, Bud and Howard wasted no time in setting up a meeting with the pilot and Gordon. Each man knew that they had crossed a very dangerous line by reaching out and saving the lives of these two agents. But it was a line that was crossed forever—there could be no going back. The two men met outside the Justice Department Building to get the meet in motion.

Bud felt that it was important for all of the men to meet at the same time, so he said, "Look, Howard, let's make it look like we are following up on the Director's orders to keep an eye on the Buffalo situation and meet out there. The pilot is already in Denver. You can send Gordon out on the next plane, and we can all meet at the Occidental in Buffalo. Since these guys are so much a part of whether we survive this operation or not, I think we should take them back to where the ball got dropped and walk through things again. What do you think?"

Howard thought for a moment, and then agreed, "Sure, sure, let's do it that way. I'd kinda like to get Gordon away from this city anyway. He's a chameleon, but there are just way too many ways to be seen here. Let's do it."

"Perfect," Bud said. "Let's set the meet for the day after tomorrow, in the Occy for breakfast."

Howard was already walking away, and said, "See ya there."

On his way to his townhouse, Bud stopped and used a payphone that was a bit out of the way, but safe. He thought of the many times that he, himself had bugged the pay phone outside the Justice Department building, and he could not afford to take any chances...lives depended on his abilities and experience. *I'm sure Howard is doing the same thing right now...calling Gordon, but always conscious of the potential for bugs,* he thought. The pilot had been instructed to always be near this number at this time every day, so Bud fully expected him to pick up, and he did.

"Hello," he said weakly into the phone.

"Hello, this is Bud," he said quickly. "We need to meet. I'll have a rental car waiting for your pick up at the Denver airport under your new name—Frank Sturgis. Make sure you have your new ID, get the car, and drive to Buffalo to meet with Howard and me on Thursday at 0900 for breakfast at the Occidental Hotel. Got it?" Bud asked.

"Got it," came the response.

"See you then," the new Frank said, and Bud hung up.

Howard's communication didn't even involve a phone call. He and Gordon had a prearranged drop spot that Gordon would check at the same time every day. Howard knew that there was no need to talk directly, in case he was being tailed, so he stuck the information for the flight and the meeting in a brown paper bag, along with a bottle of wine, and handed it to the old wino sitting on the cardboard box. The toothless vagrant accepted the gift, said, "God bless you, sir," and moved over to stand by his grocery cart filled with his life essentials. He took the wine bottle out of the sack, stuffed the sack into his coat pocket, unscrewed the cap on the bottle, and drank half of it in one huge swallow followed by an "Ahhhhhhhhh." He was immediately lit up again, but he awaited the next part of the process before he could sit back down on the cardboard remnant to finish the bottle. Soon a man came walking by, asked the wino if he could help him walk to the cardboard, grabbed his arm, and simultaneously reached into the wino's pocket to retrieve the message and place another wine bottle into the pocket. Again, the wino said, "God bless you, sir," and the drop was completed as the wino was now seated and blissfully finishing off the Mad Dog wine that Howard had given him. "God, I hate to touch that stinking son of a bitch," Gordon said to himself as he walked away to his safe house to read the message.

Bud and Howard flew together into Caspar, Wyoming, got a rental car, and headed out for the two hour drive to Buffalo. Caspar was a better drive for this time of year because of the constant threat of wintertime blizzards that routinely blew in, closing roads with generally little to no warning. Fortunately for all of the travelers on this operation, the weather was clear and surprisingly warm.

"No freakish weather today," Bud said to Howard.

"Nope, it should be a great day for travel, and our guys should have no trouble getting to the Occy either," Howard commented.

The trip was uneventful, as expected, and the conversation limited. Bud and Howard were attached together in life through their work, but had very little else in common, except trying to stay alive. If it weren't that they were thrown together in this monumental situation, they would probably have very little reason to hang out or even talk. Bud viewed Howard as the cold-blooded killer that he was—more of a knuckle dragger with social skills. Howard, on the other hand, saw Bud as more of a bureaucrat, content to stay in the background and not get his hands dirty. This seemed to cause some internal discontent, but never got in the way of the job that they had to do. Both men agreed, universally, that loose ends were bad, and that was why they were on this trip—to tie up the details that could get them killed.

"When we get to the Occy," Bud began, "we will check in to our rooms and our guys' rooms. But I don't want to talk to the guys until tomorrow morning. We need to keep our meeting as low profile as possible."

"I agree," said Howard. "But tomorrow morning, we need to spend the time wisely educating them about their future—we can't pull any punches—and we need to make them feel safe with us."

"Right!" agreed Bud with emphasis, but then the two conspirators fell silent for the rest of the trip.

After a couple of hours, they arrived in Buffalo, followed the main street to the Occidental, parked the rental car, and went in. Bud assumed that they would be checked in by Mrs. Smith and had an envelope prepared to give to her. *This will ease some of her burdens,* he thought as they walked through the dining area towards the hotel check-in. He looked at Howard, wondering if he even gave a shit about her husband, whom he had so mercilessly and efficiently dispatched just a couple of short weeks ago. He knew the answer to that: *Hell no,* he thought.

No one was at the desk, so Bud tapped the bell to call someone to help them. Sure enough, it was Smitty's wife. She seemed much calmer than the last time that he saw her, but her eyes were sad and distant. She tried to smile, though, and said, "Well, it's so nice to see you gentlemen again. When I saw you had registered for a stay, I was very pleased."

"Hello, Mrs. Smith," Bud said in his kindest voice. "It's nice to see you too. I hope everything is going better for you."

She said, "Not yet, really, my husband is still missing, and the authorities are wanting to say he is either dead or a runaway. Ha," she said. "Runaway at his age!" Her eyes started to well up with her pain of loss that was still so close to the surface, and Bud quickly changed the subject.

"Well, we are on a business trip for our historical interests and wanted to make our donation to you in person." Bud handed over the envelope and said, "Hope this helps."

Meanwhile, Howard was restlessly waiting for the bullshit to get over so that he could get to his room and relax. Mrs. Smith, though, took the envelope, looked inside at the stack of hundred dollar bills, and immediately started to cry again.

"Oh my lord," she cried. "Thank you, thank you. I was so worried that the last time you came here would be your last."

Howard finally jumped in, "Oh no, ma'am, you'll be seeing a lot of us in the future."

Bud nodded his head in agreement and said, "As I said, I hope it helps. Please let us know if there is anything else we can do. We look at this as an investment in your success, so don't hesitate to keep us informed. By the way, we will want to make our normal walkthrough tomorrow morning, at the request of our benefactors, to make sure everything is up to par. Will that be okay?"

"Absolutely," she said as she tried to pull herself together. "Let's get you checked in. I see you have two other rooms also. Would you like me to take care of them too?"

"Please do," Bud replied. "Our associates will be in a little later, and I will give them their keys. Thank you very much, Mrs. Smith." And in a matter of a few minutes, the two men were on their way to their rooms—each with thoughts of the meeting that would take place in the morning.

As usual, Bud was the first to arrive for breakfast in the hotel restaurant. He seated himself in a corner table where he could survey the comings and goings of the people in the hotel. An elderly waitress brought him coffee, and he sipped and watched, sipped and watched, and then saw Howard slowly crossing into the restaurant from the hotel side. When he noticed Bud, he quickly changed directions, went to his table, and sat down.

"Good morning, Howard," Bud said evenly. "How'd you sleep?"

Howard responded, "Good morning to you. Not bad for an old broken down hotel. I'm sure the mattress was from the early 1900s," he laughed. "But it was okay. Any sign of our boys yet?"

"Not since I've been here," Bud responded. "But it is a little early yet. I needed some go juice, so I've just been drinking coffee and waiting."

"I don't know about your pilot," Howard said. "But I'll bet Gordon has already been here and is watching us as we speak."

"You are probably right," Bud said and at that precise moment, Gordon and the pilot entered the dining area. They nodded at Bud and Howard as if to say, "Should we come to the table?" Bud waved them over; they sat down; all of the men ordered breakfast; and the meeting was on. Both men looked a little uneasy, with the pilot more so than Gordon. *After all, he isn't a seasoned agent like Gordon,* thought Bud. *But Gordon appears to be on alert, as always.*

Everyone threw out "Good morning" and "Nice to see you" type pleasantries. But everyone knew that this was serious stuff.

Bud got started. "Well, gentlemen, we called you here because of our desire to continue to keep you among the living. Earlier this week we met with the Director and the Assistant Director and came away with a very clear view of what we, and you, have to do in order to make this work."

Howard interjected, "And that means to keep you alive."

To say that the pilot's face turned deadly serious would have been a major understatement of the reality. It was obvious that he was scared shitless and unable to fathom why he was caught up in this crap. Gordon, on the other hand, was the consummate professional and just understood. He knew the business he was in, and he knew that he had played a major part in the operation. And he knew that he was a "loose end."

"So how do we fix this?" Gordon asked.

"Well, the reality is that there is no fixing this as long as the guys who set this in motion are still breathing," Bud said. "All we can do at this point is play defense and keep you guys out of sight and out of mind."

Howard jumped in to say, "Yes. The good news is that they all truly believe you both were terminated and that you are out of the picture—loose ends that were fixed."

"That being said," Bud continued. "We will protect you and provide assistance for you as long as we need to. You understand that our asses are on the line here too. The moment we pulled you two out of the line of fire, we became targets ourselves."

Howard chuckled a sinister little chuckle, "And now we have our own little club, the loose ends club or the expendable ones."

"Why are we here then?" Gordon asked. "We should be in deep cover now and forever, until those bastards are all dead."

Bud said, "Yes, we agree, but we have a couple of loose ends that we need to fix for ourselves too."

"That's why you are here," Howard said pointedly to the two men. "Gordon, you remember that this is the place where we dropped the merchandise, right?"

"Yes, sir," he replied.

"Well, part of the merchandise is still missing, and we need you to help us locate it," Bud said. "We are going to relocate you out here so you can keep an eye on this place and make regular inspections."

"Works for me," Gordon said.

"And you, my good friend," Bud said eyeing the pilot, "are going to be Howard's and my pilot and work out of the Johnson County airport. And be on call for us when we need you for what I'm sure will become lots of trips from D.C. and Buffalo. We have all the details worked out—your new license to match your identity, your reason for moving out here, and your new job at the airport."

"I can do that," the pilot responded quickly.

"Plus, you will be able to help Gordon with the investigation into the merchandise," Howard added. "But remember, this is deep cover, deep cover, deep cover. You get caught and we all pay with our lives."

Gordon and the pilot both nodded and leaned back in their chairs.

"Now we need to finish here and do our walkthrough," Bud said. "I'll introduce you both to Mrs. Smith as subcontractors for the historical group I represent. And tell her that you will be around when I can't be. The monthly cash that I will continue to provide for her will keep that door open for you."

"One other thing," Howard added. "You need to keep a low profile, but you also need to get acquainted with the gun folks of this community. If the merchandise has been taken off of this property, I'm betting that that is where we will eventually get some leads. Gun people won't talk out loud to the general public, but they do a lot of talking to their own kind."

Bud looked intently across the table at the two men that he and Howard risked their lives for and thought, *These guys hold my life in their hands—I'm forever attached to their ability to do what we ask them to do.*

"Okay," he said. "Let's go look around."

Mrs. Smith was in the saloon portion of the Occidental when Bud brought Howard and the other two guys in to introduce them and look around.

"Good morning, gentlemen," she said. "I hope your stay was comfortable."

They all nodded and said, "Yes, Ma'am."

Bud then took over the conversation, introduced the new guys to Mrs. Smith, and all of them made small talk while leaning against the bar. Mrs. Smith was quite open to letting the men look over whatever they wanted. Bud smiled and thought, *It's funny how a little cash can grease the skids.* He said, "Thank you Mrs. Smith, we will start with the basement as usual." He guided everyone behind the bar and down the stairs. *Every time I come down here, I still see Howard snapping old Smitty's neck, with no feelings of remorse,* he thought. *If only he had waited until we talked to him, we wouldn't be in this position. Oh well, water under the bridge— we can't undo it. We just have to fix it.* The same old familiar smell of the basement hit them all as they were about halfway down the stairs. The good thing about the smell was that it wasn't old Smitty's smell as he lay decomposing in the secret wall safe. *No, this smell is okay,* Bud thought. *The last thing we need is for someone to get a whiff of Smitty and start nosing around.* He even chuckled to himself on that thought.

When the four men reached the bottom of the basement Howard asked, "So Gordon, does it look and feel familiar?"

Gordon nodded his head, "Yes, it does. But it was a lot darker down here when I gave the briefcase to that old guy. I sure wish I had paid attention to where he put that thing. He could tell that it weighed more than the other ones, and so he probably got curious and put it aside."

The pilot, who had never been in the basement before, said, "This is really kinda creepy down here. It doesn't feel right— kinda like there should be secret passages or something."

Bud and Howard looked at each other, but didn't acknowledge the comment. Bud did say though, "Look around and get familiar with this place, because you two are going to be keeping tabs on anything that changes down here. And I mean anything. If you notice that junk over there moved to the other side of the basement, we need to know right away. Got it?"

Gordon and the pilot nodded yes as they surveyed the whole of the basement.

Bud continued, "You two need to become regulars in the Occidental so you won't stick out to the locals. You guys are the new locals in town."

"Okay," they both said. "We get it."

The four men looked, poked, and prodded throughout the basement until Bud said, "Okay, that's good for now. But, like I said, get very familiar with this space and the Occy in general. That way, no one should get suspicious of you asking questions. And remember you represent a historical group interested in the preservation of this old relic from the past."

With that, Bud and Howard ushered the two men back up the stairs and into the old saloon where Mrs. Smith was waiting.

"Well?" she asked. "Does it suit you?"

"It sure does, Mrs. Smith," Bud responded. "Get used to seeing my two colleagues here, as they come around to check in. They will be a couple of your newest Buffalo residents and will stop by on a regular basis to see how things are going and if you need anything."

"Thank you, Bud," she said solemnly. "I appreciate the help."

"As I said before," Bud added as the men turned and headed toward the door, "We are happy to help preserve this diamond in the rough. Until next time, Mrs. Smith. You take care. Howard and I are going to check out—and my two friends will stick around for a while."

Howard had to add as he walked away, "Good luck in finding Smitty."

As Bud and Howard prepared to leave Buffalo and head back to D.C., Bud had one more comment for the two former agents, "Remember, even though you are far away from D.C., you are never outside the reach of the Director. Take every precaution you would on a deep cover operation and keep us informed on the tiniest of details or curiosities. Our lives and your lives depend on it. We'll be in touch soon," he said as he and Howard jumped into the rental car and sped off to Caspar.

CHAPTER 30

Mike was just finishing with his chickens when his cell phone rang. He saw it was Bud and smiled to himself, *Now this is too coincidental, just get off the phone with my buddies and here Bud is calling me. I am starting to think the old fart has me tapped.*

"Hey, pardner," he said into the phone.

"Hello, Mike," came Bud's response.

"I was just thinking of calling you," Mike said. "But you probably knew that and that's why you're calling me. Haw, haw, haw," he laughed.

Bud laughed too and said, "Mike, you know I have you under surveillance 24/7. It's an old occupational habit." Mike was silent on the other end, prompting Bud to say, "You know I'm kidding, right?"

Mike shot back, "Yeah, yeah, I know that you are just full of shit, like the chicken shit I just stepped in. Just trying to get it off my boot."

Bud laughed and said, "Oh my god, Mike, you are one of a kind. That's why I like you."

Mike snorted and said, "Really, pardner, I thought it was the smell of chicken shit that drew you towards me."

Bud smiled and thought to himself, *This guy makes me laugh and that's not an easy thing for me. One of a kind,* he thought again.

Mike said, "So what's up? I know you don't like to do the small talk thing. You got a lead on your guns?"

"No, I don't. Besides, that's what I'm paying you for. I just thought we should get together and get lunch sometime soon. I'm in Buffalo for a few days. What do you think?"

"Well, pardner, if you're buying, I'm eatin'," Mike said.

"Great," Bud said. "Let's meet at the Occy tomorrow at noon. Will that work?"

"Well, hell yes," Mike exclaimed. "I can't afford to eat there normally, so let's do it."

"Okay, meet you there at noon," Bud said and hung up before Mike had time to say anything else.

Still holding the phone to his ear, he thought, *That s.o.b does that to me every time. Next time I'll be hanging up first before he finishes talking.* He smiled to himself and then dragged his boots across the ground some more, trying to get the chicken shit off.

When Mike arrived at the Occidental Hotel, he parked on the street just down from the entrance. He was actually early. *I'm just going to sit here for a while, though, and let Bud get there first and pick his table.* But after several minutes and with Bud seemingly a no show, Mike decided to go in. He was surprised to see Bud and another man sitting at a table in the restaurant. Bud noticed him enter, stood up, and waved him to his table.

"Hello, Mike," Bud said. "Please have a seat."

Mike acknowledged the greeting with a "Hey, pardner. How the hell are ya, and how did you get in here without me seeing you?"

Bud took the greeting in stride, smiled, and said, "Remember what I said about occupational habits? I've been watching you sitting in your truck, wondering what it is about you that you have to be late. And to answer the other part of your question, I came in the back." Then he sat down.

Mike laughed his laugh, "Haw, haw, haw, now I see," he said and reached out to shake Bud's hand. When he looked at the other man seated at the table, he said, "And you aren't going to introduce me to your friend?"

"Yes, Mike, this is Frank. He's my pilot. You may have seen him around town when I'm in town."

"Hello, pardner," Mike said immediately. "Nice to meetcha." Then he looked at Bud and said, "You are full of surprises. You have your own pilot? Oh my god, you must be special. I don't know anybody else in my world who has a personal pilot, or even knows a pilot. Haw, haw, welcome to Buffalo."

The pilot said, "I've heard a lot about you Mike and told Bud I'd like to meet you." Then in a solemn voice he said, "By the way, nice bib overalls. They go well with your white tennis shoes."

Mike was silent for a second, thinking, *What the hell? I don't know this guy and he says that to me?*

Frank immediately laughed at Mike's double take and said, "Sorry, Mike, Bud said you were a funny guy, so I couldn't resist."

The ice was broken, and Mike flipped the ass-kicking switch to the belly-laugh switch and thought, *This guy's all right too.* Mike looked at Frank and at Bud, and let the laughter out, and said, "Just so you know, Frank, you were a pubic hair's length away from getting your ass kicked."

Bud jumped in with a smile, "Yes, that was my fault. The only time I find humor in life is when I'm around you. That's why I like you, Mike, and I can say unequivocally that I have liked very few men in my life."

Mike raised his hand to his eyes, acting like he was wiping tears away, and said, "Aw, Bud, you're gonna make me cry," and then erupted again into his signature laughter. "Let's order lunch and shoot the shit instead of spreading the bullshit. So Frank, how long have you been Bud's pilot?" Mike quizzed while taking a humungous bite out of a bison burger sandwich.

Frank looked at Bud before answering and, with a nod from Bud that Mike noticed, he said, "Well, Mike, I started flying Bud around in 1963 and have been doing it ever since."

Bud added, "Yes, it has been quite a long time, but it has been beneficial to us both."

"Wow," Mike marveled. "You are getting pretty well up there in years to be flying yet."

"Maybe, but my health is still good, and I love to do it. Bud has taken me into some pretty interesting situations over the years. And I never get tired of the excitement." He smiled and said with a wink to Bud, "I would venture to say that I wouldn't even be here if I didn't have the opportunity to work with Bud."

Mike was in full munching mode, when he said with his lips smacking, "Sounds like a good match for you two, much like the match that my two buddies in Ohio and I have. Speaking of my buddies, they wanted me to get to you and talk about the guns again. They are working hard on the Uberti's, but just wanted to make sure that you still want us to find the other guns on the list too."

Bud responded while watching Mike eat, "First of all, Mike, you have a little food on the bib of your overalls, and second," he said smiling widely. "Yes, please continue looking for the other guns too. But my chief interest is with the Uberti's. So keep the Uberti's first, and if you come across any of the others, I am still interested."

"Great," Mike responded while wiping his beard and bibs clean of the flying pieces of his sandwich. He continued, "Bud, you said that you suspected that we might eventually have some luck in finding them out West here in Wyoming. Why?" he asked.

Bud looked at the pilot and answered, "Well, my friend, I can't tell you much, except to say that they were a part of an operation that flowed through Wyoming and that I have a strong feeling that they were lost out here. I believe that I mentioned to you that the guns could be damaging to those who participated in the operation if they were found by the wrong person. So remember, that detail must remain confidential as you men look."

"Okay, pardner, I got it. You can trust us," Mike said with emphasis.

"Oh, I think I know that," Bud said with a smile as he signaled for the waitress to bring the bill. "Say, Mike, have you ever had a full tour of the hotel?" Bud suddenly asked.

Mike responded, "Well, pardner, just on the main floor like the saloon and the restaurant. Never have seen the rooms or anything else," he added.

"Okay, if you have time, I'd like to treat you to a mini-tour of this place. I assume you know people from the past like Butch and Sundance, Calamity Jane, and Teddy Roosevelt used to frequent the old hotel."

"Yep, I've heard that, and I've also heard that my favorite author, Ernest Hemingway, came by here too."

"That's right," Bud said. "Over the years Frank and I have been coming here, we got to know the owners and they have allowed us some special privileges to come and go as we please. Do you know Dawn Wexo, the current owner?"

"Yep," Mike said. "I met them at the K of C events and got to know them a little. Nice people."

Bud continued, "Unfortunately, Dawn is not here today, but she won't mind if I show you what I think is one of the most interesting things about this place, the basement. Want to look?"

"Why, hell yes, pardner," Mike shot back. "Let's do it."

Bud led his companions from the restaurant to the saloon and walked them behind the bar where the familiar door to the basement was still located, even after all of the renovations. Both Bud and Frank had been down the stairs more times than they could count over the years.

"Looking the same, Frank?" Bud asked.

"Yes, sir, it is," Frank answered back. "But you know the stairs were easier to navigate when we were younger," he laughed.

"I hear that," Mike blurted out as he kind of took one step at a time, turning sideways to take the pressure off his bad knees.

Bud added, "Besides the stairs, the one thing that always remains the same is the smell. It always hits you about halfway down, with a cool dank smell that you can almost taste."

"Pardner, I *can* taste it," Mike said. "You sure there's nothing dead down here?"

Bud almost laughed out loud as the old memory jumped into his head. "If there is, it's from long ago," he said.

"Maybe some dead cowboys or gunslingers?" Mike continued. "Or just ghosts from the past?"

Frank said, "I'd go with ghosts from the past."

"Haw, haw, haw, well, I ain't afraid of no ghosts," Mike belly-laughed.

Bud walked the guys through the basement and thought how little it had changed over the years. He said, "You know the only real change over the years down here is the increasing quantity of stuff that got stuck down here. When Mrs. Smith and her husband owned the place, and after he went missing, this basement became the catch all for everything that was ever changed in the original building. Finally, when she died in 1976, this place was full of history, stacks and stacks of history. And no one really touched it until Dawn Wexo and her husband bought the place in 1997 and started to redo it. They reached into the basement to find treasures that you now see on display around the building. It truly is amazing that it survived the wrecking ball," Bud added.

Mike couldn't keep his mouth shut any longer and finally asked, "Okay, pardner, I get that you are interested in history, but for you to pay so much attention to this one property is kinda weird to me. What the hell ain't you telling me?"

Bud looked at Frank, stood silent for what seemed like an eternity, then slowly said, "Mike, I have never told anyone this outside those involved in that operation that I told you about. But this is the last place that anyone ever saw the Uberti Colt .45's. From here to god knows where." As he walked away from Mike and started the steep climb of the stairs to exit the basement, he slowly said, "Now you do know something that people have died over. For your safety and the safety of the people who run the Occidental, you need to protect that information."

Mike's jaw dropped, and he mouthed, "Holy shit!" as he followed Bud and Frank up and out of the basement.

Back in the saloon, Mike's mind was still stuck on the information that Bud just gave him. He couldn't wait to call his buddies in Ohio and let them in on it. But first, he had to ask something more.

"Okay, pardner, one more question," he said. "What is your real relationship with the owners of this place? Why do they seem to kiss your ass and let you do whatever you want here?"

Bud smiled, "Actually, Mike, that's two questions, but I'll let you in on it. I represent a wealthy historical interest who has helped fund the Occidental over the years. I have passed that money on to the owners since 1963 up to the present. The only stipulation is that I have final say over all renovations and any other changes to the structure."

Mike interjected, "So what you're saying is that this place would have folded long ago if it weren't for you?"

Bud just nodded his head yes.

"Haw, haw," Mike laughed. "Do you feel like adopting another project by the name of Mike?"

All three men laughed out loud, but Bud became serious when he quietly said, "I already have." With that, Bud and his pilot headed out of the Occy, leaving Mike standing in the saloon to ponder Bud's last statement.

Adopted...my ass! Mike thought as he too started to depart and headed out into the street, in a hurry to get home to call Bruce and Steve. *Can't wait to give the guys this little tidbit of information.*

CHAPTER 31

The Grizzly Bear was in prowl mode. He was anxious to hear back from his contacts at the importers and was becoming more surly with each passing day. Finally, he couldn't take it anymore and decided to press the issue with his contacts. When he dialed up his guy at Benelli, he was less than cordial.

"Hey, this is Bear," he growled into the phone. "Am I really going to have to come see you and cut your nuts off? I'm sharpening my gutting knife now."

The voice on the line was silent for a while, then quietly said, "Bear, I've been trying, but I keep getting stonewalled by those Italian pricks."

"Well, goddam it, you are the importer, and I need you to get it done," Bear growled like a grizzly on a kill mission.

If the guy on the line had received a call like this from anyone but Bear, he would have told him to go fuck himself—but that was not a good idea with Bear. And he knew it. So he meekly said, "Listen, I've got a couple of ideas, just be patient for a couple more days. Okay?"

Bear loved to intimidate, and he could sense that this guy was trying, so he slowly dragged out his growl of a voice and said, "Just get me that information. It'll be worth your while. And your nuts are safe for a while too." And then he hung up. Bear's contact laughed a nervous laugh, but was inwardly relieved. Bear didn't earn his nickname without good reason.

Bear's next call was to Stoeger importers, and it mirrored his Benelli call. Nothing new from this guy either. So it was on to his Cimmaron guy.

"Hey, Jim, guess who?" he growled his lowest and most ominous growl.

Jim stuttered for a moment, righted himself, and responded, "Hey, Bear, I was just going to call you."

Bear responded with a god-awful laugh-growl and said, "Bullshit! How did you know it was me calling?"

Jim answered, "Well, buddy, I'd know that sweet voice anywhere." Then he continued, "No, Bear, I was. I actually got something for you."

"Okay," Bear said slowly, "Make it good."

Jim continued, "I finally got my contact overseas with Uberti to look into the serial numbers you gave me. He dug deep into the company files from way back and came up with something you will find very interesting."

Bear growled, "Spare me stories and just spit it out."

"Okay, okay," Jim said. "But this is good stuff. The guy found some matching serial numbers from the early sixties when the old man Aldo Uberti was trying to get his company going. At that time, it seems that Aldo was making his replicas and sending them out to potential markets around the world as gifts to important people, like politicians and other government leaders. He was trying to build recognition of his line and of the quality that he was putting into his firearms."

Bear's patience for small talk, which he considered this to be, was wearing thin, and he growled with impatience to Jim, "Holy shit. Am I going to have to hear how he made his babies too?"

Jim laughed out loud, "No, no, Bear, I just thought you would like to tell this story to your collector when you find the guns and give them to him."

Bear reluctantly growled for Jim to continue, "All right, tell your little story."

Jim continued, "Okay great. So here's Aldo sending out special sets of his replicas around the world to dignitaries at all levels of government and business. So in the U.S. he thinks about it and decides that who would be better to receive the classic sets of firearms than the highest-ranking law enforcement officer in the country?"

Bear growled, "At that time it would have been the Director of the FBI, right?"

"Exactly, my good friend," Jim responded. "The records are sketchy at best, but that seems to be where the trail leads."

Growling back to Jim, Bear asked, "You're telling me, then, that the serial numbers I'm looking for, the classic Cattleman's Colt .45 set, were sent to J. Edgar Hoover?"

Jim answered, "Yes, Bear, that's what I'm telling you. Now, remember that the serial numbers for the sets of two were always the same for the set, except that the letter L preceded the serial number on the left gun in the set, and the letter R preceded the serial number on the right gun in the set. Also, there will be no importer stamp on the barrel of these guns, because they were sent as gifts to the government and didn't have to follow the same rules as all of the imported for sale guns had to follow."

"Okay, gotcha," Bear growled, now deep in thought. "So my serial numbers will still be 80001 and 80002 but with an L and an R in front of the numbers?"

"Precisely, Bear," Jim responded.

"Okay then," Bear mused with a deep guttural growl. "It looks like my next place to go is to Washington, D.C."

"That's where I would go if I were you," Jim suggested. "Now remember though, Bear, the information that I was given was from some Italian guy who could barely speak English, and the records were all hand written and hardly legible, according to him. Frankly, I'd be surprised if you find a match in D.C., but it's a good place to start."

"All right, Jimmy boy," Bear growled. "That's a hell of lot more information than I had before. Looks like your nuts are safe for a while again," Bear growled and then laughed his deep, "Haaaaaaaa, haaaaaa, haaaaaa."

"Thank god! I'm pretty attached to them." Jim shot back. And though he believed that Bear was kidding, he always had a little question in the back of his mind about the big man.

"Don't worry, I'll take care of ya, when I find the guns," Bear added. "I always do. Later."

Immediately after his conversation with his Cimmaron contact, Bear decided to call Bruce and Steve to give them an update and to see what they wanted to do next. He was thinking as the phone on the other end rang, *If I can get these pussies to do the leg work and go to Washington, it would be the best scenario.*

When Steve answered his phone, Bear just said, "Hey, it's me."

Steve didn't hesitate. There was no mistaking his growl. "Bear, how the hell are ya?"

Growling louder now, Bear said, "If I were any better, I'd be better than I deserve to be."

Steve said, "Well, Bear, you sound like a man who has had some good luck. Does that mean you have some good news for me?"

"You think I'd waste your time and mine if I didn't have good news?" Bear growled his answer. "Hell yes, I have some information for you."

"Great," exclaimed Steve. "What's up?"

Bear responded, "Well, it's like this. You two pussies need to go to Washington, D.C., to look around. I found where the guns you are looking for first appeared in the U.S., so now you have to go there to check it out."

"Wow," Steve responded. "That's great. But why aren't you checking it out?"

Bear responded with his gut laugh, "'Cause I don't do flunky work. That's your job. But you keep in mind, if you find them there, it's like I just handed them to you at a gun show. You owe me for finding them. Understand? I don't want to have to chase you down and cut your nuts off," as he repeated his familiar threat that was so easy for people to believe.

That was no problem for Steve. This was the first real lead that anyone had given them. He still had not heard back from Uberti and was totally frustrated. So this was good.

"No problem, buddy," Steve said. "You finally gave us a direction. What's the scoop?"

"It's like this," Bear explained. "It looks like you need to check out the FBI office in D.C. to see what gifts were given to the Director in the early sixties. The guns were probably given to the Director as a gift from Uberti Firearms in Italy. Go check out their records and see where that leads. The serial numbers should have an L and an R in front of their matching numbers, and they probably don't have an importer's stamp on them. It's a start."

"That's a great start, Bear," Steve said. "Looks like my buddies and I are going to take a road trip to D.C. It should be fun."

"Fun my ass!" Bear growled. "Keep me informed. Don't make me hunt you down."

"No problem, buddy," Steve laughed. "Let's hope we find them there."

But Bear had already hung up and was smiling at how he had dumped the trip onto them.

Steve tried to call Bruce as soon as he got off the phone, but got no answer. Feeling energized by Bear's call, he jumped into his car and drove over to Bruce's house to share his news. When he got there, he didn't bother to ring the bell, but instead banged on the door. He knew that Bruce seldom answered the door bell, but he would at least look out to see who was making the racket.

Finally, the door flew open, and Bruce greeted him with, "What the hell are you doing here?" It was unusual for either guy to go to the other's house without calling first.

"Got news, buddy," Steve blurted. "Let me in and let's talk."

Bruce said, "Come on in. I was just taking a nap. What's up?"

"You're always taking a nap," Steve laughed. He hustled his oversized frame through the door, found a seat, and plopped down. Then, with excitement in his voice, he said, "We finally have a lead on the Uberti's! Just when I was about to give up on hearing from the firearms maker, our good friend the Grizzly Bear called and snarled into my phone, 'I got information that you pussies can use.'"

Bruce laughed, "Wow, nice job—you make a great Bear impersonator."

"One of my many talents," Steve continued. "But my point is that he finally got through to one of his contacts, who got through to one of his contacts and found out some very interesting stuff."

"Well, get to it," Bruce said impatiently.

Steve kept going and said, "It seems that the guns with the serial numbers that Bud wants were given to the Director of the FBI back in the early sixties as a gift from the Uberti founder, Aldo. It was a common practice for him in trying to get recognition for his new company and his product."

Bruce jumped in, "Are you saying that they were given to the one and only J. Edgar Hoover? Are you frickin' kidding me?" he marveled.

"Oh yes," Steve said. "Bear indicated it wasn't a certainty because of the sketchiness of the old records, but at least it's a possibility for us to move on."

"That's incredible," Bruce said, more to himself than to Steve, as he shook his head back and forth. "So what's our next move, then?"

"That's what I asked Bear," Steve chuckled and again started to growl like Bear. "And he basically said we needed to get our asses out to Washington, D.C. and check it out. And if we find them, he expects a full payment for his services."

"Interesting," mused Bruce. "I guess we have no other choice. Plus, I think heading out to D.C. could be fun and enlightening. You know what?" he continued. "We could stay at my daughter's home in Takoma Park. I'll bet she'll know the lay of the land out there and could maybe help get us to where we need to go to start our search. I'm guessing it's the FBI Building, but it may be a special place like a museum or something."

"Yep," Steve added. "I'm sure they get lots of gifts and have a process in place to catalogue and store them."

"Wow, wow, wow," Bruce mouthed to himself. "This is great and I want to get started as soon as possible."

"I thought you would," Steve said. "But first, I think we need to let Mikey know what's up and see if he's got anything new from Bud."

"Agreed," Bruce said. "Let's give him a call."

Just then Bruce's house phone started ringing and when he checked his caller ID, it was Mike. "How crazy is that?" Bruce asked Steve as he handed Steve one of his portable phones and picked up to answer.

"Serendipitous," Steve chuckled.

As usual, both guys yelled into the phone, "Hey Chicken Man!"

Mike responded with, "I got both of you?" Then he added, "And by the way, that Chicken man shit is getting old."

"Not as old as you, buddy boy," Bruce said. "And any chicken shit you are talking about is probably on your shoes."

"Alright, okay, be childish while I have adult business to talk about," Mike continued. "So, are you done, or does your comedy routine go on for a while yet? If so, I'll wait 'til your show is over."

"Nope," Steve said. "We're done—let's talk business. We've got a scoop for you."

Mike said, "Really? Cause I've got a scoop for you and I'll bet mine is better than yours."

"Let's just see about that," Steve chimed in. "You first, Mikey—old age before studliness."

Mike guffawed over that comment, "Haw, haw, I got your old age right here." Both guys knew where he was pointing and laughed.

"Okay, go, Mikey," Bruce said. "Spit it out."

"All righty, then," Mike started. "I just finished meeting with Bud and his personal pilot at the Occidental Hotel. They even took me on a tour. Seems like they've been the reason behind how the Occy has stayed open all of these years. Bud has been throwing money at the old hotel as a sort of historical philanthropic thing. Says he's got some wealthy benefactor who supports Old West type of places just for the historical interest. I think that's just bullshit he's feeding me. But, I do believe he has a real interest in the Occy, and I also think it's somehow tied into the Uberti guns he wants us to find," Mike continued. "I don't know that for a fact, but it's a gut feeling I have. And here's why," he paused for a while for effect then he said, "because he told me that the Occidental Hotel, right here in Buffalo, Wyoming, was the last place that anyone saw the guns he is looking for. How about that, boys?" he asked. "How's that for a scoop?"

Steve and Bruce were silent for a bit and then both started to talk at once. Steve persisted though and said, "That is too weird. Why'd he tell you that now?"

"I have no friggin' idea," Mike answered, "But I believe he is telling me the truth about the guns, because he gave me that look like he didn't mean to tell me as much as he did. I'm really starting to feel like Bud was involved in some bad shit and that these guns could incriminate him in some way. Just sayin'," he added.

"We need to take some time to think about that for a while," Bruce said.

"Yes," Steve agreed. "We could be getting into something over our heads."

"Okay," Mike said before he asked, "What's your scoop? Bet you can't top mine."

"You may be right," Bruce acknowledged. "But we did find out the possible origination and destination for the guns that we are looking for. Our buddy, Bear, who by the way, could be your brother in so many ways," Bruce laughed, "has been on the hunt for us and finally got connected with the Uberti manufacturer in Italy. His importer contact said that the guns were most likely a gift to the highest-ranking law enforcement official in the country. Because that's what the founder of the company did when they first got started."

Mike was silent for a moment, thinking about who that might have been. Then he said, "What year are we talking here?"

"Early sixties," Steve answered for Bruce.

"You've got to be kidding me," Mike shot back. "You know who that was, don't you?" He answered his own question, "That would have to have been J. Edgar Hoover. Oh my god!" Mike exclaimed. "That's the connection between Bud and the guns. He had to be FBI and would have had access to them, depending upon his position."

Steve jumped in, "Well, don't get the cart before the horse here. That's a leap we can't make at this time. But Bud's comments and his government past make some sort of connection more likely."

"Hey," Mike suddenly said. "Do you guys hear that clicking sound on your phones?"

Both guys responded, "Nope, nothing on our end."

"Guess this new information is making me a bit paranoid," he laughed his deep laugh, "Haw, haw, haw. I just have a feeling sometimes that Bud is keeping tabs on me."

"Hmmmm," Bruce said. "That's interesting, but I don't know why he would want to do that. We're just doing what he wants us to do."

"Yeah, you're right, buddy," he agreed. "So go on. What's next?"

Steve chimed in, "Next is that we all go to D.C. to do some research. You up for a road trip?"

"Oh my god," Mike blurted out. "With you and Bruce? Absofuckinlutely!"

That made everyone laugh. But Mike added, "Only if I can drive out to meet you guys in Defiance and then we drive to D.C. I still can't get my sorry ass into a plane."

Bruce looked at Steve, and he nodded his head yes. "Okay, buddy boy," Bruce said. "It'll take longer, but having you with us will make it more fun. But we need to do it this week."

"Good deal," Mike said. "I'll get somebody to take care of my chickens, put on some clean bibs and my new tennies, and hit the highway."

"Perfect," responded Steve.

Bruce added, "I'll call Julie and get things set up with her too. She'll be a big help getting us around D.C."

"It's a go, then," Steve said.

Mike added, "I'll let you know when I'm on the road."

"Great, talk to you later," Steve said.

When the guys hung up though, Mike hesitated awhile and listened to his phone. He heard it click a couple of times before the dial tone fell silent. *I hope it was my imagination,* he thought as he started to move in high gear to get himself ready for the road trip.

Bud leaned back into his plush seat in his pickup, placed his phone on its charger, and contemplated what he just had heard. He was parked just around the corner from Mike's place, but out of sight of the house. *These boys are smarter than I anticipated.* He took his phone back off the charger and called the pilot.

"Frank, please prepare the plane for a flight to D.C. tomorrow."

"Yes, sir," Frank responded. "Consider it done."

"We'll leave at noon," Bud added. "Thank you." As he started his truck to drive away, he thought, *You know, I think I might just give my old friend Gordon a call to meet me in D.C. I'm sure this would interest him too. Just want to make sure that he doesn't want to kill anyone.* He smiled at the thought as he drove away, but it was a wry smile that had no happiness in it.

Meanwhile, Bruce and Steve began to prepare for the trip. They already knew that Mike would be late arriving in Ohio—he always was. So Bruce called his daughter Julie, to set up their visit.

"Hi, sweetie," Bruce said when she answered.

"Hey, you," she responded. "What's up?"

Bruce answered, "How would you feel about some house guests at the end of the week for a couple of days?"

"Sure! Are you and Mom coming out?"

"No, it's way more complicated than that," he said. "Stevie, Mikey, and I are coming out to do some research on that gun collection list that I told you about. And we need a place to stay and a guide to get around D.C. Would that work for you?"

"Oh my gosh, Dad, that would be great," she responded. "I haven't seen you three together for a long time. And my dog and cat would love the company," she laughed.

"Perfect," Bruce said. "I'll let you know our timeframe when we know when Mikey will get here. You know how late he always is. And he won't fly, so we are driving."

Julie laughed again, and said, "Oh that's right. Well, I'll be ready whenever you need me to be. I can take some time off work too, to help you get around. It'll be fun."

"Perfect," Bruce said. "I'll catch you later. Love ya."

"Bye, Dad, Love you too."

While Bruce was making plans with Julie, Steve was busily researching the process for receiving gifts back in the early sixties. He was checking all of the websites, legislation, and rules that he could find online that talked about that process. As he worked his way through the information, it was becoming increasingly clear, that back in the days that he was interested in, there were very few requirements. Receiving and keeping gifts appeared to be up to the receiver as to how it was handled, with a few exceptions. He thought, *Wow, it seems like this might be tough to sort out. Record keeping appeared to be half-assed at best, in distinct contrast to today's legislated list of procedures. But at least this is giving me a feel for where to start and what questions to ask. We'll hopefully get lucky.*

After researching and reading and researching some more, Steve felt pretty comfortable about where they would start the search in D.C. What he didn't feel comfortable about was finding credible records of all of the gifts that the FBI Director had received over the years. He thought to himself many times over the course of his readings, *This guy, one of the most powerful men to ever work for the U.S. government, appeared to believe that the laws of the land were for everyone else, the lesser people, and not for him. Since he was the chief enforcer, he seemed to believe that he had a special privilege and didn't worry about taking gifts from everyone, including his employees. Wow! I know it's a cliché now, but he is the poster boy for the old saying, "power corrupts, and absolute power corrupts absolutely."* He smiled, shook his head, and turned off the computer. *I feel like I'm wasting my time. We just need to get out there and poke around.*

When he called Bruce to report on what he had found and to see how the trip plans were coming, he simply said, "We have some work to do, even though we have a good lead. The guys in charge in the early sixties, before Watergate and ethics laws changed the framework of doing business, were basically on their own, to do what they wanted with the stuff they received as gifts. It was crazy how the process worked."

Bruce asked, "We still should go, though, right?"

"Oh yes, absolutely," Steve responded. "Gotta start somewhere. And we may get lucky."

"Okay, that's great," Bruce said. "Because I've arranged everything with Julie, and we can take off as soon as Mikey gets here."

"I'm ready and I'm sure Julie will be a big help getting us around out there," Steve added. "Now we just have to get the chicken man and his bib overalls out here." Both men laughed, hung up, and continued to ready themselves for the road trip.

Meanwhile, back in Wyoming, Mike was just about ready to hit the road. He went over his mental list, *Okay, let's see—chickens are covered, got plenty of cash, got food and beer and water, and got my cell phone. Oh and I've got my .44 magnum too. I'm good to go,* he thought and walked out and jumped into his truck and pulled out of his drive. He was also pulling his tiny travel trailer that he had attached to the truck. There would be no hotels for Mike. He would just pull off the highway, find a place to park and catch a few Z's in the trailer. Actually, that was quite an upgrade for Mike. He thought about that for a second. *In the old days it would be me and a dog snuggling in the back of my truck, lying on a hard mat. I loved it, though. I must be getting soft.* "Haw, haw, haw!" *In about sixteen hours, give or take, I should be there,* he thought and pulled out one of his remaining cigars from Steve to celebrate the beginning of the trip. He lit it with a book of matches that said "Occidental Hotel" and taking a powerful drag from the long dark Maduro, he exhaled and filled the cab of his pickup with a blue haze of sweet smelling tobacco. *My little slice of heaven,* he thought and laughed his laugh, "Haw, haw, haw."

CHAPTER 32

The Director pored over the private file that Miss Gandy had brought him regarding LBJ. It seemed to calm the fire raging inside him after his conversation with the President. *Well, Mr. President,* he thought to himself, *I know you don't want to accept it, but the fact is, based on this file and our mutual participation in the changing of the guard, you are mine. I control you.* His complexion changed from fire red to his normal sanguine look.

He yelled out, "Thank you, Miss Gandy. You may refile this folder. I'm feeling better now."

"Yes, sir," she said as she came in to pick it up. "I'm glad."

He gave no acknowledgment to her comment. Instead he said, "Please organize the release of the FBI report. Make sure there are copies for every person with press credentials who could possibly want one. And schedule my press conference prior to the President's. It's my report, so I should release it before he has a chance to take credit for it." Then he leaned back in his chair, placed his hands in an interlocking grip over his head, and smiled. *That hillbilly may be sitting in the President's office now. But I'll be making damn sure that he always remembers how he got there.*

He yelled out to Miss Gandy, "Please call Clyde and ask him to come by as soon as he can."

"Yes, sir," she replied and called Clyde immediately. However, she got no answer from Clyde's phone. He was already on his way over to see the Director and walked in just as Miss Gandy was cradling the phone's hand piece.

She looked up, smiled, and said, "You must have been reading the Director's mind. Go on in."

Clyde was normally very polite and professional when it came to Miss Gandy, but this time he hardly made eye contact and rushed into the Director's office. Seeing the Director leaning back in his chair with a somewhat relaxed look on his face prompted Clyde to take it down a few notches and calm himself. He knew that any agitation coming from himself seemed to light a match to the Director's mood. He didn't want a blowup. He wanted the Director to react to his news with calm and logic.

"Clyde, thanks for coming over so quickly," the Director said.

Clyde took a deep breath and sighed, "No problem, sir. I was on my way anyway. I wanted to talk about the report we are releasing tomorrow."

"Why that's perfect, Clyde, because that's why I asked you here," he said. "Are we all set? I want to beat LBJ to the press conference so we get all of the credit. And not him. We did all of the work, so we should get the credit. Right?" he asked rhetorically.

Clyde responded, "Well yes, that is right, sir. But we need to be careful here. I had the report leaked to some of my key reporters, both print and television, to get an early analysis of how the report will be taken. Sir, I'm sorry to say that the initial discussions are less than complimentary of our work." That caused the Director to immediately throw his hands down on his desk, lean forward, and look Clyde straight in the eyes with his piercing beady dark eyes.

"Just what does that mean, Clyde? Who is criticizing us and why?"

"Mr. Director, it's across the board, and honestly, it's being fueled by all of the conspiracy crap that the reporters have been spouting for days. They wanted the report to say that the assassination was a conspiracy and who was involved. Of course we didn't do that."

"Of course we didn't, Clyde," the Director said. "But this report is coming from me, the By-god Director of the FBI. Who are they, who is anyone to question my work on this?"

"That's exactly why I'm here, sir," Clyde continued. "We need to craft a response to the criticism right now and be ready when the shit storm hits during the press conference."

Now the Director leaned back again and assumed his familiar pose of leaning back with his arms upstretched. "All right, all right. What are the critics saying? Let's fix it," he said more calmly.

Clyde continued, "The biggest complaint is that the report is long on making Oswald the lone gunman and short on evidence."

The Director turned fiery red for an instant, and exclaimed, "For Christ's sake, Clyde, that is exactly what we need people to believe. We have to have Oswald as the man and the only man. Otherwise, the digging continues, and we all get put in jeopardy. Do you see that?"

"Oh yes, sir, I do," Clyde agreed. "But if we don't respond to the critics in some way to defend our report, it'll take off and have a life of its own."

"Or just get thrown aside and ignored while the President goes off and does his own report, like that commission he is putting together," the Director said. He then stared off into space for a while, calmer now than he was, but still agitated. He was considering his options. Finally, he looked hard into Clyde's eyes and said, "Well, Clyde, thank you for bringing this to my attention, but I am going to go forward just as I had planned. I will release the report, say that I believe it without question, and thank the men who worked so hard to put it together. Then I will say, 'As the Director of the Federal Bureau of Investigation, who founded this great crime fighting organization that stands for fidelity, bravery, and integrity, I stand firmly behind it and stake my reputation on it.'" He leaned back again, but with a smile now on his face.

Clyde just looked at him with disbelief, thinking, "He didn't hear a thing that I just said. He believes he's invincible." Recognizing that he wasn't going to change the Director's mind, Clyde merely said, "Yes, sir, if that is your desire, we will do it that way."

The Director said, "That is my desire and my directive. They won't question me." Then he smiled and said, "I expect you to stand beside me at the release of the report."

"Yes, sir," Clyde said. "I'll be there," as he stood up to leave and then headed back to his office.

The next day the five-volume, four hundred-plus page report was released to anyone and everyone who might have some sort of press or TV credential, and the response was as predictable as the sun rising in the morning. The Director and his Assistant withstood a withering barrage of questions regarding the lack of evidence included within the report. Finally, with an "It is what it is" attitude, they tried to gracefully, yet with an edge, defer the lack of key evidentiary pieces and hurried-up appearance of the report to the President's desire to get it out to the public. It soon became the answer to almost every question of concern. "Well, in order to help the President," or "The President needed us to move swiftly on this," became the excuses of the day.

Finally, when it was all done and the Director was sequestered safely back in his office with Clyde, he sighed, "You were so right, Clyde, but we are done, and it is now in the hands of the President. He can be the guy with the answers. That's what he's wanted all along anyway."

In an attempt to reassure the Director, Clyde said, "At least it's off our plate now. And in the hands of LBJ. His little team of handpicked politicians and friends will fare no better than we have. But I bet in the end, most of their work will revert back to the same conclusions we drew. Just watch how many times that commission will refer to our report and try to make it theirs."

"Thank you, Clyde, but truthfully, I am still happy that our report was first and served to defer for the time being any link to any kind of conspiracy. That makes me breathe easier, even though the lack of respect that I was shown by those reporters will never be forgotten." He laughed, "I may start a file on all of those bas-tards."

Clyde laughed too. But he thought to himself. *Those guys with the most questions and most lack of respect better be squeaky clean, because the Director never forgot a slight of any kind. And he never left a loose end or detail unaccounted for. That's precisely why he was still the Director and would be for the foreseeable future.* Clyde felt quite comfortable knowing that the Director was still in charge and still orchestrating the greatest covert operation in the history of this country.

CHAPTER 33

Bud got down to the Johnson County Airport a few minutes early, hoping that Frank had the plane ready to go. There was really never any reason to doubt that he would, but old habits die hard, and Bud was the consummate detail person—always thinking and re-thinking, always checking and double checking. From the time that he realized way back in 1963 that he had failed to tie up all of the loose ends, in without a doubt the biggest operation of his career, he had vowed that he would never fail in that way again. *Look what that has cost me*, he thought from time to time. *Years of looking over my shoulder, years of knowing that my failure could bring me down, as well as the people I promised to protect.* As he got older, it gnawed at his gut that he couldn't figure it out. Even when his bosses passed on, seemingly leaving him finally safe from some form of retribution, like those poor bastard unsuspecting young agents received way back when, he couldn't shake his feelings of needing to set things right. Nearly every waking minute, it was in his thoughts. *Bud, you must finish it*, he thought. So that's what he did. He plodded on. He was wired to finish things and would really never be at peace until he did.

Frank, on the other hand, had become his right hand man and only friend. Every time he saw Frank and worked with him, Bud thought, *I am so glad I was able to give this man a life*, albeit a different life than Frank had envisioned. Frank seemed to be content though. He was able to do what he loved best in life—fly, fly, fly. Working with Bud allowed him to

285

continue that. Plus, he had been able to be productive and work off the agency's books for Bud in numerous dark operations over the years. He just had to be careful to fly under the radar of those still in positions of power who could pull his plug immediately if they ever found out his real story. Living between Buffalo and Deadwood, ferrying Bud around on a moment's notice, worked quite well for him. And for Bud.

"Good morning, Frank," Bud greeted him as he saw him sitting in the cockpit of the small Cessna. "Is everything in order and ready to go?" He knew the answer, but he just had to hear it. Always.

"Hey, Bud," he said speaking as if to a best friend. "You know I'm ready," he said with a smile. "I'm always excited to head out on another adventure, especially to D.C."

"All right then," Bud responded as he climbed aboard. "Let's do it. I want to get there and get into position long before our friends do. Plus, we need to meet with Gordon to outline our expectations—specifically that I don't want him to create any bodies that we have to deal with. Our three friends have no clue what they are involved with, and I don't think they can do us any harm. We are just going to watch and listen. Maybe, just maybe, they might stumble onto something that we can use."

"Perfect," the Pilot responded. "Let's hit the friendly skies," and they taxied for takeoff. Upon takeoff, Frank's mind jumped back to the first times that he had flown into this tiny airport. It was an eternity ago, but oftentimes, it seemed like yesterday.

"Wow," he said to Bud. "Today is one of those days when my gut feeling just jumped me back to 1963. It's incredible how close those days can feel."

"I know what you're saying," Bud said. "I feel it almost every day."

"The big difference for me, though," Frank said, "is that I wasn't even aware of what really happened. It was just another dark operation that was 'need to know,' and I didn't need to know. It was one hell of a shock when I found out what the actual op was. And if not for you, I would be dead now because of it. Amazing!"

Bud smiled and said quietly, "Yes, you would be," as he leaned back, closed his eyes, and settled in for the long flight.

Frank knew that was his sign to quit talking and do his job.

Meanwhile, far below on a crowded interstate, Mike was making progress in his trip back to Ohio. "Goddam morons," he yelled to himself about the people pushing him from behind. "Go around me if you don't want to follow me. But I ain't going no faster!"

Mike was an interstate turtle. He never went over a maximum speed of sixty no matter what. "I'm doing sixty, you idiot," he yelled at a passing SUV that flashed its lights and blew its horn as it whipped around and passed Mike. His driving on the interstate was quintessential Mikey. He did it his way and "screw everybody else." This was probably a good thing, though, for the other drivers on the road. Mike could never be accused of having great driving abilities. Pulling the tiny trailer caused him to bob and weave in his lane, and going any faster would have put everyone in more jeopardy than they already were. So he was the turtle, keeping his pace and never varying it. He stopped when he needed to go to the restroom, but only sometimes. Generally, he would unzip his bibs, grab an empty coffee cup, whip it out, and do his thing while heading down the highway. When his buddies would give him crap about this habit, he would laugh that belly laugh, "Haw, haw, haw," and say it was "just a natural thing to do." And if a passing motorist inadvertently looked over at him while he was in the process, he would just smile and wave and mouth, "You ain't never seen anything big as this, have ya?"

This practice did have another downside to it. Bruce and Steve were never shy about telling the story of the three guys heading out on a road trip with Mike driving his truck. Mike had brought a coffee with him and placed it in his cup holder. The problem was that he also had a similar, supposedly empty, coffee cup sitting in the other cup holder. While driving, Mike had finished his coffee, placed it in the cup holder, and after several miles, he picked it up again to take a drink. It was empty.

Bruce would start laughing while describing what happened next. "The dumb s.o.b forgot he had finished his coffee, set the empty cup back into the holder, reached over to the other cup, swished it to see if anything was in it, and noticing that there was, he took a deep swallow."

Mike said, "Wow, that's really cold. It doesn't taste like my coffee," and took another drink.

"And then," Bruce continued. "The light came on in his brain, and he proceeded to spit it out in a solid stream that covered the dashboard and the driver's side window. You see, our good friend Mikey was drinking his own piss that he had left in the cup from the last time he used it."

Now every time Mike would use his cup for a toilet, he would remember that time. Then he would roll his window down and dump it. "Never gonna happen again!" he vowed. But Bruce and Steve never tired of telling the story of Mikey's piss cup.

After nearly twenty hours of turtling across the interstate, Mike finally arrived at Bruce's driveway and pulled in. He was beat, but excited for the next leg of the trip. He had called both of his friends to let them know his approximate time of arrival and was pretty close for a change. Bruce and Steve generally added at least two hours to any time that Mike would throw out as his arrival time. And it was no different this time. Steve pulled in just before Mike and waited expectantly with Bruce talking about their plans.

"We need to let him decompress for a while, so let's leave about 9 o'clock in the morning," Bruce said.

"That works for me," responded Steve. "As long as we keep Mikey away from the booze, we should be able to hit that time. Look, there he is now," Steve said pointing to the driveway and Mike's truck and trailer pulling in.

"Yep, there he is, cowboy hat on, chomping on a cigar, and looking good in his bibs," Bruce said. Then Bruce looked at Steve, and laughed, "Remember, don't take a swig from his coffee cup if he offers."

"Oh trust me," Steve responded. "That will never happen."

"Hey Chicken Man," they both yelled at once.

Mike waved and pushed open his truck door, threw his portly frame out of his seat, and repositioned himself by reaching down into the front of his bib overalls and then yelled, "Hey, boys, how the hell are ya?" Bruce and Steve just smiled, looked at each other, and enthusiastically responded in tandem, "Great!"

Mike shuffled up to them and reached out his paw to shake hands, laughing that signature laugh, "Haw, haw, haw." Both men opted for a quick man hug instead of the handshake. It was just too soon after watching Mike reach into the front of his bibs for that.

"Oh my god, it is so good to be here and see you guys," Mike continued. "That was a friggin' long drive. And by the way, I smoked up the last of your gift cigars. They made the trip bearable when I needed it most."

Steve responded, "That's great, because I know where I can find lots more for you."

"Let's go in and relax for a bit and talk about our plans," Bruce said. "Oh and Steve brought you a nip of Jameson's to bring you down and get you relaxed, too."

"You guys are just too much," Mike said. "My buddies and Jameson's. Wow. Now that brings back some great memories. Not that I remember most of those times, except what you told me the next day," Mike laughed again. "Haw, haw, haw."

"Those were the days all right. Yes, they were. More memorable for some than others," Steve chuckled.

Inside the house, Mike remained standing while Steve poured the Jameson's for everyone.

Bruce said, "Have a seat, Mikey?"

But Mike answered, "No, buddy, I got to stand for a while. That drive was hard on this old fella."

Steve said, "All righty then, here's a toast to the three of us being together again." He began with a bit of Irish lilt in his voice, "May God give you... For every storm, a rainbow. For every tear, a smile. For every care, a promise. And a blessing, in each trial. For every problem life sends, a faithful friend to share. For every sigh, a sweet song. And an answer for each prayer."

"Well done, Stevie," Mike said as the three buddies touched glasses and swallowed the Jameson's. Mike coughed and said, "Oh my Lord! That is so good. I'll be having a few more shots of that, if you please."

"No problem," Steve chuckled and poured Mike a second. "But let's get down to business first and discuss our plans quickly, before you fall into that whiskey haze that I know is coming." Mike acquiesced, and Bruce and Steve started to lay out the plans.

"We are going to leave in the morning at 9 and drive the ten hours to D.C. Julie will meet us at her house when we get there, and we'll spend the night there before heading downtown to check out a few places that I found on the Internet that look promising. She's taking the day off work and will guide us around so that we won't be wasting time getting lost. She knows her way around very well," Bruce added.

"So where are we looking?" Mike asked.

Steve responded, "I am sure we will need to look in a few places. Of course, the FBI Building will be on the list, followed by the old Justice Department, and then the one place that really jumped out at me, and I believe has the best chance for us, is the J. Edgar Hoover Foundation."

Bruce added, "Yep, I agree. So at least we have a good list to start with, and like most treasure hunts, we may find other trails along the way. I think it's going to be fun and interesting."

Mike joined in, "Well, anything that gets the three of us together for a few days has to be fun." He guffawed, "And I promise I will behave. After tonight that is. Haw, haw, haw."

"No problem, buddy, we've left you in many places over the years, but we'd hate to leave you in D.C.," Steve chuckled.

Bruce got the guys back on track, and after a few more details, said, "Well, I think that's it. Everybody be ready to go at 9, and 'let's git 'er done,' as the folks in Wyoming might say."

Mike swallowed a couple more shots and said, "I'm heading out to the trailer to sleep."

But Bruce said, "What? Hell no! Marlene has the guest bedroom ready."

Mike responded, "Thanks, buddy, but I'll be more comfortable in the trailer. I'm good."

Steve got up to leave and said, "Okay, boys, see you in the morning." He left and Mike went out to climb into his trailer, crawled into his sleeping bag and was out.

Bruce just smiled and thought how some things never change. *This trip will be quite the adventure.*

CHAPTER 34

Frank guided his small Cessna into his landing position as he approached the Baltimore airport. He was focused on the landing but also was in deep thought to himself again.

"Hey, Bud," he said quietly, "This feels all so surreal every time I fly into this place. It's amazing how the years have melted away and even though the events that changed my life were so long ago, this airport feels like my birthplace. It's actually where I became a new man. And it really hasn't been all that bad. You have been a great friend, and my choices were obviously limited at that time. I just want to thank you again for stepping out the way you did to save me."

Bud looked at Frank and responded, "Look, it was my fault that you ever got caught up in the cleanup in the first place. If Howard and I had done our jobs right, you would never have been in jeopardy. So pay attention and get this plane landed safely," he smiled. "I don't want to end my life in some meaningless way, like say, a plane crash."

Frank laughed out loud as the plane's wheels touched down, and said, "You mean like that stupid drug dealer who took my place?"

"That's exactly what I mean," Bud smiled again. "That s.o.b never knew what hit him, and he deserved it. And the Director bought it hook, line, and sinker."

Frank taxied the plane behind the old terminal to the little-used runway that the two had used for years and years. "Do you really think he bought it completely?" he asked Bud.

"Probably not," Bud responded. "He never really trusted anyone but Clyde. But if it had bothered him, he would have done everything in his power to figure it out. Of course, maybe he did dig around, and we were just too good for him," he chuckled.

Frank brought the plane to a stop, switched everything off, and the two men clambered out of their seats. Frank noticed the black SUV that was parked just inside the gate, smiled, and shook his head. "All these years of being retired, or semi-retired, and all he needs to do is make a call and the details fall into place."

"I suppose that car is for us?" Frank asked.

"Of course," Bud responded. "But I just had it dropped off. You will have to drive for us."

"Okay, let's do it," Frank said as the two guys jumped in behind the darkened windows and drove out through the already opened gate.

"Head downtown to Pennsylvania Avenue, SE, to that bar called Wisdom. It's where we are meeting Gordon."

"Great," replied Frank. "I'm referring to the bar, not Gordon. He scares me. But I love Wisdom. The owner and mixologist, Eric, serves up some of the best drinks in D.C."

"Yes," Bud said. "But only light drinks for us this time. We have lots of logistics to work on. And we need to check out Gordon's state of mind to see if he's capable of helping us on this little op." Bud was referring to Gordon's propensity to go off and act by himself, if he didn't like how the op was going. "We don't need our new friends to get hurt by Gordon. I just need to look him in the eyes and see if he's off bubble or somewhat centered. We can certainly use his skills."

Frank reiterated, "That's what I mean. He scares me."

As Frank drove into D.C., Bud just sat back and took in all of the old familiar sites that he had literally grown old with from his time working in the Bureau. He never tired of the looming Capitol building that rose so majestically ahead of them as they drove South on North Capitol Street. It was always, always, an imposing sight. He thought, *This is what I have worked for all of these years—to maintain this majesty and the power that it represents.*

"It's quite a sight, isn't it?" he spoke to Frank.

"Without question, Bud, it's one of the most powerful scenes that you can take away from a visit to Washington," Frank responded. "To me, it represents the might of this great country and the sacrifices that we have made to keep it safe for the average guy and his family."

Bud replied, "Yes, it does, but it also speaks to me of why we need to keep using dark ops methods to protect those families—basically, to protect those families from themselves and sometimes from the leaders that they have given their full trust and confidence to."

Frank continued, "The average guy would not understand the why's and the necessary protections that we provide."

"Far from understanding," Bud added, "they would crucify us for doing our job. In particular, we would become the scapegoats for our decision-makers. And that, my good friend, is why I am still obsessed with finding the last details that could tie any of us, our dead bosses, our departed agents, and especially those of us still kicking around, to that fateful day in 1963."

"I'm with you, boss," Frank commented, and then said, "We're here," as he pulled into one of the precious few parking spots near Wisdom.

"Bet you a ten spot that Gordon is here already, even though we are a little early," Bud chuckled.

Frank responded, "No thanks, that's a suckers bet, because you know that he is probably watching us from someplace right now."

"Yep, I guarantee it," Bud smiled. "Let's go in."

As the two men entered the bar, they quickly surveyed the few occupants, nodded at the bartender, and headed back through the darkened length of the building past an old ratty leather couch and a couple of chairs that had been strategically placed to a small cubicle, or sticking out from the wall.

"It's a good thing that the owner is such a good drink man; otherwise, why would anyone come to this dive?" Frank questioned as he slid a bench with his back to the wall.

Bud answered, "Well, that's the point, isn't it?" as he also slid onto the bench with his back to the wall in a position that allowed him to see in all directions. "For us, anyways, we need a good stiff drink, a private place to talk, and more importantly, a place where we more than likely won't be recognized. That's exactly why this place works for us."

The bartender slipped away from the bar and headed to the guys to get their drink orders.

"Where's Eric?" Bud asked him as he ordered three cocktails made with a significant amount of absinthe and one non-alcoholic drink, not knowing if Gordon was abstaining from alcohol, as he had a tendency to do from time to time.

The young man with a very manly black beard answered, "Oh Eric, he's working on another drink contract, so he'll be out for a while. Sorry, man," he said and disappeared quickly back to the unattended bar.

Bud knew that Gordon was close by—he could feel his presence. But he was content to sit and wait with Frank and sip his absinthe until Gordon decided that all was safe. Suddenly, out of the shadows, from the back of the elongated building, a figure emerged and headed towards the couch.

Bud never budged, and said, "Hello, Gordon. It's been a long time. How are you doing?"

Frank stayed seated too, and said, "Hey Gordon, good to see another ghost."

Gordon slid into the seat across from the two guys and simply said, "This must be important. What's up?" Even though it was dark in the bar, Bud was taken by the fact that Gordon had aged very badly. He looked years older than the last time they had met only a few short months ago.

Bud's first question was, "Gordon, how's your health? Do you feel up to a little fun with some surveillance?" Bud knew that Gordon didn't like to screw around with small talk, so he got right to it.

Gordon didn't hesitate and said, "Well, I'm a whole lot older than I used to be, but, just so you know, I can still kill anyone I need to," and laughed a crazy sort of laugh that chilled the other two men around the table. "Is one of these frou-frou drinks for me?"

Bud shook his head, "Didn't know if you were drinking or not so that one is non-alcoholic and the other is absinthe."

"Give me the absinthe," Gordon said curtly. "Time to get back on the horse that threw me." Gordon was referring to his on again, off again relationship with alcohol.

Bud thought to himself, *Yes, Gordon, I've often wondered if we did you a favor by saving your life from the Director.*

Gordon's life had been a series of amazing successes from his uncanny abilities as a dark op, but equally humbling failures from his only true nemesis in life—alcohol. When he failed, it was always because of the alcohol. And Bud knew the exact time that relationship started— the 1963 operation. It marked his life forever. Bud was actually using the moment to ascertain where Gordon was with that relationship because Gordon was too scary to deal with when he was drinking. Gordon sipped the drink gingerly at first, then took a larger swallow as Bud and Frank watched. He appeared to savor it as a man might who had been in the desert for an extended time without water, so thirsty that he would "drink the sweat off anyone's balls," yet find it offensive at the same time.

"Could I get another one of these frou-frous?" he asked. "Pretty damn tasty."

"Why, of course, Gordon," Bud said and signaled the bearded bartender for a second round. "Glad you like it."

Gordon smiled queerly, and said, "It's been a long dry spell."

Bud tried to keep up with Gordon on a regular basis. He was always a little afraid of Gordon being on his own. After the Director, Clyde, and LBJ had all passed, the danger to his life had all but dissipated, so Bud gave him the go-ahead to move back to D.C., if he wanted, or any place else in the country or world. So even though Gordon had lived a quiet life in the West, he quickly opted to go back to D.C. and almost immediately began to freelance for seemingly every agency involved in dark ops. *He was just so damn good at it,* Bud thought. But seeing his thin old man's frame and the haggard, worn face and jet black dyed hair, that made him look older than he actually was, Bud wondered if he were drawing to an end of a decades-long career.

"Get to it," Gordon grunted with a swallow of the drink that Bud had ordered.

"I need your help doing surveillance on a couple of guys who are doing a job for me. It's very simple. No muscle needed. Just watching and reporting. And positively no elimination necessary."

Gordon swallowed the second drink, and asked, somewhat rhetorically, "What the hell's the fun in that?" Before Bud could respond, Gordon said, "Sure, why not? Am I getting paid?"

"Per usual," Bud said with a chuckle. "I save your life, and all I get is a bill for services rendered."

"An old guy needs an income," Gordon shot back. It was obvious the booze was starting to loosen him up a little. That was precisely Bud's point in bringing Gordon here and getting him a drink. He had found that there was a point between sober and drunk that made Gordon more manageable. It kind of took the mean out of him for a bit.

Bud continued, "Great, here's the story. I have three guys working for me who are retired civilians with lots of time on their hands looking to make a few bucks. I've hired them to look for the missing merchandise from 1963, and they are showing that they are pretty sharp. They may just stumble onto something, and I want to make sure if they do that we know it and can then take the appropriate action. You with me?"

"Oh my god," Gordon blurted out. "You are actually still looking for those guns? And you think I'm nuts," he smirked as he responded. "Okay, sure, let's do it. Should be a piece of cake. And don't think I don't know what it's really about," he continued. "It's your fuckin' ego driving this—the only operation that you failed to tie up all of the loose ends."

Bud said, "You can think whatever you want. I just need to finish this in my lifetime. Call me obsessed if you want. But I prefer to look at it as being thorough and finishing what I started. It's like my final mission in life."

"Okay, okay," Gordon said. "I'm in, but there is no way of connecting the dots to that operation even if these knuckleheads find the guns. And that is my humble opinion and final word on it. Give me the details."

Bud looked at Frank as if to ask, "What do you think?" When Frank nodded his head in a way that indicated to Bud that he was okay with using Gordon, Bud continued, "It should be real easy. They are staying in Takoma Park with one of the guy's daughter. Just pick them up there, follow them, and report back to me on their progress. I have one of the guy's cell phones tapped. So that should help Frank and me from our end. I'm sure they are going to start with the Director's memorabilia either at the FBI or the Justice Department, then on to the Director's Foundation. They will probably find nothing we don't already know. Sounds simple, doesn't it?"

"Oh yeah, they all sound simple, until they don't," Gordon replied.

"They will be arriving tomorrow at this address," Bud continued as he handed over a piece of paper to Gordon. "Probably late afternoon. That's really all there is until you get back to us after they leave town again."

Gordon was already standing. He reached out and shook hands with Bud and Frank. "Actually, I wish these bozos would find the merchandise too. I would love to have that weapon in my hand once again. You know, we truly changed the course of history for this country with that operation. I've never regretted it for a moment," he said, as he walked away into the darkness of the back of the elongated building and disappeared.

Frank and Bud looked at each other and smiled.

"Bud," Frank said. "I think he's dying from something. He looked terrible."

Bud agreed, "Yes, but we all are. He just may be sooner than later. I'm just glad he's willing and able to be a part of this. He could use the closure too, even if it's for a different reason than I have in mind."

The two men swallowed the last of the absinthe, walked past the bartender, and said, "Tell Eric that Bud was here and that the drinks were outstanding as usual."

The bartender waved and said, "Will do. Thanks for coming in."

The two men exited, found their car, and headed back to Bud's safe house near the center of the city.

CHAPTER 35

Bruce got up early to get everything ready for the trip. He smiled to himself and thought, *At least we don't have to wait on Mikey. He's already here.* But then he went outside to bang on the trailer to wake him up and amazingly he found the truck was gone and the trailer was empty.

"What the hell?" he exclaimed. "Where is that crazy s.o.b?" Bruce pulled out his cell phone and called Mike's number, but it went straight to voice mail. *Oh my god,* he thought, *he's doing it to us again. Always late and always dancing to a different drummer.*

He called Steve and told him and Steve reacted much like Bruce, "Well, dammit! We can only hope he didn't leave in the middle of the night to get drunk. I'll be there on time, and all we can do is hope."

"Yep," Bruce responded and ended the call. There was nothing else to do, except to continue to get ready.

As the appointed time got closer, Steve arrived, parked his car, and carried his luggage over to the van. "Still no Mikey?" he asked knowing the answer.

"Nope," he laughed. "He never changes."

"But that's why we love him," Steve said.

Just then, they heard a horn blowing and looked up to see Mike pulling into the drive. Both men looked at each other with simulated disbelief and laughed out loud. Mike had his window down, was smoking a cigar, and was yelling to them, "Let's get this party started.

Haw, haw, haw." He parked his truck in front of his trailer, jumped out, and said, "Bet you were pissing and moaning about where I was, weren't you?" He took a long drag on the cigar and continued. "You know that I'm the chicken man, and I've been getting up with the chickens for years now. So at the crack of dawn, I got up and you lazy slackers were still sawing logs, so I went up to get breakfast at the VFW and see if some of the old guys were still around playing euchre. And they were. They bought me a couple of beers, and we talked and now I'm here—on time I might add. Haw, haw, haw."

Bruce and Steve just laughed and were pretty much speechless. Bruce did say though with a laugh, "Okay, where's Mike and what did you do with him? The beer fits but not the on-time thing."

Mike responded, "Well, I'm here. Let's get going." He went to the trailer, pulled out his bag, and threw it in the back of the van. The road trip adventure was a go.

It would take about ten hours to get to D.C., but if the first couple of hours were any indication, it would be a pleasant trip. The weather was great and the three buddies spent the time talking almost nonstop about everything under the sun.

It's funny, Bruce thought. *A guy can make lots of new friends over a lifetime, but it's never the same as the relationship you have with your old friends. My dad said it best, after he had outlived most of his old friends and was missing them. "Old friends know how you got to be who you are and where you came from. They know what you are made of and that makes all the difference. You can't hide yourself from old friends."*

Throughout the trip, the topic often came back to the quest that they were on and how they were going to proceed. Steve had it pretty well mapped out from his research on the Internet.

"We've got the serial numbers, the kind of guns, and who had them when they came into the country. So that means we start at the Department of Justice, go to the FBI, and then follow the trail to the J. Edgar Hoover Foundation."

"Frankly," Bruce said. "I'm betting on the Foundation for our best information."

"Me too," Steve said. "Based on the information on the net, it appears that the Director kept most of his gifts, and most of his memorabilia was given to the Foundation after he died."

Mike interjected, "I agree. He believed that laws were meant for him to enforce, not for him to live by. Some of the stuff that he got away with wouldn't fly today. He was like a king running his kingdom."

Bruce added, "And no one had the guts or the clean life that they would need to take him on. He had files on absolutely everyone who could possibly come after him."

"It speaks volumes about our leaders, that no one could go after him because they were hiding something in their own lives," Steve added. "Amazing."

Bruce then reminded the guys, "Remember, we have to go easy in our search and just be collectors, and the people who can help us may be more willing to help. We can't do anything or ask questions that someone might interpret as besmirching the Director's name."

Mike laughed, "Besmirching my ass! That's a pretty big word for an old retired guy."

But everyone agreed with the assessment and the need for caution.

The trip turned into a pleasant drive that moved along at a fairly good pace. Steve and Bruce took turns driving the full size van and ignored Mike whenever he offered to drive for a while. The guys knew firsthand how that would affect the arrival time.

The last time he asked, Bruce retorted, "Hell no, if you did drive, we would be calling you turtle man instead of chicken man. You have one pace, too damn slow!"

Mike pretended to have his feelings hurt, "Well, you are a mean s.o.b. Do I have to remind you that the tortoise won the race? Haw, haw, haw. Plus, my driving wouldn't slow us down any more than you two guys' prostates. We haven't missed a rest stop yet."

Bruce and Steve both laughed, and Steve said, "Can't argue with that."

"Besides," Bruce said. "We only have a couple hours left. We'll be at Julie's before 7 p.m."

"All righty then," Mike said. "I'm going to take a nip of Jameson's and take a nap too."

"Perfect," Bruce said as he continued down the highway.

Before Mike awakened from his nap, Bruce was pulling onto the street in front of his daughter's house.

He turned to Steve, "Think we should wake up sleeping beauty, or let him sleep in the van all night?"

"Well, the way he is snoring, it would be better for all of us if we left him in the van, but let's start to unload our stuff. That should wake him up."

Julie came bounding down the steps to her house when she saw the van pull up and the guys get out. "Hey there, you guys," she shouted. "So glad you made it," as she hugged Bruce and Steve. "Where's Mikey?" she asked.

"Oh, he's sleeping, but my guess is he'll be awake in a sec," Bruce said.

Just then, Mike popped out of the van and said, "Julie, how are you?" as he limped over to hug her. "Don't believe a word these guys say. You look great."

Julie laughed out loud, and said, "Well, I love the bibs and the white tennis shoes. Very non-D.C."

Mike guffawed, "I think I'll take that as a compliment."

"It is," Julie said with a happy smile. "I am so glad to see you guys. Let's get your stuff in and relax for a bit."

Moving up the steps to the house, everyone was so engrossed in pleasantries that they didn't notice the car parked a half block away with an older man slumped into a position that allowed him to see everything that was transpiring without being seen.

Gordon thought to himself as he watched and took pictures, *I really don't know why the hell Bud needs me for these bumpkins. But I said I would do it, and I will. But it looks like it's going to be a real snoozer of an operation. I'll stay 'til the lights go off and come back in the morning."*

Inside the house, the guys and Julie talked and reminisced until about midnight. They made plans for the next day and fell into the sleeping arrangements that Julie had set up for them. Bruce got the futon, Steve wanted the recliner rocker, and Mike ended up on the floor of the basement.

As he said, "That's perfect for me. You can't hear me snore, I have my own bathroom, and my back is used to sleeping on the floor at home. Can't sleep on soft mattresses anymore."

When the lights finally went out, Gordon just grunted to himself and drove away—but not before planting GPS tracking devices on both the van and Julie's car.

CHAPTER 36

The Director had turned around in his chair and was staring at the wall with his hands clasped over his head when Clyde came in. Miss Gandy had told him to go on in, but seeing the Director in this pose made him hesitate for a moment.

"Sir?" he said quietly.

"Hello, Clyde," the Director said without so much as moving even a little bit. To Clyde, this greeting had two possible meanings: Either the Director was deep in thought, or he was so livid about something that he was about to blow. *I hope it's the first option,* Clyde thought. It didn't take long to find out that it was not either or, it was both.

"Clyde, that son of a bitch LBJ is throwing us under the bus regarding our report," he said between gritted teeth. "What do you think our options are?"

Clyde studied the back of the Director's balding head and said, "Mr. Director, I think we have done everything we can do, and now we let him be presidential on this issue. You know that his interests are the same as ours here. He wants to get the conspiracy stuff stopped as much as we do. Let him move forward with his new commission. And it'll take so long and it'll use our report so much that eventually, we will look good for getting ours done. Now that's just my opinion, sir," he said respectfully. He could see the tension melting away in the way the Director was clasping his hands.

Finally, he said to Clyde, "You are right again, as always. Thank you, my good friend. Your counsel is indispensable. I will call the President, offer my input for members of the commission—the Warren Commission, I believe it should be called—and let him run with it. As you said, we have already done our part." With the tension gone, the Director turned around to face Clyde and placed his previously clasped hands flat on his desk. "Issue number two," he said.

Clyde responded, "Yes, sir?"

"I want the merchandise from the operation returned to me so that I can take them to my residence for safe keeping. I just feel uncomfortable with those guns sitting around in that little gift room area where any Tom, Dick, or Harry might venture across them and start to dig. You understand what I'm saying, Clyde?"

"I do, sir," Clyde responded. "But I worry that it is a little soon to touch them again. We just got them placed there and to get them back out now might raise a question or two."

It was obvious the Director had already made up his mind. He ignored Clyde's comments completely and spoke as if they were never said. "Please go get the merchandise and bring them to my office so that I can transport them to my residence. I want to look at them every day to know that we are safe and to remind me of what a great thing we did."

Clyde knew that the Director's tone was that of an order and that he had to comply. He briefly thought about making his argument again, but decided to just accept the order with resignation and do it. "Yes, sir," he said. "I'll have the guns to you this afternoon."

The Director smiled and said, "Thank you, Clyde."

Clyde left the Director's office and went straight to Miss Gandy. "Do you have the file on the merchandise that the Director asked you to keep?"

"Of course, sir," she replied and walked over to a row of file cabinets where she opened a particular drawer and pulled out a file. "Here it is, Mr. Assistant Director."

Clyde took the file, briefly perused its contents, grunted a quick "Thank you, Miss Gandy," and walked out with it.

Miss Gandy followed him into the hallway and said, "Sir, when you are finished, please bring me the file. The Director wants me to keep it in a special folder."

"Yes, Miss Gandy. I will when I bring him the merchandise," Clyde responded as he disappeared around the hallway corner.

When Clyde entered the gift storage room, he immediately went to the agent with the sign-in sheet and asked him to get the merchandise. Clyde didn't want to sign in as the person removing the briefcases that held the guns, so he used his position to intimidate the agent and told him that Miss Gandy would be down to sign for the Director in a little while.

"Is that okay?" he asked with authority. *What would any agent say to that?* he thought to himself. *He damn well better say, "Yes, sir."* He smiled.

"No problem, sir," the agent responded. "I'll just make a note that she is coming to sign them out."

As the agent bent over his desk, Clyde waited impatiently for him to finish and get the merchandise. Finally, the agent left and returned with the three silver briefcases and sat them on the desk in front of Clyde.

"Thank you agent," he said without emotion as he scooped up the cases and carried them out of the room.

Behind him, as Clyde walked away, the agent was making another note that said, "The Assistant Director picked up three silver briefcases that each contained one Uberti replica Colt .45 on this date in 1963."

Clyde hurried back to his office with the merchandise before taking them directly to the Director's office. He wanted to check them out personally before turning them over to the Director. Upon reaching his office, he closed the door and opened the cases one at a time by popping open the case and flopping the top back onto his desk. Inside each was the replica gun. He stared at them as if he was looking at a long lost work of art. *These guns are really pristine and beautiful,* he thought. *But the value can only be calculated by their place in probably the most significant national event since Abraham Lincoln's assassination. It's too bad they can't be displayed for the part they played in history."* He sighed. *I don't see how anyone can ever connect the dots in this operation, though. But loose ends are loose ends,* and Clyde could think of many cases that had been solved by the Bureau with less information than these guns would provide someone hell-bent to prove a conspiracy. He picked up each weapon, made sure it was unloaded, looked it over very carefully and smelled it to see if it had been fired or not, and placed each back into its briefcase. The two guns with the matching serial numbers, L and the R, were clean and like new. However, the third gun that matched up with the missing gun in Wyoming appeared to have been fired. It had a faint smell of gunpowder, and the firing mechanism appeared to have a slight firing stain on it. Clyde thought, *That's strange. Only one agent said he fired during the operation, and that's the missing Colt.* After thinking about it for a while and coming up with no plausible explanation, he decided to take the briefcases to the Director's office.

On the way, he thought to himself, *We could ask the agent who was responsible for this weapon during the operation, but oh no, the Director had to have him eliminated.* Then he sighed again and moved into Miss Gandy's outer office where Miss Gandy immediately held out her hand for the file and then told him that the Director was expecting him and to go on in.

"Hello again, Clyde. I see you have the merchandise. No problems, I assume?" he asked.

"No, sir," Clyde responded. "They were just as they were when we had them placed in the gift room. But there is one thing. It's probably nothing, but just for your information, the gun that matches the missing Wyoming gun seems to have been fired. Remember, the agents all said that they didn't fire the guns, with the exception of the missing gun."

The Director leaned back and thought for a second before speaking, then said, "Unless you can find a reason how this will negatively affect us, I don't think it will be a problem. Do you, Clyde?"

"No, sir, I really can't think of how this can hurt us. But I thought you should know."

"Thank you, Clyde, but I'll have them at my residence so they will be safely out of sight and mind."

"That will be perfect, sir," Clyde responded. "Anything else, sir?"

"No, Clyde, except will you help me carry the briefcases to my car? I want to move them on."

"Absolutely, sir," Clyde concurred.

When the Director arrived at his residence, he immediately took the briefcases into the house and into his library, as he liked to call it. It was the study room where he kept many of the gifts that he received over the years. Actually, it was almost totally full of the largesse that he expected people of all stations in life to gift to him because of his position. *These guns will fit in very nicely,* he thought as he moved the "career loot" around so he could place the guns in a position where he could see them easily. He then opened each case, placed the full briefcase that housed the gun on a slanted display shelf behind his desk, and then stood back to admire them. *Looks perfect,* he thought. *It's too bad that the guns couldn't be labeled for their true historical value,* he sighed. *But I will know what they mean to this country, every time I enter this room.* No one had ever described the Director as showing a grin on his face, but if anyone had been there to see him staring at the guns and reliving the history of the moment, that is exactly what they would have seen—a huge grin on the face of the Director of the FBI.

CHAPTER 37

Gordon was already parked in his car in the same spot he had the night before—just a half block from Julie's house. He didn't like to repeat anything when he was on a stakeout, but for this particular operation he didn't feel the need to make too many changes. After all, these guys were not what you would call sophisticated or worldly in any way that would be comparable to the operatives that he spent his life trying to stay ahead of. *Totally amateurs,* he thought. *And totally a waste of my time. But Bud saved my life, and I'll always be loyal to his wishes. And his wishes are for me to tail these people on their wild goose chase.*

Inside the house, the guys were moving slowly, still feeling the lag of the long trip. But they were making progress. Bruce and Julie were ready and sitting in the dining room talking and just waiting for the other guys to finish up so they could hit the road and get breakfast before heading to D.C.

"C'mon you slackers," Bruce yelled out to no one in particular. He just was anxious to get going.

Steve came into the dining room looking refreshed and dressed in comfortable clothes like the tourist he was. "Hey, I'm ready," he said. "We are now just waiting on Chicken Man," he chuckled.

Bruce got up and walked over to the basement door and yelled down, "Hey, Chicken Man, let's go!"

Finally Mike shouted back, "Just cool your jets. I didn't have as plush sleeping arrangements as you did. But I'm almost ready." When he did come up the basement stairs, with a kind of limp and drag motion, he looked like he had gotten very little sleep. "I'm raring to go," he said. "But I gotta tell you Julie, that dog and cat of yours kept me up most of the night." He was referring to Julie's sixty-five pound mixed breed rescue dog that was the love of her life and her rescued grey tiger cat that followed the dog everywhere.

Julie laughed and asked, "Why? What did they do?"

"Well, for starters they came down and lay next to me on my blanket, but when I woke up, that stupid dog—Sorry, Julie, no offense," he apologized. "That silly dog was lying on top of me and the cat was lying in the middle of my suitcase on my clean bibs, which I am currently wearing. Neither one would move or give up any space, so that's the way we all slept, or didn't sleep. Plus," he continued, "I thought that I snored, but that cat has real problems. I thought there was a snoring old man sleeping right next to me. So needless to say, I'm a little tuckered out. But I'll make it as soon as I get some coffee into me."

Julie responded, "Oh, Mikey, I'm so sorry. I wondered where they were. They usually sleep close to me. I bet the dog kept you warm though," she laughed.

"Oh my god! She's a furnace." And then he let out the first guffaw of the day, "Haw, haw, haw." And startled the dog so much that she started barking and howling while the cat just ran away and hid.

"So much for your friends," Steve chuckled. "Are we ready to go?"

"Yep," Bruce said. "I'll drive. We are going to the eat breakfast at the Tasty Diner in Silver Spring."

"Good food and quick service," Julie added. "And only a few minutes away."

When Gordon saw everyone jump in the van and drive away, he waited for them to get at least a block ahead before pulling out and following. *Wow,* he thought. *That van makes it even easier to tail them. I probably didn't even need the GPS tracker. But ya never know.* He continued to follow at a safe distance, and when the van parked in the garage opposite the Diner, he guessed that they were going to get breakfast there. Gordon decided to go into the Diner to get a quick bite to eat too and to place himself strategically close to where they were sitting, so that he might overhear some of their conversation. His plan worked.

"Please seat me next to that table please," he told the waitress. Since the early morning breakfast crowd had thinned out considerably, the waitress nodded and complied with his request. When he sat down, he smiled to himself and thought, *Perfect. I can hear almost every word they are saying.* So he sat, ate, and listened. But he really didn't pick up anything more than he had already anticipated. *Well, they are going to the Department of Justice first, then to the FBI, and then to the Hoover Foundation. That makes perfect sense for them and it makes it easy for me to keep track of them.* Sensing that they were almost ready to go, he grabbed his bill and carried it to the cash register near the front door. *But things never go as smoothly as you want,* he thought. The cash register was jammed, and he had to wait and that was a problem because when he turned around, the three guys and Julie were standing behind him waiting too. *Dammit,* he swore to himself. *I didn't want them to be standing behind me, watching me, and noticing me. It's just human nature to study the person in front of you,* he thought. *So now they got a good look at me, and I'm just going to have to be more careful not to be seen as I follow them around. Shit!* he added for good measure. He could only hope that they were too busy talking to really take notice of him. And it appeared that they were. Finally, the register was fixed, he paid his bill, and he practically ran across the street to his car in the garage. Okay. *Get your head in the game,* he said to himself and waited for the group to come into the garage and get in the van.

He didn't have to wait long. The group crossed the street, still talking about how great the food was and carrying their to-go cups of coffee, and clambered into the van. Then Julie took over and started to guide her dad towards D.C. and to their first destination, the Justice Department.

"Okay Julie, get us there quickly," Bruce said.

"No problem," she responded. "We are past the hour of the worst traffic, so it should be smooth sailing. We need to hit North Capitol and virtually follow it all of the way downtown." She continued, "On the right, on the grounds of the Armed Forces Retirement Home, is Lincoln's summer residence."

Mike interjected, "This town has changed so much since the last time I was here back in the late sixties when I was in the Navy. It's amazing!" he exclaimed.

"What's more amazing," Bruce laughed out loud, "is that you can remember that far back."

Mike responded, "Julie, it's a good thing you are with us to keep our conversation civil. Otherwise I might have something to say about your dad's bloodlines. Haw, haw, haw."

Julie shot back, "Don't mind me. Give him what he deserves." And they all laughed.

Then Steve said, "Hey pay attention. Look, there's the Capitol. Oh my god, that is a majestic sight." The guys were mesmerized into silence for a moment.

Then Julie said, "At night if you see the light on in the Capitol tower, do you know what that means?" she asked.

"I do," said Steve. "It means that our representatives are in session."

"Wow," Julie said. "You are good. I've actually found very few people who are not from here who know that. Good for you."

Steve added, "I'm not just another pretty face." Which made Mike choke on his coffee, and Bruce snort up his mocha.

Laughing out loud, Julie continued her tour, "Over that way is Union Station. There's a pretty good restaurant in there. And over that way, on Pennsylvania Avenue and East Capitol, are some good bars that a couple of my friends own. The Department of Justice is located on Pennsylvania Avenue and so is the FBI Building, in fact right across the street. Basically, we are almost at our first destination. Let's find a parking spot and get going. Okay?" she asked. The guys all nodded in agreement, and Bruce located a parking spot that would allow access to both buildings.

Gordon was still behind the van and was anticipating their search for a parking spot. When he saw them turn toward a parking garage, he followed, and soon both the van and Gordon were parked and ready for the next step—which, for the guys and Julie, was to go into the Justice Building and, for Gordon, was to place a listening device inside the van. He needed to hear what they had to say after their little research party was over. Otherwise, he was just guessing. Walking up to the van, Gordon pulled out a universal remote that would activate the van's door locks and unlock it for him. He hopped in, picked his spot for the device immediately, and placed it in the front slot of the ceiling TV that would ideally pick up conversation from all over the van. In a matter of seconds, he was done and back into his car and would now wait for the group to come back. He knew that it would probably be awhile, so he settled in and put his mind on autopilot.

He sighed and thought, *I really hope Bud appreciates my efforts for him. This has got to be the most boring operation that I've ever been on.* Just as that thought crossed his mind, his phone rang.

"Hello, Bud," he answered. "What's up?"

Bud was on the line and said, "Just checking in. I figured you would be hunkered down and just mostly sitting and waiting. Anything happening, my good friend?"

"Well, you caught me just as I was about to take a cat nap," he said with a bit of smartass in his voice. "I'm just waiting for them to come back from their first research expedition into the Department of Justice and probably the FBI. So you're right. I am just sitting and waiting."

"Okay," Bud said. "Frank and I will catch up to you sometime later. Otherwise, call if there is anything strange. Talk to you soon," he said as he hung up.

Gordon just frowned, and thought, *This can't get over fast enough for me. What a snoozer!* And he waited.

Meanwhile, the guys and Julie had made their way into the main entrance of the Department of Justice. It was a massive structure, befitting the might and power of the law enforcement arm of the government in the United States. At first glance, it seemed like a daunting task to get to where they needed to go, but Julie marshaled the guys towards the information desk, smiled sweetly at the officer on duty, and found out pretty quickly what they needed to do in order to get started with their research.

She told the officer that, "We are looking for some information on Hoover and the FBI."

The officer gave the trio of friends the once over, stopping his gaze for a moment on Mike, and politely, yet pointedly, said, "If you are looking for research regarding J. Edgar Hoover or anything related to the FBI, you need to go to the FBI Building across the street. There you will find two reading rooms available for research. One is actually a virtual electronic reading room that you can access from anywhere, and the other room is a physical reading room."

Bruce asked, "We were wondering if the Department of Justice had kept anything regarding the Director of the FBI since his office used to be in this building."

The officer responded, "No, sir, it has all been moved to the building across the street. That happened in 2005. They will be able to answer all your questions over there."

Steve thanked the officer, "Thank you, sir," and then asked, "Any chance we could see where the FBI was housed in this building?"

"Yes, sir, but you must call ahead to schedule the visit."

"Okay, got it," he said. "Thanks."

Bruce looked at the gang and said, "Looks like we cross the street." Julie led them out of the building and across the street towards the main entrance.

Mike exclaimed as they went, "Hey, can we slow down a bit? We ain't running an Ironman race, are we?" and belly laughed his way into the FBI Building, drawing more than a little attention.

Bruce and Steve both shushed him at the same time, and Julie just laughed out loud. "Mikey," she said. "Don't pay any attention to these old curmudgeons. They're no fun. We'll slow down for you. But really! I thought with those snazzy white tennies of yours that you'd be leading the pack."

Mike threw both hands up, kept limping forward, and said, "I'm not sure, but that sounded a little like your dad talking."

"Oops, sorry," she said chuckling. "If I'm around him too much, he has a tendency to rub off on me." Continuing on, Julie led them to the information/security desk. "Hello," she said. "We are visiting from out of town and would like to do a little research on some areas regarding the FBI and J. Edgar Hoover's legacy. Could you get us to where we need to go?"

"Absolutely," the lady at the desk responded. "We have a research area that we call our reading room, and we also have a virtual process for going online to do research. We call that the Vault. Did you have a preference?"

Steve answered, "If possible, we would like to see the physical reading room first."

The lady responded, "That is fine, but you have to call ahead and give forty-eight hours' notice prior to using the room."

Bruce responded, "So we can't get in for forty-eight hours?"

"Sorry, sir, but that is correct," the lady said matter-of-factly.

Julie said, "Let's just schedule an appointment and then get some guidance on accessing the virtual electronic reading room."

The guys agreed and the lady at the desk sent them over to another information area where they were patiently given instructions on accessing the Vault.

Bruce asked the agent who was instructing them, "Can we make an appointment to visit the physical reading room for some research too?"

"Absolutely," was the response and the guys gave their forty-eight hours' notice for using the reading room.

Julie said, "It looks like that's all we can accomplish today, so do you guys want to take a break and get some lunch?"

Mike jumped in, "I vote yes. I'm starving." Bruce and Steve agreed, so they left the building with the information that they had been given and headed back to the van.

Gordon thought the group would be gone for far longer than they were, so he had ducked into a coffee shop in one of the nearby government buildings. *This is far better than waiting in the car,* he thought as he sipped on his second venti latte. Actually, it wasn't a true venti latte because he had poured a great deal of the contents of a silver flask that he carried in his coat pocket into it. *A little Baileys and espresso never hurt anybody,* he smiled to himself. *Except me,* he chuckled to himself. He knew that this was always how it started—the bingeing and the blackouts. But right now he was so freaking utterly bored that he didn't care. *I'll be fine. I can handle it this time.* At that moment his earpiece came to life. *What the hell?* he thought. *They can't be done yet. They really are amateurs.*

The voices coming through the piece were as clear as if he were sitting in the van with his targets. He always called his assignments targets, because he found over the years that more times than not they would all become targets. That was fine with him too. He checked the GPS to see where they were headed, but it appeared that they were still sitting in the parking structure, just talking.

One of the voices said, "Well, crap, it looks like it's going to take longer than we thought."

Another voice said, "Yes, but now we know. Plus we can get started by looking at the virtual records."

Then a girl's voice, "Actually, I think you guys will be glad you checked out the online archives first. It should give you some direction and define the scope of the records that you have to dig through."

The first man's voice agreed, "Yep, it should help, but it will be a long process. You know, I think we can all work on it when we get back to your house Julie. Stevie and I have laptops, you can use your desktop, and Mikey can drink," he laughed.

Gordon laughed at that comment, *I think I like that guy.*

The girl's voice said, "But I'm going to call Mindy for some help, too. She is so much better with computers and digging up information that I think we should ask her." Mindy was Julie's younger sister.

The other man's voice said, "The more help, the better."

The rest of the conversation revolved around lunch, and the GPS tracker started to move. So Gordon took his Baileys latte and headed back to his car to catch up.

It didn't take Gordon long to catch up. The van's GPS stopped moving on Pennsylvania Avenue SE, but the listening device kept working perfectly.

The girl's voice said, "Pull in there and park if you can. That's the restaurant a block down there. It's called Beuchert's Saloon and is owned by a friend of mine. I think it's pretty good food."

Then the less refined voice spoke up to say, "I don't care if they serve shoe leather, I'm starving."

Another male voice said, "My god, Mikey, you just had breakfast a couple hours ago."

Then a huge gut blowing laugh almost blew out the hidden microphone. "Take a look at this body. It takes a lot of fuel to keep it percolating the way that it does."

Gordon pulled in to park and watched as the van unloaded. He thought to himself again, *What the hell is Bud thinking and why am I here?* Then he decided to go in even though it went against surveillance protocol. One of the targets may recognize him from the Diner, but he doubted it. The liquor in his flask that had now been completely emptied into his latte was making him a little overconfident. He rethought the situation for a second then went in anyway. He had never been in this bar/restaurant before so he didn't know the layout. When he walked in, he was relieved to see the targets sitting in the back of the elongated building. *I'll just sit at the end of this bar and try to pick up something from their conversation,* he thought. The hardwood floors and plastered walls made that an easier task. The group's conversation bounced around the building and came right to his spot at the bar. *This is almost better than a bug,* he thought. So he watched and he listened and he drank. By the time that the group was finished eating, he had had at least four martinis. Add that to the flask and the latte, and he would have been considered drunk by any standards. But he didn't show it. He had years of practice covering it up. What he felt, though, was another thing.

"I just want to kick that guy's ass," he mumbled to himself.

The bartender only caught part of what he said, and asked, "What did you say?"

But Gordon didn't respond and was now openly staring at the table of friends, and in particular at Mike and his bib overalls and white tennis shoes.

Finally Steve took notice of Gordon and leaned forward at the table and said, "See that guy staring at us from the bar? He was at the Diner this morning for breakfast."

Bruce responded with a whisper, "You're right. I'd remember that old man and his black-dyed hair anywhere. Maybe we should go."

"This is a little strange." Julie agreed and said, "Let's go. We can pay at the other end of the bar, where my friend is standing."

Bruce and Steve looked at Mike, who was focused on the old man. "Mikey, just walk out quietly please. We don't know what this guy might be up to."

"Well, I'm going to find out," Mike blurted out and made a beeline for Gordon.

Everyone yelled "Mikey!" at the same time, but it was too late.

Gordon never flinched as Mike approached. *This could be fun,* he was thinking.

"Howdy, pardner," Mike said. "Didn't we see you at breakfast this morning? Is there something we can help you with?" Gordon just looked him up and down and said, "Get the hell away from me or you could get hurt."

Mike laughed a tense little laugh that didn't begin to show how the heat was rising within him. "Whoa, pardner, I'm just making conversation. We will just go, and you can cool off."

The booze spoke for Gordon, "Too late," he said as he swiveled the bar stool around to face Mike. "I think I'm going to kick your ass."

That was the straw that broke it for Mike. Almost instantly, Mike had pulled off his glasses, thrown them across the room, and moved toward Gordon. It was a reaction from years and years ago. At the same time, Gordon was reaching into his back pocket, pulling out a small blackjack that he was going to use to bash this rube's face in. But it never happened. Out of nowhere a three hundred pound blur came blasting in from the side, belly bucking Gordon and knocking him and his barstool over. Steve picked up Gordon and the barstool and threw them both off to the side, at the same time yelling for the bartender to call the cops, and yelling for his friends to leave. Gordon was dazed by the move and by the time he recovered, he knew that he too had to get out. By that time, his targets were in the van and gone. And he was feeling humiliated by what had just transpired.

I need a drink, he thought as he jumped into his car. He felt the need to lick his wounds so for now his surveillance was over. He texted Bud, "Not feeling well, need to take a break. Need you to take over for a while."

Bud looked at the text, thought to himself that something was up, but said, "Okay, will do. But contact me when you are up to it."

In the van, there was nothing but shocked silence.

Finally, Bruce said, "What the hell was that?"

Julie said, "I've been in this city for many, many years now and have never seen anything like that. Mikey, what were you thinking? You are not in Buffalo, Wyoming."

"Hey," Mike exclaimed. "I was just making conversation. That's what you do in Wyoming. That guy was just a crazy son of bitch. I will say, though, nice move Steve."

Steve laughed out loud, "Still got it, don't I? That was my patented Club 49 move from my days of working at that bar in Payne, Ohio."

"By golly, Stevie, you're right," Bruce said. "Mikey and I were there one night when you did the exact same thing."

"Yep," Steve said. "Old dogs don't learn new tricks, but they also never forget the old ones. I'm just glad that none of us got hurt. Plus, it didn't hurt that that guy was older than dirt," he chuckled. "It's amazing what kind of courage booze can give you. Right, Mikey?"

Everyone in the van laughed at that as the tension began to evaporate.

"Oh crap," Mike said. "I left my glasses there."

"No worries," Julie said. "I'll call my friend Nathan and he'll get them for you. By the way, that was way more excitement than I'm used to. It looks like this is going to be a visit to remember. Let's head home for a while to unwind."

They all sighed deeply and said, "Perfect."

CHAPTER 38

Bud picked up the tail on the van as it headed back to Takoma Park. He was blocks away, but with the GPS tracker he knew exactly where the guys were at that moment, and he knew they were heading back to the girl's house. Because of that, he was in no hurry to catch up to them. As was his custom, he had already taken care of what he needed to do. Anticipating the morning visit to downtown D. C. by the guys, he took the opportunity to slide into Julie's house and look around. And he placed several bugs throughout the residence. Bud thought matter-of-factly, *No need to hurry. I'll catch up on everything they talk about as soon as they get there.* And as usual, he was right.

Even though the three guys and Julie talked about the event that just happened all of the way home, the conversation continued on into the house. Julie was the most concerned by what had happened.

"I can't get over it," she said. "I've never seen anything like that. Do you think the guy was just targeting us to rob us?"

Bruce answered with a chuckle, "Heck no, he was just attracted to Mr. Bib Overalls here and wanted to make a statement about Mikey's sense of fashion."

Mike grunted and said quietly so Julie couldn't hear, "Yeah, right, I got your sense of fashion right here." Then he said loudly, "He was just an old demented nut who zeroed in on us for some reason. Sometimes there is no rhyme nor reason for crazy."

"Okay, okay, we need to forget it and get down to business," Bruce prompted. "We have got lots of work to do."

"Right," Steve agreed. "First things first. Hey, Julie, could you call Mindy and ask her to start looking at the electronic reading room?"

"Yep," she said quickly. "I'm on it."

Bruce added, "The rest of us should get our laptops out and get into the Vault too."

Steve said, "Yes, and we need to compare notes as we work. No sense duplicating our efforts."

Mike, on the other hand, had decided that the best thing for him to do was to fix himself a Jameson's on the rocks. "Julie, you are such a great hostess. How'd you know that I love Jameson's?"

Julie just smiled and said, "Oh, maybe from knowing you for over forty years?"

Mike smiled and took a big swallow, "Ahhhhhhh. Let me know if you need me to kick someone's ass. Jameson's always makes me feel stronger than I am," he guffawed as he walked towards the basement. "I'm gonna rest." Everyone else just shook their heads and got to work.

Bud, who was listening to every word of the conversation, just shook his head too. "Gordon, Gordon," he said to himself. "Now I know why you aren't feeling so well."

In the house, everyone was working diligently on getting into the FBI's virtual electronic reading room, or Vault, as the Bureau had named it. Julie had gotten connected with Mindy, so the group had three laptops and one desktop all working through the FBI records.

Steve said, "I think we would all best be served by going to the 'Guide to Conducting Research in FBI Records' first. It really gives a great overview of how to access the National Archives and Records Administration. It's called NARA on the website. From what I've seen in the Guide, this appears to be where the bulk of information from

Hoover was eventually filed. And by filed, I mean made accessible to researchers."

"Okay," Bruce said. "Let's all start there, and let Mindy follow her own path. She's leaps and bounds ahead of us in her capabilities. So we can compare our results to hers as we move through the process."

Everyone agreed and got busy. For Bud, listening in from down the street, this was a cue to take a break and record any further conversations.

He dialed Frank to update him, and said, "Hey, Frank, everyone's gone to quiet work mode. So I'm going to pull off and keep the recorder on. Let's get something to eat at that Mexican restaurant in Silver Spring—Mi Rancho."

Frank responded, "Great, I could go for a margarita."

When both guys reached the restaurant, they opted to sit in the outside covered eating area that had several dark corners. It was just customary to sit in the half lit or dark part of any restaurant that they frequented, and always with their backs to the wall. Bud smiled as they sat down, and Frank instinctively knew what he was thinking.

"Frank, do you ever get tired of this?"

"Well, if I had a choice, yes. But since I haven't had a choice in close to fifty years—hell no. It's why I'm still alive—being very good at being secretive."

Bud nodded his head in agreement. "It was our choice all those many years ago. And frankly, I can't imagine another way of living."

"My point exactly, Bud," Frank said.

After the waiter had taken their orders and brought them both a margarita with lots of salt, they settled in to chat for a while.

Frank asked, "Where are we going with this, Bud? I'm not sure I get it at this point. These country boys are working hard at what you hired them to do, but why are we so focused on every step they take to get to where you want them to be?"

Bud nodded and considered the question. Then he answered slowly, "Well, it's like this, Frank. I have run out of options for tying up the one last loose end of my life and my career. It's just a personal goal that I need to finish, and I have a gut feeling that these guys are just smart enough to figure it out for me. As long as I keep financing them, they will work their asses off to get the job done. That's been their history in life, and I have to believe in them. I've gone the professional investigative route, and it didn't work—too many questions and too much potential for opening a door that I can't close again if the wrong people get involved. These guys are nobodies, yet capable of getting it done without getting noticed. At least that's what I hope will happen."

Frank smiled, "I can see that. But frankly, everybody who cared is dead, so what could possibly be the danger here anymore?"

Bud just shook his head from side to side, and said, "Oh Frank, please don't be that naïve. There are any number of ruthless assholes out there who would do anything to protect the names and reputations of the guys who made this happen in the first place. One small misstep that would tie LBJ and the Director to the operation would be enough for immediate elimination of anyone involved. And that, my friend, is why I'm paying so close attention to my friends from Ohio and Wyoming. I want them to be successful, but I don't want them to be collateral damage in any way."

Frank nodded, "It's a good thing you're in charge here. This intrigue stuff is way over my head. I just hope it works for you. You deserve it," he said as he swallowed his third margarita with a smack of his lips. "Great choice of restaurants, Bud."

Bud laughed and then got serious, "We need to put Gordon on the shelf again. He's too unpredictable at this point. He's sick, drunk, and old."

Frank agreed, "And that's a bad combination in any line of work, but especially this one."

Bud continued, "I'll let him know tomorrow that we won't need him for a while. He'll be pissed, thinking he got fired, but it's the only thing I can do now. I just hope he stays away from the operation. If he doesn't, he's going to make it very dangerous for himself," Bud said as he stood to leave.

Frank nodded again in agreement and then stood up with Bud and followed him out of the restaurant.

Back at Julie's house, everyone was busily using the FBI's electronic reading room and working through the multiple files once belonging to Director Hoover. It was a laborious process by anyone's standards, but it was the best place to begin. Steve and Julie were making the most progress in their efforts and eventually found a relevant link between the FBI's archived Hoover files and an organization called the J. Edgar Hoover Foundation.

Steve asked, "Has anyone seen the information regarding Hoover's and Tolson's memorabilia?"

Julie responded, "Yes, and I've also got a link to that foundation that lists some of the memorabilia that was donated after Hoover and Tolson died."

"Right," Steve said. "I've found where over two thousand items of memorabilia have been donated to the new Law Enforcement Museum that is being constructed as we speak."

"Yep," Bruce added. "I've found that too, but I can't find a list beyond his desk and chair and other basic stuff. I really think that there has to be another list."

Steve agreed, "It's got to be buried in this information somewhere. Keep digging."

They continued late into the night, but had no real luck in pulling out the specifics that would lead them to the gifted Uberti Colt .45's.

Finally, worn out and having no better direction, Bruce said, "Let's call it a night and start again tomorrow morning."

Julie yawned and responded, "Works for me."

"Me too," Steve said. "It's been a good start to our hunt, and tomorrow should bring us a little closer. I have some ideas that I'm going to sleep on, and, hopefully, we can move forward in the morning."

"See you all bright and early," Bruce said as they all headed to bed.

After the house went quiet, Bud quit listening and hit the record switch. He smiled, *These guys are really taking this seriously. And I am excited to see how far they get. They are going to go through doors that I never wanted to open, even though I've always felt that what they are doing is the first step on my way to finding the missing merchandise. Good job, boys,"* he thought to himself as he, too, readied himself for bed and an early morning.

The next morning came quickly and loudly. Mike had awakened first in the house and decided he was going to make breakfast for everyone. With clanging pans and the loud clatter of drawers and doors opening and closing, it didn't take long for everyone else to crawl out of their arranged sleeping areas and slide down to the kitchen to see what was up.

Wide awake and bristling with energy from a long, sound sleep, Mike greeted them all with an ebullient, "Good morning!"

Bruce and Steve never ceased to be amazed, even after all these years.

Steve said, "He drank himself to sleep last night and look at him. Unbelievable."

Mike spoke loudly, "Hey, what's that supposed to mean?"

Bruce answered that question with, "Oh my god, you should have a hangover, and yet we seem to be the ones suffering."

Steve added, "But that's because we worked most of the night, and Chicken Man here dreamed of his flock of chickens with no apparent guilt that we were working and he was sleeping."

"Haw, haw, haw. Ain't life good?" Mike laughed. "I've got your breakfast ready, and I've got a vegetarian omelet for Julie. Always doing my part to help. Haaaaaaah," he snorted.

All Bruce and Steve were thinking, though, was, "I hope he washed his hands."

But they did enjoy the breakfast and chatted about their plans for the day.

Julie said, "Thanks for breakfast, Mikey. It was very tasty. As soon as we get ready, I think we should head out for the Foundation's office and do some poking around in person."

Steve agreed, "Exactly my thoughts. But first, I think we should check in with Mindy to see where she got to in her search."

Bruce nodded and picked up his phone and dialed Mindy's number.

"Good morning, Dad," Mindy yawned into the phone. "I was hoping you'd call. I was up late working on your research, and I think I found some good stuff for you."

Bruce responded as he put her on speaker phone, "Hey, that's great, sweetie. Whatcha got?"

Mindy continued, "The Vault was very helpful. However, I was also able to find out about the existence of an all-inclusive memorabilia list from some other sources who had previously done research on the many gifts given to Hoover and Tolson."

Bruce said, "Hey, that's what we were trying to find last night."

"Great minds think alike," Mindy replied. "Now listen closely, because you have a few different places to visit that might have the list.

First, you should go to the Masonic Temple. This is where the J. Edgar Hoover Foundation was housed and where their memorabilia was kept after both men died. Hopefully, you will find the list of the gifts there. If you don't, then your next step is to go to the new storage area for this same memorabilia. The gifts are being kept in a separate location near other memorabilia that will go into the National Law Enforcement Museum when it's completed. The Hoover Foundation made a deal with the National Law Enforcement Museum to gift all of their memorabilia to the museum. From reading through some blog posts about the move, I've learned that it was moved out of the Masonic Temple and put temporarily into a storage room in a building close to the new museum. I think the building is called the Pension Building, but I can't find it on the map. I believe that somewhere between the Temple, the Foundation, the Pension Building, and the Museum, you should find that list. And actually, it should be a hard copy. I think the information in the FBI's Vault only includes parts and pieces of records, so going in person is necessary. But I'll keep looking online later today, after the kids' soccer games."

Steve jumped in to say, "Nice job, Mindy. I think we were heading in that direction, too, but you got there a lot faster than us."

"Yes, thanks, kiddo," Bruce added. "Okay, looks like we have a plan for today and tomorrow. We'll keep you informed and you do the same for us. Love ya. Give the kids a hug from me and wish them luck at their games," he said as he hung up.

Julie added, "Okay, guys, let's get ready, so I can lead you around and make good use of our limited time."

Bud looked at Frank as they sat quietly in their car parked a block away from the house and said, "Looks like it's going to be an interesting day."

Frank nodded, "Or at least a long day," and sighed.

CHAPTER 39

Bruce hopped behind the steering wheel and waited patiently for his entourage of friends to load up the van. As usual Mike was the last one in because he couldn't withstand the temptation to quickly light the huge 5 Vegas Maduro Torpedo cigar that he had been carrying around between his lips all morning—even while he was cooking breakfast. Bruce yelled at him as he hunkered into his seat, the captain's chair immediately behind Bruce.

"Mikey, no smoking in the van! Especially that cigar!"

His response was quick, "I ain't smoking—I took a couple of drags and put it out—that's my new aftershave you're smelling. Haaaaa, Haaaaaaa! Pretty good stuff, ain't it, buddy?"

Steve responded, "Mikey, I think your bibs are on fire! Your pocket is smoking!"

Immediately, Mike looked at his pocket and started smacking his chest where the smoke was coming from. "Holy shit!" he exclaimed. "I've got it." And he pulled out a smoldering cigar that had reignited in his pocket after he thought he had put it out.

Bruce joined in, "No wonder I thought you were smoking—you were!" He laughed out loud with everyone else in the van—even Mike.

Steve added, "Mikey, I love the smell of the cigar, but your bibs smell like burning chicken feathers!" Of course, that brought the house down with laughter.

"Sure, go ahead and have fun at my expense," Mike guffawed.

Julie said through her laughter, "Roll the windows down and get this chicken coop moving." It was a great beginning to their day's quest, and it was also good for Bud and Frank. The two guys were still laughing as the van pulled out and passed their parked car.

Bud looked at Frank who was just shaking his head and said, "That's my friend, one of a kind." And then he pulled out into the street to follow the van.

Julie took charge and guided the guys towards downtown D.C. again.

"Okay, Dad, the Temple for the Freemasons is located on 16th and S streets in NW D.C. near Dupont Circle. So it will take about the same amount of time as yesterday, but we will go a slightly different direction."

Bruce responded, "You guide, I'll listen."

"Perfect," Julie said, and navigated the trip downtown into an easy twenty-five minute drive. "There it is," she pointed. "It's that huge magnificent white stone building."

Everyone stared at the structure that seemed to have been lifted out of Egypt or Greece and set down intact in D.C. It was historical and breathtaking, even for three guys who really weren't that interested in architecture.

"Wow, that's quite a building," Bruce said first.

"Yes, it is," added Steve.

Mike agreed with a grunt and a verbal acknowledgement of, "Wow. Looks like it's going to be a long walk—again."

Julie said, "It won't be that bad. That's why you still have on those snazzy white tennies." She turned and went back to directing Bruce and said, "Dad, the only parking is on the street. That spot looks good. We'll get two hours at a time."

Bruce responded with, "Okay," and pulled into the parking spot about a half block down from the building. The group exited the van and headed to the main entrance. Bud, following the van from about a block away, decided to park too and pulled into one of the two hour spaces. He and Frank decided to wait a few minutes before following the group into the massive structure. He had been here many times but had always been very careful about his research. If anyone had recognized him from his past association with the Director, there would have been too many questions. And, from all of his professional contacts, he had become aware that there were many zealots supporting the Director's foundation who would do anything and everything to protect the historical integrity of J. Edgar Hoover.

He thought of this as he and Frank waited. *Who would ever think that such a charitable organization would have a dangerous element to it?*

Julie entered the Temple first, followed by Bruce, Steve, and, pulling up the rear, Mike. The first impression as they walked through the door was unanimous, "Oh my god." Then "Look at this place" and "How beautiful and artful" were some of the comments by everyone except Mike.

He just looked at the massive floor space, the huge grand staircase, and said, "Oh shit! This place ain't built for an old guy like me. You think they got a place to sit down?"

Bruce laughed and said, "Mikey, pretend you're walking on your thirty-five acre ranch and you'll be fine."

Mike answered, "Oh, I'll make it, but you guys don't wait on me. I'll eventually get there."

The group stopped at an information desk and asked about the Hoover/Tolson collection, indicating that they were huge fans of the Director.

The man at the desk was pleased to hear that, but said, "I am sorry to say, though, that the Hoover Foundation memorabilia is no longer housed in this Temple. It has been put in storage near the site of the new Law Enforcement Museum that is to be completed in 2015. But I'm sure our library would have some references to the makeup of our former display of memorabilia. Please follow me," he said as he shepherded the group towards the library.

Everyone continued to marvel at the magnificence and elegance of the building's interior as they followed the guide.

Approaching the library, the guide slowed and said, "The librarian will help you get started, and you can use the reading room for a work space."

"That will be perfect," Steve said. "Thank you so much."

When they entered the library, they were further awed by the quantity of materials on display and by the rich dark wood structures, including the tall sliding ladders that accessed the stacks.

"This place is incredible," Bruce whispered to Steve. "It looks like it came from a movie."

Julie heard him and said, "I'm sure that it has been in some movies. It's not unusual for moviemakers to use places like this to shoot."

Just then another gentleman entered, said that he could help them, and asked what they were looking for. He was rather stuffy and obviously impressed with himself and his position as the guardian of the library. But he was helpful and quickly informed the group that, even though the memorabilia collection was no longer housed there, he thought that there were some records available. He pointed the way for them to get started and the search was on—old-school style. The guys and Julie pored through the card catalogs and pulled everything that was remotely connected to the Director and his memorabilia.

It was obviously going to take a while so Julie said, "I'm heading out to fill the parking meter with quarters again so that we can have two more hours. The last thing we need is to have the van towed."

On her way out, she clearly heard someone shout, "YES!" and as she turned to listen, she ran smack dab into Bud, who had also heard the shout and turned quickly in response.

"Oh, I am so sorry," Julie exclaimed.

"No, it was my fault, I am sorry," Bud said as he turned to the side so that she wouldn't get a good look at him. "Pardon me." Then he quickly walked away towards Frank, who was also waiting outside the library.

Frank asked, "What was that?"

Bud quickly muttered, "That was unlucky is what that was."

Frank said, "No, I mean the shout."

"Oh, of course. I'm betting that that was Mike and that he found something," he answered.

He was right. In the library, Mike had been looking at old-school microfiche. It's what he knew from his past as a library aide in college.

"I've found something," he said to the other guys, only a little too loud.

Bruce shushed him and said, "That's great, but don't get us thrown out before we can check it out."

Mike said, "Okay, okay, I just got excited."

Steve hustled over to Mike to see what he had found. There it was. It was a microfiche of an old sign-in sheet from something called the FBI gift room. "Oh my god, Mikey, that looks like it could be what we are looking for."

"I hope so," Mike responded. "See, boys, I ain't just another purty face," he laughed, prompting Bruce to shush him again.

Bruce added, "Nice job, buddy. How'd you find it?"

"Well, that's what I used to do, work with microfiche at the college library. The records from the time period we are looking at had to be put on microfiche. They are probably transferred to something else now, but this was the method of choice for records back then."

Steve agreed, "You are so right. So, let's hope it's the record we need to point us in a direction."

They all gathered around Mike as he ran the microfiche, each hoping and holding his breath. "My god, the Director received a lot of gifts. And it seems that they were all kept in this basement gift room at the Department of Justice," Mike continued. "Well, not all of them. It appears that the guy routinely took things out of the room for personal display, either in his office or in his home." He shook his head, "There is an amazing amount of stuff listed." Suddenly he lifted his hand, looked up, and said, "There it is. A notation from 1963 saying that Assistant Director Tolson signed out three briefcases containing Uberti Colt .45's for display purposes."

"Wow! There's the smoking gun, so to speak," Steve laughed.

The men high-fived each other just as Julie re-entered the room. "Looks like you found something," she said.

"We think so," said Bruce.

"Way to go," Julie responded.

"We found some gifted guns, but we haven't found the serial numbers yet," Mike added.

"Right," Steve said. "So, we need to look earlier for when the guns were first entered into the record."

"Yep," Mike said deeply concentrating on the microfiche. "I'm reading as fast as I can." Then he yelled "Eureka!" which prompted the librarian to move in the guys' direction. Mike looked up at the librarian, and said, "Oh, sorry, pardner, I got a little excited there. It won't happen again."

With a stern politeness the librarian said, "If it does, I will have to ask you to do your research online. We have a certain decorum that must be followed." But before he walked away, he said, "Do you mind if I ask what is causing the excitement?"

The guys looked at each other, and Bruce nodded to Steve.

"Certainly, sir," Steve said. "As you know, we are looking for records of J. Edgar Hoover's memorabilia and finally came across what we are most interested in. We are gun collectors and are interested in a certain set of guns that the Director was given back in 1962. We think we just found evidence of their existence."

"Well, that is great luck on your part," the librarian said. "But you do know that we no longer house any of the memorabilia in the Temple, don't you?"

"Yes, sir, we do," Bruce responded. "We just needed to verify that they did exist and that the Director and Mr. Tolson received them as gifts. Our goal is to find them and see them."

The librarian nodded as he walked away. "Continued good luck then," he said. However, he wasn't smiling as he walked away. Instead, he was remembering a directive that he had received long ago, when the Temple first became the guardian for the Director's memorabilia. "If anyone ever acts suspiciously or seems to be conducting research that might be detrimental to the legacy of the Director, you must bring that to the attention of the Grand Master immediately." So that is exactly what he did. He didn't even wait until the so-called gun collectors finished their research before notifying his superior.

Meanwhile, Mike kept plugging away at the microfiche. "What we want are the serial numbers and to see if the guns are still a part of the memorabilia," he said to Steve and Bruce.

"Absolutely," Steve said. "The serial numbers will lock it down for us and give us a better direction."

"Wait!" Mike shouted with a whisper after his previous admonition. "Oh my god, here are the numbers. There's a notation that shows Tolson signing out four guns and briefcases on September 8, 1962. The serial numbers are R80001, L80001, and R80002, L80002. And now I found where they were returned by a Miss Gandy in December 1963, except that the gun with the R80001 serial was kept by Hoover for display." Mike stood up, high-fived the other guys and Julie, and said "Hell yes!" with a huge smile. "There we go boys. We are hot on the trail."

"Yes, we are!" Bruce laughed. "I think we can move on to our next stop. Let's get copies of this from the librarian and head out."

After receiving the copies that they needed, they turned to leave, but first, the librarian looked at each one of them and, with a solemn expression on his face, said very seriously, "Thank you for visiting. Please remember that it is our obligation to maintain and protect our Brother, J. Edgar Hoover's legacy, at all costs." Then, as if he felt the need to reinforce his statement, he repeated the phrase one more time with extra emphasis on, "at all costs."

When they all got into the van, Steve said what everyone was thinking, "Did you all catch the veiled threat in that guy's thank you?"

"Hell, yes, pardner," Mike said. "Nothing at all to catch there. He was telling us to be careful about what we did with anything related to the Director."

"No ifs, ands, or buts," Bruce said.

Julie joined in too. "You guys just need to be careful. This is D.C. and politics in this town can get ugly real fast and can get people hurt."

Bruce asked rhetorically, "But how is this politics? We are just looking for a gun."

Julie responded, "It's all about perception, Dad, and if someone with ties to Hoover's past or legacy feels like there may be something more going on in your hunt for the gun, it's game on for them. They will do anything and everything to stop you from doing what you are doing. It may sound crazy and paranoid, but it's a cold hard fact here in this city."

Steve agreed, "As we move on with this thing, we need to look over our shoulders and be very specific about why we want to check out the guns. The Director needs to be our hero, so to speak. We never say anything negative, and we never look for anything except the guns."

Everyone nodded in agreement as they pulled away from the Temple and started to head for the future home of the Law Enforcement Museum.

At the same time, Bud and Frank looked at each other and nodded.

Bud said, "I hope they follow that approach as they keep digging. That young lady is so right. And the last thing we want to do is put these people in some sort of jeopardy. Let's see what happens next," he muttered, as he pulled into traffic to follow the van.

As the van headed to the Law Enforcement Museum, Julie spoke up. "Dad, I think we need to change our destination," she said as she referred to her smartphone. "I think we need to find the Pension Building that Mindy mentioned. The memorabilia is currently in storage there. The building should be adjacent to the Law Enforcement Memorial, which in turn is adjacent to the soon-to-be-completed Law Enforcement Museum near Judiciary Square, however, it's not coming up on my map either. So when we get to the plaza at Judiciary Square, we need to look between Pennsylvania Avenue, H Street, and Interstate 395."

"So you think it has changed names?" Steve asked.

"That's what I'm betting," Julie said.

"Perfect," Bruce said. "Let's get down there then."

After several minutes of fighting a surge of traffic, Bruce finally guided the van into a parking spot on the street in front of a building called the National Building Museum.

Julie said, "This is it! I bet this used to be called the Pension Building, but now it's this museum."

All of the guys let out an "Oh my god," at the same time.

"Look at the size of the damn place," Mike complained. "Don't they have any buildings with easy access for us old folks?"

Steve said sympathetically, "I'm with ya, Mikey. Looks like we have lots of 'miles to go before we sleep,'" referencing Robert Frost.

"Well, let's get out and get it done," Bruce said. "Then we can take a break."

As they walked the long sidewalk leading to the entrance, they had to reign in Julie's fast walking more than once. "Julie, slow down. You're killing me," Mike said with Steve and Bruce's support.

"Sorry, guys," she said. "I have just one speed in the city. But we are almost there."

When they entered the building, they were greeted first by security and then by an elderly female information officer. After listening to their queries about the Hoover memorabilia, she graciously sent them to a young information officer named Andrew who she said should be able to help. She was right.

"Why yes, we do have memorabilia from the J. Edgar Hoover Foundation in storage here," Andrew said. "Unfortunately, it is not out for public display at this time."

Julie took over at that point and played the cutsie gender card with the young, good-looking guy. "Oh no," she said. "My Dad and his friends have traveled all of the way from Wyoming and Ohio to catch a peak at that memorabilia. We missed it at the Masonic Temple, and now we seem to have missed it here. Is there any way or anyone we can talk to and see if we can just see what's here? They won't be able to get back this way together, for maybe never," she said with a huge sweet smile.

"Well, you plead your case very well. Let me talk to my boss and I'll be back," he said returning her smile.

"Thank you, sir," she said, with sugar and honey in her voice.

"Well, that's the kiss of death," Steve said. "The boss never wants to be bothered. He probably just walked around the corner and is counting to one hundred and then will come back to say, 'Sorry, rules are rules.'"

Bruce agreed, "Yep, that seems to be how it works at all levels."

Julie just smiled and waited.

When Andrew came back, he was actually beaming. "I'm sure you didn't expect this, but I got approval to show you the room where the memorabilia is being stored. The best pieces have been set up for display, and I guess the plan is to open it to the public very soon. So, the boss said to go ahead and show you the room, as long as I have security along."

Surprised but elated by the decision, they all thanked Andrew profusely for his efforts as he led them, surrounded by gigantic pillars from the past, through the cavernous main room. Mike even invited him out to Wyoming to shoot prairie dogs.

The young man laughed out loud and said politely, "Now that would be something I've never done before. I'll consider it."

After walking what seemed like a mile and a half inside the coliseum-like building, Andrew greeted a security officer and said, "Here it is." Unlocking the door, he said, "There are display ropes in place, and I have to ask you to remain behind the ropes as you view the exhibit."

"Absolutely," came the response from Julie and the guys in unison. The room was jam-packed with all sorts of stuff including the Director's desk chair, his desk, file folders with famous names written in bold print, and all sorts of books and letters. There were rifles and shotguns and pistols—even a small Derringer. And then, almost leaping out at them from the far side of the small room, there were the briefcases with the guns they were looking for.

"No way!" Bruce exclaimed under his breath.

"Oh my god!" Steve kind of whisper-shouted.

"I'll be goddamned!" Mike swore out loud and then said quickly, "Sorry, Julie."

Julie smiled and said, "No worries. So, I take it that these are what you were looking for." In an instant, they were all standing right in front of the briefcases. They moved across the room so fast that the officer and the security guard were somewhat startled.

When Andrew caught up to the movement, he immediately reiterated, "Remember. You may only go up to the display rope—and no touching."

The security guy moved to a vantage point where he could see everything the guys and Julie would do from then on. But no one in the group noticed. They were mesmerized by the sight of what they had come so far to find and were paying no attention to anything else around them. Each gun was displayed in the same opened silver briefcase that the Director had kept it in at his home.

Steve was first to speak, "Look at them. They are beautiful, and they have the Old West finish that the guns we are looking for have."

Bruce added, "And they have the 7.5-inch barrels. We just have to see the serial numbers." He looked at the young officer and asked, "Andrew, is there any way you could jump behind the rope and read the serial numbers for those guns to us?"

The young officer looked at the security guard, moved towards him, and whispered something in his ear. The guard nodded, and Andrew said, "Yes, I can do that." Unhooking the display rope, he approached the three briefcases and bent over to see if he could see the numbers. He couldn't.

Steve spoke quickly, sensing that he was going to give up, "The numbers should be just under the barrels in front of the trigger."

The young man nodded, "Okay, I'll try," he said as he slid on a pair of white gloves and then lifted the first Colt out of the case to turn it over.

"Here it is," he said and then read the number on the first gun slowly. "L80001," and placed it carefully back in its display case. He did the same with the other two guns, "L80002 and R80002."

The guys all took a collective deep breath and Bruce said, "Thank you, buddy. Those are the numbers we wanted to hear. Especially the L80001." He continued, "Do you think there is anything in here that could tell us where the matching gun for that Colt is?"

Andrew responded, "Well, yes, as I look in this notebook, I see that there is a notation from Miss Gandy regarding the guns. She noted that the Director was keeping the matching gun with serial number R80001 for display at his residence. So I guess there were actually four guns given as gifts to the Director from Uberti Firearms."

"Wow, thank you very much," Steve said. "So if you were us, looking for this other gun, where would you go next?"

The young officer thought for a minute before speaking. "I think I would go to the FBI research library and also possibly speak to someone with something to do with the Law Enforcement Museum. The FBI is where the gift originated, and the Museum is where these guns will end up.

"Perfect," Steve said. "And one more thing, can we take cell phone pictures of these guns?"

"No problem," responded the young man. After taking the pictures and on their way out of the building, Julie and the guys thanked Andrew profusely for his help. The young man smiled and said, "My pleasure to help," and slipped Julie his card with his cell phone number on it. "Anything else I can help with, please call. Have a great day."

They all responded with, "We will now, thanks to your help."

Meanwhile, Bud and Frank had been anxiously waiting for the guys to finish up. Bud had decided not to go into this building because he couldn't afford to be seen by Julie again, or even Mike. He was disguised with a different hat, glasses, and jacket, but he didn't want to take any chances. *Besides,* he thought, *As soon as they get in the van, I'll have the bug on to find out the what, where, and when of their next move.* And that's precisely what happened. Once back in the van, the chatter began. Frank even noticed that there seemed to be an uptick in the excitement level.

"Wow, Bud," he said. "What the hell happened in there?"

Bud responded, "I believe, my good friend, that they may have found something."

Bruce confirmed it for Bud a moment later. "Well, guys," he said. "That made this trip worthwhile."

Bud, listening intently, sat straight up with the next words from Bruce. "Finding those guns is off the charts unbelievable."

Steve added, "Yes, it is. And to match the serial numbers almost gave me a hard....." he looked quickly at Julie, said "sorry" and then said, "I meant heart attack."

Everyone in the van laughed and continued the excited chatter. Bud and Frank, though, were now in full go mode.

"We have got to find out just what guns they are talking about for sure," he said to Frank.

"Absolutely," Frank said. "They'll probably tell us as they talk about it, but we need to get back in that building to check it out."

Bud agreed, "Absolutely, and very soon," he said as he pulled into traffic to maintain his tail on the van. However, as he was maneuvering through the always heavy D.C. traffic, trying to maintain a safe distance from the van and listening to the talk coming from the implanted bug in the van, he was suddenly taken aback by something he absolutely didn't want to see.

"Frank, look over there. I guarantee you that that car over there is also following the van."

Frank looked and frowned, then said, "You're right."

"Who the hell could that be? And why?" Bud added. They watched the non-descript black SUV all of the way to the van's next destination, the site of the new National Law Enforcement Museum. "Once we get parked, I'm going to call in the plate number and find out who these jokers are," he said, looking directly at Frank.

Bruce parked the van per Julie's directions and said, "Wow, look at this place. It's going to be amazing as usual."

Julie agreed, "Yep, Dad, they don't build cheap in D.C.—but this one will be unique—it will be mostly underground."

Mike jumped in with, "All I can see is more walking, walking, walking. Size matters, but why does everything in this town have to be counterproductive to old folks, like us, to get around? This is just horseshit!" he groused.

Steve turned to look at Mike and said, "Just behave or we will leave you in the van."

Mike rejoined with his "Haw, haw, haw! That won't hurt my feelings. But I am the chief investigator who found where the guns were, am I not? Can you novices get it done without me?"

Everyone rolled their eyes and Bruce said, "You go ahead and stay here and rest. We'll call you if we need you."

"Perfect," Mike said as he feigned hurt feelings. But he had no problem leaning back in the captain's chair and relaxing. "See you in a few," he said as everyone else exited the vehicle. What happened next was right out of the Twilight Zone for Mike. He fell asleep immediately and was sawing logs when the side door to the van opened quietly. Not opening his eyes, he mumbled, "How'd it go?"

"Better than we anticipated," came back a voice he didn't recognize. It jolted him to an instant awareness that someone was sitting behind him in the van. The voice said quietly, "Just relax pal," and Mike felt the cold hard steel from a gun barrel press into the back of his neck.

"What the hell?" Mike stammered. "I don't have any money, but take my wallet."

The voice shot back, "I don't want your money. I just want to know what you people are looking for and why."

Mike stammered, "Listen, pardner, we are just looking for guns for a gun collector. That's all. It's a hobby of ours."

"Well, my bosses think you've nosed around enough," the voice continued. "Let it go and get the hell out of D.C. Share that with your buddies. I'm leaving now, so close your eyes again and count to one hundred. If I see you looking around, I'll come back and put you to sleep permanently. Got it?"

Mike didn't hesitate and closed his eyes. "No problem, pardner," he said as the man left the van. Mike started to count.

Bud and Frank were parked about a block away when the man entered the van. Bud said, "Oh my god, that's not good. We need to get up there," and jumped out of their car and started moving towards the van. Both men had their hands around their weapons tucked away in their waistbands and were moving as fast as they could for a couple of old guys. It wasn't fast enough. When the man jumped back out, he immediately hopped into the car that had been tailing the van and was gone in an instant. Bud said, "We're too late. Let's hope Mike is okay and get back to our car. We can listen to what happened when everyone comes back, and we need to flag that license plate now."

Frank nodded, and both men turned back to their car and got busy checking on the plate.

Mike, on the other hand, was in no hurry to finish his count to one hundred and just kept counting. He counted slowly with his eyes closed. "Oh my god," he said quietly to himself. "I think I just lost ten years off my life." Finally, Mike reached the magic number—actually he reached it three times. He slowly opened his eyes, rotated his body to look around in the van, and sighed, "So far so good." Then he opened the side door of the van, crawled out, and stood for a moment. He reached into the top pocket of his bib overalls and pulled out one of his long, black Maduro cigars, lit it with a match from a matchbook that said Tasty Diner, and took a long drag. Exhaling the smoke, he leaned back against the van with his head the centerpiece of the blue cloud that enveloped him. "Oh my god, oh my god," he just kept repeating as he took drag after drag from the cigar and waited for his buddies to return.

Back a block and a half, Bud and Frank were relieved to see Mike crawling out of the van with seemingly no ill effects. They were moments from heading back to the van when they saw him.

Bud looked at Frank and said, "Well, he seems to be okay—maybe a little bit shaken—but okay. So let's sit tight, wait for the others to return so we can hear the story, and hopefully we'll get a hit on the plate."

Frank nodded, "Seems like that's all we can do at this point."

On the other hand, all that Mike could do at this point was to speed-smoke his cigar, think about what had just happened, and wait for everyone to return. It didn't take too much longer. He could see everyone returning from the museum site and couldn't wait to tell them what happened.

Bruce yelled at him, "Hey, Mikey, thought you were gonna nap!"

Mike responded, "Oh, I did—for a few minutes."

Julie then said, "Oh no, Mike! You're smoking another cigar. Hope you don't burn your bibs off this time," she laughed. He put out the cigar and climbed back into the van and waited for everyone to get in.

"Well, we didn't find anything here," Steve said. "Seems that even though it will be the future sight for Hoover's memorabilia, they haven't received a complete list of what they will be getting from the Foundation. So next stop will be the FBI Building again. But that will be tomorrow—remember?"

"Yeah, yeah, yeah," Mike said. "I got your tomorrow for you. Are you guys ready to listen yet?" Mike asked with a serious tone that got everyone's attention.

"What's up?" Bruce asked. "Are your bibs on fire again?" he laughed out loud.

"Hell no. This is serious," Mike answered quickly. Everyone quieted down and Mike began, "Well, I'm sleeping and the door to the van opens. I think it's you guys so I don't pay attention. The next thing I know I've got a gun pressing into the back of my neck with a guy telling me that we need to stop our search for the guns and go home."

"What?" everyone yelled at once.

"Bullshit!" Steve said. "You were dreaming."

"Like hell," Mike said. "That gun was very real. He had me count to one hundred after he left and, by god, I did."

Julie chimed in, "What are you guys doing that you have guys like the one at the bar and this guy threatening you? I've lived here for ten years and never even heard of anything like this. I don't get it."

Bruce said, "I certainly don't know, but we need to head back to your house, Julie, and sort this out. I think we may be getting into something that's way over our heads."

Julie added, "I told you, Dad. You have to be careful with politics in this city."

Steve agreed and said, "I thought you were just telling us a story, Mikey. Sorry. Are you okay?"

Mike responded, "Yes, pardner, I am. My blood pressure is probably elevated, but I'm good. That bastard was lucky that I left my .44 at Julie's."

With that, Bruce pulled out of the parking spot and headed away from downtown D.C. towards Takoma Park and Julie's house.

Bud and Frank pulled out after the van, but soon turned and went in another direction. After seeing what happened and after listening to Mike's account of the incident, Bud decided that he needed to get that plate run quickly. And he also decided to bring Gordon back into the picture.

"We need Gordon to keep an eye on these guys again, but not to spy on them. We need him to keep these guys safe," he told Frank. "So we're heading back to Wisdom to meet Gordon and see if he's up to it."

Frank nodded in agreement, "Yep, we need his help."

CHAPTER 40

Almost immediately after they entered Julie's house, Bruce's phone rang. The voice was unmistakable. It was the Grizzly Bear. He didn't say hello, or how are you, or what's up? He just growled, "Which one of you pussies am I talking to?"

Bruce sighed resignedly at Bear's insult and responded, "Hey, Bear. How are you? What's up?"

Bear ignored the greeting and growled even deeper into the phone, "You boys doing any good out there? I'm just making sure you're doing what I told you to do."

Bruce answered the question, "Hell yes, we are, Bear. And guess what? We just found three of the Uberti's that the Director received as a gift set from Aldo Uberti. The fourth one is missing and that's what we are going to try to track down in the next day or so."

Bear responded, "That's better than I expected. Keep me informed. I can smell a finder's fee coming my way," he laughed with his deep guttural growl.

Bruce asked, "You got anything more for us?"

"Hell, yes," came back the growl. "I've found most of those other guns for you, but I'll wait 'til you get back to tell you about them. Keep me informed," came the growl as he hung up.

As usual in conversations with Bear, Bruce had more to say, but couldn't get it out before the hang up. "Every damn time," he swore.

"What?" Julie asked.

"Oh, it's nothing really," he answered. "I just never get finished with this guy before he hangs up on me."

Steve jumped in, "It's because he doesn't respect you. We need to sic Mikey on him sometime. That will earn his respect," he laughed.

"Wonder how many times Bear has been threatened at gunpoint?" Mike said, "Speaking of which, we need to discuss this thing and what happened."

"You are so right," Bruce said. "Tell us again exactly what the guy said."

"Frankly," Mike said. "I can't remember his exact words. It's hard to think straight with a cold metal gun barrel shoved up against your neck. But the gist of it was for us to quit poking around and go home."

"No reasons given?" Steve asked.

"Nope," Mike answered. "Just quit and go home."

Julie jumped in, "Well, I will say that it is pretty obvious from an outsider's perspective that you are making someone nervous about these guns. First, the guy at the bar, and now this," she said.

"Plus, the veiled threat at the Foundation," Steve added.

"Right," Mike said. "And remember that Bud told me these guns were a part of an operation from the past that he was involved in, and he needed to find them before he died."

Bruce added it all up and said, "Boys, we need to decide if we want to continue with this. It could get more dangerous. And I'm not sure the money we will make is worth the risk. I tell you what," he continued with a serious tone. "We need to let Bud know what's happening and get his take on it."

Everyone nodded in agreement and Mike said, "I'll call him in a few. I don't think he wants us to get hurt, either."

Bud and Frank were in a hurry to get to Wisdom. After several attempts, they had finally hooked up with Gordon, and he seemed willing to help again.

"The question with Gordon's help is whether he can be contained and not become overzealous in his attempt to help us," he said to Frank.

"Exactly," Frank agreed. "But we do need his help and, if necessary, he can and will be the muscle we may need, albeit old muscle," Frank chuckled.

Bud smiled at this, too, thinking to himself how old he feels sometimes. But nevertheless, he felt confident that Gordon could still take care of himself. As they arrived at the bar, Bud's phone rang, and he got the call he had been waiting for. He took the information with only a few words—"Yes. Thank you. I owe you." In a matter of seconds he was done and looking at Frank. "Well, we know whose car it is."

Frank looked back at him with a questioning silence.

"It belongs to the big guy at the Temple—the Grand Commander."

Frank just said, "What?" and followed it with a "Why?"

Bud responded with, "I guess we need to find out," as they entered the bar.

Inside the bar, Bud ordered two absinthe drinks and a water with lemon as they walked past the bar towards the darkened back portion of the building. He didn't see Gordon, but he knew he was there watching them. So when he sat down and Gordon suddenly appeared from the shadows in the back, he was not surprised.

"Gordon, thank you for coming down so quickly." Gordon just nodded and Bud continued, "Do you feel ready to help us again?"

Gordon hesitated then said, "If you need me, Bud, I'll help you."

When the drinks arrived, Bud watched Gordon's reaction to the water with lemon. "You okay with that?" he asked.

"Yes, I'm good." Gordon responded. "I'm off the juice again."

"Perfect," came Bud's reply.

Feeling more confident in Gordon's ability to help, he proceeded to explain the situation. The only caveat that he included in Gordon's duties was that he could use deadly force if necessary to save his life or the lives of Mike and his buddies.

"I'm okay with that," Gordon agreed. "If there is nothing else, I'll get on it."

Bud replied, "No, that's it. Thank you."

They watched Gordon disappear into the shadows from where he came in.

Frank smiled, "I think he'll be okay for a while. So what about the Grand Commander?"

Bud answered, "I think that will require a personal visit. Let's do it now."

As they stood up to leave, though, Bud's phone rang again. When he checked, he saw that it was Mike. He debated whether he should answer it or not, but finally did. "Hello, Mike, how are you?"

"Hey, pardner, this is your old buddy from Wyoming. Are you busy?"

Bud couldn't help but smile every time he talked to Mike. "Never too busy for you, Mike. What's up?"

"Great," Mike said. "Well, I'm here in D.C. with my buddies looking for those guns you want so badly and, believe it or not, we found some of them."

"That's great, Mike," Bud responded. "Are you sure?"

"Absolutely!" Mike exclaimed. "The serial numbers match and everything else looks good. But one of the matched sets has one gun missing, so we are still on the hunt— or I should say that we might be still on the hunt."

Bud asked, "What do you mean, Mike?"

Mike started to tell the story, but before he got too far into it, Bud interrupted. "Hey listen, Mike. Are you still in D.C.?"

"Yes, pardner, I am," Mike responded.

Bud continued, "Well, as luck would have it, I am here on some business too. Can we get together to meet and talk?"

"Hell yes, pardner," Mike answered. "Just a second." He turned to the rest to make sure it was okay and to find out where to meet before responding. "Hey, Bud, let's meet at the Tasty Diner in Silver Spring at 7."

"Perfect," said Bud. "See you then, Mike. Goodbye."

Turning to Frank, he said, "That will give us some time to connect with the guy from the Temple. We'd better get going."

When they arrived at the Temple, Bud turned off the street into a small surface lot that was marked for employees only. Entry could only be made by a personal key card. Not phased at all by this, Bud pulled up to the gate and pulled a card from his wallet that seemed to be blank. He slid it into the slot at the gate, and the gate immediately popped up and open.

Frank said, "You are the miracle man. An answer for every problem."

Bud smiled and pulled into the small lot. His purpose was not to park, but to look around for the black SUV with the plates that they had run. He saw it almost immediately. It was parked in a space next to another black SUV that had signage that read, "Reserved for Grand Commander."

"There it is," Frank pointed.

"Okay, let's get out of this lot and park a little ways down the block," Bud said as he exited the lot and found a spot on the street.

On their way in to the Temple, he simply said, "Frank, this will be about intimidation. Just follow my lead."

Frank nodded, "I will. I'm with the master of intimidation."

When they entered the building, Bud flashed his FBI credentials at the security desk and demanded to see the Grand Commander. The officer at the desk tried to defer and say he was unavailable, to which Bud replied, "That is unacceptable. He is to make himself available, or I will have him arrested for impeding an ongoing investigation."

Clearly flustered, the officer disappeared for a moment, and when he came back, it was obvious he had been placed in the middle. "I'm sorry, sir, he said that he is busy and that you should make an appointment."

Without comment Bud signaled for Frank to follow and charged past the officer down the hallway. He followed a sign that pointed to the office of the Grand Commander. He opened the door, startling the Commander and catching him off guard as he was seated behind his desk.

Bud announced, "We have business to talk about." Continuing to stand, Bud and Frank looked down at the Commander. "Here is the way it will be," Bud said matter-of-factly as he flashed him his FBI badge. "You threatened a colleague of mine today who was participating in a confidential operation for the Bureau. I have no idea why you would do that, but if that happens again, I will personally shoot your left nut off after arresting you for impeding our investigation."

The Grand Commander pulled himself together and stood up. "You have no idea who you are messing with," he spit back to Bud and Frank with a glare. It was obvious he was not used to being talked to in that way. "I don't give a rat's ass about your outdated FBI badge. And I certainly don't know what you are talking about. So get the hell out of my office, or I'll be on the phone with the FBI Director in a heartbeat telling him about your pathetic attempt at intimidation."

Bud and Frank never flinched and continued to lock eyes with the Commander. After a long minute, Bud said, "You do what you have to do, and we will do what we have to do. Just consider very carefully if it will be worth your pain."

Then they turned and walked out, leaving the Commander red-faced and spitting fire. He immediately dialed an in-house number and shouted, "Get your ass down here! We have a situation."

In turn, Bud and Frank returned to their car still parked on the street. Frank spoke first and said, "Not sure that went how you wanted it to go."

Bud sighed and said, "Not really, but he's been given the option now. So whatever happens, the ball's in his court."

Frank continued, "So what's his motivation?"

Bud answered, "These Freemason guys protect their high-ranking brethren at all costs. They don't want a blight on the institution. And I think they fear what my friends may find out about Hoover, one of their most treasured legacies."

"Oh my god, over thirty years since he died, and he's still making people squirm," Frank added.

"Yes, he is," mused Bud with a wry smile.

CHAPTER 41

Gordon was back in his spot, parked a block down from Julie's house. He was bored to tears, wondering why he had agreed to do this again, when the conversation in the house jumped him to attention. After hearing Mike tell his story another time, he thought, *How in the hell did I miss that? That changes everything. My threat level just elevated itself and now I know I'm in the game again. So what I thought was a snoozer of an operation is now the real deal.* He continued to think to himself, *All I know is if I had been on the job, there would have been a body to dispose of.* Then he smiled.

The conversation inside the house was all over the board. Sometimes they all agreed to end the hunt and go home. And sometimes they decided to keep going and get the thing done. But they all wanted to hear from Bud before they did anything else and were anxiously watching the clock so they could get things sorted out with him.

Finally, Mike said, "All right already. I need a nap to decompress before the meeting."

This idea was met with enthusiastic support, and the conversation from the house subsided while they all rested. That is until Mindy called with some more information from her online digging. She had to call twice, though, before anyone picked up from their snoozing.

Bruce was the first to answer, "Hey, what's up?" he said groggily from the lazy boy.

"Hi, Dad, where is everyone?"

Bruce responded slowly trying to get his brain moving, "Taking a nap. We had a stressful day and have a meeting tonight. You got something for us?" he asked as the dim light bulb in his brain began to burn brighter.

Mindy laughed and said, "Of course. Listen to this. You need to get back to the storage room for Hoover's memorabilia. I found a notation on one of the Foundation sites that said they have most of the Director's old personal files and the Law Enforcement Museum plans to display some of them. It seems that Hoover kept a file on basically everything he did and about everyone he worked with. So I believe that there has to be a file about the guns. See if Julie can charm the officer into letting you look at the memorabilia again. I think you should go there again before you go to the FBI Building. The file should have the same approximate dates as the notes you found about the guns."

Bruce responded, "Wow! That sounds plausible. We'll let you know after our meeting tonight what we are going to do."

Mindy replied, "Perfect. I'm really excited about this clue. Let me know. Now, go rest. Love ya."

"Bye, sweetie, and thanks," Bruce said as he hung up.

The conversation gave Gordon a much-needed shot of adrenaline. When the house went quiet, it was a struggle for him to focus. *Back in the old days,* he thought, *I could sit on a stakeout for days and never even think about taking a break. Now I can't even last a couple of hours before I have to fight falling asleep. This getting old shit is getting old,* he smiled at his own words. But he was excited about the potential of a different personal file that the Director had put into play all of those years ago. The Director's propensity for creating files and keeping them hidden was common knowledge. *Maybe,* Gordon thought, *there is one that got overlooked. After Bud's meeting with these guys tonight, we will have to talk about it. I know what I would do,* he mused. *I'd go get those guns as soon as I could and then look for the files. The security in that building is old school weak. But it's Bud's call.*

Inside the house, everyone was getting ready to head out to meet with Bud. Bruce had to marshal the gang so that they would get to the Diner on time. Timeliness was not a priority for most of the group, and it always added a little stress for Bruce. He wanted to get there and be waiting for Bud, so he exhorted them saying, "Come on, Come on. We have to go!"

Finally, they headed out the door and jumped in the van for the now familiar drive to the Diner. "We will be there in plenty of time," Julie said. "Traffic shouldn't be a problem."

"Great," Bruce responded. "This should be a very interesting meeting."

Mike added, "Absolutely. Bud will tell it like it is. And then we decide what to do. And by the way, in case anyone cares, I am carrying my .44 with me. If that bastard comes around again, I will be ready."

Julie quickly said, "Mikey, don't you know that that is illegal in Maryland?"

Mike just shook his head and said, "Yes. Sorry, Julie, but I believe it is illegal to stick a gun in my neck in Maryland too."

"Point taken," she said. After that, the conversation waned until they got to the Diner and were seated.

"Well, we beat him here," Steve said as he took a seat with his back against the wall.

Mike hurried to get a similar seat, saying, "I need to see who's coming in this place. Don't need any surprises here."

So it was Bruce and Julie who had their backs to the door when Bud and Frank entered the Diner. Mike saw them first and signaled, "Hey, pardners, over here." As everyone stood to greet Bud and Frank, Mike continued, "How are ya? And what the hell ya doing in D.C.?"

Bud greeted them all, introduced Frank as his friend and pilot, and moved seats for themselves between Mike and Steve. He answered Mike, "Just some business to take care of. Even though I'm retired, I still get asked to help out sometimes in contract situations. So how is it going for you all here in the big city?"

That opened the flood gates. Mike started with his tale of the gunman and the bar fight. Steve talked about the three guns that they found. And Bruce mentioned Mindy's Internet hunt and her belief in the existence of the Director's file that could possibly shed light on the lost pistol. The only break in the conversation came when ordering and when the food was delivered. It was intense. Not only because of Bud's being there, but because the gunman and the bar fight had created a great deal of anxiety within the group. Bud sensed it and tried to calm them down after listening to their story.

"Okay then," he said. "I will admit that you've had some strange things happen to you. But I think that I can help you to make sure it won't happen again. If you will permit me, I can have someone assigned to follow you and protect you from anything like that again. And believe me, if you are under my protection, you will be safe. I think you are making some great progress in your quest for me, and I would really love for you to continue. This is the closest I have ever been to acquiring these guns. So naturally, I would hate to see you give up and not get your payday for completing the job. Frankly, you have given me great reason to be excited. What do you think?" He looked directly at Mike.

Mike rubbed the back of his neck, and said, "Well, pardner, I would hate to go through the gun thing again. But if you can assure our safety, I'm in." He looked around the table, and everyone appeared to nod in agreement.

Bud smiled, "Perfect. My man will be in place before we leave this diner. You won't see him, but he will always be close by—around the clock."

Nervous smiles appeared on their faces. It was easy to tell that even though it sounded good, there was still some apprehension.

Bruce spoke first, "Okay, but if there is the slightest danger ahead, we will be pulling out of this gig."

Then Steve added, "That's right. I'm down with your guy protecting us, but I'm still not sure who or where the problem is coming from."

Bud took a while to answer and finally said, "I'm sorry to say that there are many crazy zealots out there with causes that they have embraced without knowing why. Some of those people have created a shrine to the past Director and obviously will try to stop anyone from besmirching his legacy. There must be a sense in that community that you, we, are digging into something delicate that will do damage to his reputation."

Julie couldn't stay silent and asked, "So what community are you talking about—the Freemasons?"

Bud just nodded and said, "Over the years, they have always had some of their members in positions of power throughout the government. There are even those who say the government was created and is sustained by this group. On the surface they are a very solid organization with high standards. But they are very capable of doing whatever they think is necessary to preserve the sanctity of their members."

Bruce sighed and said, "Sounds just like some movies I've seen."

"Oh yes," Bud replied with a wry smile. "And Hoover was one of their most revered members with one of the group's highest ranks."

"Wow," Julie said and was echoed by Bruce and Steve.

Bruce said, "Okay then, what's next for us if we are to continue the search?"

"Well," Bud continued, "I'm going to check out the three guns you found for authenticity. You fellows should continue in the direction that you were already going."

Steve said, "Okay, tomorrow we are heading back to the memorabilia room, where the guns are being stored, to dig a little deeper. Then we have an appointment at the FBI Reading Room to look around there for a bit."

Bud agreed with that idea, "Sounds like you guys are doing the right things. Keep me informed."

Mike chimed in, "Wait, just one more thing, pardner. Didn't you tell me that there was a rumor that the missing gun was last seen in Wyoming?"

Bud looked at Frank and responded slowly, "Yes, I did. And actually, the story was that an Uberti Colt .45 with the serial number we are looking for was seen in Buffalo or Deadwood or Sturgis. I've never been able to get any traction on that story though."

"Okay, I just wanted everyone to hear that possibility." From that point the conversation turned to stories of Wyoming and D.C., and before long it was time for everyone to head out, get some rest, and then move forward in the quest.

As Bud and Frank exited and jumped in their car, Bud said quietly to Frank, "You know, if we can keep these guys safe, we may get lucky."

Frank nodded, "I'm kinda feeling the same way."

CHAPTER 42

The guys slept a little easier that night, knowing that someone was assigned to watch them. But that didn't mean they were completely comfortable. Just the fact that it was necessary for someone to protect them gave them some fitful moments. In fact, nobody was feeling really rested, and there was a general feeling of anxiety as they got ready to go. Even Mike was ready a little early because of it.

"Hey, we ever going to leave?" he bellowed throughout the house. "Let's get this party started. Haw, haw, haw."

Bruce just said, "In a minute, and by the way, who are you and what did you do with Mikey?" Mike just gut-laughed again and stepped outside to smoke a cigar. Finally, they were all ready and in the van. And as usual, everyone was pissing and moaning about the cigar smell that Mike brought with him into the van. Very soon, though, the conversation turned to their plans for the day and to the fact that they were being followed.

"Wonder where that guy is?" Steve asked as he looked around in front and back of the van. "I don't see anyone."

"Me, either," said Bruce.

"Well, I trust Bud," Mike said. "So I'm sure he's out there somewhere."

The conversation continued with those references until they reached their first destination. Some of the things they said almost made Gordon laugh out loud as he maintained a safe distance from the van. *Yes, I am here watching and listening,* he said to himself with a smile. *If they only knew how easy it was to stay connected to them...*Before he could finish this thought, his phone rang. "Hello, Bud. What's up?"

Bud replied, "I'm just checking in and wanted to let you know that your targets are leaving tomorrow morning. Keep them safe today and tomorrow. Then I need you to help us finish the operation here in D.C. Let me know the minute they are outside the beltway and on their way home."

Gordon answered, "Will do," as Bud ended the call.

Bud and Frank were already in place in the mega building that housed the memorabilia and the guns. "We need to be able to see things from a distance and watch our guys as they go back into the storage room," Bud told Frank.

"Gotcha," Frank responded as they picked up their pace and found a place out of the view of the security officer and the young man who let the group in the day before. They fit right in as two old fellas checking out the beautiful architecture of the aging Pension Building, looking every inch like tourists. They split up and from their separate vantage points, they could see the group making the necessary reconnection with Andrew, the information officer, and then heading all smiles and laughter towards the memorabilia storage room. The young officer was very happy to see Julie again and was falling all over himself to make the visit positive for her.

"Absolutely," Andrew said when she asked if they could sneak one last look at the room. "We'll need to hurry. I have a tour group coming in soon, but it will be no problem. I hope you folks are having a great time in D.C."

Julie responded sweetly, "Oh yes, it's been a great trip. We're almost done and were hoping to catch one more glimpse of the memorabilia. Thank you so much for making it happen."

"That's perfect. I'm glad I could help. Here we are," the young officer responded as he opened the doors to the displayed items.

From a safe distance, Bud was measuring the "lay of the land" and peering into the room with some sort of high-tech eyepiece that brought everything that was viewable in the room up close and personal. The best part was that he could also see the guns from his line of sight.

He whispered to Frank through his ear mic, "Bingo, Frank. Those are the guns—no question."

"Outstanding," Frank whispered back. "What's next?"

Bud responded, "Let's just let them do their work, and we will wait until they leave."

Inside the room, everyone focused on the gun display, as they did the last time. The guys took a few more pictures and then said, "Thank you again for your help," to the young officer.

Then Bruce said, "You know there is one more thing we are interested in, if you don't mind."

"What's that?" Andrew asked.

Steve said, "We are also looking for one of the Director's personal files that mentions the guns and how they were gifted to him. We understand that he kept personal files on nearly everything that he did."

Andrew thought for a moment, walked behind the display rope, and opened the file cabinet from Hoover's office. As he looked in he said, "I know we have some of his personal files, but almost universally they have been redacted to the point that they are unreadable. See?" He flipped open a file that had been blacked out by magic marker. "I'm sorry to say that this is how most of them look." The guys peered at a typed page that only had a few readable words not redacted.

"Wow," Bruce sighed. "So where would we go to see if we could find the original?"

The officer said, "I was told that anything of Hoover's not here would still be at the Masonic Temple or at the FBI Building."

"Oh I see," Bruce said. "Then that's where we will look."

"Thank you for showing us again," Julie said with her cutest smile. "We may be back again sometime. And I still have your card."

Andrew smiled at that, and said "I hope so," as he led them all out of the room and into the main part of the building. What he didn't do in his haste to continue a conversation with Julie was lock the room again. This afforded Bud and Frank an opportunity that they hadn't planned on. Without even a moment's hesitation and with no comment, they swooped out from their vantage points, slid into the memorabilia room, closed the briefcases one by one, and scooped them up. They carried the briefcases back to the spot where Bud had waited and settled back into their roles as the old guy tourists, watching for the moment when they could bypass the security guard and information officer and walk away with the guns.

When Bud saw a huge tourist group entering the building, he whispered to Frank, "Look. I love it when a plan comes together." Soon, Andrew and the guard were caught up in organizing the tour, and Bud and Frank just melted away, briefcases in hand.

That was just too easy, Bud thought with a smile as they exited the building and jumped into their car.

Frank said, "Wish every op was that easy," and smiled from ear to ear.

Bud looked over at Frank and said, "Yes, and they probably won't even notice that the guns are missing as haphazardly as things were put out in that room. By the way, the locks were old school. I pushed the locking button on the door as we left. So that officer may remember that he didn't lock the door, but when he gets back to it to check, it will be locked for him," he said with a broadening sense that things went better than they could have even planned. "Now we can move forward and hope that our guys find a file."

Frank nodded in agreement, "Perfect, and now we don't even have to come up with a risky plan to come back in the middle of the night to break into this place to get the guns. It couldn't be better."

"Right you are," Bud answered as he pulled out into traffic. "Let's catch up with the guys and see what's happening at the FBI Building."

When they got to the FBI Building, they saw the van parked in a street parking spot about a block away from the main entrance.

Bud said, "Let's sit tight here until they come out."

But Frank said, "You know Gordon is on this too, so let's take a break and get a coffee. He's probably got them in his sights right now." Then he laughed, "I mean visual sights, not gun sights. But you never know with Gordon."

Bud smiled too, and agreed, "Okay, let's get over to that Starbucks on the corner."

Inside, the guys and Julie checked in with the security agent and then were escorted to the physical reading room where they were going to do their research.

"Let's hope we get lucky here," Steve said. "I'm not in a real hurry to go back to the Temple. That place just doesn't feel right to me."

Bruce agreed, "Yep, that librarian gave me the creeps. He had a very threatening manner about him."

Mike chimed in, "I wouldn't be surprised if that thug with the gun came from there." Everyone nodded in agreement.

When they got to the Reading Room, they explained what they were looking for and got a quick tutorial from the staff person on duty. When he mentioned that many of the records that the guys might find useful had been transferred to the National Archives and Records Administration, they collectively sighed and Mike just said, "Oh horseshit! Sorry.

Just disappointed." He was buoyed a bit when the guy told him that they could still find information in the Reading Room, but a proficiency in reading microfilm would be very helpful.

"Haw, haw, haw! I'm that guy," he exclaimed. "Let's get to it." Mike led the way as the time flew by. Everyone else did their part too, but Mike just had a knack for it. Finally, after a couple of hours of intense focus, he exclaimed, "Look at this! I just found a microfilm that shows a redacted copy of a file where Hoover mentions the Colt .45's and where they came from. And it mentions all four guns with serial numbers that match what we are looking for."

When Steve looked at the microfilm, he said, "This is so strange. It appears to be in a file that also mentions John F. Kennedy. But there is too much redacted to make any sense of it." Bruce went over to request assistance from the staff person. "My suggestion to you folks would be to go to NARA and dig a little for this same piece. Because of the Freedom of Information rulings, many things that you find redacted here might be found in their original form there. Just an FYI for you, in 2005 all of Hoover's personal files that were tagged 'official and confidential' were sent to the National Archives."

The guys looked at each other, and Bruce asked Julie, "Can you get us over there?"

She smiled and said, "Sure, but we should get going now. Make a note of that microfilm information first, though."

They thanked the staff person for his help, said they might be back, and headed out quickly to NARA.

"Who knew that there would be so many places where records could be kept?" asked Steve. "It's incredible and a bit frustrating."

Looking back at Mike limping slowly along, Bruce asked, "You gonna make it?"

Mike responded out of breath, "Yes, pardner, I am. But you gotta give me a little more time."

"No problem, buddy. We'll be in the van," Bruce responded.

Gordon noticed the group immediately and sat back to watch and wait. *Where in the hell is the bib overalls guy?* he thought. When he saw him, he understood. *Man that guy is running out of gas. I hope they are done for the day, cause I am too.* But when he heard the conversation in the van, he sighed, *Oh bullshit! Not done yet.* After Mike finally got in the van and Bruce pulled out of the parking spot, Gordon resumed his tail and followed them to the Pennsylvania Avenue home of the National Archives. *So far so good,* he thought to himself. *Let's keep it that way.*

Inside the van, the conversation was animated and excited, even though the group was beginning to tire.

"This could be a big break," Steve said.

"Absolutely," Bruce agreed. "But it could take more time than we have."

Mike added, "We should be able to cross-reference the microfilm information from the FBI, though, and that should speed things up. If we can use the time period we found there, it may limit the scope of our searching."

Bruce agreed, "Let's hope so."

When they got to NARA and finally found a spot to park, they moved through the main entrance and proceeded to the Research Center on the first floor. After talking to a greeter, Julie said, "This may be a process. Looks like we have to go through an orientation, get registered as researchers, and get identification cards. We can do all of this in the Research Center on the first floor. So no grumbling, let's just do it and move forward."

It turned out to be a simple process. Even Mike did what he had to do without too much complaining. When they were all through he said, "Well boys, that wasn't too bad. Let's get down to work."

This prompted everyone to look at him and actually say at the same time, "Who is this man? And where is our Mikey?" Laughter echoed around the massive building.

"Shhhhh," Julie reminded them. "Don't get us thrown out of here."

Finally ready to work, they asked for some help from the archivist on duty. He said matter-of-factly, but in a pleasant tone, "You can match the microfilm that you saw at the FBI with ours, and I'll bet it will be mostly original without all of that redaction. By the way, we have almost seventeen-thousand pages of personal material from Hoover's office. So cross-referencing the time period on the microfilm should save you time." He led them to the microfilm room and turned them loose. It didn't take Mike long to make the connection. And the archivist was right—hardly anything was redacted.

Mike exclaimed, "Wow, look at this. Here we go. Hoover kept a file on the guy who gave him the guns. Assigned an agent to check him out. Our guns are listed with the proper serial numbers and here it says he decided to display them at his residence. Then later Miss Gandy added a line here saying three were returned to the gift storage room with Hoover keeping one for office display. Then later another note saying the three were removed again by Clyde Tolson for personal display by the Director and...Oh my god, this is unbelievable!" Mike's exclamation caused everyone to move closer and hover over the microfilm.

"What?" Bruce asked for all of them.

"Wait for it," Mike teased them.

"Goddam it! Just tell us," Steve whisper-yelled.

"There is a note at the bottom scrawled in handwriting that looks a lot like Hoover's that says, 'Fourth gun lost in Buffalo, Wyoming, last seen at Occidental Hotel,'" Mike said. "And then it says, 'reference chain of events in personal assassination file of Kennedy 1962.'"

"What the hell does that mean?" Bruce said quickly.

Steve said, "Let's copy this microfilm and take it with us."

"Absolutely," Mike said. "There is more, but it's really hard to read."

"What about that assassination file?" Julie asked. "Can you find that?"

Mike said, "Let's try now," and started digging through the microfilm files where it should have been. But it wasn't there. "Hell's bells," Mike whispered. "It ain't here that I can find. Let's ask the archivist if he can help."

When the archivist was finally free to help, he took the information from the guys and started to search. But he too came up empty. "It should be right here in this timeframe, but I can't find it."

Bruce asked, "Can you check to see if the original file that would have been microfilmed is available?"

The man answered, "I can, but if the microfilm isn't here, I don't think that the original file will be. Give me a minute." He disappeared for what felt like a long time and, in reality, was about thirty minutes. When he came back, he said, "It appears that the original file, which was a part of the Director's 'official and confidential files,' was on loan to the Hoover Foundation per the instructions of Hoover's will and it has disappeared somehow. There are records of other requests for the file, including Freedom of Information requests, but it has never surfaced. The records from the Hoover Foundation are inconclusive, so I think you've hit a dead end. I'd go back to the last place that Hoover's memorabilia was kept if I were doing the research."

The disappointment was palpable in the research room.

"Well shit!" Mike said. "We've got some good stuff, but that file sounds like it's got some great stuff in it." Steve and Bruce just nodded.

Julie said, "Well, I guess you have to take what you can get. But I'm not sure going back to the Foundation would be a good thing."

Bruce agreed, "We need to talk about that. Okay, let's head out. We have our copy of the microfilm and some new direction."

When they got back to the van, there was no end to the talk about what they had found. This is what Gordon had needed—he had been ready to quit again and go get a drink. But the renewed vigor coming from his targets energized him. *Holy shit,* he thought. *Could these rubes really have found the loose ends that Bud had been looking for all of these years?* As he listened to the banter in the van, he decided that he had better call Bud and let him know what was going on.

"Hey, Bud?" he spoke quietly into the phone. "Hold on to your hat, buddy. These knuckleheads have uncovered a confidential file of the Director's that describes our guns and what happened with them—even to the point of saying the fourth gun was lost in Buffalo, Wyoming." There was silence from Bud. "You there, Bud?" asked Gordon.

"Yes, I'm here," Bud said. "I'm just trying to make sense of what you just said."

Gordon said, "Okay, but there is one more thing. There was a reference in this microfilm that suggested the Director kept a separate file on the operation, with details. You know how he kept a file on everything? I don't think it's a stretch to believe that there is a file out there outlining everything that went down for the operation. That means me, you, and Frank may be a part of the file."

More silence from Bud. When he did speak, he sounded more agitated than Gordon had ever heard him. "All right," he said. "This is what we will do. If our guys decide to look for that file, we will let them and then take it from them if they find it. If they decide not to, I will get whatever information they have, check it out, and then we will find the file on our own. I'm guessing they will opt to go look for the gun in

Buffalo and not worry about a file that really has no significance in their minds regarding the lost gun. But for us, we will definitely need to find that file. So keep on them, and keep me informed of their decision. When we know what they are thinking, I will set up a meeting with them again and help guide their direction and pick their brains for what they think they know. I need to think this through a bit more. I'll be back in touch."

CHAPTER 43

Back at Julie's house, the guys kept up their discussion—stay, and look further for a maybe meaningless file, or go, and look for the gun in Buffalo. It really came down to what they were being paid to do.

"Look," Bruce said. "The only dog we have in this hunt is that missing gun. We've found the three guns, and now we need to do what we are being paid to do—find the fourth gun. Then we will have all four pistols, and we will get paid. I've got to believe that Bud will be very happy with that result. What does he care about Hoover's confidential file if he's got the gun?"

"I agree," said Steve. "Let's get back home and start to work on that fourth gun. If we find nothing, then we can come back to see if we can find the file and see if it has anything helpful in it."

Mike weighed in with, "Ordinarily, I'd say let's find that file. I smell some shit going on that may be a part of that file. But I'm the guy who had a gun stuck in his neck. So I say, let's get the hell out of D.C. before we find something too dangerous for us to handle. Soon as I get back to Buffalo, I can get started checking things out."

Julie was in agreement with that decision. "Guys, I told you D.C. is dangerous if you get involved in the politics. I think you've done all you should, and even though I love having you here, you certainly have given me some moments that I've never experienced before. Go home and be safe," she laughed. "Besides, Mindy can still poke around in the electronic FBI Reading Room for that microfilm. And who knows, she may find something."

That clinched it. The decision to leave was unanimous.

Gordon smiled and immediately called Bud.

"Hey," he said. "They are leaving in the morning. You need to set up a meeting tonight or at breakfast before they leave."

Bud responded, "That's the best case scenario. Thanks Gordon. Stay with them, though, until they leave."

Gordon laughed and said, "I got it," as he settled in for a long night in his car just down the block from the house.

After what seemed like a very short night for everyone in the house, the guys got ready and said their goodbyes to Julie.

"Come back anytime, especially when you aren't working so we can have some fun and not get threatened," she laughed. "I can take you to some great fun places."

The guys assured her that they would, gave their hugs, and jumped into the van to stop at the Tasty Diner one more time. Bud had called and wanted to meet for a moment before their departure. There was a sense of relief in the van as the guys rehashed everything about their adventure in D.C. They were anxious to get home, but they also felt like the trip was productive—even though there were a few speed bumps, or humps as the signs said in Takoma Park, along the way.

Pulling into the parking garage across from the Diner, they noticed Bud and Frank going in.

"Hey look," Bruce said. "They beat us here."

"That's unusual for Bud," Mike added. "Seems like I'm always waiting for him."

"But this is good," Steve said. "We can get done and get out of town."

As Gordon pulled into the garage too, he smiled and thought, *Almost done and I can get some rest. I'll stay with them until they get past the beltway.*

When the guys got into the Diner, they found Bud and Frank with their backs to the wall in a secluded section where a private conversation would be easy to have.

"Good morning, gentlemen," Bud said as he and Frank remained seated. "Thank you for meeting with us. Have a seat, and we can catch up and get you on your way." Pleasantries were exchanged and then it was down to business. "Please tell me about your hunt in D.C. and whether you had any further luck," he prodded with a smile, looking expectantly at Mike.

"Well, pardner, it's like this. We found microfilm that appears to be in Hoover's handwriting that says the gun we are still looking for was lost in Buffalo. Remember when you said that could be the case?"

Bud answered, "Yes, I do, Mike. But I have looked for it in Buffalo and surrounding communities and have had no luck. What's your plan?"

Mike continued, "The Occidental Hotel seems to play a part in this, and I know the current owners pretty well so that's the first place I'll start when I get home. You can come with me if you like."

Bud didn't commit to this and said, "Okay, we shall see. What about the other microfilm file from Hoover's confidential files?" This question caught everyone by surprise.

"How do you know about that?" Bruce finally asked.

Bud smiled, "Remember, I had a man on you to keep tabs on you and keep you safe?"

Mike, sensing the other guys' discomfort, said quickly, "Well, I, for one, appreciate that and understand. Thanks for looking out for us."

Bud nodded with a smile, "Just protecting you and my interests. Plus, I'd like to follow up on that if you can give me a starting point."

Steve said, "Okay, that's fine. Based on our research and the input from the archivist, we think that the file may still be at the Temple where all of the rest of Hoover's stuff was displayed. We think that they kept some of the more controversial memorabilia and confidential files. So our suggestion to you, which you probably don't need coming from amateurs like us, is to go see the Grand Poobah, or whatever he is called and check it out."

"You will probably have to use your powers of persuasion," Bruce added and laughed. "But I'm sure you know how to do that."

Mike added, "Those Freemasons seem to be a secretive and strange bunch of guys."

Bud responded, "Yes, they are. And even though they have contributed a great deal to this country, some of their tactics have been questionable."

Mike then took out a pen and jotted down the microfilm information and handed it to Bud. "That's all we got, pardner. So, as soon as you get back to Buffalo, let me know if you found anything and we can go find the fourth pistol."

"I will," Bud said as he and Frank stood to leave. "Thank you, gentlemen. Stay in touch and be safe going home. By the way, my man will escort you past the beltway and then you will be on your own."

The guys waved, finished their breakfast, and hit the highway, all looking forward to getting home and the next part of their adventure. When they reached their exit on the beltway, they turned north and almost simultaneously looked back to see if they could spot Bud's protector. They would have been quite surprised to see that it was the old guy from the bar, who would have had no qualms about killing them in that moment of drunken rage. Gordon thought about that as he peeled off and took an exit taking him back to D.C. *It's a crazy game that we are playing.* He called Bud to let him know and also to see what's next.

Bud said, "Go get some rest and when you're ready let me know. We need to meet with the Grand Commander again. Make sure to come operation ready."

Gordon lit up with that last comment. *Sounds like the old days,* he thought.

As the guys settled in for their ten hour drive back to Northwest Ohio, they talked very little. But they were all thinking—thinking about the gun in Buffalo, thinking about the three guns they found stored in Hoover's memorabilia, thinking about the file they couldn't find that may provide more information for them about the guns and how they were used, and finally they were all thinking about the foul play that they had run into. Mike, in particular, couldn't get his meeting with the mystery gunman out of his mind. And Steve and Bruce thought about the crazy scene at the bar with the old man. Needless to say, they were all happy to have survived the adventure and were looking forward to getting home.

Bruce sighed and said, "Settle back, boys, and relax. It's going to be a long trip. But we will have more adventures coming as soon as we get caught up on our rest." No one responded though, as the sound of snoring permeated the quiet of the van. "Looks like I need some music to cover that up," Bruce said and smiled to himself.

Bud, Frank, and Gordon were also trying to relax for a bit. However, they were just biding their time before they headed to the Temple to see the Grand Commander. Bud was convinced in his own mind that Hoover had made another file—a file detailing the events of the Kennedy operation.

That's just how he operated, he thought. *He probably actually wanted someone to find it after his death so that he could be declared the hero that he thought he was.* "The Director was probably the most narcissistic individual that I have ever met," Bud mused out loud.

Frank heard the comment and said, "What?"

Bud just smiled and said, "Sorry...was thinking out loud about our former boss. He was quite a piece of work."

Frank agreed and added, "Well, I don't have any love lost for him. The bastard tried to kill me."

"You are right, Frank," Bud responded. "But it was precisely because of his remorseless personality and obsessions that he was able to build the FBI into the amazing organization that it has become."

Frank just shook his head and said, "He'll always be a son of a bitch to me."

After resting for a couple of hours, Gordon was getting antsy so he called Bud, "Hey, Bud, let's get this thing going. I'm ready."

Bud wasn't surprised by the call and said, "Perfect. We're ready too. Meet us in front of the Temple just as it is getting dark."

Gordon replied, "I'll be there."

Bud and Frank arrived at the Temple first—at least they thought so. As soon as they parked, though, a dark figure came up to the car and tapped on the window. Bud rolled down the window and said, "Gordon, slide in." When he did, Bud diagramed the plan for the guys. It was simple. Bud said, "We use our FBI badges to get in the front door and past security. If there is an issue, we neutralize them, and then move forward to the Grand Commander's office. If he is there, we put the fear in him. If he isn't, we tear his office apart until we find the file. It has to be there. This guy reveres Hoover, and Hoover kept everything important and confidential in his own office. Hopefully, the threat of violence will be enough to get this done if the guy is there. If not, then you know what to do, Gordon. But don't kill him unless we are out of options, and until we find the file. Are you good with that?" Bud looked directly into Gordon's eyes when he asked this.

Gordon looked back and answered simply, "Yes, sir."

Bud said, "Okay, then, let's go."

When they reached the entrance to the massive building, Bud pushed the after-hours buzzer and awaited the security guard to answer the buzzer.

An intercom squawked and the voice said, "Can I help you? We are only open for members at this hour."

Bud responded, "Why yes you can. We are with the FBI and would like to meet with the Grand Commander for a moment. We need you to open the door and let us in."

"Sorry, sir, I'll be right there," the security guard responded. "Please have your credentials out so that I can see them."

Bud said matter-of-factly, "We do, and we are waiting."

When the guard came to the door, the three men held up their badges for his perusal. Satisfied, he unlocked the door and let them in. Bud noticed immediately that the guard was the same guy who stuck the gun in Mike's neck.

The guard said simply, "The Grand Commander is not in. You will have to come back another time."

Bud just smiled and reached into his pocket and pulled out an official piece of paper and said, "I believe this will take care of your concerns. This is a warrant for us to search his office."

The guard balked at this, took the paper, looked it over several times, and said finally, "Come this way." He led them down the hallway where the Grand Commander's office was, but didn't stop at the office.

Bud said, "This is the office."

But the guard kept on going and said, "No, sir, his office is this way." Eventually, he stopped, opened a room that appeared to be an office, and said, "Feel free to look around."

Bud said in his firmest voice, "Maybe you didn't read the warrant fully, but it is for the Grand Commander's office. And this is not that."

The security guard just as firmly said, "Maybe you didn't hear me, but this is his office. Feel free to look around." Bud surveyed the office quickly, noting that it was obviously a secondary office that was never in use and probably used for display only or for overflow needs.

"Listen, young man," he said quietly. "Unless you are looking for a ton of trouble, I advise you to adhere to the warrant."

The guard just smiled and said, "Well, you listen, old man. You three old farts are about as FBI as I am. So this is the best you get. Or better yet, you better get the hell out of here before something bad happens to you. I was just playing with you, but now I'm tired of it and you need to either go or someone will get hurt. Understand?" he threatened as he pulled out the same gun that he had stuck in Mike's neck.

In that instant, Gordon reacted. He had had his gun in his hand in his jacket pocket since they entered the building. He fired twice through his pocket with his silenced weapon, hitting him in the heart and immediately killing the guard who never knew what hit him.

"Old man my ass," he muttered. Then he said, "Sorry boss, he gave me no choice."

Bud nodded, "Agreed. You clean up the mess, and Frank and I will check out the office.

"I'll get my cleaner in here. I already warned him that I might need him, once you said to come operation ready."

Bud responded, "Great. Make it happen by the time we get done with the office." Gordon was already on the phone and setting things in motion.

When Bud and Frank got into the Grand Commander's office, they locked the door and got to work. Years of practice made their search go quickly. There were only so many places to hide things in an office, and they knew them all. The only thing they wouldn't be able access on this search would be a hidden safe. They would have to come back for that if they didn't find anything.

After a while, Bud said, "Remember, most things are hidden in plain sight. The people who hide them want to access them quickly and easily and often. So if it's a file, it may be attached to a file that has nothing to do with the one we are looking for."

Frank said, "Yes, got it." Almost as soon as he said that, Frank pulled out a file that said, "FBI Confidential Report on JFK assassination." "Look at this, Bud," he said handing the file over to Bud to look through. "This was in a memorabilia file under 3rd Degree Hoover's Freemason title."

It only took Bud a second to see that it was exactly what they were looking for. "Oh my god, Frank. This is it. Hoover did keep a confidential file that described it all—everything that happened in the operation. That crazy s.o.b wanted someone to find this and recognize what he had done for his country. Okay, let's get out of here. Leave everything as we found it. And check with Gordon."

They had been in the office for just over 2 hours when they found the file. When they left to find Gordon, they prayed that he was done with the cleanup.

"We need to get the hell out of here," Bud said. He called out to Gordon as they reentered the first office where the bloodshed had occurred. "Gordon, are we all set?"

"All done," he replied as Bud took a quick look around. "The cleaners took care of it all, including the security cameras. We need to move."

With that, the three men slipped out of the Temple and found their way to their car. Bud never put the file down. He clutched it close to his body. After all, it was the link to his role in that fateful operation in 1963. It was the loose end that the Director always preached about. And it was finally in his grasp.

He took a deep sigh and mouthed to himself, "After all these years." He turned to Frank and said softly, "Now it's down to the gun. Curiously," he said. "That's what started this whole saga. When we didn't know this file existed, the gun was everything."

Frank nodded, "Now, if we find the gun, we can definitely put everything to rest. Your buddy, Mike, and his friends have amazed me. They are tenacious."

Bud smiled and said, "Yes, tenacious, but also very lucky. And luck plays a part in almost every operation, no matter how well planned. Let's get this file back to our place, review it more fully, and get it packed away," he continued as they drove away into the night.

Meanwhile, Gordon was heading back to his place too—with a huge grin on his face. *Oh my god,* he thought to himself. *Just like the old days. Nothing gets your blood pumping like that anymore.* Replaying every second of his role in his mind, he was almost giddy from the excitement that it brought him. And excitement was something that had gone from his life long ago. He didn't even feel the need for a drink. He wanted to keep his natural buzz and feel it all for as long as he could. *I hope Bud keeps going with this thing. I need this in my life,* he continued to think. Then he laughed out loud. *We're like the last of the Mohicans—Bud, Frank, and I. The only ones left alive to know the truth about 1963.* "I love it!" he exclaimed and continued to drive to his safe house reveling in his born again feelings.

CHAPTER 44

After the ten-hour trip back to Ohio, the guys were exhausted and decided that they would go slow in the morning and meet around 10 a.m. for breakfast. Mike was chomping at the bit to get started back to Wyoming, but Steve and Bruce felt the need to go over their plans one more time. Really, it was only one plan. Mike was supposed to meet with Bud, get as much information as he could about the rumors of the Colt .45 and the Occidental, and then go see the owners of the hotel. Bruce and Steve would be on standby waiting to see if Mike needed them. If he did, they had plans to fly out again and get involved. Right now, though, they were hoping Mike could get it done by himself. And then, as luck would have it, just as the guys were heading uptown for breakfast, Bruce got a call from his favorite gun guy—the Grizzly Bear.

"What the hell, you pussies, doin'?" came the growl over the phone.

"Hey, Bear," Bruce responded into his cell. "How are you?"

He looked at Steve and mouthed, "It's Bear."

"I'm pretty freakin' good!" he growled. "That is, I will be when you pay me my finder's fee."

Bruce brushed the comment off and said, "Me, too, buddy. Here's the plan. We found three of the guns like I told you, and now we are following a lead back to Buffalo, Wyoming, for the fourth and final gun. Your payday, and our payday, will happen after we check this lead out. This gun is the Holy Grail. If we find it, both of our paydays get much better. Sound good?"

Bear was silent for a minute, almost like he fell asleep, prompting Bruce to say, "Bear, are you there yet or are you still in hibernation?"

A deep rumble came back over the phone, "You think you are a funny guy. I've castrated funny guys before!" Then silence. Bruce was just about to apologize when Bear's god-awful, bloodcurdling laugh growled back at him. "Just fuckin' with you again! You are too easy." He kept the growl going, "Listen to me. I have gun contacts all over Wyoming and South Dakota. I think I should go out there and meet with them; but you will pay for my trip."

Bruce said, "Just a second." He covered the phone and told Mike and Steve what Bear had offered.

Steve said, "I say, yes, we will pay if he finds something. If not, the trip is on him."

Mike nodded in agreement.

"Okay, Bear, we will pay if you find something. If not, it's your expense. Do we have a deal?"

Bear hesitated and then growled, "You cheap bastards. Yeah, we have a deal."

Bruce added, "I'll set up a meeting with you and my friend who lives in Buffalo. You'll like him." Bruce gave Bear Mike's cell number and said, "He'll call you as soon as he gets back out there."

Bear didn't acknowledge that he heard anything. He just grunted, "Uhhh," and hung up, catching Bruce again.

"Damn it. He got me again," Bruce fumed.

Steve just laughed.

"That guy could piss off the Pope," Bruce laughed. "We better go or we won't get Mikey on the road."

Mike wanted to eat at Cosmos, a diner-like place on Second Street that catered to old folks and big eaters. Mike qualified under both categories. By the time breakfast was over, he had eaten a mountain of pancakes, an omelet that covered a separate plate, and enough biscuits and gravy to give most guys his age an instant heart attack. Bruce and Steve just watched and marveled at his ability. The other good thing about Cosmos was that the tables were large enough that any excess food that flew out of Mike's mouth while he chewed never really reached across the table.

After watching the food fest, Bruce said with loud laughter, "Mikey, I'm buying breakfast. That was like watching a true Olympian compete in his sport."

Steve added, "You were magnificent."

Mike responded, "Yeah, Yeah, Yeah, I've got your Olympic sport for you," as he let out his signature gut laugh sending shards of omelet everywhere across the table.

"Oh my god," Bruce said. "Now I need a shower."

Finally, it was time to send Mike on his way. It had been a great adventure to D.C., with stories that would last the buddies' lifetimes. As Mike pulled out with his truck and miniature trailer, Steve and Bruce looked on, with Bruce saying, "Well, I hope the turtle makes it safely. I have a feeling that we have more adventures to come."

Steve agreed, "I'm sure of it."

When both guys got back to Bruce's place, the phone rang almost immediately. It was Mindy, wondering what was going on. She said, "I haven't heard from you guys since I gave you the information on the file."

"Hey, sweetie. Sorry. We forgot to call you back and tell you that we decided not to follow up on Hoover's confidential file. We found what we were looking for with the guns, and we were a little bit scared to go poking around the confidential files. We had enough trouble on this trip."

Mindy said, "Oh, that's okay. I figured you got tied up. I was just wondering how it went."

Bruce responded, "It was a crazy trip. We were threatened verbally, and Mikey even had a gun stuck in his neck. Plus, we got into a bar fight with some old guy. You could say it was just a crazy trip. But we found the guns, and you got us a lead on the fourth pistol from that file. It may actually be out in Buffalo, Wyoming. What are the odds of that happening? See? It was just crazy."

Mindy answered, "Crazy sounds like an understatement. You need to fill me in on the details sometime! Bar Fights! Guns! Geez, I'm glad you got home safely. Hey, I wanted to tell you that I've been digging around the Vault and have found a couple of other references to the four pistols, basically saying that they were gifts from Aldo Uberti and that they were being kept by Hoover in his home residence. Nothing really new, unless we could review the confidential file further."

But Bruce wasn't interested in that. "No thanks, kiddo, we have enough for now. We'll dig around Buffalo and try to locate the gun. But if we can't, I'll let you know, and we may want to revisit that file."

"Okay," Mindy said. "Works for me. In the meantime, I'll poke around some more in case something new jumps out at me. Talk to you later. Love ya."

Bruce responded, "That's a deal. Love ya too. Bye."

Steve had been listening to the conversation and agreed with Bruce on everything. He said, "You are exactly right. Our focus is the gun and nothing more. No use stirring whatever pot we were stirring out in D.C. any more than we already have. There are some fanatical lunatics out there."

Bruce just nodded in agreement. "For now, let's wait to see what Mikey can get done with the Grizzly Bear. We might just have to go out there to see both of them together."

They both laughed out loud. "What a pair!"

Back in D.C., the pot that Steve had talked about not stirring was about to boil over. The Grand Commander was an unhappy man. He had ordered his right hand man to find out what was going on with these seemingly too old FBI guys. But now he couldn't find his right hand man. *He had better be dead,* he thought to himself as he sat in his office. *If he isn't and I find out he just blew me off, he will wish he were dead.* In his gut, though, he knew something wasn't right. His guy had never let him down before. So based on that gut feeling, he brought in a couple more of his best men. "Listen to me very carefully," he said. "I want you to find these old guys masquerading as FBI agents, and I want to know what they are up to. And I also want you to find three other guys from Ohio who were poking around in Director Hoover's memorabilia. Things started to go south around here when they showed up, supposedly as tourists. Get as many of our security guys involved as you need, but get it done quickly. Something is up, and I need it resolved."

At the same time, Bud was studying the confidential Hoover file. "This is absolutely incredible," he muttered to himself. "He didn't leave out a single detail. He lists LBJ and himself as the chief co-conspirators. Clyde was responsible for getting the agents and the weapons. Oh my god!" he mouthed. "He lists me and Howard as the black ops agents in charge of the operation. Detail after detail is included: The deaths of the four FBI agents and a pilot to cover up the operation. Using the Occidental to hide the weapons and subsequently losing one of the weapons. And he even references a conversation with Clyde about terminating Howard and I. And it's all written in Hoover's own handwriting. This file is a powder keg that could upset the establishment in so many ways. It's no wonder that the Grand Commander had this file stashed away. It could undermine all the positive things that the Freemasons supposedly have stood for since the beginning of this country. And even though there is no note in the file detailing Freemason collusion in the operation, Hoover does note that things proceeded with Freemason support. Obviously, they wanted a Freemason back in the Oval Office."

Finally, visibly shaken, Bud put down the file and sighed, and then he laughed to himself, "Maybe I should thank the Grand Commander for finding this file and hiding it. He actually did Frank, Gordon, and I a favor. But when he finds out the file is gone, it will create quite a shit storm. I need to protect my new friends. The Grand Commander already had them in his sights for some reason, and I can guarantee they will become even bigger targets now. Hopefully, he won't find out the file is missing for some time."

Bud looked up to see Frank just watching him. "Sorry, Frank. The file completely blindsided me."

Frank responded with a smile, "No problem. I enjoyed the play by play as you read it to yourself. By the way, in my mind, for us to be completely in the clear with this stuff, I think you ought to sic Gordon on the guy and end it once and for all. Just saying."

Bud responded with a sigh, "Unfortunately, you may be right. But first, I'd like to look around a little to see if there could have been a copy made of this file. And I'd like to get the gun."

Frank said, "That's fine with me."

"So let's pack up and head back to Buffalo," Bud said. "I'll have Gordon keep tabs on the Grand Commander."

"Perfect," Frank agreed.

When Bud called Gordon to enlist his help once again, he got the answer that he wanted. "Absolutely," Gordon said. "This guy is dangerous, and I think we should make him disappear before he does us harm or your buddies from Ohio and Wyoming." It was obvious that

Gordon was back in the ops mode and willing to do anything to get the job done.

Bud responded, "I think that I agree with you, Gordon, but for now I just want you to watch and listen. Get inside his office and plant a bug so you can hear what he's planning to do. And stay close to him."

Gordon agreed to this and said, "I'm on it. I'll keep you posted. When you leaving for Wyoming?"

Bud answered, "As soon as we can get to the airport and jump in the plane. We'll be counting on you. And, Gordon, please no bodies unless it absolutely can't be avoided. Okay?"

Gordon grumbled, "All right," and hung up. Then he immediately headed back to the Temple to do what was necessary.

CHAPTER 45

Mike's trip back to Wyoming was uneventful and slow—just the way he liked it. Steve had given him a full box of new cigars, and he enjoyed one during every mile of the trip. *My slice of heaven,* he mused after taking a long drag on the 5 Vegas Maduro that he was smoking as he turtled along the highway. Every once in a while he would suck on the cigar, take it from his mouth, and stare at the burning ash. *Oh my god,* he sighed. *Life is good. Can't wait to get home, though, and see my chickens.* For Mike, spending time with his buddies meant everything to him. Steve and Bruce were his brothers that he never had, and he would do anything for them. *I'm a lucky man,* he thought. *And so glad we got this gun collecting gig to bring us together again.* He looked out his open window to the sky, made the sign of the cross and said, "Please, God, make this end well for all of us." Since the gun to the back of his neck, he had been worried about his buddies and himself and prayed to God often to protect them all. He worried that Bud had gotten them into something that was bigger than they were. But at the same time, he had a strong belief that Bud would make sure they were protected. So as he finally pulled into his drive, he felt at peace with the whole gun deal and looked forward to meeting with Bud when he got back to Buffalo too. *Oh yes, and I'm anxious to meet this Bear guy too. Sounds like my kind of guy. I need to call him right away.* But right away meant after he saw his chickens.

"Hey, guys, how are you all doing?" he clucked to his feathered friends. "Pop's home and all is well," he said as he reached to pet them and throw them some grain. "Ah, the simple life for me," he smiled.

Back in D.C., though, life was anything but simple. The Grand Commander, sensing that there was more to everything than he could see, had a sudden start. *Oh shit,* he thought and immediately pulled open the drawer where he kept the Hoover confidential files.

"It's gone!" he exclaimed under his breath. "Holy shit! Somebody took the file." He fell into his oversized office chair and tried to calm the fire burning inside him. He felt an anger that he had not felt in a long time. "I'm going to kill the son of a bitch that did this!" he muttered to himself. After a few minutes of trying to calm down, the Grand Commander called the leader of his men who were working to find Bud and the three other guys. "Come to my office, now!" he whispered forcefully into the phone.

"Yes, sir," the leader replied. "But we are at the Old Pension Building, tracking down a lead. It will take a few minutes."

The Grand Commander just said, "Get here as soon as you can." Still trying to get his emotions in check, he left his office to go to the washroom.

It was Gordon's opportunity. He had been pretending to be a part of a tour group of older folks while always keeping an eye on the Commander's office. The timing was perfect. The tour group was passing in close proximity to the office at the same time the Grand Commander was leaving. Gordon peeled off from the group, slipped into the empty office, and planted the bug on a ceiling fan located over the Commander's desk. It took only five seconds, and he was done and out of the office. *I'm still pretty damn good at this job,* he said to himself with a smile. Then he retreated back to the tour group and eventually out the front entrance to the building. *It's time to see what this guy is up to,* he thought. *I can tell you right now, it's no good.*

When Gordon reached his car and settled in, he knew the Grand Commander was back in his office because of the irritated banging around that he could hear. *Sounds pretty pissed off,* he smiled to himself. All he could do now, though, was wait—wait for some conversation that would tell him what he needed to do next. It took about an hour, but it was worth the wait. The first voices that he heard were from the Grand Commander and a couple of his men. By this time the Commander's temperament had mellowed a bit, and he was more rational.

The first words out of his mouth were, "Did you find anything on anybody?"

The response from one of his men was, "Yes, sir. We found out more about the three older guys and the young lady. But the old FBI guys are in the wind—couldn't find anything on them." The man continued, "So, as far as the guys and the girl go, we got their names from when they registered at the library here in the Temple. Our librarian said they were digging into stuff about Director Hoover—something about guns that he received as gifts. He said they were going to the place where the memorabilia is being kept until the museum opens up, and they also mentioned going to the FBI to look around."

The Grand Commander started to sound agitated again and snapped, "Listen, tell me something I don't already know. Jack gave me this information long ago, and I would have him working on it now if he hadn't disappeared. Have you heard anything yet from him?" the Commander asked.

"No, sir. We haven't," the man said apologetically.

Gordon chuckled to himself when he heard this and thought, *And you won't either.*

The Grand Commander was silent for a moment, then he erupted with curse after curse. Calming himself, he said finally, "This is what I want you to do. Go to Ohio and check those guys out. I'll go to Buffalo, Wyoming, to personally check out the guy from Wyoming. I have good reason to believe that these guys stole a file from the Temple that is extremely important to the well-being of our organization. I believe that they are also looking for a gun that is mentioned in the file—a Uberti Colt .45. Take one of our small planes and get it done ASAP. I'll take the jet and get out to Wyoming. Let me be very clear here. No harm should be done to anyone unless we find that file. It looks like this and is stamped as Director Hoover's confidential file. If you find that they have it, you get the file using any means possible. Understand? Go now and stay in touch."

Gordon just smiled to himself with this news. *Looks like we are gonna have some fun again. It's starting to feel like the old days.* As he thought about the possibilities, he dialed Bud and filled him in on the conversation.

"Bud, your guys are gonna be in the middle of this and probably get hurt unless we step in."

Bud considered his options and finally said, "Okay, you follow the guys to Ohio, and Frank and I will wait for the Grand Commander to show up in Buffalo. Do what you have to do to protect the guys in Ohio. I'll take care of Mike. When you find out where those guys are flying into Ohio, let me know, and I'll have a plane waiting for you in Baltimore."

Gordon just said, "Okay, got it. I'll tail the Commander's guys until they get to their airport and check their flight plan. You're on your own with the Commander. Talk to you soon."

As soon as Bud hung up, he looked at Frank and said, "I've got a gut feeling that things are going to heat up in the near future. It appears that the Grand Commander has discovered that his file is gone and has tar-geted Mike and his friends as being responsible. So far, he hasn't put anything together on us. He's coming to Buffalo to personally check out Mike and, I'm betting, to look into the missing gun that the file mentioned. We need to be airborne within the hour so we can beat him to the airport and then wait for him to come in."

Frank agreed, "Sounds like a plan," he said as he readied the plane for takeoff. "Let's do it."

CHAPTER 46

Mike decided to take some time to unwind before calling Bear and working any more on the gun search. *After all, my chickens have been neglected, and I'm still feeling a little stressed about the D.C. trip—in particular, the gun to the neck and the fight in the bar. I'm getting too damn old for that kind of shit anymore.* Then he smiled and thought to himself, *But maybe not—it was kind of fun too. Just glad no one got hurt.* As he sat out near his chickens, his mind kept going back to the one piece of the puzzle still missing in the gun hunt. *That missing gun has to be around here somewhere,* he thought. *I still can't believe we found the other three matching guns and that now the trail to the last one leads back out here. He shook his head and thought, That's just too weird.*

"Hey, Chicken Joe, what do you think?" he said addressing one of his roosters. "Where's that damn pistol?" Noticing that Mike was talking to him, the rooster came running for Mike to pet him. "That's right, Chicken Joe," he clucked to the rooster. "I need some answers." Mike continued to dwell on the pistol and the potential for finding it as he petted the big red rooster. "I guess we'll just have to wait for that Bear guy and Bud to get out here and hope they can give us some direction, Mr. Chicken Joe." After a bit, he finished feeding the chickens, went inside his house, and called it a night. He was exhausted.

After a solid night's sleep, Mike was literally up with the chickens. "A chicken man's duties never end," he laughed as he went out to feed his buddies again. When he was done, he decided to call Bear and see what his plans were. Bear's phone rang only one time before he answered. Mike had never spoken to Bear before, so he was unprepared for the growl that came when Bear said, "Hello." It was as deep and guttural as ever.

Mike said, "I'm assuming this is Bear?"

Bear growled back, "Ain't nobody else who would be answering my phone. Who the hell is this and what the fuck do you want?"

Taken aback just a tad, Mike said, "Well, pardner, I'm Mike. My buddies in Ohio said you might be coming out here to help look for a gun that we want to find."

"Oh, so you're the guy I need to see then," came back the growl from Bear. "Hope you're not as big a pussy as they are!"

Mike was silent for a moment, then said, "Pardner, I've been accused of many things, but nobody has ever had the balls to call me that."

The phone was silent for a moment, then Bear let loose his god-awful, deep-down, gut-wrenching laugh that always got everyone's attention, "Haaaaaa, Haaaaaaaa, Haaaaaaaaa! Mike, I'm just fuckin' with you."

Hearing that, Mike immediately cooled down and reciprocated with his own laugh from the depths, "Haw, haw, haw. Back at ya, Bear," he almost shouted into the phone.

When the growling and the laughing finally ended, Mike said, "We need to meet each other. When do you think we can get that done?"

Bear growled, "I'm up in Deadwood now, going to meet with some of my gun buddies. I can be in Buffalo later tonight. How's that work for ya?"

Mike was surprised that Bear was already in Wyoming but was glad to get things going. "That's perfect, Bear. Let's meet at the Occidental Hotel tonight at 7 for supper and drinks."

Bear growled, "I'll be there." And he hung up as usual before Mike could say anything more.

Mike thought for a moment, clicked off the phone, and thought, *Wow, I may have just met my match.* Still shaking his head, he decided to see if Bud was back yet. *It would be good to have Bear meet Bud too,* he thought. *He might be able to give Bear some more information about the gun. Every time we meet to talk about the gun, he seems to add more details. I'm sure I'm still not getting the full story.*

Bud was at the Johnson County Airport when Mike's call came in. "Hello, Mike," he said. "You must be back in Buffalo by now."

Mike responded, "Hey, pardner, yes I am. What about you?"

Bud answered, "Frank and I are out at the airport right now working on some things."

"That's perfect," Mike said. "I'd like you to come into the Occy tonight and eat dinner with me and a guy from Ohio who we sort of subcontracted to help us find the final gun."

Bud didn't hesitate at all. "Sure, Mike, that will be fine. What time?"

Mike responded, "7 pm."

Bud said, "See you there." When the call had ended, Bud turned to Frank and said, "I'm going to need you to stick around and monitor the Grand Commander situation while I go into town to meet with Mike."

"No problem," said Frank. "I'll keep you posted. I've gotta believe that the guy will be flying in very soon. From Gordon's comments, he seems to be on the prowl."

Bud agreed, "And potentially very dangerous."

When Mike got to the Occidental at just after 7 pm, he noticed pretty much the same local crowd that frequented the place. He knew most of them. However, he did see a guy who stood out from the crowd and was standing and leaning against the bar. *If that guy isn't named Bear, I'll be mighty surprised,* he thought. *My god, he's a giant—with long shaggy hair and full beard. He's gotta weigh in at three hundred fifty or more. He's actually taking up two spaces at the bar.*

When Mike walked up to him, the giant turned, looked down at him, and checked him out from head to toe. All he said was "Nice bibs, but I hate the white tennis shoes." Then he let out that blood curdling laugh again, "Haaaaaaaa! Haaaaaaaaaa! Haaaaaaaaaaa!" Heads turned from everywhere in the bar to see what the hell was going on. "You must be that Mike fella. And I'm the guy they call Grizzly Bear." He reached out his paw to Mike, who grabbed it and squeezed hard. But Bear's huge paw swallowed up Mike's smaller hand and almost turned it into mincemeat, prompting Mike to shake it off when Bear finally released it.

Bear followed the handshake with, "I was hoping you wouldn't be another pussy like your buddies."

Mike looked him in the eyes and said, "Oh, I guarantee you that no one has ever called me that and been happy with the result. Yes, Grizzly Bear, I'm Mike. Nice to meet ya."

Bear slapped him on the shoulder and growled, "Great! Slide in here and get a drink with me."

Mike happily obliged. "A shot of Jameson's ," he ordered, "and a beer."

Bear gave him a look of approval. He was drinking nearly the same thing—Johnny Walker straight up with a beer that he had dropped the shot into.

Mike just smiled at the similarity and thought, *I think I'm gonna like this guy. At least I hope so, because I know I can't kick his ass.* Then Mike dropped the Jameson's shot glass into his beer, took his first swallow, and all was well. The connection was almost immediate. It was very much like Mike was talking to a caricature of himself—only larger-than-life sized. They shared several drinks before they heard a voice behind them. Bud had entered the saloon and saw the two new buddies leaning against the bar.

"Hello, Mike," he said. "I had a table set up for the three of us over in that corner, so that we could talk privately." He looked at Bear and smiled. "You must be the gentleman that Mike told me about. Welcome to Buffalo," he said as he reached out to shake Bear's hand.

Bear responded with as civil of a growl as he could, "That would be me. Just call me Bear." Then he crushed Bud's hand just as he had done Mike's.

Bud acted like it didn't faze him at all and said, "Let's go get seated."

At the table, Bud seated himself with his back to the wall before Mike and Bear could position themselves in that same position. "Looks like we all would like our backs to the wall," Bear growled. "Must say something about our suspicious natures or how we view people in general."

Mike agreed and took a seat that was angled a bit so he could still see a somewhat inclusive view of the saloon. Bear took two seats, but was able to angle his position so that he had a pretty good view of the place too.

Bud spoke first, "So, gentlemen, it's nice to see you. What can I help you with?"

Mike started to talk, but Bear jumped in over him and growled, "I understand you are the guy paying the bills. I'm here to get your take on where you are with paying for the D.C. guns that I helped you find and where you are on paying me for finding the other guns on your original list."

Mike, sensing that Bear was trying to cut out the middlemen, meaning Steve, Bruce, and himself, said, "Whoa, whoa, whoa, Bear. You work through us, pardner. You help us. If you find something, you give it to us, and we work with Bud. He pays us. Then we pay you. Isn't that right, Bud?"

Bud smiled and said, "Yes, Mike, that is how I prefer to do it. But I want to thank you, Bear, for your good work so far."

Bear acted a little agitated with the answer but finally growled, "Ain't no skin off my ass, if that's the way you want to do it, as long as I get paid for my work."

Bud responded, "That will be no problem. How many of the guns from the original list have you found?"

Bear answered, "I got all of them if the price is right."

Bud sat up straight, momentarily energized, and asked with some excitement in his voice, "Even the fourth pistol from the Uberti set? Are you saying you have found that Colt .45 too?"

Bear seemed to retreat a bit from the question. He growled, "Well, not exactly. I have them all except the Colt .45. But that's why I'm here. I've got some good leads from my Wyoming and South Dakota contacts."

Bud slumped back in his chair and said, "Okay, you do understand that the Colt is more important than all of the rest, don't you?"

Mike said, "Yep, pardner, and that's gonna be our main focus out here. That's why we asked Bear for help. He has a great gun network out here. And I wanted to pick your brain a bit more about the last time you saw the gun here in Buffalo, so that Bear can hear it and get moving on his contacts."

Bud sat silently for a second then said, "Okay. That will be easy. Finding the gun won't be. I've looked for over forty years and have run into nothing but dead ends."

Mike and Bear fixed their stares on Bud's face until he started to talk about that last time.

"After the operation when the four pistols were used, the agents brought the guns back here to the Occidental for safekeeping. When it came time to pick them up, we could only find three of them. The old man who owned the place was supposed to take care of them, but he disappeared, and with him went the fourth pistol. He was never found and neither was the gun. We looked all over this place, in particular, down in the basement where the old man originally had hidden the guns, but we came up empty every time. We even thought the old guy's wife might have had something to do with it, but we watched her and came up empty there too. So that's all I have for forty years of looking."

Mike and Bear waited for more, but got nothing.

Bud was done except to say, "That's why I brought you guys in. I needed someone with fresh eyes to look at it. And it's the one thing on my bucket list that I just have to complete before I die."

Mike said, "That's why we wanted to meet you here. I wanted Bear to hear the story in case it might help him with his contacts."

Bud shook his head and said, "Wish I had more for you, but I guess if I knew more, I wouldn't have needed you in the first place." As Bud finished speaking, his cell phone rang and he fished in his pocket to retrieve it and answer it. "Right, okay, I'll be right there." He stood up after hanging up and said, "Sorry, gentlemen, but I have to go. But I'll be in town for a few days, so we should be able to get together again. I hope this helped us all." He shook hands and headed out of the saloon. Mike and Bear picked up where they left off when Bud came in and eventually headed back to lean on the bar.

"Let's meet back here tomorrow for breakfast at 9," Mike said.

Bear growled his approval and said, "Unless we are still here!" as both men let loose with their signature laughs that startled nearly everyone in the place.

"That works for me too," Mike said. From that moment until closing time, the whiskey and beer flowed so freely that the bartender had to dig out more bottles from his stock.

Meanwhile, Bud was speeding back to the airport. Frank was on the call that Bud had taken at the Occidental. He said that a small jet had radioed in for permission to land and that he suspected it was the Grand Commander. Bud wanted to be there for the landing so that he could see how many thugs the guy brought with him. Frank was waiting for him, when he pulled into the airport.

"I think this is our guy's plane," Frank said.

Bud nodded in agreement and said, "Yes, I do too. Let's position ourselves in that hangar, so we can get a good look." He pointed to a seldom used older hangar that would give them a perfect vantage point.

Frank said, "They were about an hour out when they radioed, so we won't have to wait long." When they entered the old hangar, they found a couple of chairs and sat and waited. Bud never was much for small talk, but he would talk about each and every detail of any operation that he was involved in. No more loose ends in his lifetime. So that's what he did.

"Listen, Frank, I fear that this will get ugly before it's over. As soon as you can after these guys land, I want you to call Gordon and get him out here. We are going to need the firepower."

Frank agreed, "I hope it doesn't go that way, but over the years, you have always been right on."

Bud sighed, "I can feel it in my gut." At that moment, both men saw the jet circling the airport.

Frank said, "The pilot is probably making sure it's big enough for his plane. It is. He should have no problem."

Bud added, "When he lands, we will just watch and then follow them. No contact at this point."

"Got it," Frank said. When the plane finally landed and the exit door opened, there was no mistaking who the pilot was.

Bud whispered, "Look, it's the Grand Commander himself." After the Grand Commander deplaned, he waited for the rest of his associates to exit and bring his luggage.

"Very little luggage," Frank said. "Not planning to stay long. And I count three other guys."

Bud shrugged and said, "That's workable on both counts. Best case is they look around and get the hell out." He continued, "But I'm betting they will stop at nothing to not leave empty-handed. He appears to be the kind of guy who isn't used to losing."

Frank said, "He hasn't dealt with us before," and chuckled.

It didn't take the Commander and his men long to move into the tiny terminal where they worked at making arrangements for a car. Frank took the opportunity to call Gordon.

"Gordon, this is Frank. We are going to need you to hurry up in Ohio and get out here as quickly as possible. We need some back up."

"Hello, Frank, that won't be a problem," Gordon responded. "I'm finishing up right now. And the best part is I didn't have to leave D.C. because my targets never left."

Frank relayed this to Bud, who instinctively knew what that meant.

Gordon chuckled into the phone, "Yea, it looks like they are tied up with something else. So I'll get airborne within the hour and see you later tonight."

He hung up before he had to answer any questions from Bud. He had already cleaned up most of the mess and didn't want to be chastised for doing what he believed he had to do. The mess was the two bodies that were tied up and wrapped in plastic on the plane that they were planning to take to Ohio. After Gordon found out their plans, he decided that if the goal was to protect the amateurs from Ohio, then it would serve no purpose to let these guys go there. He simply followed them to their plane, changed into some coveralls, pretended to work at the airport, slipped onto the plane behind them, and shot them both.

Pretty nifty piece of work for an old guy, he thought to himself as he awaited the cleaners that were always on his speed dial. He rationalized, *Now I can go help Bud and not waste my time going to Ohio. This was an inevitable ending anyway. These guys weren't going to go easy on the Ohio guys,* he smiled.

As soon as the cleaners arrived, Gordon was out the door of the plane and heading to his own plane to get himself airborne and on his way to Wyoming.

CHAPTER 47

All the way home from D.C., Bruce and Steve talked about what had happened and what the next step would be. Bruce wanted to make just a quick stop at home and keep on going out to Buffalo. However, Steve resisted this idea because he was flat out tired of traveling. So when they got home, it was still an unsettled issue. Bruce called Steve the next morning after a good night's rest in his own bed.

"Hey, buddy, listen. You know we've been leading this thing all of the way. Don't you think we should at least try to be there in case Mikey and Bear are able to find the gun? We need to head out to Buffalo to help Mikey and to get this done one way or the other."

Steve was well rested from his own good night of sleep. "Absolutely," he said. "Let's do it."

Surprised and shocked, Bruce said, "What did you say?"

Steve laughed and said, "I said yes, let's do it. I'm good to go. I agree we need to be there when this finishes."

Bruce exclaimed, "Tremendous! Can you be ready so we can leave by noon?"

"Yep," Steve said. "I'll be ready."

When noon came, Bruce was at Steve's and raring to go. "Only twenty more hours of driving."

Steve shuddered but said, "Let's git 'er done," as Bruce pulled the van out of the drive and into the last leg of this adventure—at least they both hoped it was.

It was 9 a.m. Wyoming time when the guys left, so they decided to call the chicken man and let him know they were on their way. Steve dialed Mike's number and put the phone on speaker. No answer. They tried an hour later. Still no answer.

"Where the hell is chicken man?" Bruce said. "He's always up and around taking care of his friends."

Steve persisted along the way. Finally, around noon Wyoming time, he got an answer.

"Hello," came an obviously still sleeping response from Mike.

Steve said, "Get your ass up, chicken man. Your friends are starving."

The groggy voice said, "What? Who is this? What time is it?"

Bruce laughed and said, "Oh my god, Stevie, he's still in bed and hung over."

Mike said, "Hey! I heard that and yes, I am. Oh shit, I was supposed to meet Bear for breakfast at 9. Am I late yet?"

Both guys laughed.

"Oh, yes, buddy. You are sooooo late. You stood up, Bear? Wow," Bruce laughed again. "Not a great way to start a friendship or build relationships."

Mike could barely speak. His throat was so dry. "I've got hot pipes and feel like shit. And it was Bear's fault. He tried to outdrink me, but finally, at last call at the Occidental, we both called it a draw. Just a second, I hear something." Mike got up and the guys heard him say, "Oh my god, he's here sleeping on the floor."

"Who?" Steve asked.

"It's Bear," Mike whispered.

With that, the guys burst into laughter.

"Wow," Steve said. "Mikey found his clone."

Mike said, "Hey, look, I gotta go. I'll call you back when I get things figured out here."

"All right man. Good luck," Bruce said. "Shades of the old days with Mikey," he turned and said to Steve. "I'm just glad it wasn't us sleeping on the floor."

"Been there, done that," laughed Steve.

While Bruce and Steve were traveling and Mike was drinking and sleeping in with the Grizzly Bear, Bud, Frank, and Gordon were busy following the Grand Commander around. Gordon got in late, but was in go mode as the three men split up surveillance of the Grand Commander and his men. It was a tricky surveillance because Bud and Frank were known to the man because of their attempt at intimidation in D.C. Gordon, on the other hand, may have been spotted in or around the Temple on security tapes, but that was probably unlikely. Either way, those connections made it tougher to stay close. However, the small size of Buffalo also made it possible to maintain a somewhat safe surveillance perimeter. For example, after the Commander and his men left the airport the night before, it was easy for Bud and Frank to follow them back to town and to the Occidental, where they had booked rooms for the night. From there, it was up to Gordon to maintain an internal position in the hotel and up to Bud and Frank to watch for outside movement. As always, one of the first priorities was to place and position a listening device in each of their rooms. This was one of Gordon's specialties, and he accomplished it like the professional that he was, when the men went down to the restaurant to eat.

When he was done, Gordon connected with Bud and said, "It's done. We should hear everything from the room now."

"Perfect," Bud responded. "This just got easier. Now see if we can somehow get a bug in the restaurant and also in their car. Then we'll be in even better shape."

"Can do and will do," Gordon shot back. Within the hour, Gordon connected again to say, "Car is bugged. And the table in the restaurant that they used last night is bugged. It's large enough for them, and it's in a place where they think they can talk. I'm betting they use it most of the time."

"Okay, thanks," said Bud. "Nice work." *Now we just sit back and listen to what they have in mind,* he mused.

In the meantime, Mike was finally able to rouse Bear.

Mike smiled and thought, *It's almost like the big fella went into hibernation. Very appropriate,* he chuckled. Coming out of that hibernation, he was even more like an awakened grizzly. "You are a surly son of a bitch," Mike finally said, tiring of the big man's attitude.

"Just get me more coffee," Bear growled in his deepest voice. "How'd I get here, anyway?"

Mike responded, "Well, you tried to outdrink me at the Occy, and as you found out, that just doesn't happen. But, to tell you the truth, I don't know how we got here either. Someone obviously dropped us off, because neither of our vehicles are outside."

Bear was finally starting to feel halfway alive again after several cups of coffee. "Hope we had a good time. I'm sure whoever dropped us off will tell us sometime. How am I going to get back to town?"

Mike responded, "I'll get you there as soon as you're ready."

Bear thought for a minute and growled, "Let's do it. I've got work to do."

Mike asked, "You want to shower first?"

"Hell no," he snorted. "The guys I'm talking to would think I was un-American if I showered to talk guns. And that suits me fine. Haaaaaa. Haaaaaaa. Haaaaaaaa," he gut-laughed. "Let's go."

Mike said, "Okay, gotta take my old car since my truck is missing. What a night!"

They went out and jumped into Mike's ancient, rusted out Ford Falcon. Both men had to be careful where they put their feet—the floorboards had rusted away, and Mike had covered the holes with old metal signs cut to fit. But the car ran and it always started.

He dropped Bear off in front of the Occy and asked, "Who are you meeting?"

Bear almost cordially said, "Got some gun contacts up in Deadwood who cover this area and beyond. They think they might know something about the gun we're looking for."

Mike said, "Want me to tag along?"

Bear just laughed his huge laugh again and growled low and slow, "I like ya, Mike, but hell no," and walked away.

So Mike turned his old Falcon around in the middle of the street and headed back home to take a shower. As he turned, he saw his truck and thought, *Okay, I'll get that later.* He didn't see Bud and Frank sitting in their car a few parking spaces behind the truck, but they saw him drop off Bear.

Bud turned to Frank and said, "Frank, I think we need to split up. Let's get the other truck, you come back here, and I'll go watch Mike's back. I guarantee that sooner or later these guys will make a move on Mike, after they scout the lay of the land."

Frank agreed and they left to make the switch.

Meanwhile, Gordon was playing the role of an elderly tourist in the Occidental Hotel. He talked to other tourists, spent time looking around the in-house museum, ate in the restaurant, and tried very hard to stay out of the saloon. The rest of the time he spent lounging in the main foyer of the hotel. It was easy duty, but boring beyond belief for him. He was more than ready for the game to really begin. *Patience, patience, patience,* he had to keep telling himself.

After Mike got home and got himself cleaned up, he felt halfway human again. *Damn, I'm getting too old for that crap,* he thought as he headed out to feed his chickens. His cell phone, ringing in his jacket pocket, stopped him.

"Hello," he answered.

"Mikey, how ya doing?" Steve asked.

"Hey, buddy, what's up?" Bruce continued, "Stevie and I are only a couple hours out from your place. Are you ready for us?"

Mike shouted into the phone, "Hell, yes, I was born ready! I just dropped Bear off uptown to go see some of his contacts. He's pretty optimistic. When you get here, we'll make a plan of attack and make one last attempt to find that gun."

"Perfect," Bruce said. "See you in a while."

Mike hung up and thought, *This is kinda crazy. Everybody who's been working on this gun thing is ending up in Buffalo. I think that's a good sign,* he chuckled. *All roads lead to Buffalo, Wyoming.*

CHAPTER 48

The Grand Commander and his men were making good use of their time in the Occidental Hotel. Even though their major focus was finding Mike, they also wanted to dig around for the lost gun that was mentioned in the missing confidential file. It was the proverbial "smoking gun" that linked the confidential file to Director Hoover. One without the other was not conclusive to prove a conspiracy, but both together, plus the guns in D.C., were. And he was committed to putting an end to it right here in Buffalo.

Acting the part of tourists, but still looking out of place, the Commander and his men scoured the old hotel from top to bottom, with the exception of the basement. Memorabilia from the storied history of the Occidental was displayed throughout the hotel, and they noted all of it. They talked to the employees, and they even talked to the current owner, Dawn. Nobody seemed to even remotely know what they were talking about when they mentioned the lost gun. But Dawn said that she would give them a tour of the basement as soon as she could find time. The Grand Commander had to use all of his personal skills to get this done.

"Dawn, I know that your basement is probably like most basements—full of stuff and probably in a fair amount of disarray, but that doesn't matter to us. We just want to get the complete feel for this place, and historically speaking, that basement probably hasn't changed much since the place was built. Am I right?"

Dawn answered, "Yes, you're right. But it is such a mess. I'd be embarrassed to show it to you."

Undeterred, the Commander continued to press, "All we will notice is the history. We only have a short time here so we really need to do that to give our trip the historical link we came here for."

Dawn considered his comments and said, "Oh, all right. But I want to put it in a little better order first. How about tomorrow afternoon?"

The Grand Commander felt like he had won a small victory and said, "Thank you, Dawn, for your hospitality. That means everything to us."

Gordon saw the exchange from his seat in the lounging area of the hotel near the front desk and heard the owner give her permission. He immediately contacted Bud for instructions.

"Just stay as close as you can," Bud said. "I'll let you know what we do next."

Almost on cue, the listening device started to pick up a conversation from the Grand Commander and his guys. They had taken their familiar seat in the restaurant to talk. Bud listened intently to the discussion. Actually, it was just the Commander talking and giving orders.

"Now that we're familiar with this place, I need you to go visit that Mike guy. Talk to him about our thoughts about what he did in D.C. and help him to remember. Hopefully, he'll crack, we will get back the file, and then we can take one last look for the gun tomorrow in the basement. After that we get the hell out of here. So it is absolutely imperative that you get him to talk about the file. Understand?"

Grunts of "Yes, boss" and "Will do" came to Bud from the bugged table. Then it fell silent.

Bud quickly connected with Gordon and said, "Are they moving?"

Gordon responded, "The two thugs are. The Commander is sitting tight."

Bud acknowledged the information with, "Okay, you stay with him. We'll follow the other guys."

Gordon just said, "Got it," as Bud and Frank spotted the Commander's men and began to tail them.

Right away it was apparent that they were heading in Mike's direction. But Mike wasn't home. He had already left to meet Bruce and Steve on the outskirts of Buffalo as they came in from their long drive. He thought that they could eat first at one of the local diners and then head to his house to relax. It had been a long but fairly quick trip for Steve and Bruce, and they were starving and ready to get to Mike's. Both guys were feeling exhausted from the combination of the trip to D.C. and then on to Buffalo.

"Maybe we bit off more than we could chew," Bruce said as he struggled to find a comfortable way to sit.

"I'm with you, buddy," Steve agreed. "What a long-ass trip! Hope Mikey's on time so we can eat and get to his place to crash."

"Agreed," Bruce said as he maneuvered the van into one of the parking spaces at the diner. "There he is." And he pointed at Mike waiting in his old Falcon.

It was a fortuitous stop for Mike and his buddies. While they were at the diner, the thugs were pulling into Mike's drive looking to cause a little mayhem. Unfortunately for them, they didn't know that Bear had just stopped back to Mike's place to talk about the gun and his contacts. So when they kicked in Mike's door to surprise him, it wasn't Mike they surprised, but it was Bear—the Grizzly Bear. They came in with guns drawn, but Bear picked up Mike's favorite recliner rocker and threw it at them before they could even begin to react.

"What the hell?" one of the guys shouted. And then Bear was on them, three hundred-plus pounds of pissed off Grizzly just reacting, not thinking.

"No one pulls a gun on me," he growled. And he proceeded to beat the living hell out of them. After taking the beating of their lives, the guys finally were able to scramble out the kicked-in door and limp/crawl to their car and speed away, leaving Bear to smile at his victory and say to himself, *What the hell was that all about?*

He looked around Mike's unkempt house and just thought, *They couldn't be thieves. There's nothing here worth stealing.* Then he went to Mike's fridge, grabbed a beer, and chugged it all in one huge swallow.

The thugs sped back to Buffalo, licking their wounds. Both were pretty busted up, and they were worried what the boss would do next as a result of their failed mission. They were so focused on what happened that they didn't even notice when they passed Bud and Frank heading out to Mike's. Bud turned to Frank and said, "Well, that was quick. Wonder what happened," and proceeded on to Mike's place.

When the thugs got back to Buffalo and entered the hotel, Gordon almost choked trying to mask his laughter. He thought, *Either those guys wrecked their car, or Mike kicked the shit out of them.* He looked away as they took the stairs up to their room to clean up and then talk to their boss. Gordon knew the boss was in the saloon, so he took the opportunity to call Bud. "Hey, your boys just got back and it looks like they got their clocks cleaned," he chuckled. "What happened?"

Bud chuckled too and said, "They ran into a Grizzly Bear. Our new friend Bear stopped by to see Mike, and they didn't know it and thought he was Mike. Mike wasn't home so Bear was the welcoming party. That's what happens when you leave details to chance. We're heading back."

As Gordon watched, the Grand Commander answered his phone, slammed his hand on the bar, and almost ran towards the stairs. Gordon thought with a smile, *There goes a man who is having a bad day. I can only hope it gets worse.*

When Mike, Steve, and Bruce finally got to Mike's place, they immediately saw the front door busted off its hinges. "What the hell?" Mike yelled and pulled out his .44 magnum from under his seat and signaled for the guys to be careful. He pushed through the door and saw Bear. "Bear?"

Bear just looked at him and growled, "You're the third guy to come through that door with a gun out. The first two didn't fare too well," he growled and gut-laughed at the same time. "I don't believe they'll come back," he said, taking another swig from one of Mike's fast-dwindling stock of beer. After Bear told his story, the guys just looked at each other for a moment.

"Trouble seems to be following us ever since our D.C. visit," Bruce said.

"Following me!" Mike exclaimed. "Let's recap here—fight with the old guy at the bar, gun to the back of my neck, and now two thugs with guns busting into my house. What rat's nest have we opened up?"

Bruce and Steve agreed that something was up and that they needed to speak to Bud as soon as possible. Bear agreed too. "Listen, that Bud guy seems to be the guy who knows what's going on," he said. "He's either gotta fix it or get you guys off the hook. He ain't paying you enough to find guns if it's gonna get ya hurt or killed. I came back here today to tell you my contacts have all heard rumors about a missing gun used in some bigtime assassination thing years ago. If that's true, it's no wonder anyone involved would want to stop any investigation. A couple of my guys even mentioned the Kennedy shooting. It's probably bullshit rumors, but rumors get people killed sometimes. The one common thread is that the gun was lost in Buffalo at the Occidental Hotel. I think we need to go there to look around. I know your friend Bud said that he already had, but fresh eyes find things that someone too close to the situation can't."

Bruce and Steve agreed.

Mike said, "I know the current owner, Dawn, real well. After we get rested, let's go there tomorrow and see if she'll let us look around. I need a beer. Anybody else?" No one hesitated. It was a good time to drink a beer.

Back at the Occidental, the Grand Commander was not having a good time. He burst into his hotel room to find his guys all bloodied and battered. "What the hell happened?" he screamed under his breath.

His two guys just shook their heads and said, "That guy is a monster. He was waiting for us, surprised us, and got the drop on us."

One of the guys added, "He woulda killed us if we hadn't run out of there."

The Commander was furious. "You guys are supposed to know what you're doing. My god!" he exclaimed. "You guys are worthless. I should have done it myself."

The other guy said, "We're sorry, boss. We just didn't expect this amateur to be a problem. We're going to get cleaned up and get back out there."

The Commander shook his head, "Hell no, you are not. We'll finish here first tomorrow and then get out there. Get yourselves back together, and we will tear apart the basement tomorrow. This is just amazing!" he fumed as he left the room and slammed the door.

Gordon couldn't contain the size of his smile as he listened in on the conversation. "These guys are the amateurs. They haven't seen anything yet." He was feeling so confident that he even nodded at the red-faced Commander as he came back from his room and crossed the hotel lounge area.

On their way back to town and after talking to Gordon, Bud decided that he needed to see Mike and his buddies to alert them to the potential danger they were in. He called Mike's cell number. "Hello, Mike?" he said.

Mike responded, "Hey, pardner, we were just talking about you. Can you come out to the house to talk?"

Bud answered, "Absolutely, that's why I called. We need to get together. I understand you had a situation. I'm on my way right now with Frank."

Mike wondered how he knew about the fight, but just responded, "That's great. See you in a bit," and hung up. He turned to the other guys who by now had had several beers and said, "Bud's on his way," as he took a deep swallow from his last remaining bottle of Jameson's.

When Bud and Frank got to Mike's and entered the house, Bud looked at the broken door and frame and just thought, *Those guys were serious.* "Hello, gentlemen," he said, as he and Frank came in and sat down. Even though the guys were fairly well lit up, he could tell they really wanted to see what he knew of the situation.

Bruce said, "Bud, we are more than a little concerned. If it wouldn't have been for Bear, Mike could have gotten hurt, or it could eventually be one of us or all of us." He was rambling a little from the booze, but he wanted answers, as did the rest of the guys.

Bud was silent for a bit then said, "This is the story. From your visit to D.C. and the success you had, you have stirred up a long dormant hornet's nest. There was a huge conspiracy from the early sixties that involved the Director of the FBI and the President of the United States at the time, LBJ." The guys, including Bear, were hanging on every word. "You found the only link in existence to that conspiracy."

Mike said, "Oh my god, pardner, you put us in the middle of this shit. Is this the operation you told me about?"

Bud nodded and said, "Yes, it is, Mike. Frankly, I never anticipated that you men would be so successful. It was just a shot in the dark for me. I wanted to clear up some loose ends before I died, so that I couldn't be implicated in any way. It's too long of a story to tell now, but the bottom line is that you found three of the four guns used in the conspiracy. And then you led me to a confidential file that Hoover himself had put together that detailed everything about the operation, including who was involved and what was done."

He paused for what seemed like a long, long time to the inebriated guys and then continued with a sigh, "I now have the file, and I have the three guns. And I believe that I can find the fourth. The guys who came to see you, Mike, were brought here by the Grand Commander of the Masonic Temple where Hoover's memorabilia had been stored. He and his predecessors at the Temple were sworn to protect the integrity and legacy of Hoover and LBJ as high-ranking Freemasons. You guys opened a door that they never wanted open. Hence, you have become targets, and it is my fault."

All of the guys gave Bud a universal stare of disbelief—except Bear, who was really only a small part of the equation. He simply growled, "It's simple. We eliminate them before they eliminate us."

Bud looked at the other three guys and said, "Unfortunately, Bear, you are absolutely right." He continued, "It will be done without any connection to you. And you won't even know what happened. It's always better to have plausible deniability. But the most important thing here is that it needs to be done, or you gentlemen will always be looking over your shoulders for the next shoe to drop. They will come after you."

By now the drinking had stopped. The guys were looking at each other, trying to come to terms with what they had just heard Bud say. Finally, Bruce said, "Don't tell us any more details. None of us are equipped to be a part of this. All we want from you, Bud, is for you to get this done and to get it done without our involvement."

Steve and Mike agreed.

Bear, however, growled, "I'll help if you need me. Sounds like fun." His comment brought a little levity to the seriousness of the situation and allowed some fresh air into the room that Bud had just sucked all of the air out of.

Bud added, "I'll let you know when you are safe again. But first, I'm going to need your help at the Occidental tomorrow. Mike, I need you to set up a tour of the basement for you and your friends sometime before noon. I'll show up too. The Grand Commander and his thugs are going to tour it later in the afternoon."

Mike said, "Okay, I'll talk to Dawn in the morning."

Bud nodded and got up to leave. He turned to look at the guys again and said, "I'm sorry I've put you in this situation. It is not my nature to involve innocents in my operations. I promise I will make it right," he continued as he and Frank walked out the broken door and headed back to Buffalo, leaving the guys looking at each other and wondering what was going to happen next.

CHAPTER 49

The next morning came quickly for the guys. The anxiety mixed with the previous night's booze made for a fitful night's sleep for all three of them. But chicken man was up and doing his chicken thing with the first crowing of the roosters. He was feeling it though. *I'm way too old to be doing that shit,* he thought. Then he laughed out loud, *And I say that same thing every time I do it. Oh well, I'll make it,* and he chuckled as he spread the grain for his flock.

When Mike was finished he went back to the house expecting to have to wake up the other guys. "Time to get up!" he yelled so that he could be heard throughout the house.

He was immediately shushed by Steve. "My god, Mikey, easy boy. Some of us had a little too much to drink last night." He was seated at the kitchen counter on a bar stool, nursing a supersized cup of coffee.

Bruce was next to him, leaning forward, holding his head and sipping from the same size coffee mug. "WTF," was all he could open his mouth to say.

Mike took in the picture, decided he was in pretty good shape compared to them, and proceeded to make eggs and bacon for breakfast for everyone. "So where's Bear?" he asked whoever might answer.

Steve was first and said, "He disappeared sometime last night without a word. I guess we'll see if he comes back."

Bruce added, "I wouldn't mind having him with us this morning, though, when we go check out the Occidental."

All three guys nodded in agreement at that.

Bruce looked up at Mike and asked, "Okay, what's the plan? Are you calling Dawn, or are we going to go to the Occidental to see her?"

Mike nodded his head, as he finished swallowing the eggs and bacon on his plate, and said, "We need to go see her and talk her into it. She likes me, so it shouldn't be a problem."

Bruce and Steve said, "Great," at the same time, finished their breakfast, and went about to get ready.

Bud, Frank, and Gordon were already in position at the Occidental. Gordon had kept tabs on the Grand Commander and his guys throughout the night with the bug he had placed in their rooms. He was tired but got some shuteye when both rooms went quiet, and it was currently obvious from the snoring that his targets were all sleeping.

Bud and Frank were also outside listening and waiting for Mike and his buddies to get there. Bud had slept very little. He was anxious and had a feeling deep in his gut that things were going to happen today—things that he might not be able to control. He thought to himself, *This could very well be the day when the loose ends get tied up, or it could be the day when all hell breaks loose. It could be my very last chance to clean everything up from all those years ago.* He and Frank sat and waited and listened. It wasn't long before Bud heard stirring in the rooms of his targets. He connected with Gordon, "You getting that?" he asked.

Gordon said, "Yes, I'm on it. It'll be awhile before they are ready though."

Bud just grunted, "Okay. Let me know." At that same time, he saw Mike and his buddies pull up in front of the hotel. He and Frank got out of the car and went to meet them. "Good morning, gentlemen," he greeted them. "Are we all ready for some action today?"

Mike responded, "I hope we are as ready as we need to be," and laughed a laugh that was nothing like his gut laugh that everyone knew so well. It was a laugh filled with uncertainty and anxiety.

Bud caught it and said with a smile, "Relax, Mike. It will all be good when we are finished."

Mike and the other guys just nodded in a less-than-confident way.

"We better get in to see Dawn before she gets too busy," Mike said as he directed the men into the hotel.

As luck would have it, when the men entered the Saloon, they saw Dawn slip into the basement door behind the bar. Mike pointed and said, "That's where we need to get to. Let's wait 'til she comes back up from the basement. This could be perfect timing."

Everyone, including Bud, agreed, as they crawled up on the barstools closest to the basement door and ordered coffees from the young lady doing double duty as the early morning bartender and breakfast waitress in the dining room. The men didn't have to wait too long before Dawn reappeared from the basement door. She immediately recognized Mike, then Bud and Frank.

"Hey, guys, how are you all doing this fine morning?" she bubbled with energy. "It's nice to see you."

Mike spoke first, "Good morning, Dawn. It's nice to see you, too. Your place looks great," he schmoozed.

She responded quickly, "Thank you. I think so, except for that damn basement," she said with a friendly laugh as she pointed at the basement door.

All of the guys smiled or laughed with her.

She turned to Bud and Frank to say, "Now, fellas, is it time for your inspection again already?"

Bud answered, "No, Mrs. Wexo, we are just here with some friends of Mike's from Ohio and are showing them the historical sites. And, of course, the Occidental is at the top of our list."

She turned to Bruce and Steve and said, "Welcome. I hope you are having a great visit. And thanks for coming to see us."

Mike took the opportunity to interject, "I hate to ask this, Dawn, but Bud tells me that you have a ton of Old West memorabilia stored in your basement and my friends asked if maybe you'd let us all go down and look around."

She looked at Mike for a second, then said, "Oh, Mike, it's such a mess down there. Nothing is in any order. But you know what? I'm showing it to some other people this afternoon, so it's not quite as bad as usual. If you give me a few minutes, I'll move some more stuff around and let you take a sneak peak."

Mike smiled, "Why, Dawn, that is very nice of you. We'll be patient and drink some more coffee."

Bud smiled, too, but he was smiling because his plan was coming together.

Unfortunately, at that moment, Gordon connected with him and said with some urgency in his voice, "You need to make yourself scarce for a while; the targets are moving out of their rooms and heading down for breakfast."

Bud just said, "Okay."

He turned to Mike and said, "Let us know when you are heading down to the basement. Frank and I have to take care of something." He didn't wait for a response, but tapped Frank on the shoulder and simply said, "Let's go," and hurriedly walked out of the saloon and left Mike, Steve, and Bruce at the bar alone.

"What was that?" Bruce asked Mike.

Mike just said, "Who knows? That's just what he does."

Outside the Occidental, Bud and Frank jumped into their vehicle and waited.

Bud looked at Frank and said, "The last thing we need to happen is for the Grand Commander to recognize us from our D.C. visit. Gordon was right on top of that for us."

Frank agreed, "Absolutely. Hopefully, those thugs will be out of the restaurant by the time Mrs. Wexo finishes in the basement, and we can slip by them when our guys go down."

"Yes, but I'd feel better going down with them," Bud said. "I don't want our friends surprised and defenseless."

Frank agreed but didn't say anything more because he saw the Grand Commander and his men coming out of the front door of the hotel. They climbed into their rental car and took off, clearly heading in the direction of Mike's house.

Bud smiled seriously, "Looks like they are going to take another run at Mike. These guys are not your typical ex-agent types."

"Yes," Frank said, laughing at their ineptitude in missing Mike at the saloon. "They appear to be dumb, dumber, and dumbest, but with big guns. And they are persistent."

Gordon appeared at the main entrance to the Occidental, walked over to Bud and Frank, bent down, and said through the window, "Listen, I've got them on my listening device and everybody else is in the Occy, so I'm not going to follow them. Okay?"

Bud agreed and sent Gordon back in to listen and wait for them to return.

After several cups of coffee and some exceptional pastries from the restaurant, the friends saw the basement door finally open, and Dawn walked out.

"Well, Mike, it's okay to go down now. Is Bud still here?"

Mike shrugged and said, "He said he'd be right back—had to take care of something. Should we wait for him?"

Dawn laughed and said, "No, go right ahead. Just don't mind the mess of one hundred years of stacking and hoarding."

Mike replied, "No problem—the history is all we care about."

Dawn added as the guys moved around the bar to head down, "Just be careful of the stairs. They're old and steep."

Mike laughed, "Haw, haw, haw. So are we."

Dawn left the guys to head over to the hotel part of the building and said as she left, "Take all the time you want."

As the guys headed down the stairs, Bruce and Steve were regretting that they let Mike lead the way. He was dragging and dropping his feet on each step. Bruce said, "What the hell is the hold up?"

While Steve added, "He's handicapped, remember?"

"In more ways than one," Bruce agreed.

Mike didn't change a thing about his descent—except maybe to become more deliberate to piss his buddies off more. "Just bite me!" he exclaimed to his friends and continued on.

When they finally reached the end of the stairs and looked around at the wide expanse of the basement, the guys took a minute to just look around.

"This is it," Mike said.

Bruce added, "Wow, there is some old stuff down here. And it's all in piles. Let's split up and spend some time poking around some of the piles and the small rooms."

Steve agreed and they quickly understood why Dawn was concerned about how the place looked. It was like a time capsule of the old hotel—ancient history in pile after pile.

Mike yelled out to the guys, "Be careful of big rats!"

Bruce responded, "You're the only big rat we have to worry about."

Again, Mike said, "Bite me."

Steve laughed and said, "You've got to get a new line, Mikey. You've worn that one out."

As they continued to look around, Mike said, "You know, I would bet anything that there are secret places down here, like rooms or hidden walls or hiding spaces in the ceiling. Back in the old days, it wasn't safe to just store things out in the open."

Steve agreed, "Yep, so as you walk around, look for something that might be a lever or a hinge or anything that could be a key to something secret."

At that moment, the guys heard the stairs creak and groan with the sound of an obviously heavy person coming down to the basement. The guys turned and were surprised to see Bear.

Bruce called out, "Hey, Bear. How'd you know we were down here?"

The growl came back, "I saw your friend Bud and the other guy sitting in a car in front of the hotel and scared the hell out of them when I shook their car from behind." Then he let out his gut laugh that echoed throughout every inch of the basement. "Some secret agents! Or whatever the hell they are. Anyway, they told me you'd be here."

Bruce asked, "So what's up?"

Bear scowled and growled back, "I was checking on some more contacts, but got nothing. Seems that there are plenty of rumors about this hotel and the gun, but nobody really knows nothing. You boys having any luck?" He dragged out the question like he knew the answer.

Mike responded, "No, pardner, not yet. We're looking for anything that might open a secret hiding spot, like a false wall or false ceiling or floor. Feel free to check it out. The owner gave us all the time we need to look around."

Bear didn't respond, but he thought to himself, *Yeah right, all the time we need to find something that probably doesn't exist—it's needle in a haystack time.* That changed in a heartbeat. Bear was a head taller than the other three guys and, after looking around for a while, leaned against a wooden dowel at the corner of one of the basement walls. *What the hell?* he said to himself as he felt it move a bit. He jiggled it, pulled on it a little, and then let out a growl that any grizzly in the woods would be proud of. "Hey, pussy boys! Is this what you're looking for?"

Bruce, Steve, and Mike came running and watched as Bear pulled out the dowel. They almost fainted when the wall popped open a few inches. In that moment, even Mike forgot about Bear's insult.

Bruce said excitedly, "Pull it open, Bear—go ahead."

When he did, dust from years and years ago flew into the air and hung like a winter fog, temporarily keeping the men from seeing inside. The false wall was obviously meant to hide something and opened up to a good-sized area about the size of a large wall safe. But the flying dust and the dark interior kept the men from seeing what was inside.

"Anybody got a flashlight?" Bear growled.

Steve stepped forward and said, "Just my cell phone flashlight app." He tapped the app on his phone, and the light brightened the whole interior. "Oh my god!" he exclaimed.

The other guys shouted "What? What?"

He just said, "Will you look at that?"

Everyone pushed forward to see and there it was—a briefcase that looked exactly like the ones they found in D.C.

"That's got to be the gun!" Bruce shouted.

Bear reached in to pick it up, but Bruce said, "Wait, wait, Bear. We need to document and take pictures first. And we need to get Bud and Frank down here."

Bear reluctantly backed up and said, "It's your deal." Then he growled, "Look at that thing next to it. It looks like a bag of some sort."

Mike jumped in and said, "Actually, it looks like a body bag. When I was in the Navy I saw a lot of bags like that."

Steve spoke up and said, "I agree with Bruce. We need to get Bud down here. Close it up 'til he sees it."

Bear growled his displeasure with that idea, but he reluctantly complied, pushed the wall shut and replaced the dowel.

Mike immediately dialed Bud's number. "Hey, pardner," he said when Bud finally answered. "You've got to get down here fast. We found something you need to see."

Bud looked at Frank and mouthed, "They've found something."

At the same time, Frank pointed at the rental car that was pulling up in front of the hotel. "Hey, Bud, the Commander and his thugs are back," he said quietly.

Bud acknowledged Frank, and said quickly to Mike, "We'll be right there." After Bud hung up, he said out loud, "Where in the hell is Gordon? He was supposed to tell us when they were coming back."

Frank just said, "Don't know, but we better get in there. It won't be good if they find Mike and his buddies in the basement."

Gordon was on the job—sort of. He had gone into the saloon to wait for the Commander to return, and eventually it got the better of him. He was like the proverbial kid in the candy store. He started drinking coffee, then added whiskey to the coffee, then finished the coffee. It was all downhill from there. Before he knew it, he was pouring from his own bottle of whiskey and slugging it down. The whiskey, coupled with his lack of sleep and age, soon left him pretty useless for his assigned duties.

By the time Bud found him in the saloon, Bud knew that he and Frank would be on their own. Bud addressed Gordon, "What the hell are you doing?"

Gordon slurred back, "I'm on the job. Just trying to relax a little. I've got you covered. When those thugs get back, I'll let you know. They will be no problem."

Bud responded, "Listen to me. Do not engage with those guys in any way. Just let me know when they come in to the hotel. Got it?"

Bud's tone immediately pissed off Gordon and he slurred back loudly, "I said I would and I will. Leave me the hell alone and do your own job."

Bud looked at Frank and said, "Let's go down to see what our guys have found. I think Gordon's okay enough to let us know if the Commander and his guys show up back here."

Frank agreed and both men entered the basement stairway.

Down in the basement, everyone was chomping at the bit to find out what was in the briefcase. When the stairs creaked and groaned with the weight of Bud and Frank, their anticipation level rose accordingly.

Bud saw the guys standing around looking all agitated. "Hey, gentlemen, what's up?"

Mike was the first to speak, "Pardner, we think we found what you've been looking for."

Bud shot back, "You mean the gun? The fourth pistol?"

Bruce jumped in, "It sure looks like it. But we wanted you to be the one to check it out for sure. It's behind this hidden wall."

Bruce pointed to it, and Bud turned pale for a moment. He thought, *Oh my god, they found Smitty's body.* He looked at Frank before he spoke, trying to get his thoughts in order. "What's in there?" he asked Mike.

Mike responded, "There's a briefcase that looks just like those we found in D.C. and a peculiar bag that looks strangely like a body bag."

By now Bud had regained his composure and said, "All right, how do we get into the wall?"

That was Bear's cue to pull on the dowel. The wall popped open again, with far less dust this time. Bear growled, "There's your fuckin' gun case."

For a moment, Bud was stunned. His mind was racing. *How can that briefcase be in there?* he asked himself. *We checked it before we closed it. It can't be.* He moved forward, took out his cellphone and snapped pictures of the hidden space and everything in it.

Bear couldn't wait any longer and growled, "What the hell you waiting for? Open the damn case."

Everyone else had the same thought. Finally, Bud reached in, lifted the case out, and sat it on the floor. He ignored the body bag. In his mind he was resisting the idea that this could be the gun, the lost detail that had consumed so much of his life. He noticed the lock had been broken as he bent down to open it. His heart was pumping so fast and hard that he could feel it pushing up against his chest. Then he flipped the latch and pushed the lid of the case open.

There it was—the last detail, the loose end. Inside was the Uberti Colt .45, the gun that Howard had fired to finish off the President under Bud's supervision. The operation flashed through his mind. The motorcade, the first gun shots, the grassy knoll, and the neck shot that came from this gun—the fourth pistol. Plus, the subsequent hand-off of the briefcase to Gordon.

This seems so surreal, he thought. *But everything is still in place just as I left it so many years ago—the police badge and the police revolver—all there.* The guys were quiet as the scene unfolded, not understanding the real significance of the gun to Bud.

Then Mike spoke, "Hey, pardner, look at that. That looks like a letter of some sort." Sticking out from underneath the Colt .45 was the corner of an envelope.

Bud slowly and methodically raised the gun and pulled the envelope out. It wasn't addressed to anyone. Just as before, the guys pushed forward to see if they could see what it said. Bud read it to himself first, then after several minutes of reading, said, "It's from the previous owner of the Occidental Hotel, Margaret Smith."

Bruce said, "Read it out loud."

Bud shook his head, "Sorry, I can't. But the gist of it is that her husband had put the gun case in the safe upstairs because it felt different from the others. He told her about it and the other guns, and he also told her about the fake wall. After he turned up missing, she took it out of the safe and, eventually remembering the fake wall in the basement, she decided to hide it there."

What Bud didn't tell the guys was that she also wrote in the note that she found the body bag with Smitty's body in it and decided to let him rest in peace in the wall of his beloved hotel. Plus, Mrs. Smith had put two and two together and decided that Bud was providing the so-called historical money to her because he wanted to find the gun too. And she decided to keep the money flowing.

One line of the note struck at Bud's heart. It simply said, "If it was this guy, Bud, who killed my husband, I hope he spends eternity in Hell." Mrs. Smith ended the note by simply saying, "And to whoever finds this note, if you have to move Smitty's body, I would surely appreciate your reburying him next to me."

It was obvious to the guys that Bud was moved by the words in the note, but they still wanted to know more. They started to throw questions at Bud. But he didn't answer. Instead, he said, "Listen, gentlemen, you have accomplished what I hired you to do. You have finished what I never thought would get done in my lifetime. I owe you, and I will reward you handsomely for your amazing work."

Still, their curiosity was overwhelming, and they kept asking for answers. But instead of answers, all they got was the creaking and groaning of the basement stairs again. It was obvious that someone else was moving very quickly down the stairs. By the time the guys turned and saw who it was, it was too late.

The Grand Commander and his thugs appeared with guns drawn and mayhem on their minds.

"Don't anyone move!" the Commander shouted as he waved his 9 mm at the guys. "Move up against that wall! All of you! Now!" he continued.

His thugs moved swiftly to push everyone face first against the wall.

"Wow," he continued. "It seems that fate has brought us all together to finish this little bit of historical fantasy that you have all been looking for. And I seem to recognize so many of you."

One of the thugs pointed at Bear and said, "That's the son of a bitch that we ran into yesterday."

The Commander nodded and the thug walked up behind Bear and said, "Your time is coming big man." Bear let out a growl that would have curled the thug's hair if he wasn't holding a gun on him. He was still in pain from the beating Bear had given him the day before.

The Commander kept talking, "This is how it will work. I want my confidential file back. I will keep that gun. You will also give me the other three pistols you stole from D.C. If I don't get an agreement in thirty seconds, I will let my assistants pick someone to shoot in the kneecap. Are there any questions? Oh, and we will do that until we get the answer and the merchandise we want. The clock is ticking."

Bud responded quickly, "These guys have nothing in this. I just hired them to find the gun. So leave them out of it, and let them go."

The Commander just laughed and said, "No such luck. You have ten seconds."

Bud waited a second and then said, "It's a deal. The other guns are in my car trunk with the file."

The Commander said, "Really? That sounds too easy, but my assistant here will go look. Give him your keys."

Bud threw him the keys and prayed to God that Gordon would snap out of whatever he was doing and notice. He didn't have to wait long. Before the thug even got to the top of the stairs, he was met by Gordon coming down. Gordon was obviously inebriated, but still mobile, and his years of experience and training kicked in—literally. He kicked the thug in the throat and watched him tumble end over end to the bottom of the stairs, startling the Grand Commander and the other thug just long enough for Bud, Frank, and Bear to move on them.

Bear got to the Commander first, knocked the gun from his hand, and almost snapped him in half with a true Grizzly Bear hug. Bud went after the other thug with a gun and was able to knock his weapon away too, but not before Mike, who had thrown his glasses across the basement, blasted into him with his own version of a belly buck. By that time, Gordon was down the stairs with his gun drawn and ready to kill somebody.

Bud waved him off and then, seeing that everyone was okay, he said, "Well done, gentlemen. Now, if you are all okay, I'm going to have to ask you to leave while we interrogate these criminals."

Bruce, Steve, and Mike didn't have to hear it twice. They practically flew up the stairs. But Bear wanted to help with the interrogation. He wasn't done with the fun yet. Unfortunately for Bear, though, it wasn't to be. Bud told him it was now an official FBI operation and that he wasn't cleared to be a part of it.

"That's just plain bullshit!" Bear growled, but left anyway.

Now alone in the basement, Gordon and Bud knew what had to be done. Frank would soon see.

Bud spoke to the Grand Commander and his thugs, "You know if I were to let you go, there would be more loose ends to deal with. And that would go against everything your great brother, the former Director of the FBI stood for. I know you understand that it must be finished here."

Gordon was standing behind the three men who had been positioned on their knees near the false wall. Bud nodded and it was over in seconds. Pop, Pop, Pop.

"No more loose ends. End of story for the three of us," he said to Frank and Gordon. "Let's get things cleaned up before Mrs. Wexo comes down here."

Gordon asked, "How do we get them out of this basement?"

Bud answered, "We don't. Smitty has been lonely for a long time."

CHAPTER 50

Once they got back to Ohio, Steve and Bruce settled into their retirement routine. But there was never a day that went by that they didn't talk about the magical adventure with Mike. It became the moment in their lives that defined them and said to them, "Even though your professional careers are finished, you do have value and can still contribute." It was a great feeling for the two friends and, if the truth be told, they both craved a bit more. Bud had taken care of all three guys very well financially.

"After all," he told them when he handed each a fifty thousand dollar check, "How do you really put a value on something that has been such an all-encompassing part of your life?" And he left the door open a little for the guys to help him if he needed it in the future.

When he told the guys that, Mike gut laughed and said, "Don't wait too long, pardner. Our futures are getting shorter by the second."

Bud laughed too, and added, "For me too, Mike. But we will see each other quite often if that is all right with you. You are a good friend."

As for Bear, who turned out to be so consequential in the success of the whole operation, Bud decided to put him on a retainer. The Grizzly Bear had become a larger-than-life figure in the operation, and Bud had always been a great judge of talent. He wanted him somewhere close by when, and if, things ever got dicey again.

As for the guns and the confidential file, Bud decided to create a mechanism that would kick in upon Frank's, Gordon's, and his death.

The confidential file and fourth pistol, the kill gun, would be sent to Mike for safekeeping. It would be up to Mike and his buddies as to whether the world would ever know, or should ever know, the real truth.

Finally, in one last gesture of his trust and appreciation for the guys, Bud sent them each a gift. It was a couple of months after they all got home. A man in a black SUV pulled into Bruce's, Steve's, and Mike's driveways. At each house, he rang the doorbell and proceeded to return to the back of the SUV. He opened the trunk and pulled out a large locked box and handed it to each of the men, saying with great respect, "Compliments of Bud. Thank you again."

Each man brought the box into his house and opened it immediately. Inside each was one of the Uberti Colt .45's, that Bud had looked for, for so long, and that they had helped to find, still in the original briefcase.

Bud's note simply said, "Because of you, the history of the four pistols remains intact. Display discreetly. Thank you."

Four Pistols is the first work of twice-retired Bruce W. Goodwin. Before venturing into the world of writing, Bruce worked for thirty-six years in education as a teacher, a coach, a guidance counselor, and an administrator. After retirement he ran for public office and served six years as a state legislator. He started to write *Four Pistols* after his final retirement to fulfill a commitment he made to himself years ago as an English major and high school English teacher. He often said that "One day when I finally have time, I will write a book—not a great literary piece, but an entertaining piece using my life experience as a guide and a source for inspiration." He has accomplished this with his first novel; and now that he has started his writing career, Bruce has no plans to stop. He is currently working on a sequel and has several other creations in mind and plans to continue his literary adventures with his friends.

Find out more at www.weauthors.net.